MW00413884

FREEDOM SUN
IN THE TROPICS

BRAZILIAN LITERATURE IN TRANSLATION SERIES

SERIES EDITORS
Dário Borim & Cristina Mehrtens

EDITORIAL BOARD
Bela Feldman-Bianco
Lilian Fontes Moreira
Robert Moser
Vivaldo Andrade dos Santos

Rubem Fonseca, *Winning the Game and Other Stories*
Translated by Clifford E. Landers

Jorge Amado, *Sea of Death*
Translated by Gregory Rabassa

Cristovão Tezza, *The Eternal Son*
Translated by Alison Entrekin

J. P. Cuenca, *The Only Happy Ending for a Love Story Is an Accident*
Translated by Elizabeth Lowe

Rubem Fonseca, *Crimes of August*
Translated by Clifford E. Landers

Luiz Ruffato, *Unremembering Me*
Translated by Marguerite Itamar Harrison

Moacyr Scliar, *Eden-Brazil*
Translated by Malcolm K. McNee

Ana Maria Machado, *Freedom Sun in the Tropics*
Translated by Renata R. M. Wasserman

FREEDOM SUN IN THE TROPICS

Ana Maria Machado

Translated by Renata R. M. Wasserman

TAGUS PRESS
UNIVERSITY OF MASSACHUSETTS DARTMOUTH

Tagus Press is the publishing arm of the Center for Portuguese Studies and Culture at the University of Massachusetts Dartmouth.
Center director: Paula Celeste Gomes Noversa

Brazilian Literature in Translation 8

Tagus Press at University of Massachusetts Dartmouth
Original Portuguese text © 1988 Ana Maria Machado
Translation © 2021 Renata R. M. Wasserman
English-language translation published by arrangement with Base Tres,
https://base-tres.com.

All rights reserved

Manufactured in the United States of America

Executive editor: Mario Pereira
Series editors: Dário Borim & Cristina Mehrtens
Copyedited by Dawn Potter
Designed and typeset by adam bohannon
Printed by Books International, Inc.

For all inquiries, please contact:
Tagus Press
Center for Portuguese Studies and Culture
University of Massachusetts Dartmouth
285 Old Westport Road
North Dartmouth, MA 02747–2300
(508) 999-8255, fax (508) 999-9272
www.umassd.edu/portuguese-studies-center/

ISBN: 978-1-933227-95-5
Library of Congress control number: 2020941188

CONTENTS

Brilhou de novo o sol da liberdade
A luz renasce sobre a serra
O mundo volta à tranquilidade
Findou a Guerra
A paz se estende sobre a terra
Foi vencida a tirania
Pela democracia

(SALGUEIRO SAMBA, 1946)

A freedom sun shines anew
Light peers up behind the hills
The world returns to peace
The war has ended
Peace covers the land;
Victorious over tyranny
There it is: democracy

FREEDOM SUN
IN THE TROPICS

I

A vida é amiga da arte
É a parte
Que o sol me ensinou

(CAETANO VELOSO)

Life is a friend to art
That's the part
the sun taught me

The house was solid and sunny, its windows open to the
wind and the verandas strung with hammocks. Welcoming like a hen spreading its wings to shelter the chicks
from the rain. That, the woman knew. Had always known. And all that
hospitality even bothered her, with its lack of respect for the privacy of
those who lived in the house. As a child, she had enjoyed the ruckus
made by lots of cousins and friends gathered for vacations, sleeping in
rooms full of bunkbeds, hammocks, mats on the floor. She had loved
it as a teenager—coming home from parties late at night, everybody
whispering in the dark till sunrise, careful not to wake parents or
younger siblings in other rooms. But even then the girl had known
that the price she paid was to feel invaded, always. The house always
had room for one more, and none of its rooms was hers.

Strange, to return to the house now, so many years later, in search
of her place. Or in search of quiet, of all things. She knew there would
always be a place for her there, so long as her mother lived in it. It
could always be arranged. But, for her, quiet had never been part of the
furnishings.

Nevertheless, she had come, on impulse. It had been easy. A phone
call, a flight, a fifteen-minute drive with her mother from the airport,

and in less than two hours the big city was far away, the small town was a landscape left behind. And the woman could lie in the sun, her foot raised, for as long as she pleased, nobody to jostle her and interfere with healing the broken toe. The house was as solid and sunny as ever. But this time it was empty, it was not vacation time, she was not playing or going to parties. She was just a bruised woman who needed to hide away in a cave and lick her wounds till they started healing.

She could have done that anywhere in the world. She had no idea why she had chosen that house. Maybe she wanted to curl up in her mother's lap, odd as it would be to acknowledge that. She did not know how to ask, and her mother did not know how to give. But when she had suddenly felt like coming, she had come. It had to mean something. Everything meant something. Even the broken foot—literal, no off-tune poetry about it. On the day she broke it, after bandaging it, she had called her analyst:

"Look, I can't come today. I broke my big toe."

"No problem. Come when you can." There was a faint tone of mockery in his voice.

"Don't laugh. It's true. I really did break it. This morning."

"May I guess how?"

She was sure he would recall some similar case; her friends had told her at least half a dozen in the last couple of hours. But she agreed:

"Sure. Go ahead and try. But I doubt you'll hit it . . ."

She recalled what the orthopedist had told her when he saw the foot. It was a typical fracture from kicking the leg of the bed or of the couch, very common, no big deal, all you had to do was rest it up, there was no need even to put it in a cast. A classic case of a toe being bent back as it collided with furniture.

"You hit the wall of your own home, from the inside."

"Of course," she joked, "it's an apartment . . ."

But she felt caught. She recalled the phone ringing all of a sudden, and her getting up from the couch, startled, running, and, she still did not know why or how, making a mistake about the width of the door to the hallway, kicking the corner of the doorframe with all her might, crying out in pain as the toe swelled up and turned purple.

She noticed there had been a long silence on the phone and asked:

"How did you guess?"

"I did not guess. I know you . . . You are always doing this. Only this time it was literal."

"Stop bugging me. I'll call later."

"Fine. Don't worry. Come to the next session. Or let me know if you can't."

She thought it over. Was it really that clear? Maybe it had just been a lucky guess. Maybe she was really always banging against the walls of her house, pushing against limits, trying to cross borders and increase her territory, always headlong and reckless. Something to think about, later.

And now, lying on the ground in the yard, with her foot on a stool, she tried to think about it. But couldn't. And anyway, what for? No need for it now. Right now, she had to live the moment of being there. Feel the sun on her skin, that trustworthy remedy for all ills. All she had to do was close her eyes and feel the heat. If the bugs let her. Not the mosquitoes, for so long as the wind blew that hard from the sea, no mosquito would come near. But ants. She swept away the ones climbing up her shoulder. She opened her eyes. Small red ants were hurrying around the sun-bleached hairs on her arm. The light bothered her. Cover the face with the straw hat. That was better. Looking up, she could see little sun-stars through the weave of the straw. The stiff fibers tickled the skin on her face, and she smelled their wildness mixed with the ancestral tang of the sea that impregnated every object in the house. She turned her head a bit, and watched the ants.

Weird to be lying there, contemplating bugs at that point in her life. Again. It seemed she had always been doing that, day after day. She remembered that, at this same beach, when electricity had not even reached them yet, her maternal grandmother would tell stories in the evenings, lying in the hammock that creaked, back and forth. There was the story of Mikey, the boy who stopped anything he might have been doing to watch the ants. She remembered nothing else about the story. But she remembered that it was her favorite. She had to ask her mother if she remembered. Later, when she got up, went in, talked. Not right now. Right now, all she wanted was to look inward. Or outward, to see what was to be seen. Like those bugs coming and going, one ant coming, one going, meeting, stopping. She was sure they were saying something. She had always known they did, even before reading about the adventures of the charming *Narizinho* and entering the realm of marvels the books opened.* Even before university and learning how Frisch studied the language of bees. Even before the house. Still in the old house, her grandmother's, she remembered one carnival when she dressed up as an ant for the costumed dip in the ocean, covered with chestnut leaves pinned to her bathing suit. A horrible woolen bathing suit, that scratched when dry and chafed her thighs when wet. But today's ants were much less interesting than the leafcutter ants and the fire ants. They were just common ants, boring ants, scurrying from the recently watered grass to the rocks, over the loose sand of the yard.

The rocks. How could that be? The woman thought that she knew everything about the house, its sun, its solidity, its solitude. But now she was surprised by the stones that peeked out from behind the broken cement of the steps, under the little paved walk leading to the veranda. The rocks that held up the house. The rocks that had always been there, though she had not remembered them. Precisely those rocks, of whose presence she had always known. After all, they had been her first sight of the house, when the yard was nothing but a lot planted with corn, right by the sea. When they still surprised the child, like a strange thing, a line of reefs anchored in a cornfield. For the rocks, in truth, were not rocks. Not even foundations. They were reefs on dry land, brought in by a fisherman.

Shortly before then, her father's father had died. Maybe two years earlier—it was hard to know for sure, those childhood times were always a bit mixed up. All she knew was, it had been long enough that the inventory of the estate had been completed, and construction had begun, on the day she first saw the lot. With the money he had left them, which was not much, her parents had decided to start construction on the land the mother's parents had given them, close

---

*Landmark children's book by Monteiro Lobato, first published in 1931, in which two cousins—a boy and a girl—along with an outspoken and subversive ragdoll and a scholarly corncob doll, have fascinating adventures and engage in productive mischief ("reinações"). The title *Narizinho* translates as Snub-Nose, the girl's nickname. The book inspired generations of readers, was developed into a series, and was made into a TV serial.

to their own house, at the very end of the beach, jutting into the sea, windswept, and backing onto the clump of pepper trees and Surinam cherries that almost closed the trail leading to the spring, where the village women met for endless chat while they washed dishes, scoured pots, rubbed or beat clothes against the rocks, or just walked over to fill their earthen jugs with fresh water, carrying them back balanced on a twisted cloth on their heads. For the little girl, that was a land at the end of the world, in the middle of the forest. At first she did not like it much, and worried about what might happen:

"When the house is ready, will we spend vacations there?"

"We will, my child. And we are building a good house, comfortable. That way, when mom and dad get old, we might even go live there . . ."

"But then, aren't we spending vacations at Grandma's? Are we going to be all alone in that house, far from everybody else?"

"Not alone. There are a lot of us. And every uncle will have his own house, a piece of that land, one beside the other. There is not enough room any longer in Grandpa's house. You are growing, the family is growing, there is no room . . ."

"But we will be so far . . ."

The girl realized it was a lost battle. The grownups had decided. She did not even know why she still insisted. She was hearing what she expected to hear, as if she had lived through it before.

"Not far at all, you are being silly, Lena. It's just over there, at the end of the beach. You can run over any time, in a second, or you can take your bike to your grandfather's house."

Compulsively, she continued to argue: "But what about at night? I won't be able to go alone, in the dark . . ."

"But you won't even want to. Everybody will want to go to the new house. And you know why? We are going to put in a motor, a generator, and our house will have electric light. You'll be able to read, listen to the radio, do a lot of things . . ."

"When will it be ready?"

"Oh, gosh . . . That will take time. We have to clean the lot, draw the plan, we have to buy the building materials, put in the foundations, we'll have to . . ."

That calmed her down. Even when the grownups said right away, it still took a long time for things to happen. Much more so when they said it would take time. No need to worry. She'd still be sure of vacations at her grandparents' house, with all the commotion of the full house, where everyone helped himself at meals and took the plate outside, under the tree, because there was not enough room at the table.

Father and Mother had been dreaming of a house for a long time. They drew up plans upon plans, argued, showed them around, she understood nothing. One day, she went to have a closer look. Her father was holding some papers, sitting on a strange armchair in the grandfather's house that they called a sitting duck: it was wooden, squat, with broad arms, very straight, a treacherous chair because if you sat wrong on its arm it could suddenly overturn, chair and child in a heap. But only when there was nobody sitting in the center, to keep the balance. That day, her father was sitting there, ensconced, a sister on his lap, her mother beside him, and she and a brother took up the other side.

"See here what our house will look like."

She looked and it was not at all like a house. Before she could say anything, her brother volunteered:

"Want me to draw it for you, Dad? I can make it much more like a house than that."

The father laughed and explained that what they were looking at was a drawing as if the house were being seen from above, without the roof. The lines were walls, the holes were doors. And he pointed:

"This here will be our room, and on this side the big girls' room and to the other side of that, the little kids' room . . . This is the living room. On the other side of the house, the boys' room and a guestroom."

"And this here?" her brother wanted to know.

"These are the verandas."

It was all there, on that paper. Like an enchanted house, it all fit into one drawing. And when they arrived for the next vacations, the land had been stripped of vegetation and planted in corn. In a flash the brothers and cousins discovered how wonderful it was to play cowboys and bandits in the cornfield. From time to time the rocks, like reefs in the ocean, intruded on their game. But they did not know what they were for or about. One day, however, parents and grandparents all went to see the house with the children, and with their explanations Lena began to understand that the reefs, all lined up on the ground, made up the same drawing she had seen on paper with her father, though now the outline was the size the house would really be. Those lines of reefs marked the path of the walls, established the division into rooms, anchored the house from the inside and from the outside, and made up all the places that would be there one day. But for the time being, they were nothing but rocks.

And now, many years later, lying in the sun, the woman looked at the ants coming and going on the reefs that hardly showed, buried like treasure. And she realized that her urban eyes were seriously deformed. These were not boring ants. True, they were tiny. But life effervesced in them. They moved incessantly, from the grass to the reefs beached under the house, from the moist earth to the dry sea. They were a whole world.

Maybe that was why the house was solid. Because it had been planted in the ground, in the middle of the corn, sun-ripened, wind-swept, on ocean sounds made into stone, speaking of the Atlantic and its history. Rocks. Purplish, almost red at times, at times going toward black, twisted, encrusted with old shells, softened here and there by a more insistent beat of the waves. Riddled with little holes that were once the hiding places of fish among the algae. In front of the house, in the water, the line of reefs continued and did not seem to miss the chunks old Mr. Joaquim had brought in one day in order to build the house on them as if by biblical injunction. Even now anyone could go play among the rocks in the sea with the children, carrying a little bucket to catch small fish and shells, or put on a snorkeling mask to watch the dense silent dance of changing colors in the salty water. But no longer did anyone gather lobsters in the ocean off the front yard with the precision of the old-time fishermen who followed the moon and respected the spawning season, who knew every hiding place, and would hold the animals with an unprotected hand and still be safe from their pincers and their sharp shells.

The sun was heating up.

It would be nice to take a dip in the sea. But since she had to keep her foot immobilized, and could not walk to the water or enter it, the only thing she could do was refresh herself with the hose curled up in the garden. Soon, perhaps. With the back of her hand, Lena wiped off the sweat where it bothered her most, on her upper lip.

The movement shifted the hat, widened the field of vision and revealed the almond tree, with the children's swing hanging from one of its branches, and the large table of rough-hewn wood planted in the ground under its shade. The woman smiled. If some day she had to write a song of exile, she would say that her land had almond trees.* If on some other day she had to choose a tree to house her personal god, she did not doubt the tree would be an almond tree. Her totem. A wild unkempt tree, prone to seasonal hallucinations. It could create its own fiery autumn more than once a year, at times you'd least expect it. It could shed its leaves like dry tears and decree its own individual winter in the tropics, revive in a glorious soft spring of tender pink buds and then create deep shadows in a crazy exuberant green, according to its own calendar ruled by the sap pulsating through it. Who knows, maybe someday the woman would be able to learn from the tree how, when necessary, to get rid of dead leaves, and how to search in her heart for the will to be born again and start a new cycle? Who knows? And if any almond tree were able to teach her that, it would be this one. Her old friend. Not as old as the rocks, since it had been planted after them. But better attended to, ever since it arrived in the form of a sapling brought from the forester's, with the other three. All more or less the same size, planted on the same day, by the same mother's hands, in the same yard. One of them never made it: it stood right in the path of the leafcutter ants that came from afar to go at the leaves of the poinciana tree; the ants ate it several times. It shriveled. Another never even took, nobody knows why. The one behind the house leafed out, beautiful, solemn, dense. But it had grown more slowly. This one, beside the house, where she could watch it from the window in her room, among the palm trees, this one was *hers*.

*"Song of Exile" (1843) by the Romantic poet Antonio Gonçalves Dias may be the best-known Brazilian poem, written when the author was studying in Portugal, nostalgic for Brazil. It starts "My land has palm-trees / Where the thrush sings . . ." It is widely quoted and often parodied.

FREEDOM SUN IN THE TROPICS

There was no way of knowing whether it had flourished because the seed had been in some way special, or whether there had been a particularly nourishing substance in the soil, but the fact was that this particular almond tree had stood out right away, among all the other saplings on that first day when they were planted in the yard. At the end of the vacations it was already sturdy and growing fast. A few months later it had turned into a reasonable-sized bush, almost as big as the girl, as verified in the photograph still to be found in the album. The following summer it had grown taller than the teenager. And now it was amusing to imagine that one day the woman, frail as she was, lying on the ground, had thought about comparing her size to that of such a tree, that looked centuries old with its rough and creased trunk, raising its crown so high that the fishermen could see it from afar, from the ocean beyond the bay, and set their course by it to return to the village. And for that the tree was perfect. A point of reference, well planted, the north of a homegrown compass that always showed the way back and rolled out the welcoming paths. Solid and sunny like the house, with which it made a harmonious and well-proportioned twosome. Protective shade.

Right now she thought shade would be most welcome. The heat was becoming unbearable. The sun declared it was time to break the spell, set a term to the frozen moment, move, talk, leave. Lena realized that she would not be able to get up by herself, and would need help. She called toward the house, loudly.

"Mother!"

The voice responded so close and soft that she was startled.

"Here I am, my child. You want help getting up?"

"I do, please."

And while her mother rose slowly from the chaise behind her, the woman felt a slight irritation creeping up in her. For how long had she been watched like that? Of course, she was well aware that her mother's nearness could have other meanings. For how long had her mother been beside her, keeping vigil in silence? Why did Lena always have to react with that touch of roughness, guarding her territory, feeling invaded? Everything could be so much simpler . . . But why had Amalia not said anything, not given any sign that she was there?

"Have you been here long? I never saw you come . . ."

"You were so absorbed that I though best not to interrupt your thoughts. I was sitting there, looking at you, you are so thin, my dear, you have to eat better."

The years passed, the refrain was the same. This girl does not eat, I don't know what else to come up with, every day at mealtime it's hell . . .

"Has it been long?" she insisted.

Her mother was vague about it: "More or less . . ."

"Why didn't you talk to me?"

"I thought it was best for you."

Of course, that's what mothers are for, always to find what is best for the children and do it. Lena felt that the tenderness was real and strong. And this time she did not even disagree.

The irritation was different, archaic. At least as old as the time of her first boyfriend, maybe when she first became conscious of it, at fifteen, when her mother read the letters she had kept in her drawer, without asking, always "it's for your own good; it's best this way." But there was no sense getting annoyed about these things so much later in life. She should have made a fuss at the time, confronting her, marking her territory. She had swallowed so many things for so long that there was no point in vomiting it out all of a sudden. She had much more urgent problems. And she needed the calm and the tenderness to sweep the cobwebs from her mind. Better channel the affection toward the concrete.

"The heat is crazy, isn't it, Mom? I think I would like to go in for a spell. We could make some lemonade the way you like it . . ."

"I had them get some cashews for you. If you like, we can squeeze them in a jiff."

And the two women went to the kitchen, like so many human females along the centuries. This time they would not stew over things unsaid, or season with pent emotions the food they prepared for the offspring or the warrior. But the chosen silences, picked out from among impurities like beans, followed them, in the best feminine tradition, to be stored, always at hand, in a well-stocked pantry, or carefully frozen for future use.

Even though, apparently, they were just two beautiful animals, escaping the heat, and quenching their thirst with the juice of pressed fruit.

II

Traduzir uma parte noutra parte
que pra mim é questão de vida ou morte
Será arte?

(FERREIRA GULLAR)

To translate one part into another part
that for me is a question of life and death
Would that be art?

Early in the morning, amid the rags of fog rising from the ground, she had seen a boar stepping suddenly onto the trail, in the middle of the woods, to drink at the river. That was the truth. She had really seen it. Even she was astonished. Of course, in the world of an Asterix cartoon the boar would not surprise anyone. Or if the woman were a character in a medieval story—or even in the eighteenth century in Europe, who knows when the growth of cities and ecological threats had driven boars away—she would have been able to deal with the situation more matter-of-factly.

But at this point, however logical and absolutely convincing the explanations, it was difficult to avoid a feeling of wonder. She, of all people, from the land where the thrushes sing, wandering in woods where boars drink . . . She, of all people, who had received from Alonso, one Christmas, a beautiful twentieth-century art book with the inscription "For the most XXth-century person I know." Well, yes, of all people. But she should not be surprised. After all, even if she had not lived through the war that was so well documented in the photos of the big book, she had seen much more astonishing things than boars in those twentieth-century years allotted to her—not that there had been so many of those years. But at that moment, before her. There was the boar. Undeniable, solid, heavy, panting, covered with muddy bristles. And she was astounded.

She could not avoid the sudden wonder at that unexpected animal, a survivor, protected by the hunting preserve, right by the side of the narrow road that wound up the slope where the *paesino* perched its eight hundred inhabitants in old stone houses embraced by a wall that spoke of seven centuries, in the middle of a field where Roman ruins and Etruscan tombs were not as astounding as the vision of the panting animal. And above all there was her surprise at that astonishment, the intuition that she ran the risk of becoming like all the others, of turning into another kind of being. One of those who are astonished when they see an animal drinking water when it felt safe, and who anesthetize themselves against the knowledge that defenseless men are dying of hunger. In her country it was like that. The poem and the national anthem sing: "Our woods have more life." But life can be a manner of speaking. It depends on what you call life. A form of life where routine violence did not astound anyone. But where protected animals drinking clean water in a wood would really be an astounding sight. Sad land, sad times.

Rhetoric. Sad was what had come before. At the time of exile without romanticism, an exile that had nothing to do with what Gonçalves Dias sang about in his poem, his lines incorporated into the national anthem. Does it really make sense, thought the woman, for a country founded by deportees, that even in its national anthem remembered the pain of banishment, and quoted the song of exile, to banish people in the middle of the twentieth century, scattering exiles around the world? "Dear God, do not let me die before I return." Same poem, another anthem, same longing.

Even now, when the trip is to last only a few weeks, a working trip, and when exile is no more than a desecration back in time. Far away, hurting in a dusty corner of the soul, with a huge boulder on top. But even so, reverberating. Despite the round-trip ticket in her pocket, despite the assurance it gave that two Sundays from now she would be once more wearing the hot sun of home, away from this grey exile sky.

That was it. As soon as she was far away, longing set in. Maybe a bad habit from other times. But Lena could not really complain. Her exile had not been that long, or involved as much deprivation as others'. Strictly speaking, it had not even been real exile, but more like a voluntary absence, before absences were imposed and limitless. She never actually thought of that time as exile, exactly; it did not really deserve the name. The others were exiled, those who had had no choice. Not her. It was a season. A long season, almost four years, but a season. She had had the chance to get truly interested in many things about the adoptive countries, to wear as well as possible the borrowed skin of other languages, of other kinds of humor.

A true exile had been that of Honorio, for instance. What a coincidence, thinking of Honorio at this point, because right away her traveling companions would be mentioning him.

In the front passenger seat, Maria turned back and said:

"How nice that we get to bring you here, Lena! This is not at all touristy . . . This place is on no guide to Italy, nothing important happened around here, there is not a single work of art. Just a small, comfortable house that we rented, as I was telling you yesterday. You'll like it. The village is graceful. It is simple and does you good. Like the visits from friends such as you. Every time you come, one feels one has not interrupted anything, even if we don't write."

"Every time you come," Antonio added, "it is like a bit of Brazil that comes with you. Of the better Brazil, of course . . . There is another one we are not at all eager to see. But it ends up being the one that comes most often. To shop at Gucci's and sit in a café on the Via Veneto."

Lena, who had been thinking about longing, asked the question that had been worrying her:

"How do you manage to stay away for so long? Don't you ever think about going back? This exile of yours, even if it is voluntary and atypical, is getting a bit too long . . ."

Maria's answer showed a touch of nostalgia:

"No idea." When my parents were still living, I thought about returning. But now . . . What for? We are doing so well here. People get more respect. And now the children are married, we have the grandchildren around here too. The people I love most are here."

But Antonio's answer was conclusive, its jokiness disguising anything else it might include:

"I can't return. I cannot live without soccer and Brazilian music. All the best Brazilian players are playing in Italy. And every time I go there, all I hear on the radio is rock. Only here do they play our music every day. What am I going to do over there?"

Lena laughed and explained:

"I see. But I keep asking because I would like to have you closer. We see each other rarely, and I am not a great letter writer, I know, but the affection is always there. You know that . . ."

Funny, she thought. She liked Maria and Antonio very much, they were rare and true friends, but it is so difficult to say what one feels. The moment was one of declarations, however, and Antonio went on:

"Go figure. Did you notice? Time passes, and it is as if we were getting closer. Even when we spend a long time without seeing each other, without writing or talking. When we do get together then, we don't have to fake anything. We understand each other, even if we disagree, even if we changed in some ways. I felt just the same way when I ran into Honorio, after all those years, for instance . . ."

It was no more than a passing thought, a spark of affection, there was no need to say more. A good emotion breaking through the fog.

They drove on in silence for a few more kilometers; the road cut through fields of small daisies and poppies. And in the silence, she recalled Honorio and their last conversation.

It had been soon after his return to Brazil. Ten years of real exile. During that time, they had managed to talk a couple of times on the phone, but they had not seen each other. They were always in different countries. And after she returned, every time she went to Europe, she tried to meet with him, but he had always just left that town or not yet returned to it.

Even so, while she was still living in Paris, they had managed to fight at a distance, despite their fondness for each other. Something about his having given her address to someone for correspondence meant for a third party she did not even know. Lena felt invaded and was very angry. The letter reached its addressee, but she saw right away that the thing had Honorio's fingerprints all over it; he always thought he could count on people without consulting them. She called him in another country with an international scolding:

"I do want to return, you know. I am not going to let anyone complicate my life and interfere with that. I do not want to receive a fifteen-page letter, a brick in a tattered envelope glued together with tape by the men, in a ridiculous code full of underlined words, any idiot can decipher it at first sight. You had no right to get me involved in this. I will not allow people to use me . . ."

The fight did not get more serious because his reaction was gentle: "Sure, kid, you are absolutely right, I promise it will never happen again, you can relax . . ." If he had reacted with self-criticism or defiance, Lena would not have been able to take it, and would have been really mad at Honorio, even though she liked him. But there was no danger of that. Honorio had always had a winning style and the gift to match his words to his audience. He would not have let her down that way. So all went well. And ten years later, at his return, after the parties for the exiles and the first conversations that were all about everybody's happiness, when the time came for a real talk, it was a good meeting.

They spent hours at dinner at a seaside restaurant, enjoying the fish, talking slowly, and suddenly Honorio said:

"I am finding this all very nice, but I confess that it is a surprise and a mystery that I am unable to understand."

"What?"

"Your history. Your trajectory. I don't know. You here, today, this way."

Now it was Lena who did not understand.

"Why?"

He took a sip of his orange juice, looked at her, saw again the conventional person he had left taking care of husband and home, so many years before, writing her little charming and sophisticated articles for the culture section of the newspaper, and tried to explain:

"It is strange, and surprising; we had known each other for about three or four years, right? Then we did not see each other for ten. There is something I don't recognize in you. You turned into someone who does not jibe with my memory of you."

"I see. But we never knew each other all that well, there was never that kind of intimacy, don't you agree? We moved in the same circles, had a lot of common friends, and all that. But we were not exactly friends."

"Despite a great unconfessed tenderness," he joked.

She corrected him: "Maybe even because of that great unconfessed tenderness. And on my part, perhaps even an unconscious erotic desire. I would never have admitted that, but I think I was deathly afraid of becoming conscious of its existence. But we always had each other's back, and that was very important. We both knew that we could count on the other in case of need. But without any intimacy . . . Isn't that how it was?"

"That's right. We were not really close. You are right. But we always had a kind of distant affinity, we did not even have to speak of it. I remember clearly the last time we saw each other, before everything happened and I had to vanish—do you remember?"

She smiled, the image very clear in her mind.

"Of course. It was Carnival, in '69. We had agreed to go with a bunch of friends. You came by the house (Marcelo was hiding there, remember?) and we all went to watch the parade of the samba schools, it was still on President Vargas Avenue. I will never forget you dancing and singing "Freedom's Heroes." The float and dancers of Imperio Serrano were fabulous . . ."

She remembered and hummed:

Freedom is rising like the sun
Like the sun, freedom rises . . .
It's a breeze caressing the young
It's a flame that hatred can't douse
In the universe
It's the revolution
With legitimate justification . . .

Now Honorio was smiling, thinking back.

"Right. The text, approved by the censors, actually said "*evolution*." But everyone on the avenue was singing "*revolution*," it was just great."

She chimed in: "Man, it was beautiful. You were singing like someone who already knew of the double life you'd be leading, semi-clandestine, the works. But I did not know anything of all that. I just thought it was beautiful, you singing. You were giving yourself up completely to the music, with your entire body, just into that samba. I will never forget it . . ."

"See?" he broke in, "the image of me that stayed with you was of a guy singing and dancing in the middle of the street. Crazy! That's what I mean. Everybody else kept that image of me as militant, political, the guerrilla, the terrorist, whatever you want to call it. Or when they want to avoid all that stuff, they talk about the unimpeachable professional, things like that . . ."

Lena looked up from the fishbones on her plate and apologized:

"Wait a bit, man, that was not what I meant . . . I have that image too, I mentioned singing and dancing because the memory just came up, so powerful. Don't get upset . . ."

"I'm not upset. I'm enjoying it, Lena. It confirms what I was trying to say earlier. What puzzles and fascinates me about you. I'll tell you a secret."

Now she was curious. She bent forward a little, to listen, as if he had to whisper. But he went on in the same tone of voice, quiet, calm, warm.

"I'm just loving to be back, to see the old places, smell the smells, taste the tastes, hear the language, the music, everything. But one thing depresses me. The only people I can really talk to are my friends' children or the very young. Among the old friends, people of my generation, I don't think there are half a dozen with whom one can talk. They have nothing to say, you know? They are all solemn, serious, whatever. It's a different point of view. You are one of the few with whom I have really enjoyed talking for a while now, it's amazing. You think the way I view things, the way I dress, the food I eat, are entirely natural. And before I left, I would never have thought that this very conventional woman, so housewifely, would turn around this way, become a rare, really interesting, new person. That's the mystery I am talking about, the trajectory. You need to write this up, a kind of deposition . . ."

She decided she'd make a joke of it; she did not want him to know he was making her ill at ease.

"This deposition business is for the prisoner before the bar."

"I'm serious. Tell your story, be a witness. Have you never thought of it? After all, writing is your profession. Has been for years . . ."

Lena told him the truth:

"No, I had never thought of it. My profession is being a journalist, not writing personal accounts. And I don't believe in this. I think it is more honest to declare from the start that this personal-account business is a fiction, a part of the romance genre, if that's what it is called in literature. That is, an invented way of telling things, making believe that they happened just like that, but in fact they did not happen like that. And you know that better than anyone."

Now he really disagreed.

"That's nonsense, Lena, and you know it. Of course, there are certain conventions. When you select, you leave out certain things. One can't tell all."

"But it isn't just that. There are all those people playing hero, telling things they did not do, making up charming epics with other people's actions, not to speak of more seriously dishonest things."

"You are being too severe. Often the guy who writes is in trouble anyway, and if he takes responsibility for something another has done it's because he feels there is no point implicating his comrades by telling the exact truth. It is also a question of security. Or would you rather he told on others for the sake of being faithful to the facts?"

Her question showed a certain skepticism, and her voice had a tinge of irritation:

"More than ten years later? With amnesty and all on the way? You are bullshitting me, Honorio. Don't even try. This kind of talk can fool someone who's out of it. But you and I know that the problem lies deeper. If you can't tell the truth, don't. Fine. But then don't tell lies dressed up as truth, pseudo-factual testimonies to feed future historians."

She was veering into sarcasm, almost aggressive, and was getting openly irritated as she went on:

"It is more honest to admit from the start that you are not going to tell the truth, and embark on a fictional narrative; get the characters all mixed up, combine situations, invent new things, cut what is of little interest. Then it's a very different matter. Too much grass for my mare, as my grandmother used to say. I'd have to be an artist, let language impregnate that testimony, so it could turn into something more productive than a testimony about facts, so it could move into another sphere, if you like."

Honorio's insistence took on an affectionate tone, maybe a bit paternalistic, but at least he stopped being confrontational:

"Listen, Lena. What I am saying is that somebody has to tell about this trip. And you could do it well. If you don't want to do it as a testimony, or a deposition, fine, don't. But you are not getting out of it in any case. It is all the same. Everybody will think that any resemblance to real people, living or dead, is *not* coincidental. You say it is fiction and everyone will want to find out to whom those stories refer, who is the model for whom in the book. In the end they will accuse you anyway of being autobiographical, confessional, whatever, all those literary sins. In the end I think it is still best for you to choose to be journalistically objective and tell what you saw and what you lived through."

"Tell the story from the periphery?"

"Periphery? No. Tell your own story. Little middle-class girl, university student, glitzy South Side in Rio. Don't start talking to me about the working class at the city's periphery, alternative culture, all that junk, I can't stand those clichés . . ."

She laughed. She realized she had used a word from her own personal code, remembered it was a term Adriano's parents had invested with that meaning. Better explain:

"No, I am not talking about the geographic periphery; I am talking about the historical periphery. This is not about the outskirts of the city."

"That's the fashionable one; everybody is running around with brilliant plans for the working-class communities at the outskirts."

"You know that's not where I'm at. I was thinking about that time, just before and just after you left, what we can now call the turn of the sixties to the seventies. For me it was the time on the periphery, when I was always gravitating around what was going on. I had the impression that I was on the periphery of all the most dangerous things happening. I ran the same risks as those at the center. Maybe more. Because I had no protection, nobody to have my back. But at the same time . . ."

He interrupted: "On the contrary, you had the backs of the people at the center."

She agreed. "Precisely. Everything was dangerous, always. And it was not necessarily divine-wonderful. Because I had not chosen it. And more and more clearly I saw that I had no choice. I had to go on, move on, because I also knew I had not chosen to be neutral, no way, all the time I was in complete solidarity with all of you. But that was the only thing left for me, solidarity. Because I did not want to take the same road you had taken. Except that there was no other. And that it was impossible to stay put. At the speed everything was coming at me, that would have been a spectacular smash-up . . ."

It was like a return of that old need to solve the question and the problem. Lena made a move to indicate the end of the meal. She crossed her silverware, pushed away the plate, even took the napkin off her lap to place it on the table. All she needed to do was push back the chair, get up, and leave. In the air, after all those years, there was the same anxiety, the wish to disappear, the need to protect herself.

Honorio, attentive as ever, noticed her actions and went back to the charge:

"And then you left."

"Of course. And I was not the only one. But many did not even have that choice and were sucked in directly from the periphery to the center."

Her friend was getting excited about the turn the conversation had taken. He insisted: "See what I mean? You are very clear about it all. It is obvious you have been thinking about it. Sit down at the typewriter and start telling it. We already have a lot of stories by and about the gang that was looking into the whirlpool, into the eye of the storm. Tell your own tale, Lena. This thing that you call the view from the periphery. How an action you did not choose affected your life."

"What happened to me is completely unimportant."

"It is not. It happened to a lot of people."

"That's true," she had to agree. "In that case, it could be interesting. I could do a report, I can see that. A collection of recollections from those times. A map of different trajectories. I would write down those recollections, a real journalistic enterprise, maybe even a book."

"Nonsense, Lena. Don't be so naïve. This is not a subject for a newspaper or magazine article, or even for a book making believe it is reportage, as in a newspaper. Now it is my turn to tell you that you know better than I that newspapers are the biggest providers of fiction in the twentieth century."

At this point they started to talk newspapers, tell funny stories, and the conversation changed course. But months later, when she was traveling around in old Italy, while Antonio's car rode through the nature preserve where she had just seen the boar, Lena smiled and thought that this time Honorio had been right. "Our pain won't show up in the newspaper," as it said in the samba. Many things are never published. And some are, the devil knows why. At least in some of the rags. But she felt that a paper could be different, that many of her fellows were doing their best to make that happen. And some day the whole country would be different, who knows? And in a new context, it would have a different press, all part of the same whole.

She also felt that fiction had nothing to do with this, whether it was something invented or something that had happened, that's not where the difference lay, despite the kinship with the Latin word for pretending. Where was the difference? Maybe in the need to spit something out, to translate into words the eye of the writer's inner storm, to let the language be more important than the facts or the plot. That must be it. Something like that. As if it were a disease, an obsession with turning words around and around, under all sorts of light, transparent or shadowy, under all kinds of lenses and mirrors, deforming them, inverting them, glittering, reverberating. Something that spurted out uncontrollably, irrepressibly. Like hunger, thirst, or sex. Like an animal crashing through the trees. Like that boar that just now had surged out of the woods in the fog. An animal so otherworldly, so much of this world, from a universe so different from that of the fauna that inhabited the distant world of the newsroom.

III

Falo somente para quem falo:
quem padece sono de morto
e precisa um despertador
acre, como o sol sobre o olho:

que é quando o sol é estridente,
a contrapelo, imperioso
e bate nas pálpebras como
se bate numa porta a socos.

(JOÃO CABRAL DE MELO NETO)

I speak only to those I speak to
Who suffer from death-like sleep
And need an alarm
Sharp like sun on the eye:

Which is when the sun is strident,
Against the grain, arrogant
And punches your eyelids
As one knocks on a door, with fists.

The fauna at the newspaper included, for instance, Barros. But Lena knew that she would never be able to stick that character into a book or onto a stage for the play that, at times, she thought of writing. It would be unrealistic, clichéd, unabashed typecasting. Nobody would believe that such a stereotype could really exist—sliding right over into caricature. He cared only about samba, soccer, and women. Truly. The rest was camouflage to take in the dodos. He directed a samba school, never missed a game of his favorite team (from the VIP section, since nobody is made of iron), loved to do a spot of ogling when any likely girl crossed his field of vision and to gossip with his friends about who-was-laying-whom. Yet he was taken as one of the mythical old-time professionals, and might even once have been a good reporter. Once, very long ago. When he had still had the mythical fire in the belly, and the desire to rise. Before he went over to administration and wearing the owners' starched shirt. He was so completely on the side of power that, though he put on liberal airs and made the occasional show of personal solidarity to friends who got themselves into trouble with the repression, he was perfectly able, at the same time, to be friends with a torturer who was a frequent guest at his home.

When Lena learned of that, she could not believe it; she thought it was nasty gossip, that he would not do something like that. She thought it best to ask the man himself at the first chance.

"Barros, do you know that guy is connected with the repression? That very reliable sources state that he personally tortured Celso?"

He assented. And justified himself:

"There is nothing wrong with that, Lena. When it's a matter of friendship, one cannot be radical. What matters is not politics, it's the human being . . ."

"Precisely. It's as a human being that the guy . . ."

"He is a very good person, you have to know him better. A very good father, good family man, incapable of harming a fly."

"Only a prisoner who falls into his hands and cannot defend himself . . ."

Barros was still defending him: "That's inside, it's his job. It does not interfere with his relations with anyone. You have to see him here, outside, Lena. He is an incredible person, gentle, learned, very polite, refined, a great person. I insist on your meeting him, so you can overcome that prejudice of yours."

She could not control herself: "Barros, I know it's none of my business; it's your house, your life, you choose the friends you want. But, damn it, you can't impose that guy on your other friends, who also come to your house and don't suspect anything and risk running into him. You can't close your eyes to his 'job.' You just can't, Barros."

He protested: "You are always the radical."

"Don't change the subject, Barros. I am actually shocked. I am amazed that you, who are such good friends with Honorio, are doing this when your friend is living in exile. You, of all people. When Honorio was jailed, you behaved wonderfully, found out where he was, broke through the news blackout, kept him from being tortured on the operating table while they extracted the bullet, all that stuff. How can you be having lunch with a guy like that? Barbecuing for him? Allowing him into your house, with your kids? Callado said once that one has no business having lunch with people who want to eat us for dinner."

His explanation was the big surprise, the greatest shock: "There is no difference between him and Honorio, don't you see that?"

"How come no difference? This is absurd. You are out of your mind, Barros; do you realize what you are saying?"

Barros must have liked her. Patiently, almost fatherly, he explained what to him was obvious, held no mystery: "That's just it. And if you stop a moment to think, without being radical, without playing the little Manichean girl, without looking at your world as divided among cowboys and bandits, you will see that I am right. He and Honorio are both patriots, each in his own way. Both love Brazil and want progress for our people. Both think one must not waste any more time waiting for things to fix themselves. Both are impatient to find a way to change what is wrong in this land of ours. One of them thought that terrorism offered a shortcut. The other thinks that torture is a way of saving lives."

She was indignant: "What do you mean, saving lives? You must be joking. A very bad joke, by the way. You can't possibly believe this, Barros."

"Of course I believe it, Lena. It's logical. And you, a smart girl, will follow my reasoning. If, by torturing a guy, you manage to get out of him information that lets you block new acts of terror, information that could not be obtained in any other way, then torture is a way of saving lives."

She realized that the boss was not teasing her, or joking, as she had thought. He was serious. She felt disgust, and a growing anger, but she tried to keep her cool and argue it out.

"Barros, nothing justifies torture. Nothing at all. No reasoning, however tortuous. And to begin with, what you call terrorism isn't terrorism; it's an armed struggle, urban guerrilla, whatever. Terrorism is to spread terror, attack the innocent, defenseless people, take up violence when there are other forms to protest, a free press, a functioning legislature, freedom of speech and of assembly, right to strike, all that stuff. Terrorism is what the Red Brigades were doing in Italy, or those German groups, the Basque separatists, those groups in the Middle East. Or, around here, those bombs at the Press Association, at the Brazilian Law Association, at newsstands, at the National Bishops' Conference. That has absolutely nothing to do with the activities of those men who were tortured. Damn it, you have the example of Mateus, your dear friend, your child's godfather, I know that much, that wonderful, sweet person, who was jailed, tortured, broken, for nothing, just because one day he gave surety for an apartment where some guy the police was looking for spent one night . . ."

"Well, yes. Shit happens. It's life. Both sides can make mistakes, but that does not invalidate anything I explained to you. The torturer, just like the terrorist . . ."

"It is not terrorism," she repeated. "Terrorism is something else, completely different. It's resistance . . ."

"There you go, with your little semantic games. It's all the same thing."

She saw it was useless to argue. And useless to tell anyone anything about it. They would not believe it. The image of Barros was that of the old, friendly, liberal reporter. Those who did not know him swallowed that reputation. Few came close enough now to learn what he was really like. One day, some intern would find on his daily reporting chore list: "Barros is dead, a former staffer here, a journalist of the old guard. Cover the funeral." And probably he would hear a lot of people praising the old bohemian friend, the good carioca, a boon companion, fun to talk to at the bar or in the sauna. But when he went to interview his ex-wife, the girlfriend, the child's godfather, the people who really knew him, it would be embarrassing. Because they would know that Barros was not being buried that day: he had been dead and buried for a long time, and what remained was just the name and the fame. They had mourned him long before, and often. Their eyes would be dry.

For Lena, as she thought about the conversation with Honorio at the restaurant, Barros was a symbol. He proved that it was impossible to write

FREEDOM SUN IN THE TROPICS

about real people as they are, show on a stage the facts as they had really happened. Nobody would believe it. Fiction needs the kind of plausibility that reality seldom achieves. Things have to seem true in a play or in a novel, even if they aren't. They have to look like facts that could have been reported in the newspaper. And Honorio was right; newspapers were the greatest fiction of the twentieth century, even as a setting.

But she, too, was right. She could not follow Honorio's advice and make believe that she was writing an objective report when, dealing with real people, she would inevitably give her own private opinion about them and create enemies, or else lie to preserve civility.

On the old road, climbing the hill in the car, the woman remembered those conversations and thought more deeply about all that, convinced more and more firmly that she would end up writing. It was cold, and the wind was chilling her ears, when, at the top, they came to the wall with which, so many centuries before, the inhabitants of the little town had protected themselves from their enemies. Far down there, the plain held ancient tombs and vineyards as yet leafless. Up here, the wind blew around a head that could not stop thinking about the growing need to retrace the trajectory Honorio had talked about.

The longer she thought about it, the more clearly the woman saw that what interested her was not exactly writing a testimony, as he had suggested. It was the dizzying sensuousness of the word itself that attracted her. She could tell this or that, it did not matter that much. But ever more clearly she saw that just as those ancient inhabitants of the village had cut the stone to build, in the form of houses and walls, an urban book that would bring them alive again so many years later, she, too, wanted to sculpt and chisel the rough stone of everyday language, shared in the common life of her fellows, in order to build a shelter that would protect them all from the cold and fog of winter, from the onrush of wild boars in the night, who don't see where they go or what they tear up as they speed along. For herself, too, a shelter that would be her own territory, safe from invasions, contamination, the editor who cut out sentences or inserted punning subtitles, as they did in the newspaper. A place where simply putting her foot to the ground would renew her strength, as with Antheus of Greek myth. Or the bull in his corner in the arena, where no bullfighter may kill him. Like a wild animal who marks his territory, pees all around it, and woe to him who does not pick up on the scent and dares to enter.

A dike against invasion, marking her own territory of personal freedom. No wonder that, so many months later, back in the sun, in her mother's house, the same strong desire to raise walls around herself made her remember the visit to the *paesino* with Antonio and Maria.

She was bruised, sick, at her mother's house, listening to the tick-tock of her grandfather's old clock on the wall, with the chime that, every quarter of an hour, brought back the music of her atemporal childhood. She was at home. Her mother's. At the same time, a place that was very much hers, and that had no place for her own self, thought Lena. Especially now, at such a delicate time, when she had left her job at the newspaper to work on her own writing, placing the mortar on each brick, for each wall, of her own home and shelter, and having to face the reality of her illness, that pushed things out of plumb and distorted the straight edge.

But that she could not bear to think about. At least, not yet. Maybe in a few days. Or a few hours. She knew that, in the end, she had come to search for the kind of quiet that would allow her to look her situation in the face. As if she had to refuel by going back to the past in order to be able to face the future. An attempt, perhaps, to rediscover the unthinking security of childhood, which she had known between those walls, and among those trees, caressed by that same breeze that at times was even somewhat irritating in its constancy. In the end she might well still nourish the hope that the sea breeze would carry far away the web of reality that, on the one hand, recalled the doctor telling her she would never be able to have children and, on the other, the realization that words no longer obeyed her, and only heeded her summons when and if they wanted to. Or even, at times, would send other words in their places.

The future was all fenced in. Neither creation nor procreation.

No wonder that in the present, she bumped into walls and had trouble standing upright. Or that she kept turning her fabric inside out, trying to stitch together scattered bits of weaving, searching for some point in the past that would provide a frame. If only to use up the leftover bits of fabric for a homemade quilt.

Her mother's voice interrupted her: "Isn't it time for your medicine?" Was there something for it? Even now? Could something from the outside help her, take away the pain of opening her eyes?

Her mother insisted: "Take it, child, to go on getting better."

It was less trouble to open her mouth and swallow it than to argue. She did not know whether she was getting better. Or what it meant to get better.

True, she was no longer falling over all the time. Come to think of it, that hadn't happened for weeks, that sudden not knowing what was up and what was down, a loss of orientation, of vertical and horizontal, and finding herself on the ground, eyes open, seeing all, hearing all, not unconscious or out of it, not dizzy, but also with no idea of how it had happened. So she must have been getting better. And it must have been because of the medicine. Or of all the prescriptions, there were so many. But she kept forgetting more and more things. Not those from before, which seemed invigorated and rejuvenated. But she forgot everyday things, was living inside only and finding herself suddenly, to her surprise, on the street, with no idea of where she was going, where she had just come from, or what she was about to do. Or startled, in the middle of a conversation, with no idea of what people were talking about, or what she was supposed to be saying next.

The doctor explained that she was running into white spots. Given the usual racism of the language, the expression was surprising. What she felt was that she was running into black spots, regions of total darkness, the color of pitch, where she could not make out anything. And then suddenly she broke out into the light, blinded, without knowing how she had gotten there.

These moments were still frequent. She even had the impression that she was having more of these "episodes," as somebody had called them. She was not getting better at all; she was getting worse. And she was also getting worse about words; she knew that. Even if she concentrated before speaking, she noticed that often she said the wrong thing, without feeling it. Other times, she did not even notice. But she saw the puzzled expression of the person she was talking to. Once again she had said something that made no sense.

This knowledge hurt more than the nausea, the headaches, or anything else physical she felt. How the hell could they think she was getting better? Was that any kind of getting better? Did getting better mean being divided between two worlds? Did it mean looking pretty and obedient in the outside world where everybody saw her, like the exemplary little girls of the old children's books, while in another world, inside, the wheels turned endlessly in her head, thinking and remembering ceaselessly, and she could not share her vertigo with anyone?

And on top of it all, this was happening precisely when she was coming to the conclusion that she would indeed do her work, gather the interviews, analyze the letters and statements, blend the facts from the newspaper clippings with her own painful memories, try to organize the fragments into a play, lay out the drama, tell on stage that trajectory of a woman on the periphery of events.

Could it be that her illness was just a way of transferring to her body the fear of all the impediments and obstacles she predicted and knew she would meet? Could it be fear, laziness, panic? Or was it because of her situation with Alonso? Off she went again on her merry-go-round. Her analyst had even examined her brain scan and declared that it was not just an emotional or psychological condition. But what if it were? What if he were wrong? What if something in her inner world was managing to deceive even him—and her?

But she wanted so intensely to defeat this, she wanted to win this one, she did not want to lie fallow.

"Who is it you don't want to follow, child?" Once again, her mother's voice cut into the darkness as if someone were lifting a curtain slightly and letting a sliver of sunlight invade the room. Just a sliver. It blinded her suddenly, without shedding real light.

"I don't understand. What are you talking about, mother?"

"I am the one who does not understand, Lena. You said you had to follow . . ."

"Me? I didn't say anything. This is weird."

"Sorry, I thought you had. I must have misheard."

Of course she had said something. Her mother was trying to gloss over it, not to hurt her. But she knew she had said something, aloud, and she did not know what it was, had not the least idea what it was.

Lately she kept doing things like that. Saying things that did not make sense. Isolated phrases that made her vocal cords vibrate unknowingly, sounds she articulated on her tongue and that came out of her mouth. Or she would forget to say what she had just thought, and fall silent, waiting for an answer to what she had not said.

Even worse was what had happened the week before, with the release for Paulo's show. She did warn him, when he asked her: "I can't, Paulo. I have not been able to write."

She liked him so much, loved the work he had been doing, as he found his own style, inventing a new way of doing things after his return from exile. She really wanted to support him on that first show, which was so important for her friend. She did not want him to think she did not appreciate it. That was why she did not give him the usual excuse that she was so busy and had no time, as she had been doing for a while, to get rid of all possible engagements that might endanger her relative safety. No, to Paulo she had told the truth, though somewhat attenuated, placing the blame on her medication: "The thing is, I am taking some meds that disconnect me. I can't write."

"Nonsense, Lena. It's just a paragraph, to distribute to the press. You know me well, know my life, my work. You'll do this with one arm tied behind your back."

Was it possible to joke about it? To say that the arm was broken? She did it. It was really a small job, fifteen lines, max. She wrote it, reread it, approved of it. And when Paulo came to pick it up the next day, she gave him the page.

"I think you gave me the wrong writeup, Lena. This is something in code, or some kind of text that does not make sense."

She took it back, tried to understand what was written, and couldn't. She read it again and started to cry. She knew it was the same thing she had written the day before. She was sure of that. But where were the words she had thought and arranged so well, with so much care? Why had they turned into something else on their way to the paper? How come she had been able to read it right after writing and now she no longer recognized it? It was like a mother not recognizing her child.

Paulo had already shared many difficult moments with her. At the university, at demonstrations, along the thin threads that connected a clandestine life and life within the law, exile and being inside. He did not have to say anything to show he cared for her. He put his hand on her shoulder, stroked her head for a moment. Then he got up, went to the bathroom, and returned with a box of tissues.

"OK, cry as much as you like. Then, when you calm down, you'll explain it all. Want a cup of coffee? If you tell me where things are, I will make some for us."

"No, thank you."

"Then I'll make one for myself. We'll let some time go by."

Paulo went to the kitchen and she followed him. He was opening cupboards, filling the kettle with water, rummaging in drawers. She let him, trying to hold back her tears. She did not want to be a drip. But how was she going to explain? What was there to explain? She didn't know either.

All she could say was: "This is what I wrote, Paulo. Or it was. I don't know what happened. But it has been like this for a while. I think one thing and write another."

He sat down beside her, with a steaming cup of coffee in his hand. He opened the typed sheet of paper on the table, and observed: "I see. Here is my name, you can tell that. But this sentence is sort of complicated: 'There hesitates an alien of the resigner Paulo Filgueira that is bilinguist . . .' That's complicated. Are you sure this is about me?"

Lena had a glimpse of something taking shape: "Wait a minute, Paulo. I just remembered something. This 'hesitate' at the start is 'exist.' It started with 'exist,' I am sure of that. I remember that I did not want to use the verb 'to be' so it would be different from the second paragraph: 'there exists'—'there is.'"

"Well, if that is the case, then the 'resigner' must be 'designer,' which is what I am." That was it! With all their sense of humor and deductive ability, they eventually decided that the text started with "There exists a line by the designer Paulo Filgueira, that is distinctive . . ." On they went. With some more effort and much laughter and some choking up, they finally deciphered, more or less, what she had written.

"See, girl? It wasn't that difficult. What you have to do is read aloud, looking for the sound, that makes it all easier. The important thing is that you are thinking straight, the ideas are perfectly connected, your logical thinking is not affected. It is something formal, it can't be serious, it's just on the surface. The structure of your thought is cool."

She said nothing. There was some hope. For the first time she noticed what kind of distortion was happening. At least in writing. Speaking was different. Either words disappeared completely, impossible to retrieve them, or they tumbled out on top of each other, in a gobbledygook that nobody could understand.

Paulo continued to joke, trying to make her feel better: "See, just go with Shakespeare—there is method in your madness."

She did not much like the word "madness" in that comment. But she knew that Paulo's help had been important. Not just because of the affection, but also because of the keen observation and the aptness of the joint discovery. She would have to think it all through.

That was when she had decided to give herself some time, drop everything, and go to the beach, to her mother, using the pretext of the recently broken toe. Because she did not dare ask shelter for the internal cracks.

Before he left, Paulo made one more suggestion. "Look, Lena, could it be that they are doping you with all that medication? Why don't you try something different? A homeopathic treatment, acupuncture, something like that . . ."

"Good idea. I'll think about it."

She did not want to tell him that she had already gone on that particular pilgrimage. Maybe she should have been more patient with that homeopathic treatment. But since she had continued to fall after some days of treatment, she had given up. As for acupuncture, that had been her great hope; she had had such good results on so many other occasions. But this time the thing may have been too radical. She had had a little run-in with Professor Zanotti, who had made her give up those lines of action once and for all.

It had started pretty well. She had gone to his house one sunny morning. Just going there had made her feel she was getting better. It was up on a hill, and you reached it by climbing a road through the forest, past old fountains from the time of empire. There were glory trees in bloom, and the golden splashes of the canafistula amid the silvery trumpet trees mottling the forest.

Climbing this road always made Lena feel better, and she thought it was because of the landscape itself and had nothing to do with her having been born up there, having her umbilical cord buried in that ground, having played on those streets and run up and down that hill in the meadow or after the goats. It was her mountainside that balanced the sun madness of the beach that she had always adored. It was more than that: it was the territory of the other grandparents, memories of her father's side.

She climbed in silence, thoughtful: these good memories must be a sign of good hope, of something positive happening. She was not even surprised to realize that Professor Zanotti lived in exactly the same apartment house and the same tower where she had been so often as a child to see her grandparents. She recognized the entrance, the dark marble of the solemn lobby; she even felt that the metallic grind of the elevator door echoed in her memory.

More than a coincidence, it seemed to her a good omen. It could only be good. It was as if her grandfather were there with her, taking care of her, with his heavy Portuguese accent, teaching her to chew toast with her mouth shut and notice the noise it made as it was crunched, or to unwrap and eat the candies from Lisbon, in the warm complicity of eating between meals, in secret, together.

While she waited to be seen by Professor Zanotti, she looked out the window. The green forest, the city in the distance, all so peaceful. She found herself almost praying. Not the Catholic prayers from the catechism, from the mass, from life before exile. A different prayer, like a conversation with the grandparents who had lived there.

Suddenly she noted, with a tightening around her heart, that there was someone else in that conversation, invisible among the leaves of the jack tree in the forest. Of course! How could she not have known that he had been the one to bring her there? She could almost hear him with the rolling *rr*s from his Paris childhood, his slight cough, his vibrant voice. Dearest old Luis Cesario, who for many years had lived in a house a few streets over, till his painful death a few months before. Eternal Luis Cesario, the old warlock with the magical powers, magus with his ancestral wisdom, Merlin of her heart, laic Saint Francis who stood on his verandah, white mane in the wind, in the perfume from the jasmine tree or under weeping ferns, pouting kisses to the afternoon till the hummingbirds came to drink from his lips.

There he was now, invisible to the naked eye, joking and optimistic as ever, the companion for mysteries, pathfinder. Serene as when he asked her, on the eve of his death, in between the morphine shots that helped him bear the pain, to wear bright colors and a low-cut dress when she went to take leave of him at his funeral: "I want a beam of beauty!"

And with the same kind wisdom with which, as he was dying, he sent her a message: "Tell Lena that I am thinking of her, that beauty exists, and is worth it all."

That was what the leaves were murmuring again now, while the woman waited to be seen, to try to find health again. She smiled. It was good to feel him close. Old Luis Cesario always managed to be by her side during difficult times, always just like this, unexpectedly, arriving without notice and making himself present. Being his friend had been one of the blessings of her life, and it was very good to know that he was near now. He surely had approved of her going for acupuncture. It was as if he had led her there by the hand. And while she waited, she chatted with her friend.

But soon she was called.

Professor Zanotti asked a few routine questions and filled in a form, just like any doctor. Name, address, age, profession. Then he took her pulse, attentively, and asked: "Did you know that you have a slight prolapse of the mitral valve?"

She knew. But to learn it, she had had an electrocardiogram, a test in an echo chamber, and a lot of things. She could not imagine that someone would be able to find such a subtle variation by just touching her wrist with his finger. She was very impressed with the professor, more than ever disposed to trust him, to follow his orders and get well soon.

He asked some more questions. She told him everything she had been feeling, how the falling had started, she told him about the lapses, whiteouts, absences, the whole arsenal of terms she had been learning from the doctors. Then he wanted to know what she ate. The woman described, in detail, what she had for all her meals. She imagined he would suggest changes, prescribe a different diet, but thought it would be worth trying. Probably he would order her to stop eating red meat, sugar, white rice, all that natural nutrition business. To get well, she was ready to experiment.

"You eat all wrong, no wonder you get sick," he said.

She sat back in her chair and waited for the rest.

"Let's cut out all that meat, replace the sugar, and balance this diet. There are *yang* foods and *yin* foods, as in everything, following the principles that govern the universe."

Attentively, she listened and tried to remember everything, though he had told her he would give her everything he had said in writing. If that was the price to pay so she would stop falling down, recover her words, be able to dream of having a child with Alonso, then she would sacrifice and say farewell to a nice barbecue, to the sweets and pies she loved, to a well-seasoned feijoada that made her mouth water just to think of it. She could not have felt more docile, ready to submit to anything, just so she would get better.

Suddenly, in the middle of all those explanations, Professor Zanotti said something that took her aback: "You will also have to cut out milk, cheese, butter, cream, cottage cheese, all milk products."

She questioned him: "Any type of cheese? Even white cheese, all fresh? And ricotta? Fresh milk curd?"

His answer was cutting: "Any cheese. Any milk product. I spoke clearly and you heard me. I don't need to repeat myself. Milk is poison. Only mother's milk is not. Cows don't drink milk—they eat grass."

Feeling suddenly lost, Lena tried to argue: "OK, no milk. But every once in a long while, a little piece of cheese, wouldn't that be allowed?"

"I have told you no, and you understood me perfectly. There is no point coming to me for help if you are going to be stubborn."

Something rebellious was growing inside her. It was still diffuse, but would not let her be silent. She remembered a house cheese Carlota had made once and they had eaten for lunch at old Luis Cesario's house, white, wet with serum but not much, with long holes, perfectly salted, and she asked: "And why can't I?"

Old Luis Cesario smiled and winked at her and Professor Zanotti never noticed: "Look, if you are going to argue about my recommendations, there was no point in coming. I am a busy man and we are wasting a lot of time, yours and mine. I am telling you that you are not allowed to eat any type of cheese because I know you must not. I know what I am talking about. Either you trust me, put yourself into my hands, do what I tell you, and get rid forever of all those infirmities, or you run about out there eating cheese and die in a short while."

Lena waved a white flag. "OK, I will think about it and decide. But in the meantime I will do the rest of the diet, cutting down on cheese, and we have a few acupuncture sessions, which is why I came here. Would that do?"

Professor Zanotti looked at her, very serious, and said: "I don't think you understood me. There is no point wasting time in a treatment that won't work because the patient is not collaborating. There are lots of people waiting their turns, even without an appointment; my time is precious. Either you commit yourself never to eat any kind of cheese again or ingest any kind of milk product, or we stop fooling ourselves. I am a responsible person, a scholar, not a charlatan. If you don't change all your nutrition radically, and that includes the end of ingesting any kind of milk products, you have no chance of getting healthy again, and there is no point in arguing. It is in your hands. It is your choice: health or illness, life or death."

When she realized what she was doing, Lena was standing by the door in her best insolent style, the one from when she was healthy: "Fine; I choose death. I am not interested in living without cheese. Have a good day."

In the waiting room she could hardly keep her tears from spilling while she filled out the check to pay for the fiasco. Then she walked down in silence, shattered. But also proud. Not because she had not given up on the pleasure of a good brie, a bleu, or a gruyère from time to time. But because she had not subjected herself quietly to the arrogant authoritarianism of the professor. That was the first time in weeks that she had been able to stand up to someone. Except, that this had left her exhausted, done in. And what if he was right? And what if she had just wasted her last chance to get well? *No!* Something told her that illness and death were allowing someone to silence her and take away her word and her desire, as the professor had wanted to do. After all, that was what was making her sick; that was what bothered her so much, and why she had sought treatment. She felt she was right. It was not the cheese; it was the word. To live without the word did not interest her. But deep down she also knew that living was always of interest, the rest was just talk. She remembered a passage in a book by Clarice* that said there is more life in a dead dog than in all of literature. And she knew she wanted that bit of life left to her, any kind of life, however frayed and tatty. Or didn't she? What was she to do with a life in which she was no longer able to say what she wanted, or write, just as, more and more clearly, she was discovering the sensuous pleasure of stringing words together?

Her head throbbed as if it were about to explode. She was afraid of falling again. With difficulty, she managed to hail a taxi. She went home. She thought she should make a meal, a slab of beef, rare, and cheese for dessert. But she would not have been able to swallow while her throat was tight like that. She lay down on the floor in the sitting room, trying to relax. She cried till she fell asleep. And the way to acupuncture closed behind her. It was impossible to explain all of that to Paulo at that point. Better just to assent to his suggestion, say she would try, no details. And stay within the safety of the more conventional treatments, in the hands of a good neurologist, whom she trusted, and who was a friend.

Unless it was indeed all in her head. That was why she had gone back to her analyst after they had discharged each other some years back—if that was what you could call it. It was helpful for holding the fort, someone who would listen, make instructive suggestions, and she felt less alone, less lost in the darkness. But he insisted that what she had was physical. And had finally advised her to go to a general practitioner.

"Lena, there is something very real and concrete wrong with you, a node, that appears very clearly on your EKG. In addition, the clinical examination by the neurologist found a whole series of things, which is more important yet than the simple result from the EKG, showing something that you might have had all your life. But we need to know

---

* Clarice Lispector; her readers and admirers always call her by her first name.

why it is manifesting itself now. You are being treated and medicated, and that is good. Only, I think you started from the wrong end, by consulting a specialist. It was you who decided you needed to see a neurologist, you who took the reins of the situation, controlled everything, and sought out a doctor. All that omnipotence does not change the fact that you have not been seen by a general practitioner, and I think you are missing something there that could be very useful."

She tried to justify herself: "But I was falling down all the time, I could not wait, it was urgent. I thought that it was an inflammation of the labyrinth, and went to find a specialist."

"Well, but it wasn't. It was something else, and he saw what there was to see in his field. Starting from the hypothesis or a diagnosis that *you* came up with, which one should not forget either. Now you are following his directions like a good person, but you need to see a clinician."

"You talk as if I wanted to control everything . . ."

"And you don't?" he asked with a smile.

She was a bit irritated: "No, I don't. I understand that there are other things involved. So much so, that I came to you, told you what was going on with Alonso, how I feel about it all, all these recent experiences that stirred me up. I know that, very likely, I am falling down because I cannot stand up to what is happening to me. I am humiliated, shattered, prostrated, whatever. Damn it, I have been talking about this for days; you know that."

"I do know. I am listening and we are working on it. But none of that changes the fact that you started to feel ill and to have those crises while you were traveling, far from here, and did not know that Alonso was falling in love with another woman."

"Right. I did not know. I did not even suspect. But I could have noticed from a distance; I am very close to him, you know? It could be a case of extrasensory perception. And then I could not take it, I lost my balance, I fell over; literally, I went splat."

He did not give up: "It is an interesting possibility. We have talked about it and could go in deeper. But this does not mean you can't see a clinician."

"I don't know a good one. One I can trust."

"I'll give you the name of a colleague; he is great."

"It's no good. I have to fix things here, inside my head," she insisted. "Live through the losses."

She was silent for a while. Then she heard him repeat: "Losses?"

"Yes, this loss of Alonso, that I have to face."

"And what else? You used the plural."

She would have to talk about it, she knew, but she did not feel like it right now so she went off on a tangent: "My father, about whom I only found out on the trip. We'll talk about it another day, today we are out of time."

"Fine. Take the doctor's address. It's in this same building."

She took the piece of paper with the address and left. In the waiting room she made up her mind, called the clinician, and made an appointment. Then she walked toward the beach, sat on a bench on the promenade, and pondered, looking at the ocean. She could not count the times she had done just that, ever since she was a child. Sitting by the beach, contemplating the vastness of the ocean, that immensity of water and sky, and meditating. When she was a child, at the beach house, at the fishing village far away, she had tried to trace the changes on the surface of the sea, make out the ripples where there were rocks, a lighter stain where a sandbank had formed, a different burbling movement indicating a school of anchovies. Often she also ended up imagining what there might be on the other side of all that water, farther than the line of the horizon. Then, at school, she learned it was Africa. It then had been necessary, as an adult, to go to Africa for a series of reports in order to discover how her life might be connected to that land on the other side of the ocean.

It had been a month of unforgettable discoveries, of unexpected similarities that suddenly jumped out at her, of a reencounter with something ancient and from far back, that she herself had not been aware of. The sweetness of the local languages that had so strongly marked Brazilian Portuguese. The general tenderness toward children. The elegant gait of the people, walking as if their feet were simply caressing the ground. The touching pride that they were conquering their own independence and starting to build a new nation. The twisted trunks of the baobabs bursting out of the savannas. The clear waters of the sea, warm and free of any impurities, so transparent that she could see everything from a boat: fish swimming at different depths, even equally crystalline medusas, visible only by how they propelled themselves with their tentacles thrown back like long hair in the wind. The difficulties of the civil war, the curfew, the scattered shots in the night, the daily encounter with people carrying weapons, the obstacles to finding supplies, sabotage, attempts on people's lives. The huge line of ships carrying foodstuffs that went rotten in the harbor as the ships waited for their turn to unload among strict security measures that tried to keep the only two operative docks functioning. The island with the coconut trees before the town. The old Portuguese fort, dominating the entrance to the bay, so much like the relics of Brazilian history, yet so very colonial, operating and deadly such a short time ago. The herb vendors and fortunetellers near the foodless market, since roads had been blocked and fields destroyed. The amulets hidden under the cloths covering their stands so they would not be suspected of witch-craft and criticized in the name of the new revolutionary culture that was paying with the best of its blood for the dream of independence. The children who ran through the dusty streets playing at war with wooden machine guns. The songs and poems, since everybody was a singer and a poet; the twenty-four hours of each day, from dawn that came from the land till well after sunset in the sea, marked by music and verbal images, rhythm and words, a flame that managed to keep on its feet a people who fought for a dream against the will of the power-ful. And all of that with a Portuguese accent. Not the heavy consonant-laden Portuguese you hear in Europe. But that somewhat tropicalized Portuguese, sweeter and hotter, more rhythmic, yet still indisputably Lusitanian, that she remembered in her grandfather's speech, inter-rupted by a cough and wrapped in the smell of strong tobacco.

It must have been because of that. The simultaneous familiarity and strangeness in the same language with a different accent affectively known. The fact was that Lena had started to dream, often, of her grandfather when she was in Africa. And suddenly it was no longer the grandfather, it was her own father, who resembled him more and more as he aged. Until, suddenly, in the middle of a night in which she woke from a nightmare she could no longer remember, Lena realized, with anguish, that she had lost her father and had not even cried for him or known that he had been dying. Dying to her, of course, because he was still very much alive to his other children, especially those from his second marriage. But he had gone far away, distancing himself intentionally, turning his back on her. In particular, destroying loyalty. She was sure that from this point on she would never again share a secret with him, and that was what pained her so—the end of a place common and exclusive to them. She knew that, seen from the outside, all of this would look like a ridiculous instance of jealousy. Regressive jealousy of her father, by an adult woman. But it was more complicated than that. Or simpler. It was death. The man who had formed her character and her tenderness was no longer interested in her, no longer sought her out, did not hear her anymore, did not know what she was doing or dreaming, could not even remember the name of the man she loved, her partner for three years. And, should she want to talk to him, open her soul to him, he would listen absent-mindedly and pay no attention. And then talk about it, superficially, with his wife—Lena was sure of it.

When he got involved with her and left home, Lena avoided taking sides and judging him, however much she wanted to stand by her mother. But she realized that what was happening to him could be something that made him very happy, a renewal, a thrilling rebirth. And she admired his courage, so rare in his generation, not to lie, not to maintain a hypocritical façade, and to face all kinds of social pressures so he could live what his feelings told him to. In the middle of the family upheaval of the period, she never spoke a word against him, never said anything unkind, even when she felt that this apparent neutrality hurt her mother, something that also pained her. But then, as time passed, she felt him distancing himself, and realized little by little that in this new life into which he had been reborn there was no place for her. But Lena only really understood this, all at once, over there, in Africa. On the other side of that immense ocean that she was now contemplating from her bench by the beach. Far away, in the middle of one of those beautiful and strange African nights, that came on after the sun set in the sea, sprinkled with the same stars arranged in different spots in the sky, shuffling all those immutable Brazilian directions that had till then seemed so trustworthy.

She was thinking of that now, again, and trying to sort out her ideas. She felt a couple of raindrops on her arm but did not rise. She looked at the horizon, the leaden sky, the sea as motionless as a mirror. It was going to rain hard. She had to go home. But she did not hurry away. She did not need to run, there was transportation nearby.

It was good to be able to go home, to watch and listen to the rain fall outside, without having to fear it. At least, not personally. But she always ended up worrying when these heavy rains came on. After all, she lived in a city of tropical storms, entirely unprepared for them, with blocked storm drains, garbage piled up on the streets, underground lines blocked. And in particular, a city full of the homeless, and people living in makeshift shacks on the slopes of the hills. It was impossible to be indifferent to this and to react naturally, like a healthy animal in the rain, uneasy but enjoying the relief of tension, letting itself be washed, like the earth, by the water from the sky. Any rainstorm like that one could mean pain for a lot of people in the sequence of events that would then be on TV or in the newspapers: houses collapsing, landslides, the heavy runoff carrying everything along with it, people left homeless, losing everything, sometimes even their lives. She lived in such a distorted country, in such a sick society, that if she did not anesthetize herself, like so many, she ended up feeling bad for such a simple thing, a straightforward reaction to a storm, enjoying the falling water, its volume, its weight, its sound. And she felt as if she had been struck. The same unfair system that kept so many people in misery was robbing her of one of her most basic rights: a guiltless integration with nature. She remembered how she had always loved to watch the rain on the sea or the woods, ever since she was a child, with her brothers, counting the seconds between seeing the lightning and hearing the thunder, in order to figure out whether the bolt had hit close by or far away. Even now she loved to watch the storm gather and then unleash itself, when she went to the house by the sea, feeling the nearness of the rain, following the path of the wind, listening for the thunder in the sky, feeling almost on her own skin the turmoil in the waves, as if she herself were one of the little fishing boats tied up in the domestic safety of the little cove.

IV

As coisas estão no mundo
Só que eu preciso aprender . . .

(PAULINHO DA VIOLA)

Things are in the world
I just have to learn them . . .

When you live in a place like that, on a farm and by the sea, you learn to live differently, according to the weather outside. Amalia was used to it, after many years, but thought that, for Lena, it could prove difficult one of those days, if she were trapped in the house, could not go outside to lie on a mat in the garden, and sun herself with her foot a bit elevated, as she had done for the last two days. Amalia looked at her daughter in silence, lying in the hammock, on the verandah, watching the rain run down the windowpane, and could not think what to come up with to help. She felt that Lena did not really want to talk. But it would be so good if she could feel better.

In the past, when the children were small, rainy days were not easy in the house on the beach. Cooped up, the kids grew restless. After a while, one of them began to tease the others, there would be arguments, she would have to scold, punish them. It was only when they were a somewhat older that they began to use the time to read, draw, or play checkers, play Battleship or Monopoly. Lucky that they had always loved reading. Fernando and Lena read anything that fell into their hands, ever since they had discovered Monteiro Lobato. Teresa preferred books with big print and lots of dialogue. Marcelo was also a great reader. He liked biographies. Of course, he also liked all the stories Amalia used to tell, especially when they involved giants and dragons. And he adored the adventures he read about in the books, those set in the jungle, in castles, on desert islands, or on the high seas. But he preferred the stories that had really happened. He could spend long hours, at night, fighting against sleep while his grandfather recounted incidents from the building of the railroad, things that had really happened. And he loved reading biographies, especially the lives of people who had changed the world in some way. People who knew what they wanted and were stubborn, insisted on doing it their way, faced everything and everyone in their stubbornness.

Amalia remembered once that her mother had said of someone: "He is as stubborn as a mule . . ."

Marcelo was very intrigued by that notion, asked everyone a thousand questions about mules and stubbornness. Then he declared that you should only take the road you want, and if anyone tried to force you to do anything against your will, it was really better to balk. After that he kept coming back to stubbornness. Little by little, Amalia realized that the boy did not understand that stubbornness could be considered a negative thing. As he grew up, he kept reading more and discovering new dimensions of stubbornness. Every once in a while he talked about it.

Slowly, Amalia understood where her son's ideas were wandering about. If Columbus had not been pig-headed, he would not have discovered America. And if Galileo had not been obstinate, and if Osvaldo Cruz had not been obsessed, if Gandhi had not persevered, and if Christ had not had an idée fixe . . . As he got older, the cast of characters grew, and so did the list of synonyms. But the grip, the impulse to fix what was wrong, that was always there. Without it nobody would change the world, nobody would help to make life better. Marcelo worked on that theory. Amalia noticed that it was mostly what he saw in those biographies he kept reading. First there was a phase in which he read saints' lives; he had the whole comic-book collection of "The Sacred Series," he knew it by heart. Saint Dominick Savius so young and determined; Saint Augustine, able to change his life. Saint Francis, giving everything he had to the poor. Saint Lawrence, facing martyrdom without giving in. People who were not afraid of kings or of any powers on earth.

Sometimes Marcelo considered following in their footsteps, dedicating his life to God and to his fellow man; he thought he wanted to study to be a priest. Then, as he got a little older, he saw that the life of a priest would not work for him. How could anyone not go out with girls? Never marry? Decide never to have children? No, it wasn't for him.

At about that time, as Amalia remembered, her son discovered Rondon.* He had never thought it possible that there could be a Brazilian as saintly, as stubborn, resolute, obstinate, persevering, determined, obsessive, obsessed, deserving of all the adjectives of that kind. And damned courageous, wow! To take off on foot, with a small band of men, through all the jungles of this Brazil just to stick some telegraph poles in the ground and help people talk to each other and understand each other, that was something. But Marcelo thought that Rondon was especially wonderful because of that stubborn insistence that nobody should harm an Indian. "Die, if necessary; kill, never." After years of watching Westerns at the movies, with all that killing of Indians, when Marcelo read that order of Rondon's to the men under his command, he thought he had before him another saint's life. The Indians were the first owners of the land. Their descendants were all those hungry backlanders who had no land in the countryside, no home in the city, nothing anywhere that belonged to them in that land that was theirs. They really needed someone determined like Rondon, who could do something for them with no fear of confronting the powerful. And if Rondon had to join the army so he could do his work, then Marcelo decided he, too, would join the army.

"A son of mine? In the army? No way!"

Amalia would never forget her husband's reaction to the new plans of his teenage son. When the subject first came up, the thing turned ugly: arguments, threats, shouts; it seemed that nothing would make the kid change his mind. Then the father had a brilliant insight and settled for a chat, with the ultimate argument:

"Think about it, son. You don't take orders from anyone. If you

---

* Marshal Candido Rondon (1865–1958) was famous for his exploration of the western Amazon basin and his lifelong support of indigenous populations. The state of Rondonia is named after him.

choose a career in the military, you are choosing a life of obeying orders, often from people who are not as smart as those they command, don't know as much, are not as discerning. By the time it gets to be your turn to go through the ranks and start to give the orders, you will be old and embittered, tired of having spent your whole life obeying. And think of whom you'd be obeying . . . Is that any kind of life to be wished for?"

Marcelo was quiet, thinking. He surely realized that he could easily be a stubborn mule but had no talent for being a sheep. He never again mentioned going into the army. He went to the public high school, like his siblings, was soon well adjusted at school, cultural director of the student association, working at the school newspaper. Heaven knows what would have become of him if there had not been the '64 military coup in the country, truncating the cheery playfulness of his fifteen years that dreamt of some generous holiness at his eclectic altar. An altar where, three years later, he installed, in the central alcove, the selfless and heroic martyr Che Guevara. Another mule . . .

But deep down, Amalia thought, Marcelo was still her boy who thirsted for God, and who, as he grew up, removed from inside himself the God she had shown him and took him with him into the streets. He needed space in his heart for another god, a collective one. Marcelo was still, of all her children, the one who thirsted for holiness. Even when he was on the lists of the most wanted with his picture on posters everywhere, her mother's eye saw him clearly, transparent—one of the chosen, thirsty for justice. In the Sermon on the Mount, Christ had said of people like him that theirs would be the kingdom of God.

Amalia remembered vividly each phase of her growing son's life, proud memories despite the pain from which they were formed. With her other children everything had been less dramatic as they grew up, things had flown more naturally; they changed and became different. It was not as with Marcelo, in fits and starts, with clear anniversaries, definite crossroads.

Lena, for instance, now beside her, her marriage dissolved, her foot broken, sickly. (It must be nerves, she had always been an emotional child who cried about everything.) What was going on in her daughter's head? One beautiful day she had announced that she was going to separate from her husband. She never said anything bad about him and was unable to explain her decision, but it was obvious that she had been the one to make that decision. Then, instead of trying to put her life back together, to remarry, find some established man, well off, who might offer her stability and help her start a family, no. She just had relationships, vague and mysterious affairs, nothing really solid. Where had that thoughtful and somewhat tomboyish girl gone, always serious and studious, who was never any trouble? Amalia missed the time when the children were all small, her husband had not left, life had not started to punish her. Sometimes she had one of those fits of longing; they did not last long. But today she thought it might be a good idea to take advantage of this mood to help pass the time on a rainy day. She asked Lena:

"Child, I have been meaning to organize the photographs. Would you like to help?"

"Good idea, Mother. I'll go in with you. Where are they?"

"No, stay, don't bother; I will bring out the box. Only maybe it's better to sit somewhere else because if you are in the hammock it's difficult for us to be side by side and look at the pictures, what with your broken foot. Come, I'll help you to the sofa. Then I will go get the box."

Soon they were both settled on the sofa, looking at the old photos, trying to recognize people, classify the images according to date, the identity of the people in the photos, the place where they were taken. Or by theme, as Lena suggested.

"You have real thematic collections, Mother. You could make collages. Or albums that group them by subject. For example, all the pictures of children's birthdays, there are a lot of them, really good ones. Or all the baptisms. Or all the first communions, look here . . ."

Amalia looked with tenderness at the fan of pictures that her daughter was showing her. That's right, it might be interesting to group all those photos taken in the studios of professional photographers, with the prayer bench, crucifix, rosary, the scenery all ready. How strange to see all those pictures together, side by side. Each child, at seven or eight years old, dressed in white, the girls with veils and wreaths, the boys holding candles, all looking a little sad, serious, slightly scared, perhaps intimidated by the camera and the atmosphere of the studio.

She smiled and showed another one, quite different this time: "If we look, we will find others like this one to make up another series. This idea of yours of putting together similar pictures is funny. I think all of you took some like this one at school. Look."

Lena looked and smiled. It was a picture of Claudia, the youngest, in her little public school uniform, with a crest embroidered on the pocket of her blouse, sitting at a desk, with a pencil in her hand and a notebook open in front of her, as if she were writing something. In the background, hanging on the wall, a large map of Brazil. On the table, in the foreground, a small Brazilian flag. Her hair was neatly combed and held together with a barrette to complete the stereotype, but none of that could break the intensity of her glance and her roguish smile.

"How old was she then? Is there a way to find out?"

"Very precisely. She was six. This was taken in '68. August of '68. I remember going back to the school especially, to pick up the picture that was all paid for, a few days after the whole confusion. Claudia was no longer going to school. So, September."

Lena remembered what had happened, but had gotten the dates and facts a bit mixed up. She thought it had all happened a bit earlier.

"Wasn't it June, Mother? Or May? Yes, May. May of '68. There were student demonstrations in France and here, too, a huge coincidence, two such different processes . . ."

"No, my child. It was August. I remember it well. Because of Soldiers' Day, August 25. May and June were the beginning of the demonstrations. But I am speaking about that other case, when she had to leave school."

"I thought that was the time of the encampments at Botafogo, when there was the invasion of the university administration building."

The memories came back clearly, to both of them. Amalia agreed: "Yes, right, it must have been the beginning of June. But the demonstrations here had started way before May, before those in France. When the police shot that boy at the university cafeteria . . ."

That had been in March, Lena remembered. The beginning of the academic year. A commonplace, routine demonstration by students against an increase in the price of meals. The police came in shooting and killed a boy and then wanted to take the body somewhere, far away, and have it disappear. The students did not let them. They fought over the body and finally won. And the poor humble boy, who had come from the interior of the country to study in the capital, ended up murdered by the police and mourned by a multitude in the great hall of the city legislature, more and more people arriving every minute, everybody staying all night for the wake, rumors flying that the repression was coming to get the body. A tense and nervous vigil, and a general feeling that this time they had gone too far. But all knew that it was only the beginning. March of '68. Beginning of the school year. Beginning of a deadly year.

Then there was the funeral of the boy. There were people from everywhere, despite the government's threats that they would not allow the funeral march to proceed, especially not the long parade on foot, a multitude crossing the whole city, a huge distance to the cemetery. There was a full day of negotiations between the student leadership and there were messages from the government, with mediation by politicians, religious leaders, intellectuals, journalists. In the afternoon, while the crowd grew in front of city hall, those in power had to bow to popular pressure and allow the procession to leave.

It was a tense procession, shouting slogans and singing anthems learned in school, as if it they were some rhetorical flourish set to music and suddenly you noticed that they spoke to the deepest emotions that every person was feeling at the time:

Liberdade, liberdade,
Abre as asas sobre nós . . .

Freedom, freedom,
*Spread your wings over us**

---

*"Liberdade, Liberdade" is from "Anthem of the Republic" (1890), with music by Antonio Miguez and lyrics by José Joaquim Medeiros e Albuquerque. The verses that come next in the narrative are from the national anthem (1831), with music by Francisco Manuel da Silva and lyrics by Joaquim Osório Duque Estrada.

Those words that had sounded hackneyed, read again and again on the covers of student notebooks, mouthed at elementary school music lessons or in the schoolyard where students lined up on the first day of classes, were suddenly no longer empty but became a challenge to the military government, to the usurpers who arrested, tortured, killed. And the multitude followed the coffin through the streets, shouting the national anthem as if to defy the authorities:

Mas se ergues da justiça a clava forte
Verás que um filho teu não foge à luta,
Nem teme quem te adora a propria morte,
Terra adorada
Entre outras mil
És tu Brasil
Ó Patria amada

But if you raise the heavy mace of justice
You will see a true son of yours won't flee from strife,
Neither does he who loves you fear death,
Oh, beloved land
Among thousands,
You are Brazil,
The country I love.

From the windows people threw scraps of paper and applauded. From the apartment houses, along the way, more and more people came out to swell the march that proceeded slowly. Along the Flamengo beach, on the side lanes, buses stopped and passengers got off to join the protest. The entire city was moved by the death of one boy. The sky darkened; night was falling; soon the lights would go on.

But they did not. When the funeral march was leaving Flamengo to enter the Botafogo beach, it was dusk in that postcard landscape of Rio that is the entire bay ringed by lights against the outline of the Sugarloaf in the background. Yet it was dark. A more lyrically inclined spectator could even have thought that the city had put on mourning dress to protest against the violence, refusing to wreath itself in lights. But what was obvious was that the government had resorted to other tricks to form an arsenal that would prove inexhaustible in the coming years, and had ordered the lights to be kept off along the way of the march, hoping, it seemed, the darkness would make the multitude disperse. Now the cars stopped along the road, here and there, began to turn on their headlights. Then someone found a newspaper and improvised a torch. In seconds they multiplied. But they burnt too fast. At the apartment windows, on different floors, people started to light candles, whose faint light broke tentatively into the darkness. Many threw more candles down to the marchers or came down themselves offering flashlights. At the door to one shop a merchant was distributing candles and matches. Lena's throat was tight, she felt like crying as she looked at those miles of faint lights, stretching out of sight, endless, singing the national anthem; her heart constricted. She would never forget, and she could not understand how so many people had forgotten so soon. She remembered every detail. The gates to the cemetery had been closed when the procession arrived—"orders from above." At that point Lena became afraid. She felt the ambush, the trap, the preparation for a massacre. She could not imagine that any responsible authority would think it possible to contain the energy that had driven that multitude to that grave, the force that pushed them forward, despite the distance, against the orders, the darkness, the conspicuous police presence circling them the whole time, with all kinds of provocation. The closed gate was a lure, an invitation to violence, to the start of a catastrophe. New negotiations were necessary to make the burial possible, late at night. And then, the way back home, trying to understand what had happened, gauge the meaning of those last twenty-four hours, trying to imagine what would come next.

But it was impossible to predict that. The seven-day mass, the thirty-day mass, the cavalry let loose against people on the stairs to the church, soldiers unsheathing their swords and marching upon the people, priests holding hands and forming a human chain to protect the faithful against the brutality of the police.

It was not possible to forget or to get the dates wrong. More than any other time, this one had left its mark on the living flesh of all mothers.

Amalia did not forget.

The year moved on, the pages of the calendar were torn off, it was April, then May, one could sense that it would be a restless time among students. And at that precise time the government decided that it was going to take a stand and deliver the nation's educational planning to foreigners. They worked out an agreement between the Department of Education and USAID, an agreement that nobody in Brazil wanted, except for the government, to be implemented right away, an agreement repudiated by the students, the faculty, the scientists, the technicians, all of them, who wanted to be heard, to have more of a discussion, to know what kind of technology was going to be imposed, what changes the Americans would demand be made to the curriculum, what would become of the sovereignty of Brazilian education, whatever else; that was what they were talking about the whole time, as Amalia remembered. And there were meetings to discuss the agreement, ask for more debate. They wanted dialogue. Then it was June. And a meeting was scheduled at the administration building of the university.

The whole calendar was clearly impressed on Amalia's memory. One does not forget things like those. One remembers when a child has the whooping cough, when he breaks an arm, when he spends the whole night with a high fever that won't go down. That meeting had been like that. A vigil waiting for the children. Some of them, at least. Lena certainly would not have gone, since she was no longer a student. Fernando was a journalist, working in another city, so he was safe for the time being. But Amalia was sure that Teresa and Marcelo, and perhaps Cristina, had gone to that meeting at the administration building. One more, like so many others, she thought. Like the editorial meetings of the school newspaper, like the rehearsals for the year-end play, like the countless meetings at the university. But this time it was different. Her husband, who was a lawyer, called:

"I'll be late for dinner, no idea when. I am going to the administration building, which is surrounded by troops. It seems that there is a threat of a takeover and the students are inside. We are going to try to negotiate permission for them to leave, support the university president."

Her heart tightened. She managed to ask: "Do you think it is really serious?"

"No doubt about it. These guys are aching to show that they are in charge; they have still not gotten over all those people protesting in the streets when that boy died. I think it could get really ugly . . ."

Amalia warned him: "Marcelo is there."

"I thought so."

"Teresa too."

"I wish she had not gone," said the father. And after a pause: "Do you know where Cristina is? It seems there are a lot of high school students there too."

Another punch to the heart. Cristina was so rebellious, so independent, always, though only fourteen, refusing to listen to anyone. "She said she was going to study with some friends, and then they might go to some meeting."

"Then she must be there too. Well, I'd better be going. But I don't know when I'll be back. Don't wait for me."

She did nothing else that night but wait. Wait for them to come back, to send news, for the telephone to ring, for news to come up on TV; for the door suddenly to open and the whole family to come in, smiling; for the doorbell to ring and someone come with bad news. Finally, her husband arrived with Cristina. They told a tense and nervous story. The university was surrounded, the students under siege. A heavy climate all afternoon, till the president, politicians, lawyers, and professors managed to negotiate that the students be allowed to leave. The leadership had come out then, protected by this negotiating committee—by daylight, still—through a side door giving onto a street where there was traffic. The others hesitated, the siege closed up again, and they were left behind, surrounded, at night, in a part of town dense with schools but with no traffic, no business, no night life, ideal for a massacre, no witnesses.

Good thing that her husband was a well-regarded, well-known

lawyer. He had been able to go there and help. As he himself went on telling: "In the confusion, Cristina saw me and managed to get close to me. She left with me, at the end of negotiations. She did not suffer anything apart from the scare and some pushing around."

Amalia was still worried. "Alberto, tell me. Did you see Teresa around there?"

"Only right at the start, from afar. She was with Adriano. Then I lost sight of her."

"What about Marcelo?"

"He is OK. I confess that I was very afraid for him. Those guys are aching to get their hands on the student leadership. If they catch them, they'll skin them alive. But all of them managed to get out with us, guarded by politicians, professors, and journalists. They have their own security. I took three of them myself to Copacabana, and traffic was horrible. That's what took me so long."

What about Teresa? God in Heaven, where was Teresa? What right did those brutes have to push around and threaten all those girls and boys, promising to beat them up and punch them out? One carries a child for nine months, puts them out into the world, nurses them, feeds them, helps them grow up, prepares them for life, and there comes some abusive officer and gives his orders to a bunch of criminals and they start to beat up those children one loves and that have not done any harm to anyone? Amalia realized she would be ready to kill. She had to do something, she did not know what, she, who had always been meek and quiet. She swallowed and prayed to God that he would give her strength and patience. And she said: "We have to get news of Teresa. Even if we have to go back there. I called her at home several times and nobody answered."

They called again. The phone rang and rang; there was no answer. It went on like that all night, agony. Alberto thought there was no point in going out at random, it was best to wait a while. She conceded. Her husband was more experienced in those things. But it was nerve-racking. Where is my daughter, oh God? What have they done to her? Don't let anything happen to her, I implore you . . . Look, we'll swap— you save my girl and have something bad happen to me, in exchange, nobody has to know. Please, take care of her, my God . . .

In the small hours, the phone rang. It was Teresa. "Mother, I am just calling to say that I am well. It was horrible, but I was able to escape. Do you have news of the others? I lost track of them, but it was not possible to look for them or to wait. I had to escape . . . I was lucky. But I did not see anyone else, I don't know what happened."

She was agitated, her speech disordered, almost crying. Calm with relief, Amalia could put her mind to rest. "They are all well, child. Cristina left with your father and both are here; they arrived a short while ago. And they left Marcelo where it was safe, in Copacabana."

Teresa relaxed and began to tell: "Mother, it was horrible, you can't imagine. It looked like a concentration camp, I thought I was going to die. And the shots, Mother. They were shooting, they were going to kill us."

She could not stand hearing a daughter crying on the phone, far away, needing her, and be unable to put her arms around her; all she could do was repeat like an idiot: "Take it easy, my dear, don't cry, it's over. And Adriano? Is he all right?"

Little by little, through her daughter's sobs, Amalia heard and reconstructed what had happened, the part that Teresa had lived through.

She had tried to leave with the first group, with her husband, right after the student leaders. But in the pushing and shoving, they had fallen back a bit and were unable to take advantage of the relative protection that the leadership had benefited from. When they managed to get out, they saw that the street was a battlefield and that the siege was tightening. Everybody retreated. They had to return to the university building. As the night went on, it became clear that they had been driven into a trap, a perfect ambush—the place was going to be invaded and the massacre was a question of time. They decided to try leaving again, or at least look for an open space, maybe they could face them and flee. Inside, the tension was unbearable, and the students were beginning to fight among themselves.

They eased toward the exits. Again, Teresa and Adriano were among the first ones. They started to walk across the wide space before the gate, in the middle of the other students, surrounded at a distance by the military police. Suddenly, the shooting started. At first she did not even realize those were shots; she had never heard real shooting, only in the movies, and she thought those dry pops were odd, not as noisy as the firecrackers she was used to on Saint John's Eve or any celebration of a goal in a soccer match. And they were aimed at the ground, hitting the asphalt, just to scare them. But very efficient at spreading panic. Everybody ran off, screaming, and the police amid them, beating them up. Complete confusion, shouts, people falling, being trampled. Somebody saw that the gates of a club nearby were open and thought they would be safe in there. They all started to run that way. And it was just what the police wanted. What had been negotiated inside was that they could leave freely. But the agreement was not being respected; their word was worth nothing. As the police had not been able to get their hands on the leadership, they would have the others pay. As they left, always being beaten, they were all being herded toward the stadium and corralled in the soccer field. All amid a horrible confusion, screams, clubbings, shoving, and all in darkness because the lights at the club were out.

The darkness had eventually saved them. Adriano realized it was a trap and suddenly pulled Teresa by the hand, behind a fence that had some loose boards. From there they sneaked to an empty lot behind it, waited a while, and finally fled to the middle of a road, further down. A car slammed on the brakes right on top of them. A man jumped out. "Are you out of your minds? Jumping in front of a car at this time in the morning . . ."

Desperate, Teresa begged: "Please, get us out of here! We are students and the police are beating up everybody."

Adriano tried to hold her back—after all, that driver could well be from the police too, circling around. "Hop in. I'll leave you where you want to go."

They thought it best not to go home, which was farther away, and stay with Adriano's parents, nearby, on the other side of the tunnel, in Copacabana. But they did not know what had happened to the others.

They learned the following day. The whole city learned during the following days. Despite the horror, it was still a time when one could learn what had happened. Journalists could tell, photographers could take pictures, newspaper owners were disposed to publish. Everybody read the reports, saw the photos; the TV showed live footage. The shock was universal. That same soccer field where a short while before Garrincha's bandy legs had gladdened the Brazilian soul dribbling toward a goal was now the opposite of festive. The photos showed hundreds of young people with their faces to the ground, lying among soldiers who did not allow them to get up and kicked them in the head with their heavy boots or with the butts of their weapons, peed on the faces of the helpless students, and threatened them with machine guns. The brutality of the scenes, the crudeness of the accounts, the sadistic and odious excess of it all, the disproportionate show of force, the cruelty of the whole thing, in short, was like a blow to the head of the city. In the days that followed nobody talked of anything else. It was the only topic at bus lines, at the butcher's counter, at the bench on the little square while the children played, anywhere Amalia went. And from what her husband and her children told her, it was the same everywhere. At the meetings that teachers called at different schools, worried about the fate of education. At the encounters that actors and directors called in various theaters, after midnight when the shows were over. At union halls. At factory gates. At assemblies of priests and nuns in convents and monasteries. At the houses of intellectuals who opened their doors to friends and friends of friends so they could discuss what might be done against all of this, so it would not go by without a word of repudiation. And of course at schools and universities in all parts of the city.

So there was nothing surprising about the fact that even a six-year-old would learn about the events. But Amalia still felt the shock when for the first time she saw little Claudia playing at Botafogo field, with all her dolls lined up, faces to the ground as one of them, held by the child, walked among them kicking them and Claudia shouted and ranted. Amalia could not control herself, and left the room to cry. She wanted to cry all the tears caught in her throat those last few days. But she could not afford that luxury. She was so worried about her older children that she had not even noticed the harm it was all doing to the youngest. She returned to the room, put Claudia in her lap, and talked to her. She saw that the girl was very upset and scared. She played with her, sang to her, told her a story, and then together they put the toys away. But the mother understood that her daughter needed to exorcize those demons, and that the macabre game had been a way to deal with the terror she felt. She decided not to make any direct reference to the fact.

A few days later she was called to Claudia's school. The teacher said that all the children wanted to play those days was Botafogo field. Some would lie face down in the schoolyard and others would walk around them threatening and cursing them. The principal had given orders to find out who had had that idea, afraid of negative repercussions and reprisals against her. The teacher was not sure but thought it might have been Claudia's idea. She was not going to say anything, but she asked for Amalia's help to work around the situation so that the game would not be repeated. She, too, was very shocked, wanted to do something to protest, but did not know what. She was going to get together with some colleagues, people from the union. Maybe they would go the following week to deliver a document to the secretary of education. Everybody wanted to do something, show that they were not in favor, but nobody knew what to do. Amalia remembered those days very well. One of her neighbors, a sweet and quiet old lady, had said to her one day: "I am going to tell you a secret, because I have to tell somebody, and I trust you. I am now standing in line everywhere all the time." Amalia did not understand, but she went on: "I stand in any line, at the bank, at the butcher, at the bus stop. When it is my turn I make some excuse and leave. But while I am in line, I speak ill of the government, complain about the police, have myself a little rally. It's the only thing I can do. The people think I am a bit crazy but with this white hair I can play dumb. And it always starts some kind of discussion—some people tell me to shut up, others support me, and when I leave they are all arguing away. I think tomorrow I am going to the convent of Saint Anthony, there is a novena, many people will be there, and I'll do some agitating there . . ."

As she thought of it, Amalia confirmed once again that it had been June, the feast of Saint Anthony. The calendar for 1968 was all marked up with scares in her memory anyway. It was in June that everybody wanted to protest against the invasion of the university administration building. But it was not yet when things became complicated for Claudia at school. That beautiful, gap-toothed smile she saw now on the photo, that left hand with its dimples open on the notebook, that was August. In the meantime, many things had happened.

V

Ponho no vento o ouvido e escuto a brisa
Que brinca em teus cabelos e te alisa
Pátria minha, e perfuma o teu chão . . .
Que vontade me vem de adormecer-me
Entre teus doces montes, pátria minha,
Atento à fome em tuas entranhas
E ao batuque em teu coração.

(VINICIUS DE MORAES)

I hold my ear to the wind and listen to the breeze
That plays in your hair and caresses you,
Country of mine, and perfumes the ground . . .
How I long to fall asleep
Nestled in your sweet hills,
Aware of the hunger in your entrails
And the drumbeat of your heart.

So many school photos. Different classes, year after year, in neat rows, a teacher sitting amid them, surrounded by thirty or forty children, the same faces repeated and renewed from one year to the next. Lena sorted the pictures, some with signatures on the back, others identifying the subjects by means of numbers and lists, others leaving all the characters buried in the dust of forgetting: it was an effort to rescue one or another. There were also pictures of year-end programs. Stages with adolescents in costume and make-up, playing at putting on a play. Perhaps that was where her passion for the theater had come from—from the realization that a text could be eternal, with ever-renewed readings as it was inhabited by living people. She remembered that she did not like to actually go on stage.

She had done it twice and both times she had felt sick, exposed, with those lights on her. But she had felt an almost sensual pleasure working as a stage manager, imagining the blocking, composing the scenes, inventing solutions, creating movements and situations for the words that throbbed on the printed page. And rehearsals: repeating, repeating, starting with something shapeless and raw to arrive at polished perfection. Maybe that was why, when she decided to write a fiction about her trajectory, as Honorio had suggested, Lena quite naturally decided on a play. She would write something about her experience. She did not know how to write for the theater; she had never tried. She was fascinated by the challenge of stage time, how to condense the action, by the economy of means, the clear definition of characters, the setting up of the conflict. Then, above it all, was the challenge of the crisis. She could imagine a crisis situation, where everything moves toward the inevitable conclusion. She had decided: she would write a play, and not a report, a testimony, or a novel. Even if she had to ask for help from someone to work on the text.

On the other side of the bay, Sonia had agreed to collaborate, to work with her as a team. They had talked a few times. Lena was taking notes, collecting accounts, interviewing people, selecting the material. She wrote a few scenes. The plan was they would sit down and discuss it some more and she would start to put it all together. She would start. She would have started. If her illness had allowed her. How can you weave sentences if the word thread keeps breaking, as on a bad bobbin in the sewing machine, tangling up the yarn so that the needle bites into nothing? She had to get well so she could go on. But how? She was ever more convinced that the medication that kept her from falling also kept her in that kind of cotton-wool cloud where she lived now, a soft torpor that did not let her bump into things. Either that, or she was anesthetized by the illness and not by the medicine. What she lacked was the courage to experiment, to jump into the dark. She was afraid of falling once again, and not being able to get up.

The doctor had made an interesting observation after listening to her in silence: "I did not quite understand how you fell on that plane. Could you tell me again?"

"I had just got on, carrying the hand baggage that I was going to place in the overhead compartment, so I was standing by my seat. When I was about to open the compartment, I got confused by the lemon I was holding, and when I came to myself, I had fallen."

"I see. What I don't understand is that lemon."

"It was not a whole lemon; it was just a slice, a round."

"And what were you doing with a slice of lemon as you were boarding the plane?"

"I don't know either. I was not paying attention. I took it without noticing as I went past the galley when I entered. I think I felt like sucking on a lemon."

"And do you usually suck on a lemon, just so?"

"Not me, God forbid, a sour thing like that. But that day I felt like it. I remember that before they called us for boarding I was thinking how good it would be to have that tomato juice that they would serve. I think I was thirsty because of the heat. Then I went past the galley as I entered, saw the little rounds of lemon, and took one without thinking about it. Why? What does this have to do with my dysrhythmia?"

"I don't know," he said. "I am still trying to find out. Tell me something. What did you eat over there? Can you remember?"

Lena felt a bit impatient. "Look, all of that has been checked. I took all my meals at the hotel, just because there was food rationing and nobody could invite me to lunch or dinner. The country is at war; there are no functioning restaurants. And there is nothing to buy at the markets or in the stores; I could not find a single cookie, a single piece of chocolate. I looked everywhere and could not find a piece of fruit for sale. And all the water used at the hotel kitchen was clean and of good quality; the government is very proud of that; the hotel is their calling card, where all the official guests are housed, and it cannot be found to be spreading amoebae, or giardia, or whatever else. In addition, I brought the results of all the tests I had done—I have nothing from that side. It was one of the first things everybody thought of, some parasite, some tropical disease; after all, I was returning from Africa. But it is proven that this was not it."

"That is not what I am thinking. I want to know what you were eating there. Do you remember?"

"Simple. There was no variety. Basically, rice and fish. With wonderful Portuguese olive oil. Fresh fish, caught every morning, in front of the hotel, right there. And rice. Every day. Lunch and dinner. Every once in a while a noodle soup."

He kept at it. "What else?"

"That was it. The supply crisis is very serious. The roads were totally blocked and there wasn't any way at all for product from the provinces to reach the capital. You can't find a single vegetable, a single egg, a single piece of fruit. And there is nothing canned, not a thing. It is a country at war, and without money. But one does not go hungry; it's just that there is no variety. Rice and fish, as much as you want."

He thought for a while and then asked: "So you spent a whole month without any kind of fruit or vegetable?"

"Precisely."

"And then you started falling. Then as you entered the plane, you were dreaming of tomato juice, and stole a lemon from the galley. I think you were craving vitamins and minerals."

Lena agreed: "True. But if this caused people to fall, there would not be anyone left standing over there. There are lots of people who have been on this diet for a while and are standing up."

"People differ. What I am thinking is that there is some factor in your metabolism that uses up vitamins and minerals very rapidly. You are not able to store them for very long. So at the end of your stay you had exhausted all your reserves. Somehow this must have made your propensity to dysrhythmia manifest itself, though till then you had never shown signs of it."

"And on the basis of what do you conclude this?"

He smiled: "I am not guaranteeing anything. It's just a hypothesis that seems plausible to me."

"And so?"

"And so I will propose something to you. But no guarantee. You will start on a diet that is very rich in vegetables, greens, and fruit, and gradually reduce the dosage of the medication, half a pill a day."

"No. If I do that, I will fall. I will do anything not to fall again."

"A quarter of a pill a day, or every two days. A very slow reduction. We will keep track. Any kind of dizziness or vertigo, you tell me. Try it."

Lena was distressed. "I can't. I don't have the courage. As you say, it's just a hypothesis. There is no guarantee. On the other hand, the neurologist guaranteed that if I take that medicine conscientiously, and never forget to take it, I will never fall again. I'll be able to go out on the street again by myself, walk around, go to the beach. After a while I will even be able to drive again and dance, even round and round. And swim. I'd rather take the medication. Sorry."

"For the rest of your life."

"That's it. For the rest of my life. I will spend the rest of my life not falling down for nothing, ever. Even if to have that I have to take three pills in the morning and three in the evening every day."

"Helena Maria, I can see you are still very fragile, so go on with the pills for another while. I have already told you that I cannot give you any guarantees. But think of it. You mentioned that you would like to have a child. With that medication you could never get pregnant; it would be too dangerous."

"I know. The neurologist told me it would be completely inadvisable in my case."

"Right, but not because of the disease; because of the medicine," he insisted.

She was feeling cornered by his insistence, insecure, distressed; she felt like crying.

"Please," she asked, "don't insist. The idea of falling puts me into a panic. I can't do it."

"At the moment you can't, I agree. But you need to. It will depend entirely on you. You will have to show courage; you may still have a couple of falls during the process. And maybe my hypothesis is wrong; it is just an experiment. But I think it is too bad to condemn someone to an entire life of being medicated without checking all the alternatives. Think about it. When the time comes, you'll decide. I will be here to help you."

"You will help by encouraging me, I know. But if I fall, it's me that falls, right? It is as if you were encouraging me to cross on a narrow log over an abyss. It won't be you crossing. What if I fall?"

"That's the language of fear. And if you don't fall?"

"I'd rather not try."

"Fine. It all depends on how much you want to get to the other side."

Now Lena was thinking about it. On the other side was the possibility of a child, which Alonso wanted and she did too. Even with all this mess now, him involved with another woman, his reaction when he heard of the impossibility had been intense. He had cried in silence. But that was not the most serious thing at the moment. The worst was that on the other side of the abyss and the narrow and dangerous bridge there was also the embryo of the play and of all her future texts. She could not write the way she was now. Lena felt that sooner or later she would have to decide for good. Either she gave up writing or she risked plummeting. But she still did not dare. In the end, she was probably still acting like the girl who wanted a miracle, a magical solution, the fairy's magic wand, the enchanted formula that would turn that risky crossing on nothing but a narrow log into a serene walk across a broad and safe bridge, just the way she liked it. As she had not done since falling sick. Since right before her trip, when for the last time she had met with Sonia to discuss the play.

She always thought it wonderful that there should be a big solid wide bridge over the sea from Rio to Niterói, so you could go from one side of the bay to the other without having to bother driving all around it, without ferries or boats—no ruptures or unnecessary detours. It was always something of a magical crossing, free in space, with no houses or fields on the sides of the road, nothing on the same plane, cut out against the blue, or submerged in the night or in the fog. Those where moments when time was suspended, hovering. She liked to take the trip by herself, windows open to the wind and to the smell of the sea, the car radio playing music. That day it was playing Chopin; perfect. During those minutes she did not think of the work that expected her on the other side, of the meeting with Sonia for another discussion about the text of the play, about the rehearsal-like atmosphere that had already begun to arise in their group. She could turn off thoughts about the before and after, and just cross the blue distance between two points, amid the notes from the piano. At least she could turn off the immediate before and after. Because often she was invaded by some dreamt-of and not-yet-existent after. Or some very ancient before.

Like this one now, that came with the piano. Suddenly, Lena was very sorry she had never learned how to play, that she had left way behind in her childhood all the attempts to make music flow from her fingertips. Nonsense, she should have been more determined, not have let the exercises and punishments and scales get her down, and sought out the pleasure she always felt when she managed to play something by ear, combine the sounds of both hands into something musical, enjoy the force of chords or the lightness of the fingering, seek out the charmed time that resided in the percussion of the little hammers and the vibration of the strings in that treasure box. She had not had the willpower. She had been too young, unable to imagine where the piano could lead her, so she had abandoned the instrument. As had all her siblings, one by one, giving up under the repressive ways of the teacher, who would not allow them to play music if the scales were not perfect and who execrated every sound of popular music. The piano was abandoned in one corner of the living room, then was relegated to the porch, a blunt image of decline, suggesting symbolism that nobody wanted to think about.

Coffin and body. A casket for itself, ready to trundle to the grave on its own wheels, a heavy trunkful of high and low notes, two metal handles looking like ears. Its legs wobbly and chewed by termites, its eyes opaque as in the unlit candelabra that used to shed light on the music; it opened its mouth, toothless with the keys that had lost their ivory above the two huge pedals; the bellows vomited from its insides. The bellows were shriveled, torn, past the remotest memory of the faint breath of the gears that had played dance music for breathless couples and that now, instead of piano rolls pregnant with sound, showed only, in its third eye, open in the middle of its forehead, the rotted-out machinery, the broken strings, the termite-eaten hammers, the stump encrusted with lizard eggs, the dissonant skeleton. The piano, may it rest in peace. There was a time when fingers spun chords and wove harmony and melody. There was a day when, around it, girls sighed, boys dreamt, children were enchanted.

One day. Many days ago. In her grandmother's day. Then the aunts ran their fingers up and down the mechanical scales on its keyboard, pounded out Hanon and Czerny, showed off their talents. The cousins played some boleros and song-sambas. Lena herself risked some jazzy theme by ear and was thoroughly beaten by the arrival of bossa nova, with its dissonances and odd rhythms. Only the nephews and nieces were left, playing chopsticks and ring-around-the-rosy. Nobody played any more.

Fernando showed an interest in the instrument, asked for it, got it, but did not take it with him. He had no place to put it. But he insisted that he wanted it, did not allow anyone to get rid of a piece like that, he really, really wanted it, and even joked: "I want it! Even if I end up throwing it into the ocean." But he did not throw it out. He could have. If, as they had learned at school, the ocean was the only tomb worthy of a Batavian admiral, it could well receive with honor a German piano. But this was all talk. Everything remained as it had always been. Only the termites made their progress in the silence of the dead sounds, gnawing, digging tunnels, creating hollows, making lace out of the emptiness.

Since nobody played it, they could sell, give away, rent out, lend the big music box. They could even do nothing, and leave it in the corner of the porch, waiting for the occasional music-gorged fingers. But at least they should care for it, tune it from time to time. Above all, call in the exterminators. How could they have let it get into that state? Throw some poisonous kerosene on it.

It was only when she finally caught herself alone in her mother's house that she really looked at the piano as if for the first time, with its candleholder eyes and its pedal tongue, a monster stripped of the finery in which affection had wrapped it. She looked at it closely and saw the deterioration. She opened it and was faced with the boiling termites. Nothing to be done. Or, maybe there was one last chance: she could call a company that bought old pianos. Nothing doing. It was not possible. They would not take it for free.

Lena and Amalia had to get rid of the body. Call the junk men to take it to the garbage dump. On the way, along the alley at the back of the house—it was not even a street, just an old easement—its legs gave for good, turned to powder by the termites. And now, forever unable to re-create the E-D-E-D-E-G-C-A of the eternal *Für Elise*, the piano fell to its knees in the easement. But it did not help to beg. Lord of all the easements, time has no reason to spare family keepsakes. And as she watched the dismemberment of what was left so it could be loaded onto a cart, Lena felt as if she were trying to rid herself of something even heavier. It was not just a monument to the frustrations of her childhood, but also an unbearable symbol of the decadence that was striking the family and of the melancholy end of lost harmonies.

Now the photos of those schooldays brought all that up, pell-mell. The excitement of the rehearsals and the year-end play. The solemn poses on the day of the piano auditions, the boys in suits, the girls in organdy dresses, sashes decorated with pink and blue artificial flowers. The illusion that they were all talented, educated in the arts, as required by their social standing. The flower arrangements by the grand piano, a sphinx with its jaws and entrails wide open, behind the group of children posing for the photographer on the little stage in the hall of the Brazilian Press Association—the same association where, years later, as an undergraduate, she had watched so many classic films brought in by the film club. And where, in the horror days of Brazilian history it had been her assignment to live through, there would be so many courageous meetings, so many resistance vigils, so many protest assemblies.

Like those following the invasion of the university administration building.

Nobody had had to call that meeting.

The next day there had been protest demonstrations in the streets, a lot of disturbances, barricades, beatings in the center of town. It was violent and ended with four dead and dozens wounded. Lena remembered the first page of the *Correio da Manhã*—the Morning Courier—the striking photos, the press calling the military police cavalry "The Horsemen of the Apocalypse" and designating that day Bloody Friday.

The city was even more deeply shocked. Two days in a row of such violence; nobody could remain indifferent. Everyone thought that someone had to put an end to this somehow, Rio de Janeiro was not that kind of a city, Brazil was not that kind of a country. But it was all isolated indignation; nobody knew what to do.

As they left their newsrooms, the journalists went toward the hall of the press association quite naturally. Just as, at all the colleges, classes were called off so that students and professors could discuss what was happening. Just as, at theaters scattered through town, artists and intellectuals were gathering into the small hours. As was the case at hospitals, factories, offices; in every household the outrage was the same. And everywhere, with small variations of tone and style, the same comments and proposals followed each other:

"This can't go on!"

"This time they have gone too far."

"You can't do that! This is too much!"

"We have to defend our children."

"I think we need to send a protest telegram."

"To whom? To the government? To the president? To the pigs? Don't be stupid . . . Brasilia could not care less about any of this."

"Let's put together a petition, a manifesto, gather thousands of signatures headed by important people . . ."

"Hand a document protesting this to the secretary of education. He happens to be in Rio."

"Let's hold a civic vigil in front of city hall."

"An open letter to the population, published in all the newspapers, posted on walls and fences, pamphleteered on the streets."

"A peaceful demonstration, with banners and posters, on the steps of the municipal theater. That way we can also denounce the censorship."

"A demonstration going through the center of town."

"A protest rally."

Little by little things started to converge. The students were going to hold a demonstration. The artists were going to sit on the steps to the theater. The teachers were going to deliver a document to the secretary. Each group was going to do what came naturally, choosing its own way to protest. For the sake of safety, fearing the repression that promised to be violent after the latest events, each felt it would be wise not to isolate oneself or scatter. So everybody set their protest for the same afternoon, the following Wednesday, which was when the students were going to march.

The result entered Brazilian history as the largest peaceful popular protest ever seen in the city of Rio de Janeiro: the March of the Hundred Thousand. Of course nobody would ever be sure how many people were out in the streets, ready to defy the regime; it was not possible to count them. But they filled squares and streets, as far as one could see. Some reckoned about 200,000, with some exaggeration. Others lowered it to 70,000, with obvious ill will. But the name, the March of the Hundred Thousand, stuck as a proper name, in capitals, denoting the civic celebration held that day, that the military had had to swallow, in amazement. Lena could not think of it without an ironic smile. She remembered clearly how Barros had remarked, at the paper—and perhaps for the first time she noticed how snugly he was already wearing the boss's uniform shirt:

"A hundred thousand your ass. Did you count them? Did anybody count? A good journalist is objective, only writes down what he has checked personally. And does not allow himself to be used for other people's propaganda. These agitators, who only want to manipulate public opinion . . ."

It was not the count, really, that irritated him. It was that the students had booed the big newspapers, denouncing what they called the "bourgeois press" for distorting the facts. The criticism irritated the newspaper owners. And Barros, a sensitive thermometer of the bosses' moods, detected right away that the wind was changing and that the heavy artillery was being brought out, and he scrambled onto the fence. He directed the coverage so that it would report on what it could not leave out of the paper, but at the same time, and subtly, he began to shrink the size of the protest and to introduce distinctions between the "good guys," the liberals who were indignant about the violence, which went against the peaceful and cordial feelings for which Brazilians were known, and, on the other side, the "bad guys," students, agitators linked to the Left, to unions and spurious parties, interested in promoting disturbances and street riots to reach unspeakable aims. And in the days, weeks, and months following, when that manifestation had become a watershed and, with whatever analysis of the situation it was obligatory to refer to the March of the Hundred Thousand, under that name, Barros infallibly cut in: "No way in hell a hundred thousand. The first duty of a self-respecting journalist is to be objective! Write 'the March of June 26.'"

It was a year of many marches. In June alone there were several. As the reports approved by Barros only identified them by the date, Lena thought it would be fun to ask him today whether he still remembered what had happened that day and find out where his "journalistic objectivity" had taken him.

In any case, a hundred thousand or not, the march showed the regime that there was a lot of discontent. The government had announced that any protest would be forbidden and repressed, and still those hundred thousand had gone into the streets. Faced with that, the authorities had retreated and allowed the demonstration, in order to avoid a massacre. For an entire day, the city was crisscrossed by an organized multitude chanting anthems and shouting slogans, under steady showers of bits of paper that fell from the tall buildings in the center of town. They even had a public assembly in a square. And that assembly voted to designate a delegation to go, in its name, and take the city's protest to the presidency of the republic in Brasilia. The commission included a philosophy professor, a psychoanalyst, a priest, two student leaders, and a mother. That, thought Lena, was appropriate, for the whole thing boiled down, to a great extent, to a matter of mothers and children. If some day, as Honorio wished, someone were to write the history of the Brazilian woman on the periphery of events, and then of her gradual awakening to a political consciousness, the story would have to include the student movement of 1968. And in that, they had to consider the March of the Hundred Thousand, where the crowd had elected a mother as a representative, a forerunner of the countless mothers who, in the years following, suffered their stations of the cross through the cellars of the regime, looking for news of their children, and who, if in Brazil they did not arrive at the state of organization of their sisters in Argentina, later known as the Madwomen of the Plaza de Mayo, did not, nevertheless, suffer a lesser nightmare. As if there were a thermometer for nightmares, or a Richter scale on which to measure the loss of a child.

Emerging from her thoughts to rejoin the outside world, Lena observed: "Mother, I was looking at those photos of the piano recitals at the press association hall, and thinking of the meetings we held there, later on, and the march. I think it was the greatest shock of my life to see you that day, in the middle of all the marchers. I had never even imagined that you might have the idea of turning up there . . ."

Amalia smiled. "It was my place. I knew that at least five of my children would be on the street that day: Marcelo, even Fernando who had come back to Rio, you, Teresa, Cristina. And everything was forbidden, the government was threatening, it was right after that day when they had shot at the people outside the university building. I could not stay home knitting."

"Right, I remember your saying that when we suddenly bumped into each other in the crowd. And from that point on, I did not leave your side."

Good Heavens, how could something that in experience had been so tense and fearsome turn into a tender memory? The brain does peculiar things. Or the heart.

"You didn't and neither did the others. It seems impossible that, in the middle of a crowd like that, almost all of my children should have found me. When it ended I had a guard of four children around me."

"Of course," Lena laughed. "We all wanted to be right there when Marcelo made his speech. And when he started, we all moved forward, little by little, to be near him. And suddenly the two of you were there, you proud and looking right at him, and Aunt Rosa shrinking, glancing from side to side, looking scared as anything."

"Well, when Marcelo started to speak, I went forward with Rosa. Then you started to surround me and she was left behind with my friends. But we went just the way the pamphlets had told us to. A group of five. And we were carrying wet handkerchiefs in our purses, and a tablet of fizzy vitamin C, in case of teargas . . ."

"I never knew that, Mother."

"Didn't I say you didn't have to worry about me? I did many things I never told anyone about; you'd be worried that something might happen to me; it was best you should not know. We did finances, for instance."

Surprise after surprise, at this late hour, thought Lena. "Finances? We?"

"Well, yes, me and my friends. We made preserves, jams; we knitted and we crocheted booties, little sweaters; we embroidered baby shirts, things like that. And handicrafts, like covering hangers and stuff. Then we had ourselves a bazaar and sold it."

"And to whom did you give the money?"

"To a priest, who gave it to the people."

"And your friends had no idea?"

"What do you mean no idea? They all knew, of course. We were not fooling anybody. We did it out of conviction; it was a political choice, what are you thinking? We wanted to help and did not know how. If we had gone out painting slogans on walls or distributing pamphlets, it would not work. So we did what we did. And we stirred up the waiting lines, as I told you. But our families did not know; you always thought that mothers were to stay out of it. It was good, because we were practicing courage and resourcefulness."

Closing the box with the photos as if it held a crown, Amalia smiled and recounted: "On the day of the march I, too, was scared, frightened to death, in a panic lest all of a sudden somebody would shoot at him, so handsome, speaking so beautifully from the top of that balcony, or staircase, whatever it was. I was scared to death. For him, for you all. Not for me, strangely. I felt that my place was right there, that if all the mothers came and stayed there with their children, the police would not be able to shoot at them so as not to hit us. And if they did shoot, I'd rather be there. Maybe I would be able to help."

Lena understood. She knew that's how it was. She remembered that a few months later, at the beginning of August, when Valdir, the president of the local association, was arrested and the other student leaders had to split up the tasks of replacing him, there was a highly forbidden march in Copacabana, at dusk, directed by Marcelo. It was going to be rough. Everybody knew that. And she had gone, not as a journalist but as an older sister. To be close to her boy, as Amalia would have said. She stayed around him, in the middle of the security detachment—a group of twenty-year-old judo fighters, ready to take on with their skills the sophisticated weapons of the police goons, a memory that still made her heart skip a beat and that filled her with tenderness for each one of those young guardian angels that life and the recent redemocratization was now scattering to divergent and even mutually antagonistic parties and platforms. Marcelo had climbed on the hood of a little VW beetle and was making his speech. Suddenly she noticed everybody running away.

She looked and saw, about three blocks away, on the avenue that had just been teeming with a flood of people and was suddenly empty of traffic, the approach of a metallic blue wave: the men of the military police running, with shields, helmets, and huge clubs lifted high. In front of them also running were two or three rows of soldiers in uniform, without shields but leading police dogs by the leash. It had all happened so quickly! Somebody from the security group yelled: "Run toward the police, to gain time and allow the leadership to leave . . ."

Few demonstrators remained. But nobody hesitated. It was quick, but seemed to happen in slow motion, like in the movies; you could see every detail, pay attention to everything. The sight of the police and the dogs ever closer. The sound of barking and growling, of the soldiers' boots, rhythmic, as they ran along the asphalt, the cries coming from all sides. Suddenly, a louder shout, from one of the security people among them: "Scatter! Quick!"

It was no longer necessary to run toward the dogs that were getting closer and closer, their mouths open, their tongues hanging out, their teeth bared, pulling the soldiers at the other end of their leashes. They were so close . . . Lena threw herself through the door of a confectionery store, ran among the tables, behind the counter, and out through a back door into a side street, still hearing the barking and the shouts, ran as she had never run, thinking about entering a church further on, but it was closed, there was a school, closed as well, barking and shouts at a distance, she ran into the garage of an apartment building, the guard saw her and ordered her out, she left, running, arrived at a street where there were buses, signaled, one, two, three, no bus stopped, she went on running, along the sidewalk, in the street, running in the middle of traffic, still hearing the dogs, farther and farther away, farther, running, till she could no longer hear anything and realized she was on the other side of the tunnel, close to her mother's house. She had never been so afraid as on that day. And she had never been so brave. All she knew was that Marcelo needed time to escape. And that was something she could give him, play fox running in front of the dog pack. She was happy she had been able to help.

"I don't know. I just thought that, if I were close, I could help, should he need it," said her mother, still thinking about the march. "But I was afraid I might be in the way, so I went prepared."

Lena was taken aback. "Prepared? How?"

"I told you. I had seen the pamphlets in Marcelo's room, calling for the march. I kept one for myself, with all the instructions. I did everything right. I did not go by myself, but called Rosa and three friends to go with me . . ."

Her mother was always full of surprises, thought Lena. Not only did she stand up when things really got rough, but every once in a while she showed things like this, little episodes of unexpected initiative, small but steady. For example, writing poems or little fiction sketches in the recipe book. Or, like another one of her friends, Dona Lúcia, the mother of another bunch of children involved with the student movement, who one day was sitting at the sewing machine when, from the second-floor window, she saw the police coming to her home. She told her children: "Quick, go down and gain me some time."

That was still in 1968, before the repression got even more violent. There was still *habeas corpus* in the country. The constitution, though constantly violated and amended, was still in force. The family was in the opposition, but well connected, with a nice home in a middle-class section of town in the South Zone, so nobody was expecting a confrontation or immediate physical violence—if the police did not find anything special. But only if they did not find anything. If they did, everything changed. And the children knew that, the day before, they had brought home a huge pile of pamphlets, just off the press, to be distributed around various schools, and that at the moment they were stashed in packages under all of their beds. With their hearts in their throats, they did what Dona Lúcia told them. They talked to the police, offered them coffee, tried to draw out the search downstairs and gain time. From above they heard the intermittent noise of the sewing machine, interrupted from time to time, probably to cut out a pattern, or sew something up by hand, with a needle. Finally they could not hold the men back any more and the police went upstairs. Dona Lúcia interrupted her sewing and went with them as they turned out drawers, looked into closets, searched under the beds. They did not find a thing and went away.

Then she called her older son and said: "Don't bring these things home again, or you will kill me with a heart attack."

"But where are the pamphlets, Mother? What did you do with them? I was scared to death when the guys looked under the bed, I thought right then I would fall, and it seemed a miracle."

"Sure . . . a miracle of your mother and her Singer sewing machine," she answered. "Find them."

It was not easy. Finally one of her children noticed that the beds, perfectly made, with the covers stretched tight, all had two pillows. And that the big linen closet in the hallway, where they normally kept the pillows the family used at night, and that were not kept on the beds, was also full. Two thirds of all that volume were pillowcases with pamphlets sewn into them, rolled up in sheets so they would look round and soft. But all somebody had to do was pick up one of those false pillows to feel their weight and find everything.

"Wow, mother! How inventive! And how cool-headed to do all that with the men downstairs! How did you get that idea?"

"But I have done that all my life!"

"Done what?"

"Sewn and taken care of all of you."

This incident was now almost picturesque, having been overtaken by the generalized violence. When the police had come to Amalia's house in search of Marcelo, for instance, they did not even trust the cabbage in the refrigerator, stabbing it repeatedly with their bayonets, as if it were possible to hide a weapon in it. And no pillow or cushion on the sofa or the armchairs escaped being cut open and having its stuffing pulled out. In other houses it had been worse. The paintings on many people's walls had been torn, works of art had been stolen as well as any valuable appliance. And when they did not hurt a person, the mothers thanked God. All you had to think of was the pilgrimage of those caught in the eye of the storm, going from the army to the police trying to get news of sons and husbands, so often returning empty-handed. Still, Lena could not think of it without a stab to her heart, a knot in her throat, a feeling of impotent rage and indescribable pain, an overwhelming shame that she was part of a nation where things like that could happen and were never punished—sometimes not even made public after democratization.

And that nobody was taken to court for that kind of violence against defenseless people. A country where there had always been the fiction that people were sweet, cordial, and gentle.

"When all of this is over, we will still remember it with horror, as if it were a nightmare, and could even begin to doubt that it really happened," she had once said to old Luis Cesario, chatting on the porch, in the rattan chairs, under the ferns and surrounded by the incredible perfume of the jasmine bushes.

He took her hand, stroked, and sighed: "My child, I am sorry to contradict you in your innocence. But trust an old man who was born with this century and has seen a lot. When all of this is over, everybody is going to forget, except for those who paid with their own blood. And whoever speaks of it will be called a liar. Will be criticized for being importunate. Or ridiculed, called old-fashioned. What people want is to follow fashion, be part of the vanguard, things like that."

Lena did not believe him. "You are being too pessimistic, Luis Cesario. It's not like that."

"I lived through the Vargas dictatorship. And years later I saw the dictator hailed by the entire Left, all horrors forgotten."

"Are you talking about Prestes? OK, there was the supreme leader of the Brazilian Communist Party and as soon as he got out of the dictatorship's prison, he publicly gave his support to the dictator who had delivered his own Jewish wife to be killed by the Gestapo. It is really shocking. But that's an isolated case."

The old man smiled and passed his hand over his white and unkempt hair: "My child, I am not speaking of any particular person. I am thinking of all the people who think of themselves as being part of the Left vanguard, well intentioned and progressive, and who found it convenient to forget about the dictatorship of the dictator, to build an image of him that was progressive, nationalist, and false. And I am not even thinking about Vargas himself. What interests me is our people, the man working someone else's land with his hoe in his hand, the man who faces a four-hour commute by bus to get from his home to his work in this big city every day, the woman who hears her children cry with hunger and does not have anything to give them to eat. We have an obligation to all these people."

"A lot of obligations," said Lena.

"Sure," he agreed. "But I am referring to the first, fundamental obligation. Not to lie. Not to cheat. Not to dissemble."

"It is hard, in all of this, to tell what comes first, my dear. Maybe it is feeling the injustice and hating it."

Luis Cesario changed his focus a bit and explained: "Look, I am talking of ethics, first of all. It is not just politics, or economics. One needs clarity on that ground. A moral reflection."

Suddenly, while old Luis Cesario spoke with his heavy accent of rolled *rr*s, that ineradicable mark of a childhood and youth spent in France, Lena felt very strongly that there was really a very European side to that very dear friend of hers. She had always known that, of course, and you could certainly not forget it when you heard him speak. But intrinsically, the soul and passionate heart of Luis Cesario were so Brazilian that, despite the accent, she always forgot his experience of the Old World, which came to the surface from time to time. Especially this irreducible ethical stance, that at times felt like some prehistoric remnant, something archaic that survived in him, made him seem like a walking fossil, living in that atmosphere of moral flippancy that underlay human contact in the country.

For Luis Cesario, the only quality one could use to judge anyone was his dignity, his moral stature. The rest did not interest him; it was always secondary. That was why, as he was talking that evening on the dusky, moon-laced, and jasmine-perfumed porch, Lena could not avoid shivering, not so much because of the cool breeze and the hour, as for the clear feeling that her dear friend might die at any moment, according to the natural laws of life, and that with him others of his generation were dying, and they would leave a big emptiness. Not only for those who loved them painfully, but for an entire country that had lost its way, its points of reference. All that would be left would be a time of lightness and flippancy where only the surface was important and good and evil were outmoded concepts, dusty and covered with cobwebs.

That was precisely what her friend was saying now: "We need some deep moral reflection in our society right now. I know that at this moment there are very urgent things to be done; the hour belongs to the men of action and not to the moralists. But one thing cannot live without the other. Have you noticed that the word *moralist* has turned into a term of derision? It's almost a curse word. But we need ethics; we need to think about these values that separate civilization from barbarism." He was gathering steam: "Think about a writer like Camus, for instance. He was a great moralist, but that did not keep him from being a very brave man of action, a hero of the Resistance. Yet he never abandoned his notion of justice, his concept of what constitutes the good, the supreme value he placed on human dignity. They could not make him swallow Stalinism, for instance, not for the sake of any alliance or convenience."

Up till then she had been sitting silently in her corner, listening to the conversation, but at this point dear Carlota came in to support her husband's opinion, in her low but vibrant voice: "And Romain Rolland, Lena. Do you think it was easy to be a pacifist in the middle of the war and correspond with the enemy for the sake of peace? You need great moral courage to do that . . ."

"What is that story?" Lena asked.

Carlota explained, animated, how Romain Rolland had some idea about energy without violence, and how, during World War I, he had exchanged letters with other writers, including Germans, to denounce the war and fight for peace. She talked with energy, almost exaltation, as if all that were still going on, as if it were contemporaneous with our sad tropical dictatorship. And while she talked, everything really did become contemporaneous, so great was the power of her word, that had spent such a long time contained and restrained, maturing in silence, and now came to light, plain and magnetic. More than the story itself, what fascinated Lena was the magical radiance of that old woman, older than her husband, bruised by life that had taken so many of the people she loved, including her young daughter, and who, instead of finding shelter in some sullen, grumbling discouragement, set aside any bitterness to renew herself in sweetness and enthusiasm, completely absorbed in the present and the future of her own country and of people from all countries.

But Luis Cesario went on: 'My dear, we cannot allow people to throw sand in our eyes. You may not have found out yet, but you are an artist, like me. We have to bother people and bring them something new and beautiful. Nothing is as beautiful and new as a moral sense. That is what points us toward truth."

"Well, yes, but under the present circumstances, so much is urgent, that this discussion gets very abstract," said Lena. "These are concepts, categories, things like that. There is nothing concrete."

Luis Cesario opened his tobacco pouch, took out a pinch of the special tobacco she had brought him the other day, rubbed it with his right hand into the palm of his left, and went on: "It may not look concrete, but it is. Because it is the foundation of everything, the bedrock. And there is a lot we have to look at directly, without lying, if we want times to get better, if we want to fix all this. For instance, the fact that we are very violent and bloodthirsty. We have this habit of make-believe, of saying that our history is not written in blood (as if anemia were a reason for pride), whereas our Spanish and Spanish-American neighbors were so cruel. It is a lie. We were as cruel as they, but greater hypocrites. And in addition to being cruel, we are also great thieves."

Lena was shocked by the brashness of the diagnosis: "Are you referring to the corruption of the colonists, the usurpation by the dominant classes?"

Pressing the tobacco slowly and firmly into his pipe, he answered, with complete tranquility, as if he were seeing it very clearly, something he had thought about again and again: "No, Lena. I am old, I have no more time for lies. Unless I wanted to die in a lie, which I don't. I am talking about general thievery. Everybody here in this Brazil wants to con everybody else, get the better of them, take advantage, as in that TV ad. Everyone thinks only of himself, and nobody has the least notion of the rights of others, of the respect due to other human beings and to life in general. Everyone lives as if the whole world has been created to be his slave and his property. Which means that everyone can steal, use, spoil what is not his, throw garbage on the ground, fell trees, park on the sidewalk, spend other people's money without accounting for it. In short, get on, as one says now. It may even be because the colonists gave the example and the dominant classes taught it. But these days all have learned that lesson."

"And there is nobody to teach otherwise," said Carlota.

"Except for one or another priest, some crazy professor, or marginalized artist," Lena smiled.

"That's it," said the old man. "But it is still too little. One has to multiply this."

"If only to confirm the understanding of the simple people, who do know wrong from right, but have no chance of being able to live accordingly," added Carlota.

There was a pause. One could hear clearly the faint whistle with which Luis Cesario sucked on his pipe. Taking it out with his left hand, while the sweet smell of the tobacco filled the night, together with the jasmine and the moonlight, he replied: "Maybe, but I would not put too much faith in that. I think it might be another one of our favorite myths, a kind of new tropical, twentieth-century Rousseau— everybody is a good savage so long as society does not corrupt him. No, my child, I refuse to write a new fairy tale for myself. I don't know: the more I see all this violence stored in each one of us, added to our inability to react effectively against this ruthless dictatorship, the more I ask myself if, in the end, this is not a form of cowardice and collaboration. A general one."

"Boy, you are not cutting anybody any slack, are you?" Lena joked.

"Nobody. Only the eternal individual exceptions that confirm the rule. But at times I think of that shapeless crowd that we call the Brazilian people, and I am ashamed. How can such a small number of goons take over a country this size, and 90 million Brazilians let them do it? Everyone thinks that the other one should do something about it, everyone thinks only about getting away from the line of fire, taking his stuff and running—sorry, can't get involved, stay out of it."

Lena objected: "Wait a little, Luis Cesario, it is not quite like that. There is a huge imbalance of power. The military have weapons, ammunition; they have tanks, they have support from the outside, they have money, they have no kind of scruples; they arrest, torture, kill."

The old man was getting sufficiently excited to rise from his rocking chair. "And what about Vietnam? Is there a greater imbalance of power? The most powerful army in the world against weak little men? They could be decimated, but they are making trouble. If I were Vietnamese, I would not be ashamed of my people. But as a Brazilian? A people who are so violent, so bloodthirsty, and unable to channel this into some constructive action . . . What is everybody waiting for? That the generals will destroy each other and go home? Or that they will get tired and return power to the good guys and then everybody will be able to fuck as much as they like, attack whomever they like, rob and kill one another on the streets till they get rid of the anger they repressed for all these years? If that is what will happen, then we will all be destroyed and there will be nothing left."

While he was speaking, Carlota was looking around. Then, with a worried expression on her face, she got up, walked along the porch to the front of the house, looked up and down the street. Returning, she said: "Luis, you'd better be careful. You are speaking very loudly, some neighbor might hear, somebody may be passing in the street . . ."

He shrugged and made a dismissive gesture. "Let them!"

"It is not prudent. You know that we all have to be prudent. It is more important to be careful and help in some other way. Let us go in and have something to eat. The table is set, all we have to do is boil water for tea."

"OK," he agreed. "I am not into bravado. This is just indignation."

And they went in for one of those unforgettable teas of Carlota's, with its special mixture of leaves, the home-made jabuticaba jam, the tablecloth embroidered in cross-stitch with soft-shaded thread, the ironed napkins, the fruit cake made from a family recipe, the fine china, a silent celebration of centuries of women's work in the quiet of ordinary days, helping to put together a civilization that could gather around a table a few human beings in communion.

VI

A minha pátria é como se não fosse, é íntima
Doçura e vontade de chorar; uma criança dormindo
É a minha pátria. Por isso, no exílio
Assistindo dormir meu filho
Choro de saudades de minha pátria.

(VINICIUS DE MORAES)

My country is as if it weren't, it is an intimate
Sweetness and a wish to cry; a sleeping child
Is my country. That is why, in exile,
Watching my child asleep,
I cry for my country so far away.

"It is on the table, child. Come eat something. After lunch you will rest some more, in bed, where it is more comfortable. There, on the sofa, it's awkward."

Amalia's voice came from far away, the sultry sun breaking through the cloud cover.

"I knew you were napping, but you also have to eat right and take your medicine at mealtimes. Come, you'll sleep better after eating. I'll help you get up. Hold onto my arm; careful with your foot . . ."

"It's OK, mother. Now I am completely awake. I'll just go wash my hands and face and then I'll be ready to charge at this table that's waiting for me, covered with all the little vegetables from the garden."

"From the garden and from the farm. Come, don't let it get cold."

There were collard greens, okra, yams. The day before there had been taro, cassava, plantains for lunch, breadfruit and Jerusalem artichokes for dinner. Probably the next day there would be pumpkin or yet another kind of yam. All greens and vegetables one did not usually eat in the city. Here everything came from the neighbor's yard, and was the result of a lot of work: turning over the soil, fertilizing, making the seedbeds, transplanting, pruning, watering every day, hoeing around it so it would not be choked by weeds, and above all, watching it all the time so the caterpillars would not eat it, the ants would not eat it, the grubs would not eat it. Lena looked at the plate on the table and felt she was eating the leavings of insects. Just as sapodillas were the leavings of bats, guavas and mangos were the leavings of birds, a chicken could be the leavings of a skunk, and so on. That was very different from the supplies in a supermarket, where foods were the leavings of herbicides or pesticides, or were animals raised on rations and hormones. There ought to be something between the daily war against insects and the massive dusting with insecticides. Or between the cleanliness of the chicken coop and the natural way of chickens ranging freely in the backyard. But, to the ordinary person, this was neither relevant nor urgent, for the country had other priorities; ecology is a luxury, a foreign import, or a wish to be original and different. So the small farm was abandoned, relegated to the past, forgotten by a society that turned its back on it or that modernized according to corporate models— huge monocultures for export, while the population was hungry and diseased. Or, instead of planting food to fill the bellies of people, they planted fuel to fill the tanks of cars, and food plantations were replaced with sugarcane plantations for the production of alcohol. And all that to fatten an archaic model of development built on the car industry that was of interest to the metropolis and left railroads and short-haul shipping to decay, which was called modernization. The farm people, ever more marginalized and deprived of resources, kept moving to the cities in search of opportunities that were not there.

Sometimes Lena thought that the government ought to create tax incentives for people who moved from a big city to a smaller one, and create a counter-force to the great human migrations in the country. But this implied the belief that the people in government were actually concerned about the wellbeing of the people and thought of politics as an opportunity to serve rather than to exercise power for their own benefit. She recognized that the notion was utopian. She was ever more fully persuaded that in this transition, when the country was exiting the dictatorship without quite getting to be a democracy, there was a complete lack of understanding of the notion of a *republic*, in the etymological meaning of a *res publica*, the public thing, and they thought that being in power was the same as turning public assets into private ones. And the situation in the countryside was the most pressing, generating all the misery that radiated throughout the land. But she knew that all this was very complicated, much too complex for a straightforward solution. It involved the question of land ownership and of underdevelopment in general, with the retinue of misery that follows a dependent economy. In any case, one thing was clear, visible, palpable: everything was wrong, unfair, cruel to people, and destructive to nature. Which, apparently, was going to be finished and turn into a literal still life.

Absent-mindedly, she said: "Still life."

The mother thought she was referring to the arrangement of fruits that was coming in for dessert. Papayas, pineapples, mangos, and bananas in a ceramic bowl, and the jar of orange juice on the checkered tablecloth. A tropical still life. They both smiled. Amalia looked over to a picture on the wall and said: "To me, no still life is more beautiful than this one of mine. That is, I don't even know if it qualifies as a still life. But for me, it is. I like it a lot."

Lena looked carefully at the painting she had helped choose some years before and that she still liked very much. A work of the old and dear Luis Cesario. Charming, like everything that came from him, in pastel colors unexpectedly vibrant, its unique texture tempting you to touch, its shapes precisely distorted, its crazy, playful perspective. It was titled *Artist's Studio*, showing an interior with paintings scattered everywhere, a dog sleeping on a cushion, and, in the foreground, a table with a still life reflected from another angle in a painting on its easel in the righthand corner. Now that she thought about it, it was not only a tribute to Matisse and his studio with its large window, but also a joke on the *Meninas* by Velasquez, without the mirror, but with the mirroring. And it also echoed those primitive Italians who painted sacred scenes while at the same time exploring the techniques of perspective that they had just discovered: through an open window in the background, that took over almost half the canvas, one could see a landscape. Actually, a double landscape: in front, houses climbing down the hill and, behind that, another hill, with palm trees rising above the vegetation that covered them and gave way to a view of the sea and of the bay on the distant horizon. Just like Luis Cesario: under the apparent placidity of a domestic calm, the vertiginous complexity of creation and the opening to the outside world. It was so pleasing that it turned into beauty, and entered a different dimension.

Lena sighed and looked at Amalia with tears in her eyes. Her mother noticed: "You liked him a lot, didn't you?"

"I can't even tell you," the woman thought. And did not say anything, only nodded and started to peel a mango. Alonso had asked that same question one day, in a more direct and jealous form: "You talk about that guy as if you were in love with him. Are you sure there was never any hanky-panky with him? Some heavier weather?"

Lena had been almost offended by the question, denying vehemently, explaining that she had had an equally intense tenderness for Carlota, and concluding by saying that Alonso had a dirty mind, thinking of just one thing.

"OK, I believe you," he said, "since you are so sure. That is, I believe that there was never anything concrete. But I think it is because you repressed it. Because you can't deny that, with sex or without sex, there was something like being in love."

"But I always loved Carlota just as well.

"One thing does not exclude the other, Lena, as you know. And you know what? I think that was very good for all three of you, with or without psychoanalyzing it."

Amalia broke into her thoughts: "I always pray for them both, for him and for Carlota. Before, I prayed that they should be happy. Now I pray for their souls. But I know that they are in peace. Anyone who did what they did is with God. I will never be able to thank them enough."

She had, however, made, with her own hands, a living symbol of that gratitude. A bedspread, crocheted, huge, for a double bed, each stitch hooked with the tenderness of her thoughts for them, who had saved her son's life. As if God had sent her a pair of white-haired angels to help her fulfill her duties as a mother. She had not even known them, had only met them later; they were her daughter's friends. She asked: "How did you meet them? I've always been curious, but never got around to asking."

"It was funny," said Lena. "It was just after I'd graduated from university and was beginning to work at the newspaper. One of my first assignments, that they published prominently, was an interview with a poet, and we had an excellent talk, he was very relaxed, talked about how he created his works; I was lucky as I wrote it all up, and somehow it came out really well. In the afternoon I was at the office and they called me. It was Luis Cesario, that I only knew by name and he wanted to congratulate me. He said he wanted to meet me because I was a sensitive artist, just think of it! I explained that the artist was the guy I had interviewed, a great poet, and I was just a journalist who loved poetry. So then he said that he was going to be my friend and show me that I really was an artist. I thought it was just crazy talk. But he wanted to meet me that evening, and I said I couldn't, I was covering the opening of a play. Full stop. In the evening, at the theater, I suddenly saw an older couple, both had white hair, he was a bit bent, she was holding onto his arm, and they were walking toward me. Before they said anything, I got that feeling that it was him. They came up to me, and he asked, 'Helena Maria de Andrade?' When I said yes, he introduced himself and Carlota. They sat down beside me and we talked for a long time. I fell in love with both of them. The next day, I went to their house, and we dropped all the Mister and Mrs. and Miss, and became friends for life."

"How did he know it was you?"

"I have no idea, Mother. He always knew what he wanted. I used to tease him, saying that he was a warlock. But really truly I don't think it was just a joke. I saw him do things that had me flabbergasted. He was acutely aware of everything, and had an extremely developed intuition that he trusted completely. Sometimes it seemed that he came from another world."

Led by her gratitude, Amalia suggested: "Like an angel."

Maybe, Lena thought in silence, while she got up to help her mother clear the table and wash the dishes.

Then she picked up the bottle of medicine and hesitated. What if she did not take it? What if she started right away to reduce the dosage, little by little, as the doctor had suggested, till she stopped for good? She closed the lid that she had already opened. When she was about to put the bottle back on the old sideboard that had come from the grandparents' house, she changed her mind. And if she were to fall? If, once again, everything started to turn slowly around her, while her hand groped for something to hold on to, and, thinking she was leaning against the wall, she suddenly found herself lying on the ground? No way; she would have none of that. The medicine was the axis, the plumb line, the ballast, the compass, the straight edge, the guarantor of verticality. She could not let it go. She put the pills into her mouth and swallowed, without water. Only then, feeling calmer, did she seek a horizontal position, voluntarily.

She lay down, closed her eyes, and tried to sleep. But the images and memories of the morning conversations were too insistent, and came without being called, as if answering an invisible appeal that gathered them up, till they were like living blood in her body that, at the least puncture, starts to flow, reminding her it was always there, beating under the skin, assuring her she was alive. So long as it did not turn into a hemorrhage . . . it would be so easy to flow away in a continuous flux, to succumb to a sudden spurt. But memory-blood did not work like that, this current of remembrance that irrigated with capillaries every little bit of life, feeding every cell, renewing every tissue. It was more like permanent irrigation, soaking, moistening daily life, impregnating with its sap every act of future time. But flowing half-asleep. And when there was a cut, like this morning's conversation with her mother, all the memories rushed to the site of the cut. And then they clotted. The present reasserted itself. But the scar opened at the least touch.

Her eyes closed, Lena tried to sleep. She was seldom able to fall asleep in the middle of the day, even in a darkened room, in a quiet place. Thus, now, above the constant murmur of the sea, she heard noises that pulled her up to the outside world—a dog barking, the wind carrying voices from afar, somebody sweeping a paved yard nearby, her mother putting away the pans in the kitchen. But why that? They could not have air-dried so fast. She reasoned that Amalia must have dried the dishes so she would be able to clear them off quickly. Or to make room on the counter by the sink. What for? Suddenly she got it: it was all that milk that had arrived early in the morning in a huge jar. Her mother was going to make cheese; she could get up to see. Not help, since there was not much to help with at that point: pour all the milk into the large pot, put it on the fire to heat slowly till it got to the right temperature. Then add the rennet and let it rest. Wait. Only later, when the curds had solidified, would there be a lot to help with: cut, let it rest some more, work it with one's hands, drain off the whey, and alternate kneading and letting it rest in the mold. And then enjoy the pleasure of a very fresh cheese, seasoned just right.

Though she had just left the table, Lena's mouth watered as she imagined the result. If you thought of it, it was just milk, but so tasty . . . Well, not just milk. Milk and time. Milk and work. Three so very female things. A woman's life was just like that: work and wait. And meanwhile, give birth, nurse, feed. OK, maybe she was exaggerating. A man's life, too, is made of work and wait, but less. Or, rather, not so involved with everyday matters. Meaning, a man in the middle of an existential crisis does not have to consider, twice a day, what he will cook for the family, check whether all the ingredients are in the kitchen, or cut short an explosion or a reflection because of an urgent call: "Mommy, come wipe me!" But perhaps that was also why women like her mother found an unexpected strength in difficult situations, a certainty that life is stronger and will go on. In the middle of everything, the police breaking into the house, her child on the wanted list, her husband arrested: well, there were things that could not be left for later. Bathing the children, going to the market, making up the menu. When hunger comes, however worried everybody may be, nobody cares, they sit at the table and eat, and don't ask themselves how the food got there. Women know that life demands interruptions, occupies before it preoccupies. The Indians say that you cannot hurry a river along. A woman knows that from the inside. You can't hurry a child out of the womb; there is no point in running; there is a time for everything. For gestation and for cheese. Chemistry and caesarians can only hasten it a little, interfere on the surface. But time is lord. Of the baby and the cheese. Of the rennet and the clotting, all the same thing, in some languages the same word, if different histories. In memory, too, there is rennet to stop the flow. And Lena knew that, if she managed to work and season this mass of memories that had been brought up, if she could drain it properly, separate the whey from the solids and wait for fermentation and ripening, she might get herself some good cheese. The kind that Professor Zanotti called poison, if made of milk, without which she did not want to live.

Letting the memories come, sieving, sorting, necessarily implied feeling the pain again. And facing it. Now, for instance, lying in the dark, pretending that she wanted to sleep, pretending, rather, that she could not because of some noises outside, Lena could no longer pretend that she did not hear the noises inside. And it was not only thoughts about the demonstrations and the early days of the dictatorship brought back by the conversation with her mother. These were the memories she picked up and scattered on the ground to disguise the burning sand where she did not want to step. But down there, it burned, she knew that.

The bed without Alonso burned her. Lena missed him, his smell, his voice, his warm, fresh skin, his way of whispering in her ear: "Swim to me, my little fish." She missed the muscles in his thigh, against which she liked to rub, his hands squeezing her breasts, his breath on her neck, nibbling her nape, licking her whole body, the embrace that dissolved her, the way he entered and made himself comfortable in her, his place, waves breaking on the beach, sea soaking the sand. Being away from Alonso was very hard. Especially because it was he who wanted to be away. And much, much worse than all else was to imagine that all this, which she missed so much, was now being given to another woman. In some other way, in another style, with other words, since she knew that every twosome was unique. But he was with a woman who was not her, because he chose to be. Because that woman attracted him and gave him something that he wanted and needed at that moment, and she did not know what it was and could not give it to him. Because his heart beat faster when he saw that other woman, heard her voice, saw some little thing she did, her walk, her glance, her gestures, how could one know what it was?

Something in Lena asked, "Why just now?" But that thought made her pitiable, a poor thing, abandoned in her illness, left to face by herself one of the most difficult times she had ever lived through, helpless, lost, with sudden impulses to give up and let herself be carried by the current. It was good that Lena had other notions in her head as well, which told her: "One does not choose these things. It's now because it happened now." And that refused any idea of pity. After all, pity was not what she wanted. She wanted love—and she never doubted that Alonso loved her. It was just that he was also loving somebody else at the same time. How long it would last, she had no idea. Neither did she know how it would evolve. But she knew that it was possible. It had happened to her as well, for a while. There is nothing one can do, except to live intensely and wait to see what will happen. At this moment, a single thought held her up—the certainty of his love, despite the absence. Love so strong that it was loyal, did not lie, told everything it wanted to do. And whatever she asked, if she wanted to know. That was her only trump card. Maybe Alonso was with his other girlfriend right now, but Lena was the one with whom he had a relation of complicity, to whom he could tell whether he suffered or was happy, what he felt and what he feared. Of course, she would prefer it if his organs of speech and of lust were there for her alone, just for her. But if she had to share at all, let it be the one for lust. Every time he called her or came to her place without telling the other, every time he let her know he had dreamt of them together or something of that sort, which he could not mention to anyone else, Lena felt that she was right: she loved him and was loved and could not allow ambushes along the way to turn into a halter on Alonso, a chain around his neck or a cage that kept him from flying. She could be hurt at this moment. But she was not going to use that as tar in a snare. He had always respected her freedom, and had once hung in while she spent a month in another town with another man, till that had passed. He was a very extraordinary man, a wild horse with whom she wanted to gallop through unfenced fields, or be as two seagulls following fishing boats and diving after the glint of a fish in the vastness of the ocean. It was a gift from the gods that they had met. She could not now throw it all away to make a scene like a poor helpless little thing, or show impatience, trying to force his time to be like hers, or force him to live her illness instead of her passion. But she missed him and it hurt, badly, even though he called and talked to her all the time.

Actually not; at her mother's, they could hardly talk when he called. The phone was in an open space, exposed to general curiosity; there was no privacy. And in those matters, her mother had always been indiscreet and invasive. She placed herself right beside her, listening to the conversation. Once or twice the daughter had asked: "Mother, could you excuse me a moment? I want to talk."

It did not do a lot of good. Amalia stepped away, but left the door open. And soon she was back, to put something in its place or to look for something in the living room. The calls were long-distance; one could not whisper. Alonso kept asking her to repeat what she had said. That archaic irritation Lena felt about having her territory invaded started to rise. The calls became frustrating, though they showed that he missed her and thought of her. Anyway, they were worth it, and they gave her some of her few moments of joy those days. It was good to hear Alonso's voice, so tender and laden with good things. A voice is there to be heard. But the sensations Lena felt at this sound mingled with those from other senses. The voice was sweet, warm, soft. Perhaps that was because everything about Alonso touched her whole body, nothing to be done about it. It was good to give her mind to it. But it was also good to try to forget him for a while, not think about him all the time; she would miss him too much, get upset, and sad. Her father used to say that God blessed man with two big gifts: the ability to remember and the ability to forget. Lena had always thought there was truth in that. When one of them became too intense, as her memory was doing now, it was time to resort to the other, for balance.

She decided to get up, and leave her bed, which was such a dangerous place for that mixture of regret and solitude. She did not feel like reading. The best thing would be to avail herself of the other store of memories, brought up by her conversation with Amalia that morning, and see if she somehow could go back to her work on that play. No writing, since Lena was not about to risk that yet; her last experiences had been too disastrous. But she could reread, put in order the fragments that had been written. She had not touched them since before her trip, when she had revised some passages, after her conversations with Sonia about the difficulty of meshing all those rough drafts and scattered notes into a dramatic form that would work on stage. After the meeting with Sonia she had rewritten some scenes. Then she had gone on her trip, had gotten sick; it was a long while since she had looked at it.

Maybe it was time to dive into the material once again. She had put the folders and envelopes into her suitcase to bring them along, with a spark of hope. Maybe now she could risk a test, take it up again for a bit. Nothing complicated. She did not need to pick up the letters, statements, newspaper clippings, or anything that demanded too much decanting. She could, however, for instance, go over some of what was already in play form.

(Setting: a tiny apartment in Paris, bedroom and sitting room in one, sink and stove against the back wall. A plastic curtain hides the shower by the kitchen sink. On the other side, two doors, one leading to another bedroom, and the other, which looks like a closet door, revealing the toilet. A woman is making the bed, which, with a quilt and pillows will turn into a sofa. Under it, two suitcases. Clothes racks and a coat rack with garments hanging from them. Trunks serve as dinner- and side tables. Ricardo is washing his face at the kitchen sink and turns on the shower while watching the water that is heating for coffee. Vera makes the bed, stows away some clothes in suitcases, and takes out others. Suddenly Ricardo leaves the sink, turns off the shower, and rushes to the toilet.)

RICARDO: Keep an eye on the water, Vera; it is almost boiling. Shit, this business of having a sink and shower in one corner and a toilet in the other is killing me. When I start running the water for the bath, I feel like peeing, but that's so far away . . .

VERA: We were lucky to find an apartment with a bathroom.

RICARDO: *(from the toilet)* What are you calling a bathroom? The kitchen sink? That bucket with the tiny showerhead that looks like a telephone and gets the whole room wet?

VERA: Please, Ricardo, don't start on this again. You know very well that there are lots of people who only have a bathroom down the hall, sometimes even on another floor. Didn't you hear Tania say the other day that they finally bought a chamber pot so she would not have to go out at night, in the cold, all the time, and she with that huge belly?

RICARDO: Have a look at the water there.

VERA: It has boiled.

RICARDO: Put the Nescafé in the cup for me, please. The way I like it, a little water first, just to dissolve it.

VERA: (*as she stirs*) Look, I try, but I can never get it to be thick with that bit of foam you like. But weren't you going to take a bath first?

RICARDO: It will have to be later. The water boiled too fast. Shit, I can never organize my time properly.

(They sit, one of them on the bed, the other on a pillow on the floor, by the trunk that serves as a table. As they start to cut into the baguette, the doorbell rings.)

VERA: (*startled*) This early? Who could it be at this time?

RICARDO: (*getting up to see*) Take it easy, girl, no need to be scared. The men are far away; they stayed over there, in Brazil . . . It must be the concièrge, or somebody ringing the wrong bell. (*He opens the door a crack, leaving the chain attached.*) Oh, it's you. Wait, I'll get the key. (*He turns to Vera.*) It's that couple we met the other day at Silvia's, that psychoanalyst with his wife, what was her name?

VERA: Diana.

RICARDO: That's it. (*louder*) I'm coming.

SERGIO: Please excuse the invasion at this hour, but we did not know whether you had a phone and we knew that you lived here. The other evening Vera explained that it was above that store . . .

DIANA: Well, we just wanted to get Bruno to go for a stroll with Pedrinho.

VERA: He is still asleep in there, he came into our bed in the morning. But it is time for him to get up anyway.

RICARDO: Where are you going?

SERGIO: I have an interview with a professor somewhere in the outskirts of the city, close to some woods. So I thought I would take Diana and Pedrinho along. We are taking a train, so I thought I would call to take your son. Didn't you say the other day that they were more or less the same age?

VERA: Yes, Bruno will be four.

DIANA: Right, about the same. It is good for them to play together. The children are so isolated here, can't speak the language, nobody to play with.

VERA: But Bruno may be shy. He does not know you. And then he may interfere with the interview.

SERGIO: No, no, Diana and Pedrinho are going to wait for me somewhere, in a square or a café. After that we are going for that walk. Why don't you come too, Vera?

RICARDO: That sounds like a good idea. What is the weather like? From our window all we can see is this wall and that filthy *cour* down there, smelling of mold, you can't even see if the sun is out.

SERGIO: It's the usual grey. But at least it is not raining.

VERA: OK. Let me wake and dress Bruno. We'll be ready in a moment.

RICARDO: Do you want a cup of coffee? It's instant, because that is more practical. Sit down here. Look, there is not a lot of room, but we'll find a way.

SERGIO: It's the same where we are, except we are the ones who sleep in the living room, and Pedrinho sleeps in the entrance hall.

Well, that would do for the scene showing the beginning of the friendship; it was more or less like that. Lena had rewritten the passage, because in the first version the child was in the scene, and Sonia had noted that it was really hard to have children on stage. So Lena got the idea of taking the boy inside. But then there was the other one, Pedrinho. Maybe if Diana did not come in and waited for them downstairs. But Lena was interested specifically in showing them as a couple; it was important to start building the relationship between the two couples, and then how they became closer, became friends, first because of the children, then because they were almost the only ones in their community of exiles who did not belong to any organization, did not have a party or a movement supporting them. She had to slowly stage the mental frailty of Diana and Sergio's constant and tender concern for her. And the different stages of this construction of the characters would be these fragments of their everyday lives, binding the friends together. At first it would be through the children. But it was very difficult to show that with the permanent ban on bringing children onto the stage. Yet Sonia was right. Actors who were four years old, or looked four years old, would bring an unnecessary complication to the play. She'd have to resort to some artifice. Maybe even a theatrical solution, nonrealistic, two ragdolls, or have other characters speak as if there were children on stage though in fact there were none. But the tone had to be consistent. There was no sense in doing something completely realistic and then suddenly dropping in some make-believe. For the fragments that followed she had found a solution. Vera had discovered a kindergarten for the boys, but could only enroll them at the beginning of the next school year, four months hence. And meanwhile Sergio and Diana had made a great find: at that very period they were starting, on Wednesdays, a *garderie en plein air* in the Luxembourg Gardens. A kind of open-air nursery school, once a week. It was a great opportunity for a transition. The boys would play with other children, would start learning some French while engaging in games and activities, and run around under somebody's supervision. And the first times the parents could hide behind some plants, observing from afar this new experience for their children, poor things, suddenly on the loose in a foreign city, hearing a strange language, wearing coats, boots, scarves, and hats, all so very different from Brazilian warmth and affection. But, thank God, with no risk that suddenly the police would invade their house and take everybody away; it was life without the threat of prison and torture, without the permanent fear that the police would do something to the children to make the adults talk.

The difficulty in these fragments came from something else: how to show, little by little, that Diana never relaxed, never calmed down, never forgot her terror, without giving the impression that she was half mad. As of now the play condensed the action into a few scenes, and everything became too compressed, whereas what she had in mind was subtle, gradual. Diana tried to feel free, but she was always afraid, her memories were too strong and her pain too recent. She had been treated very badly in prison, really tortured. She felt such dread of Police Chief Fleury that, though she really needed a job, she had been completely unable to apply to one likely place because the address was somewhere on a street called de Fleurus. That was enough to upset Diana to the point that she found the most outlandish reasons not to go there. If she heard a police or ambulance siren she would freeze, stop whatever she was doing, fall silent, sometimes start trembling. Apart from that, however, she was adorable, sweet, affectionate, supportive, with an enviable sense of humor. How would Lena indicate all these nuances in a play? It would have to be incremental, but clearly and decisively done, so as to prepare for the following scene:

(Vera's and Ricardo's apartment. Vera is sitting on the floor, writing on the trunk-cum-table. Suddenly she raises her head, listening.)

VERA: Somebody coming up at this hour? Would they be coming here, to our place? *(She waits; silence.)* No, it must be to the neighbors' . . . *(pause)* No, wait; there is somebody out there; I can hear the hard breathing. *(She rises and goes to the door.)* It sounds like crying, as if someone were sobbing. *(She opens the door. Diana is sitting on the floor, crying by the door.)* My God, what happened? Come, get up, I'll help. Come in. What happened? *(Diana allows herself to be brought in, crying almost silently; she sits on the bed, hands clasped together, with a look of terror on her face.)* Do you want some coffee? A cup of tea? Brandy? Sugar water? Diana, dear, say something. What on earth happened?

DIANA: Pedrinho . . .

VERA: Did anything happen to him? Did he get hurt?

DIANA: No. Pick him up at school, I can't . . .

VERA: Sure, of course, it's fine, I'll bring him here with Bruno; he can even sleep here, they'll love it, but tell me, what happened?

Diana says nothing. Vera gives her a glass of water, talks to her without getting an answer; Diana looks straight ahead without crying, twisting her hands.

VERA: Here, drink this. Boy, I should have some kind of tranquilizer, like those my mother had, passiflora, valerian, things like that. I can't give you anything stronger, I don't know what you are taking, all Sergio said was that you are taking medication, I can't mix drugs. I'll call him and ask. What's his work number? Diana, are you listening? I'm talking to you . . . What is Sergio's number? Do you have it in your notebook, in your purse? May I look? Well, if you don't answer, I will look anyway, pretty soon it will be time to pick up the boys, and I can't leave you here in this state, you need help, a doctor. *(She looks, does not find anything.)* Silvia must have it. *(She dials.)* Hi, Silvia. I need to talk to Sergio; it's urgent, Diana is here, and she is not well. You'll talk to him? OK, tell him to come right away, or call . . .

(She hangs up, goes to Diana, puts her arms around her, helps her lie down, takes off her shoes.)

VERA: OK, I've spoken to them. Sergio will be here right away, rest up, and relax. It's all over, then you tell him what happened, and you don't have to worry about Pedrinho, we'll let him stay here as long as necessary . . .

(The lights dim while Vera holds Diana, cradling her and singing.)

VERA: Rock-a-bye baby,
On the treetop,
When the wind blows,
The cradle will rock . . .

(There is a knock at the door; the lights go up; Vera rises and goes to open it. Sergio enters.)

SERGIO: What is it? Silvia told me and I ran over here. *(Reaching Diana, he addresses her.)* What happened? Tell me, come, I am here.
VERA: She's been like that since she came. That is, no, first she was crying a lot and she came to tell me to pick up Pedrinho at the school,

and by the way, I have to go, it's time. But after she managed to say that, she got like this, quiet, what I said did not register, open eyes, fixed stare, sometimes a few tears. But she does not speak.

SERGIO: Are you leaving now?

VERA: Yes, it's time to get the children.

SERGIO: Then let's go together. I'm taking her home; I don't want Pedrinho to see her like this. Can he spend the night with you?

VERA: Of course, Sergio. And anything else you may need.

SERGIO: Thank you, Vera. This is a big help already. I'll call later to let you know. *(To Diana, while Vera helps put her shoes on.)* Come, my love, let us go, it will pass, let us go home, then you'll tell me, come . . .

(They leave, close the door, the light goes out. When it comes back on for the next scene, Ricardo is finishing up a phone conversation, alone in the room.)

RICARDO: Well, look, don't worry, we'll find a way; he can wear Bruno's clothes and they'll love the mess and sleeping together. You have to take care of Diana. *(pause)* Sure, of course, call him any time you want. *(pause)* I know, I know. If he gets uneasy, I'll call. However long you need to. And we are rooting for her. Bye. *(He hangs up.)*

VERA: *(entering from the bedroom)* Finally! They are asleep. Was that Sergio on the phone?

RICARDO: It was. He wanted to know if Pedrinho could stay here for a couple of days. And if, tomorrow morning, after taking them to school, you could go there to stay with Diana while he goes out for a while.

VERA: Sure. I'll find a way. I'll cancel whatever I was doing.

RICARDO: He called two colleagues, who went there, and everybody thinks she may have to be committed. Tomorrow morning he is going to look at the hospital, or clinic, or whatever it is. And he will try to stay with her at least for part of the day.

VERA: What a bummer! And she has not said anything? Does anyone know what happened?

RICARDO: She did talk, and that's what's worrying him most.

VERA: What was it then?

RICARDO: She swears she saw Fleury at a metro station.

VERA: That's absurd! Poor thing . . . This really goes deep, doesn't it? She never gets rid of that nightmare. How long do you think she will go on imagining these things?

RICARDO: For something just imagined, it was pretty vivid. She says she was on a train, stopped at a station, and saw him on the platform on the other side. She said she covered her face with a scarf, all except her eyes and stared out the window. It lasted a few minutes, and she is sure it was him but does not know whether he saw her or recognized her, and at that point she went into a panic and couldn't speak.

VERA: That's horrible! To go off like that, suddenly, and start to hallucinate on the street from one minute to the next . . .

RICARDO: But she did control herself quite well. From what she says, she looked till she was sure, had an impulse to run off but did not run, thought that if he was on the other platform it was because he was going the other way, stayed put, continued on the same line, and, when the train started and she saw that she had rid herself of him, started to cry. She saw that she was two stations away from our place, decided to get off, and came here because she felt that she was losing control and was worried about Pedrinho.

VERA: Good thing that she managed to look for help. But it is terrible to start seeing things this way, having such a strong, clear image.

RICARDO: Sergio says what worries him most is that this is not at all like an account of something imaginary. She went into shock when she was here and could relax. But when she arrived at her home she told everything in order and with perfect logic. He even says that, if he were not sure that Fleury was still in São Paulo, he would have believed her. So I told him that the other day Teixeira mentioned the newspaper had hinted to him that there was a possibility Fleury would be coming to Paris, or even that he was already here, I can't remember exactly. It seems they have the information but are not sure, and wanted him and Maria Alice to try and ask around here. Teixeira even replied that he was a journalist, not a spy.

VERA: Then what if it is true? What does the paper want?

RICARDO: Well, that was just what he was saying. If the guy is here, secretly, and does not want anyone to know, in order to set up an agreement, cooperation, whatever, Teixeira could actually try to find out, but it will be difficult.

VERA: They will have to have the French journalists go into action, because it is very hard for a foreign correspondent to find out about something like that by himself. And if he does find out, that won't do any good. If it is a secret, the newspaper won't be allowed to publish; the censor won't allow it.

RICARDO: Somebody could publish it over here.

VERA: But here it is not news. Any representative from any country can come to France as a tourist, right? But, whatever the case, it would be good for us to know.

RICARDO: And for the newspaper to learn about it.

VERA: Does this mean that maybe Diana was not imagining anything? That would change everything.

RICARDO: It does not change the fact that she is not well and needs treatment.

VERA: But it changes something fundamental. She would then be in shock because of a traumatic experience but would not be hallucinating about things that are not real.

RICARDO: In any case, it's serious. And Sergio said something that struck me.

VERA: What? Did she see anything else?

RICARDO: No. It was something *he* said about torture. He said that torture can create a relationship between the torturer and his victim that even looks like some demonic possession. As if the torturer had set up permanent residence inside the tortured, so the victim will never be able to get rid of him. And this is what he fears the most, because the victim begins to think that there is no possible exorcism for that demon.

VERA: I can't imagine the anxiety something like that would cause . . .

RICARDO: He spoke about anguish, pain, despair, things like that. And he said he is afraid the victim might conclude that the only way out is death.

VERA: How awful. Does he think that Diana is thinking of suicide?

RICARDO: No, Vera. He was not quite as explicit. He was speaking in more general, abstract terms; he was speaking in general, about victims of torture, not about Diana in particular. But evidently this goes through his mind too. And it hurts; he is suffering a lot. It is not only her.

Lena did not know whether she should take that discussion further in the text. She thought it was too many words and not enough action; it might not work on stage. Theater has to show more and talk less, as she well knew. Rather than this conversation, based on a real fact that she had lived through while in exile, a scene had to show, to exhibit something, as if it were a big keyhole. The pleasure of the spectator in the theater has something voyeuristic about it. Maybe she should replace this dialogue with something else that would have the same meaning. The suicide of Friar Tito, for instance, had been as real a fact as Diana's breakdown that Vera/Lena had witnessed. A Dominican priest so thoroughly tortured by that same Fleury had killed himself later, after being freed and sent into exile, despite the absolute prohibition and condemnation of suicide by the church. Because the torturer had never again left his victim alone. Just as Sergio had explained it to Ricardo, and as she had shown, in that scene. And even in a monastery, among his brethren, in the south of France, the only way out for the monk had been to seek death by his own hands. So he would be able to escape from torture.

But Friar Tito's suicide, though it meant something very similar to what Lena wanted to tell, was not the fact that she wanted to put into her play. She knew that she had to select, limit the space she wanted to cover. Many had already written about torture—that was not what she intended to bring up. She would rather concentrate on exile as she had seen and lived it, share the experience with those who had stayed, the dream and the nightmare. An episode like the friar who had hanged himself in a French field was a journalistic fact, historical, documented, and broadcast. And she'd also rather speak about women. She might replace that long conversation scene with another, also taken from what had happened—a young exiled girl, in Germany, who had thrown herself under a train, under very similar conditions. And there were other instances. She could take her pick. It was always the same mechanism—a former victim of torture, who could not get rid of the memory of the torturer and of his power, ends up deciding to kill him inside and through his, or her own, death, escape the horrors of hell through that one horrible crack.

She had to think this through, resolve these problems in the play, even if she did it just in her head, without getting anything down on paper, only rereading parts and fragments, turning it all over in her mind again. This, thank God, she was able to do, despite the illness and the medication. What was really complicated was any attempt to get it out, to put it into words, to open up this trip into herself for anyone else. That's where she balked, got bogged down, sank. She couldn't. Even talking was hard. Writing, at the moment, unthinkable. She really could not make anything out, afterward, of what she had written, and got so anxious she despaired. She could feel it was not good for her. It was not yet time to go back to her experiments. So much so that she had not even brought along her typewriter.

She did have the visions, the hallucinations, her memories; the dream and nightmare in herself. She even had the words that would build the bridge, the parachute for the leap in the dark; all that was already there as well, sentence embryos, phrases in gestation, a germinating harvest. But it was all still potential. And it might not live ever, if she were really sentenced to sterility, to bear having all that universe inside her dry out, waste away. Abortion. Rotten egg. Desert. Wasteland. A kind of madness, self-poisoned by the very images she carried. At bottom, that was the threat in her illness. And the possibility of not having a child was just its symbol. She kept returning to the same idea: neither creation nor procreation, the medical verdict. The price she would have to pay for not falling. What she had to decide was whether it was worth paying that price to remain standing. Without the word, what was the point of being a biped? If she could not use language to invent something and share what she had invented, she was nothing more than a monkey, repeating, imitating, regressing to the cave. Unless she were able to use some other language, like colors or shapes, lines, textures that built other bridges from the inside to the outside. Maybe that was the way out. Search in paint or sound for the way to charm the monsters, like the magic wands in fairy tales. Or magic words. She kept returning to them.

Too bad Luis Cesario was no longer there to talk to about all that. Lena had often heard him mention this kind of thing, but, interested as she might have been, she did not, at that time, know such doubts and needs as living, ripened things inside herself, and the conversation seemed theoretical, abstract. Then, she had not yet found out that she was condemned to dive into her own dream and almost drown in it, so much so that she absolutely needed to open a sluice, an escape hatch, let it come out through the safety valve, so she would not crack. Neither had she known that a dream was so tightly woven out of reality, that the embroidery of desire can only exist if it is anchored in the tissue of memory, or it will just float away. Only lately, and slowly, had she come to understand that it was her fate to take this leap outward, from herself to others, in a phantom community. The problem was that she could not share that interior world without words. And words fell away from her with that illness. Or with the medication that kept the ground from falling away from her. It was as if she were forced to choose between losing her words or losing her balance. As if that moment were rushing upon her. And frightened as she was, she knew she would not have a choice; there was only one road she could take. But for as long as she could, she was delaying the decision.

It was best to go on rereading passages, organizing her papers. For instance, she could have another look at the letters. She did not think she was going to use letters as a vehicle; it really did not work on stage to have a person standing there reading aloud from a piece of paper—one of those huge monologues that she'd heard an actor friend call a slab of meat and a brick. The letters served to remind her of facts, of atmosphere, of a climate. But she would have to fuse several events brought back by the letters, condense into a few characters all those disparate experiences. And so far she had not had the heart to read most of the letters; all she had done was take some out from among her papers, especially those kept by her mother. Almost everything came from there. After all, it was Lena who had written from exile, and Amalia who had gathered it all. From among her own, she had only selected some thin sheaves. One, a letter to Marcelo that she had never sent, because she had lost contact with the bearer and did not know how to get it into his hands. It was more recent, and though it was not dated, she knew it was from the '70s, maybe '75 or '76, when she had already returned, and her brother was still lost somewhere in the world.

In any case, this was not the right time. She had had enough for the day. The whole morning recalling things and the afternoon rereading and remembering. She decided to leave her room. She was really confined, with that aching foot, unable to walk, step on the sand, go for a stroll on the beach. It had stopped raining and the sea was very calm; she could see it from the porch—it looked like a lake. Above the line of the horizon the sky was getting lighter, especially in contrast with the darker grey of the sea. The air and the things in it looked very clear. If this lull presaged a change in the wind direction from the southeast to the northeast, it meant the weather was not only going to change, but firm up. Maybe the next day would be sunny. It would be nice to lie in the sun again. Maybe that would also help to lift that heavy greyness Lena felt in her soul—or in her heart, since who knows where that inner fog might settle.

VII

Se me perguntarem o que é a minha pátria, direi:
Não sei. De fato, não sei
Como, por que e quando a minha pátria
Mas sei que a minha pátria é a luz, o sal e a água
Que elaboram e liquefazem a minha mágoa
Em longas lágrimas amargas.

(VINICIUS DE MORAES)

If anyone asks me about my country, I will say:
I don't know. Truly, I don't know
How, why, and when my country,
But I do know that my country is the light, salt, and water
That create and melt my sorrow
Into long, bitter tears.

Você corta um verso
eu escrevo outro
você me prende vivo
eu escapo morto
de repente olha eu de novo
perturbando a paz
exigindo o troco

(MAURICIO TAPAJÓS—PAULO CÉSAR PINHEIRO)

You cut one verse
I write another
you jail me alive
I escape a corpse
suddenly, look, it's me again
disturbing the peace
demanding my change

It was still dark when Amalia woke up. With age, she was waking earlier and earlier, and had gotten used to that. She would turn on the bedside light and read in bed. But today she could not concentrate. The conversations with Lena had upset her, her sleep had been restless, she had dreamt something about Claudia and did not quite remember what, but it had left her vaguely distressed. She started to pray for her youngest, who perhaps was in need of some special protection.

But it could also be that she had Claudia on her mind because she had recalled those things that had happened to her at school, with that idea of playing "Botafogo Field." And of what had happened after that, in August, when Valdir had been arrested and Lena had arrived home breathless from running from the police dogs and the little girl had been deeply impressed by it all. She liked Valdir, used to play with him when the young man came to see Marcelo. The big guy and the little girl—they had a special tenderness for each other. Now everybody was talking about her friend having been arrested. It was something she could not understand . . .

And because Claudia could not understand, Amalia had been called to the school again. This time the teacher looked even more serious. And the principal was by her side, and directed the interview.

"Dona Amalia, the subject of this conversation of ours is very delicate and very embarrassing, but you are an experienced person and will understand that we have no choice."

The principal nodded, and the teacher started to speak: "As you know, next week we have "Soldier's Day" and it is our custom to celebrate the occasion. You know, it's a tradition, not just this year, but we always . . ."

"It is part of the curriculum," intervened the principal.

"Yes, I know," said Amalia, because she felt she should say something, but she had no idea where they were trying to go.

"That's why," said the teacher, "I was explaining to the children that soldiers are the defenders of the country. So then Claudia asked me what a *defender* was. And I explained that it is someone who protects, takes care, so that the enemies of Brazil won't harm the people who live here."

The teacher hesitated, cleared her throat, looked at the floor, and could not go on. The principal stepped forward: "And your daughter called her teacher a liar!"

"Excuse me," the teacher corrected her, "it was not quite like that. She did not say I was a liar; she said that was a lie, that the soldiers don't arrest the enemies, they just arrest friends. When I thought that was strange and asked, she explained that the soldiers had arrested Valdir, who was not anybody's enemy, but a friend."

Amalia swallowed; she should have known it would be something like that. She remembered her mother saying, "God speaks through the mouths of children." She was worried, but also proud. Though it hurt, it was good to know that she was raising a daughter who could think for herself. But it sure made for problems. The teacher went on:

"Well, since I thought that nobody else in the class had ever heard of Valdir or knew what that was all about, I decided to go on, and only said that it was not the soldier's fault, he was only doing what he had been told. A boy asked who told soldiers what to do, and I said it was the corporal, and then the sergeant, and so on, and mentioned the whole hierarchy, as if it were a game, till we arrived at the general. Then Claudia shouted: 'Then the soldier may be good, but the general is a bad person because instead of taking care of Brazil, he is telling them to arrest friends!' I thought it best to change the subject and we went on to another activity."

"I have already told you that you did very wrong, Jurema. You had to do something right away. We will talk about this," interrupted the principal.

Amalia said: "Please excuse me, but it seems to me that Claudia is just a small child, and did not want to call anybody a liar or disrespect anything. It happens that we know Valdir personally and he is a very nice and well-behaved young man, and he always plays with her, so it is difficult for a child . . ."

The principal interrupted her firmly: "I am the one to ask you to excuse me, but it seems you do not grasp the seriousness of this fact, or its repercussions . . . We are not interested in listening to you defend that young man."

"I am defending my daughter and it does not seem to me there is anything particularly serious in such a simple thing, said in a classroom by a six-year-old."

"But the general does not think so," said the principal.

Amalia was startled: "General? What general?"

"A general of the Brazilian army, madam, who has the right not to be identified."

"But what is an unidentified general doing in a literacy class?" asked Amalia, having swallowed, just in time, the rest of her question as she had thought of it, with the suggestion that the gentleman under discussion might really need to improve his knowledge and finish his education.

Embarrassed, the teacher explained: "He is the grandfather of one of the students. Apparently his grandson got home and said he had learned at school that generals were bad people because they had arrested Valdir. So he came here to ask for an explanation."

Amalia was sorry for the teacher, and did not know whether to laugh or to cry, horrified at the importance the thing had taken. Dona Jurema went on:

"I had to explain that it was a misunderstanding, a distortion of something another child had said. But he demanded to know who that child was."

"What?" said Amalia.

"Don't worry. I would never give up a child."

"My God! This is crazy!"

The principal took over: "You have the right to think what you want; we are in a democracy. But I can't have the fatherland disrespected in the middle of a classroom, in *my* school, without doing something. As Dona Jurema insisted that I should not reveal who the child was (and at the moment I did not know it myself), we agreed on a compromise. Nobody would be punished. But at the end of the year, the teacher will ask to be transferred to another school. And this school, through my person, engaged to appeal to the parents to take the child out of here, since her influence could be pernicious to the other children. Of course, we will facilitate all the paperwork to hasten the transfer."

Amalia could not believe it: "This is unreal. If this is how nobody will be punished, what would it look like if they were? If somebody were to be punished, what would happen?"

The principal said, frostily: "I am not sure you really want to know the answer to that question. And now you will excuse me. Some people are waiting to see me."

She left the room and Amalia was floored, torn between disgust and amazement. All she managed was to say to the teacher: "But this is absurd!"

"I think so too, but I can't stand up to it. If you had seen how angry the man was, I thought he would have a stroke. He was talking about the symbol of the fatherland and national security. They have the knife and the cheese in their hand, and one can't do a thing. And the principal went smooth as silk, saying he was absolutely right. I was the one who proposed that formula, that I and Claudia would leave. But it was not just to avoid something worse. I think that it really is not possible to remain somewhere that will subject you to this. If I were you, I would find a private school for her. A public school now is a place for brainwashing. These days . . ."

Amalia was thoughtful as she went home. More than fifteen years later, she still remembered the episode, and it made her think. For her it was a landmark. She understood in one moment how fascist mechanisms can take over a society. These things she had seen in movies, read in books, about World War II, she was suddenly living now, with her little daughter. Good heavens, could it be that Brazil was moving toward this kind of terror, and she had just now noticed? Despite all those characters in all those movies she had seen, who had not suspected the approaching horrors? Even now Amalia knew that it was then, that very day, more than during any student manifestations, or any police brutality, that she had realized the degree of violence at which her country had arrived. And for the first time in her life, she had cried for Brazil.

Outside, the birds started to sing, all at the same time, greeting the rising sun. Judging by the light filtering through the slats in the blind, the weather was fine. Amalia opened the window. Many of the little boats in the cove had already gone out fishing, a sign that the fishermen believed the weather would hold. The few boats still there had their poops turned to the beach, their prows pointing northeast, and lines tying them to the bottom. Without checking on the direction of the faint breeze that rustled the leaves, Amalia knew that it blew from a good quarter. The weather was really going to be fine.

Lovely, to get up in the morning and greet the day this way, opening the window, looking at the sea, the plants, feeling the wind. It was so natural to live this way. She was lucky that, at the end of her life, after so many years in the city, stacked away in an apartment, she could come to live in this place where she had spent her childhood, where she had brought her children on vacations almost every summer of her life. She would not have been able to bear getting old locked away, walled in. She needed the horizon, the open sky; her heart contracted when she thought how horrible it must be in a prison. She had never been jailed. But she had lost count of the times when her husband had been jailed, both in the Vargas dictatorship and in that later one. And the children, too, in turns, Marcelo, Helena Maria, Fernando. They had been very lucky. So many political arrests, and no torture; God had protected them. But it was always nerve-racking, with no news, not knowing what the children were going through. The two eldest had been in for just a short time. Marcelo stayed in longer, for two months. But the good thing was he had been caught only that one time, before things got really ugly, when all he was accused of was being an agitator and a student leader. If it had been later . . . they would certainly have tortured him to death; she could not even think of it, the fear she had lived with for so many years.

But even when Marcelo was arrested, Amalia could not have known then that they would do nothing to him. Neither did she have any idea how long he would spend inside that army fort. By law, it could not be for longer than sixty days without a charge. But the law was consistently flouted, so you could not count on it. The first moment, when he was arrested with hundreds of other boys and girls at that clandestine meeting of the National Student Union, hidden away on a farm, inland, she tried to keep calm by repeating to herself what her husband was saying: "It's for a short time. They can't keep that many people locked up without a reason. The public outcry would be too strong."

It was and it wasn't. Public opinion was learning not to cry out, after the latest demonstrations had been dispersed with bullets and deaths, and people had begun to disappear mysteriously. The press—at least the big newspapers—were perfecting the technique of hinting that the student movement was not about young people clamoring for greater freedom, but simply consisted of a mass of innocent, well-intentioned youngsters manipulated by a gang of hooligans and professional agitators betting on conflict and financed by gold from Moscow. So of course it looked very plausible that this distinction would also be made among the young prisoners from the failed student meeting. Good heavens, could the men not see that the idea of hiding hundreds of people in a small rural town was so absurd, showed such lack of judgment, that it could only have been thought up by totally inexperienced adolescents, and that any professional agitator would have laughed his head off at the ridiculous plan?

But no, the government saw what it wanted to see. And it performed a triage. In the end they released everybody, keeping nine young men in prison, and, among them, Marcelo. They were considered the dangerous leaders. And then there were the pilgrimages, attempting to see her son in another town. First, to a police station in a different quarter of town. Then at an army fort, where even to go shit the boys were accompanied by a soldier pointing a machine gun at them. And when, finally, they got permission to go out in the sun and play ball for a spell, they gave up when the ball burst as it fell on the fixed bayonets of the guards surrounding the yard. And the days went by, the two months before they had to be charged were coming to an end, the jailers said nothing about freeing the boys. The lawyers thought it best to appeal to the Supreme Court for the law to be enforced. And the *habeas corpus* petitions for the nine leaders went to trial on a glorious summer day, December 12.

That day changed Amalia's life, and Marcelo's, and the entire family's. It also changed the life of the country. Sometimes, years later, like now, looking out the window at her retreat by the beach, looking at the rocks that surfaced at ebb tide, Amalia also contemplated the slabs of memory that surfaced, thought of everything she had lived and wondered how her own personal and family times were entwined with those of the country. She saw the fishermen push a boat into the water, the farmers walk to their fields. She knew that each one of them was one life, with many happy or dramatic moments, but she felt that they lived in a landscape, while she also lived in history. For them, their country was, above all, the piece of land where they had been born. For her, it was, above all, the times in which she had lived. Of course, the Brazilian space was also a part of her existence: nature, the common language, the holidays, the customs, the shared culture, the memories from her childhood. But she could not help feeling that there was a kind of curse that condemned her to live so enmeshed in the political events of her time that she could not think of them as something external to herself. All came from inside herself, like children from her womb. Curse or blessing, how was she to know? More motherland than fatherland, all giving birth and being born from the same entrails, as if Brazil were at the same time her mother and her child, a woman emerging from the open legs of history, and conceiving the future of the land inside her. A female and fruitful sequence of pain, blood, and milk.

September 12, 1968, had been that kind of day. From early morning on, she had known it would be the day of the decision on the *habeas corpus* petition for her son, and she had had no doubt that justice would prevail. Depending on when they released him and on whether there was a plane ticket available for his return to Rio, maybe he could even have dinner at home. She was going to cook one of his favorite dishes, prepare a special dessert, and make his bed with scented sheets, hang a clean towel for him in the bathroom, and gather all the magazines from the last few weeks for him to read. Far from her and from him, in a palace built to house the highest court of justice in the land, justice would be done. And nine mothers would be happy with the return of their sons.

But September 12, 1968, was something more as well, as the history of the land continued to entangle itself with Amalia's flesh and emotions. In that same capital, on that same square, in a palace built to house the parliament that represented all the inhabitants of the land, another decision would be arrived at, on the same day, democratically, through the free votes of the representatives of the people. On that day the representatives were going to say whether they would or not permit that one of them be prosecuted for crimes against national security because of what he had said in a speech a few months earlier, which now they were saying had offended the army. Amalia did not even remember what kind of an offense that had been. Something about how it used to be that girls liked to dance with cadets, but that now nobody liked a uniform anymore. In fact, the details of what the representative had said, that had been considered such an enormous outrage, were so insignificant that nobody remembered what exactly they were. But she remembered quite well why that particular pretext had been chosen. That representative had written a book denouncing and proving the use of torture and, with other representatives, he often spoke up in Congress to reveal to the country the cases of abuse and mistreatment against prisoners. And, like everyone else, Amalia knew very well that something like that could not remain unpunished. That is, torture could. Denouncing it could not. So the powerful had to find a way to prosecute him. However, according to the constitution, a representative could only be prosecuted if the others allowed it. It was necessary to get permission. Or to do away with the constitution.

There, in the capital, on what was known as the Square of the Three Powers, on September 12, 1968, the judiciary granted *habeas corpus* to the student leaders and ordered that they be released immediately. On the same day, on the other side of the same square, the legislature refused permission to prosecute a representative for an opinion voiced in a speech given in the small chamber of the House, a few months earlier. The next day, the third power, mistaking the meaning of the adjective "Executive" in its name, turned into the executioner of what was left of freedom in the land. It put an end to these ideas of independence within the other branches of government; it tore up the constitution it had itself invented a year before, repealed the mandates of representatives and justices of the Supreme Court, closed Congress, censored the press, arrested the opposition, and once and for all installed the blackest dictatorship the country had ever known. And Amalia heard all that on the radio, while Marcelo had not yet come home to sleep on his soft pillow and his scented sheets, well fed on Mother's specialties and dessert.

Claudia, Marcelo were all grown up now. But it must have been the force of habit of so many years that made Amalia wake up thinking of them, and of their brothers and sisters. A child is forever. Now she was going to take care of Lena, who was nearby, a bit sad and strange, silent for long stretches, talking little, always sleepy; sometimes it seemed she spent more time with her eyes closed than open. Well, she did have that broken foot, and could not walk a lot or go to the beach, and was as if hemmed in. Especially with that business of her nerves. Of course it was nerves, she had that chronic fatigue, was fainting all the time, no use coming to her with those explanations about neurological problems, electro this and that, focus, and whatever else. Amalia thought that, deep down, what Lena felt was the need for a stable home, children, a husband to take care of her and help support her and take care of her family; she was too overloaded and alone, and those boyfriends she kept finding were not of the type to marry and settle down.

Of all her children, Lena was the most distant, in a way the most different, the most difficult to understand in her insistence on independence, in her silences, in her standoffishness and her secrets; she had always had things she hid and would not tell, ever since she was a child, writing in her secret diaries, corresponding with faraway friends, changing the subject when her mother approached. There was a phase during adolescence when Lena went so far as to secretly visit a friend of Amalia's, cutting English classes to go to her house and staying there for hours, talking, as if she wanted to choose a different mother for herself. The girl used to write things that she kept under lock and key, and would take them all for the other woman to see, as if Amalia were not good enough for that. It hurt; it hurt the mother a lot, to feel that her daughter fled from her that way. Now she had that mysterious boyfriend, had had him for quite a while, had never introduced him, never brought him home to meet the family, and he kept away, telephoning long distance every day, without stop, and never saying anything about coming and meeting her mother, however often Amalia had invited him.

Amalia tried to understand, to learn more about all those mysteries, to know the secrets that could be making her daughter so nervous, but it was as if Lena had built an invisible wall around her. The other day she had gone so far as to ask her mother to leave the room because she was talking on the phone. As if a child should have secrets from her own mother. Even worse if it's a girl. It hurt. It had always hurt. Amalia could not accept or get used to these barriers. That way her daughter had of suddenly closing her notebook or hiding the paper on which she had been writing. The glance with which she froze her, if she started to ask something Lena thought should not be asked. The speed with which she changed the subject and deflected a conversation. The care with which she put away any letter, always locking away, hiding. She did not know from where her daughter had inherited this; neither she nor her husband were secretive like that. For instance, the letters Amalia received were part of the general conversation at the dinner table. They were left open, within everybody's reach; anybody in the house could read them. Lena was so secretive that one day, when she noticed Amalia's letter habit, she asked her mother to destroy all the letters she had ever written her. Or to return them. Amalia had to promise to collect them all, separately, in a box, out of reach of the family. But she did notice that, afterward, Lena avoided writing to her. Always plenty of hiding places for that Helena Maria of hers, even as time passed. It took her forever to open up, to say what she thought. And when she did speak, it often sounded as if she wanted to irritate, even provoke. Like the business of thinking that her father had actually been very dignified when he left home to go live with another woman whom he had already been seeing openly, with a scandalous lack of respect: "But, Mother, he is actually being honest, taking responsibility, not lying. And he has a right to happiness."

And didn't she have a right? What about the public humiliation of being exchanged for another? And all the years of her life, when she did not have a career, just taking care of him and all the brood, living for the man she had married, who had come to take her from her father's house, and then to leave her that way, for some little thing who did not have half her qualities? And what was that honesty Lena had seen in her father, when he had lied so much, and cheated on her so much, and only left her because she, Amalia, had had it with all that double-life hypocrisy and had put an end to it? It was she who had been dignified, she who had been honest; and as for the right to happiness, God in heaven, she had it too, and lots of it. But how? At her age, how to start all over again? A professional life, marriage, a new family: none of that is open to a woman in her sixties as it is to a man of the same age. It was not as if she wanted it. What she had really wanted was to grow old in peace by the side of her life's companion, finally tranquil after the battle for subsistence, with the children all grown up, and enjoying the grandchildren. She was not asking for much, was she? And then she had to hear that he was honest and had a right to be happy, knives in the form of words, from the mouth of her own daughter. It was too much . . .

Yet it was with Amalia that Lena stayed connected; it was to her that she came all the time; it was the mother who received the awkward gentleness of that daughter who seldom saw her father. When she thought of this, Amalia wondered about the mysteries of Lena's heart. She felt her closeness, her half-hidden tenderness, her presence. But, hang it, if her daughter wanted to be with her, did she need to say those things that hurt her so much? She was really hard to understand, and always had been, that Helena Maria, with her strange temperament, like a house with an attic and a basement, nooks and crannies, trapdoors and cellars, woodpiles and small rooms full of bats and cobwebs, with high ceilings, creaking floors, and half-hidden by trees. Just like her own father's house, Amalia thought, with a smile, where she had grown up and been so happy, that unique house where her dreams took her back every night, to those solid walls now demolished and murky; the only living link remaining was that old grandfather clock that had just pealed seven times in the living room, indicating that it was time to start the work of feeding another day.

She left her room and, in the kitchen, found her daughter, up already: "Good morning, Mother. Did you sleep well?"

She lied: "Very well. And you?"

"Me too."

She, too, was lying, Amalia knew that. She was hiding something again. During the night she had heard Lena get up several times. And she had seen that the light in her room had been on for a long time. But she wasn't going to press her.

They had breakfast, ate fruit, chatted lightly, as if the beauty of the day, coming in the window, had chased away the ghosts of the night.

Or of the soul. Lena filled a glass with milk and started to take her pills, one by one. Amalia looked on in silence, thought it best not to mention anything related to sickness. She suggested: "Today you could lie outside again; the sun is nice, feels great, and since it is early, it is not that hot. It will be good for you."

"Good idea, Mother. It will be great."

They spread a mat on the grass and the woman lay down. Really, it did feel good. The sun. Always a source of life. In exile, it was one of the few things she had truly missed, that warmth on the skin, the brightness on the landscape. "God's painter," Luis Cesario used to say, "it paints us too." Lena learned from her friend to appreciate in particular the golden colors of the late afternoon. She remembered a day when he had taken her to see the city from the top of the hill: "Look, my dear, every minute is a brushstroke in a different color. The color that is now on the water or on the forest will not be used again; it is unique. Even tomorrow there may not be anything like it, there could be more humidity in the air, the sun's rays might be more oblique. At this time, in this kind of landscape, every moment is absolutely unique."

"It's a magical light," Lena had said, dazzled.

Old Luis Cesario corrected her: "Not magical, natural. Alive. And therefore miraculous." And he added something Lena had never considered: "At this hour, time plays with the light. This is why the beauty does not come only from the simultaneous colors, as one usually sees it. It comes from the sequence of colors, that one has to keep in one's memory as they are being replaced by others. It is like the sounds of music that only make sense when they connect to the sounds that have already gone and announce those that have not yet been played. This is the real magic secret of this hour, the enchantment that you were feeling: it is the point where music and colors meet."

"There is a poem by Vinicius that speaks of a color that can only be found in the third minute of dawn," she recalled.

Luis Cesario was delighted: "See? That's just it. A poet knows, a musician knows, a painter knows these things. My child, everybody thinks one is an artist because one creates something beautiful and different. But few know that it is not quite like that. An artist can create only because before that one learns to perceive, to see, hear, smell, touch, feel space, dive into time. And one has to practice—don't ever forget that."

"All right. I will try."

"You will try and you will succeed. The whole secret is in the perceiving. The rest is technique, anyone can learn that with a little perseverance, even the least disciplined artists. But first you have to perceive. So that the color which can only be found in the third minute of dawn, that your poet was talking about, can become beautiful, and a joy forever, as another, much older poet, put it."

"Get off it, Luis Cesario," she had joked. "There is no such thing as an old poet. A poet like you has no age."

"The heart may not, but the body does . . ."

And smiling, silent so as not to disturb the sounds and silences of the sunset, they had stood at rest till night fell.

But the colors of such a morning had a different beauty, brash like the brasses in a big orchestra, everything clear, flat, defined in the air that had been washed by the rain the day before. And the sun offered itself not just to the eye, but to the skin, with a pleasant heat all over her body.

Lena found it perfectly understandable that so-called primitive people should have worshiped the forces of nature. But she felt a special kinship with the Incas, Aztecs, and other sun worshipers. In a way she did not understand, she felt very close to all that, in a hidden nook of her soul. She was a solar woman, not at all a night person, not the bohemian sort; she got sleepy early in the evening, had never been able to go out bar hopping, sipping beer till the small hours, like the rest of the newspaper people; she had been a bit ashamed of it. Her eyelids got heavy, her muscles relaxed, as if every fiber and every cell in her body retained the ancestral memory of civilization as it had flourished before electricity, and followed the natural rhythm of the days, violated only so recently in human history.

Though she felt very clearly that the phases of the moon and the tides alternated cyclically within her, it was with the sun that Lena had her own vital connection. When the sky was blue, she would wake with music in her head or a song on her lips, like a bird. She liked to make love in the morning, lazily and languorously, sleepily, lust awakening slowly, little by little, slipping into the act, like the sun rising luminous from the sea. She wrote at her best early in the morning, at the start of day. Though she made no chlorophyll, she needed the sun to turn her poisons into breathable oxygen and expel all that was toxic. It was always in the sun that she found herself growing, expanding into the universe, swelling with juice, a pomegranate slowly spiking up, a Surinam cherry coloring, fattening into ridges, distilling into sweetness the bitterness of the past and ripening the seeds of the future.

Juice indeed. She smiled at the recollection. Once, driving with Alonso along a sparsely inhabited stretch of coast, they stopped to bathe at a lovely beach, with rosy sand, a line of coconut palms rippled by the northeastern breeze, fishermen's huts in the distance, some reefs forming natural pools of clear, warm water. After strolling for a while, Alonso decided to run the length of the extensive beach, and she lay down, with her face to the sun, her legs wide open, to tan the inside of her thighs. It was getting on to noon and they were almost at the equator. The dark bikini bottoms concentrated the heat of the sun and Lena thought she would not be able to stand it much longer in that position, because she was beginning to feel a burn. She closed her eyes, breathed slowly, paid attention to the noise of the breaking waves, and to the occasional screech of a seabird. And somewhere beneath those clear sensory impressions, she began to feel a pleasant heat between her legs, an ember between her legs, a fire rising and enveloping her, penetrating sharp and sudden, and she realized that the wetness she felt was not just sweat, as she had thought. It came from her, responding to the sun god who had caught her unawares, ready to come any moment, in an ancestral orgasm that surely would make of her the perfect sister of all the pagan mortals possessed by Apollo, by whatever name he took, from the beginnings of life itself. The arrival of Alonso made the godhead into flesh and introduced Neptune into the triangle. And the entire mythology dissolved in the ocean, in an embrace that turned into quick and tippy lovemaking, like an amusing children's game.

The ancient sun, in all its majesty and power, had visited her before as well. One occasion was unforgettable. It was in Mexico, in the ruins of Teotihuacán, that monumental stone celebration of the forces that govern life. She had gone there in the morning with friends; they had walked everywhere in what was left of the ancient sacred city, talking about Aztec, Toltec, and Mayan legends, connecting the surviving architecture to the scenes they had seen the day before in the Rivera murals at the Palacio Nacional, which celebrated the splendor of the civilization that had flowered there, where they were now walking. After a while, her friends, who lived in Mexico and had been to the site several times before, declared themselves tired, and suggested leaving. Unless, they said, she wanted to climb the pyramids. She balked at the plural.

"No pyramids. One will be enough. But I do want to see. I'll climb to the top of the tallest and look around. You don't need to come along."

"OK. We will wait for you down here, in the shade. And you don't have to hurry, go slowly, because at this altitude, and in this heat, you'd better be careful."

Lena started the ascent slowly. Soon she figured out that it was easier to climb diagonally—the ledges were too narrow and steep for a safe footing if she went straight up. Little by little, as she climbed, she could see farther and farther along the plateau, the radius of her view increasing as she rose. She also became aware of the stones she stepped on, the precision with which they fit together. She saw the grass and herbs that grew in the cracks, little yellow daisies; from down there one would not even have suspected the presence of the flowers.

When she came to the top, she could not help but feel the majesty with which the building dominated the surrounding landscape. More impressive still was the perfect harmony with which the pyramids replicated the shape of the conical mountains that rose from the plateau, like a visual and rhythmic echo. On the landing that topped the monument, by the side of a huge stone bench, she realized, surprised, that along the centuries the wind had been bringing in soil and had created a bed. Suddenly, she saw one little heap of that earth move. From inside a small rodent came out, looking around as if startled. Maybe a marmot, or a field mouse, she could not really identify it. Right in the middle of the little yellow daisies. It looked like a scene in a cartoon, unreal and idyllic. The sensation was of absolute peace, and integration with nature and eternity.

She knew she did not have to hurry back down. She had come from so far away, the moment was so tranquil, it deserved to be enjoyed fully. She sat on the large, wide, and tall stone bench that crowned the monument. She was tired from the climb, breathless from the effort in the thin, high air. She decided to lie down and relax, give her heart time to slow back down.

As she lay back, she was immediately hit by the Sun. Just so, with a capital letter. Strong, fierce, hot, shining straight into her eyes, forcing her to close them reflexively. She raised her arm to shade them and allow her to see. In the darkness of her closed eyes, she saw suns of every color, multiplying and gliding slowly. She let the impression fade and, little by little, started again to look through a crack between her lids, letting the light come in gradually till she could see again. And then she saw. Clearly. The hands on her watch, right in front of her eyes, dominating her field of vision, showed noon, exactly.

In a flash, Lena realized. She understood it all. A one-time event. She put together all the external, objective coordinates, the concrete data she had at hand and had not noticed before. She was a woman, lying on the sacrificial stone of the Pyramid of the Sun, on the summer solstice, the sun at its zenith. She leapt up. She felt her blood, heard it beating in her fright. It pounded in her neck, in her temples. It was the effort, the altitude, she told herself. One more time, she looked at the stone altar where she had been lying and that so many, many times had been bathed by the blood of prisoners whose still-beating hearts were offered to the heat and the light that determined life and death. She shivered. She turned her back on the stone and climbed down in silence, haste, and fear. She claimed exhaustion and refused to go out for the rest of the day, closed in upon herself. She had never told anyone about that episode, but every once in a while she thought of it; and even as she laughed at herself for that irrational fright in the middle of the twentieth century, she still could not help respecting that primitive woman who had suddenly erupted from the very depth of her self.

But now everything was very civilized: the well-tended garden, the neatly cut green grass growing all the way to the wall, the gate opening to the sand on the beach. And lots of shade. All she had to do was move a bit to one side, and she was out of the sun, framing and containing it with trees, roofs, beach umbrellas. A good idea, by the way. She had been lying there long enough, might as well sit at the table on the verandah, in the shade, and read the newspaper. She had to read the paper every day, kept feeling there was something missing when she did not, that time would develop holes and become rarefied, that she was being sidelined, had fallen off the boat and was being left behind, if she did not know what was happening in the world.

She rose with difficulty, because of her foot, on which she could not yet put her weight. She went to the verandah, took up the newspaper, and sat in one of the wicker armchairs.

She read attentively, noticing that they were no longer talking about some big financial scandal that had made headlines the day before. It was most unlikely that there should have been no follow-up to the news, some "suite," as they said in the newsroom (and in France). Probably management at the paper had no interest in saying more about it. Lena always felt frustrated and sad when this kind of thing happened. It was almost a physical pain whenever she noticed the press denying information to the public, for whatever reason—external violence, professional incompetence or insensitivity, private interests. It had been very hard to live for so many years with the censorship notes from the police that came, almost every day, to stifle their words and destroy the very reason for being a journalist. Lena remembered those years with a tightening in her chest. The telephone would ring and an anonymous voice, vaguely identified as agent So-and-So or Such-and-Such, no chance of ever finding out who it really was, declared that "by orders from above, it is absolutely forbidden for the means of social communication to publish any news, reference, interviews, or commentary about subject x." For those working in radio or TV, it was even worse. Since the newscasts and prohibitions were more numerous than in the case of a newspaper (published only once a day), the clock became one more element of threat and blackmail. A radio or TV journalist could always be accused of having disobeyed a censorship order and aired a story at a given time when, in fact, the prohibition had been issued later. There was no proof. And that journalist could be indicted for a crime against the press law or national security. But it could go further and he could be punished for disobeying an order that had never been forwarded. Or that had been phoned in to the wrong extension, answered by an office boy, a technician, or a mechanic, as had often happened. At a newspaper, with only one edition a day, it was possible to arrange with the censors that only one or two people in the newsroom would be authorized to receive the censorship notices—and the more daring editors demanded that the notices come in writing and be signed by someone, which could be negotiated since, in serious and urgent cases, it was not even necessary to have the note from the police; a call from some authority to the owner of the paper had the same effect.

On the other hand, at that time, it was clear who the enemy was, so it was possible to attempt to dribble around the prohibitions, attempt to hint at the news item in some other way or at least establish a relation of complicity with the readers so they would get the idea that something had been censored. Some papers published recipes, passages from *The Lusiad,* cartoon strips, drawings in the place of the vetoed stories. In this way, it was at least possible to indicate to readers that information had been withheld, play clean, and not betray professional dignity and trust. And in the last resort, if one could not even do that, if one could do nothing at all, it was always possible to hope that this would not last forever and that one day it would end. And this was why, in a way, when external control by the police was replaced by internal recommendations, many journalists thought that was even harder to take. In most cases, these internal recommendations came from editors who wanted to be more Catholic than the pope and, on their own initiative, spiked any news that they imagined could possibly go against what might be the interests of advertisers or of newspaper owners, with an exaggerated and senseless zeal. Lena was a collector of scraps of paper. Even now, among the papers she had brought to select material from, she kept finding lots of things. She had kept copies of all the notes from the censorship office received while she worked at the newspaper. And also copies of many of the innumerable memos Barros had sent to the newsroom every day, after he had attentively read the paper. It was a collection of critical remarks, scoldings, observations, and prohibitions that drew a clear picture of this informal censorship, particularly if one considered that all these bits of paper were only the visible part of the iceberg, for the vast majority of the vetoes had arrived by the evening before, before the news matter had been approved, in the form of emotional verbal outbursts never recorded for history. It was even amusing to look at these bits of paper now. In more recent years there had been ever more notes from Barros and fewer from the censorship office. Official censorship had become superfluous, replaced by the actions of that kind of journalist. Lena reread a few of those notes, from the time when Barros was still at the paper. Funny to watch him playing liberal now; he was even involved in the Workers' Party's bid for the governorship of the state.

"Enough talk about amnesty. You are editorializing. This is not news."

"Calling a riot a demonstration is an exaggeration. Let us be objective."

"Shall we stop giving so much space to Teotonio Vilela? There is no point in giving a forum to this old madman."*

"It's not necessary to cover a union meeting. If they paralyze the city, we'll cover it."

"Why do you call the truck drivers' strike a lockout?"

"Stop talking about that hunger strike by the prisoners. So long as there are no new developments, the subject should disappear. If one of them dies, that's another matter . . ."

"Why write up this fire at the shopping center construction site? Nobody died, and the building's owner is big advertiser of ours."

"Everybody knows that representative is a pinko. We don't talk about him."

"Since when does this paper publish opinions by guys whose mandates were revoked?"

The collection was huge and varied, and included, among notes and memos, a recent article by a colleague at the political desk who was fired even as the redemocratization process was going on—maybe for the simple reason that management wanted to protect him against possible future turnabouts that could bring threats of reprisals. After all, the passage to democracy was taking place in accordance with certain tacitly agreed-upon conditions. Thus, no torturer was ever pun-

*Teotonio Vilela, a politician from the northeastern state of Alagoas, became a member of the government party but in the late 1970s began to speak in favor of redemocratization and eventually switched to the official opposition party; after liberalization he stayed in the party that succeeded the latter.

ished. No attempted right-wing murder was ever publicly investigated. No crazy terrorist plan concocted in the cellars of the dictatorship ever took any of its authors to jail—not even the failed attempt to blow up the stage where some artists were putting on a May Day show, in a closed auditorium with thousands of spectators. Or the insane plan to blow up the city gas works and blame the communists. Those responsible remained unpunished. Still. Ever.

Maybe that was why, to avoid possible dangers in the case of a political veer back, the editors of the paper preferred not to publish the article by a colleague, a copy of which Lena was now rereading:

There is something among us, called a sphere, which must be preserved.

This transcendental statement was published in this paper precisely one week ago. It did not come from a mathematician or geometrist, concerned about possible threats to solids. Nor did it come from an imaginative sports broadcaster, worried about a hypothetical invasion of our soccer fields by rugby, with its egg-shaped ball. Nothing like that. It was uttered in an interview by a police commissioner especially chosen in Brasilia to investigate accusations that torture had been used against prisoners in Rio de Janeiro, in the detention centers run by the federal police. And it referred to the judge of the 33rd circuit who, the day before, had seized, in that building, a collection of very strange objects that seemed most inappropriate for use in an office charged with upholding the law. "Office" in a manner of speaking: two soundproof rooms.

Among those objects there was no sphere. But there was a prod. According to the lawyer who filed the charge and gave the precise address where the judge would find the material, this stick with a metal hook at one end was used to deliver electric shocks to the prisoners or to lift snakes up to the prisoners' faces. There were also some drips on the floor, which the judge took along with him for forensic examination because they looked like blood. There were also two tires, old stockings used to tie up hands and feet, and a two-meter-long iron bar wrapped in a Chilean newspaper—all of that according to news reports. According to the charge by the lawyer and the suspicions of the judge, these would be the necessary parts for putting together what became known as the "parrot's perch,"* a pole passed over a prisoner's arms and under his knees as his wrists and ankles were tied together, the whole contraption then suspended from two metal platforms. The police officer on duty when the judge arrived tried to bar his entrance. Because he entered anyway, he found everything the existence of which had so far been denied. That was where the sphere came in. Because the first thing the policeman uttered was the brilliant expression above, of which he himself gave a translation: he thought the judge should not have entered the room because that was going to interfere with the investigation, since he was part of the state judiciary and had no authority to invade federal venues. They were not in his jurisdiction, in his sphere. That is, if nothing wrong were found, that was judge's fault.

Facts evolve, and the judge himself resolved to respond to those statements. But what is really difficult to understand is how it happened that, two days after the discovery of that room with its objects, the man in charge of the inquest is still stating that: "Honestly, he does not know" what they could possibly have been for, though he knows perfectly well that it is important to preserve the sphere.

Perhaps an attentive perusal of the newspapers could help the police investigator to investigate the charges. The police themselves explained that the iron bar is just part of a musical instrument, the berimbau. And another judge, Osvaldo Lima Rodrigues, Jr., as he expressed his support for the courage of his fellow judge Eduardo Mayr, said that one year earlier he had tried to perform a similar investigation, in analogous circumstances, of the building occupied by the military police on Barão de Mesquita Street, known as the "Cecilia Meireles Room," which, as everybody knows, is the name of one of the few places

---

* The parrot's perch was a torture technique used by the Brazilian dictatorship that consists of placing a tube, bar, or pole over the victim's biceps and behind the knees while tying the victim's ankles and wrists together. The assembly is suspended between two metal platforms forming what looks like a parrot's perch.

in the city where one can listen to good classical music. Well, as an official note by the military police in Paraná states, in answer to other denunciations of torture in that area, "Soon there will be air conditioning and piped-in music in the buildings of the DPF—the federal police—for the greater comfort of its possible occupants." Thus, it is clear that all of this is nothing more than a program for public musical education. The confusion is due to that standard refrain from capoeira* which, as everybody knows, cannot do without a berimbau, that goes "Zumzumzum, zum-zumzum, capoeira kills me one . . ."

Or could it be that reporters, famously frivolous, have misunderstood? Maybe the sentence was "We have something called an ex-fear, which must be preserved."

But in that case, the country would like to know more about this prefix: "Ex- . . . Since when?"

As she read the article, Lena realized once again that in one way or another censorship was still in force, though the dictatorship had ended. Even in the newspapers. As well as in other sectors. There was the film that the government would not allow to be shown because of pressure from the church or from conservatives. Or a play that had problems being allowed on the stage. Though the parties of the Left were now allowed to exist, and though there was greater freedom of thought and speech, and to start investigations, it was clear that there was still a long road ahead.

Perhaps that was inevitable. The Brazilian rhythm for history making was slow, with many advances and retreats. But more and more often she found herself surprisingly impatient with these delays and obstacles. The transition to democracy was taking so long, was still so far from complete, that it was lasting almost longer than the dictatorship itself. And though the woman knew very well that historical time is different from lived time, still, given the time she had left to live, these years were too many. It was time stolen from her, for which there was no recovery. Wrenched away by the greedy raven of time, it would return *nevermore*.

* Afro-Brazilian martial art that combines elements of dance, acrobatics, and music.

VIII

Fonte de mel, bicho triste, pátria minha
Amada, idolatrada, salve, salve!
Que mais doce esperança acorrentada
O não poder dizer-te: aguarda
Não tardo!

(VINICIUS DE MORAES)

Honey spring, sad beast, country mine,
Beloved, idolized, hail, all hail to you!
What a sweet, but chained hope
That I cannot say to you: wait . . .
I won't be long!

She leaned back in her seat. She looked at the garden, her mother in the middle distance checking out a weed that had invaded one of the flowerbeds, the sea in the background, behind the low wall.

The sight of her mother touched her, despite all the difficulties they both had showing their feelings, despite her irritation at her mother's intrusions, despite the restraint both showed when sharing that space. She would like to learn from her mother how to age. Dignified and active, Amalia kept herself up to date, connected to the world, pulling crabgrass from the flowerbeds though she knew the weeds would come back, quickly and vigorously. It was a metaphor embedded in daily life. A strong woman, like the matriarchs in the Old Testament.

Lena watched her mother from a distance, almost spying on her, not letting on, and allowed her mind to roam: if she managed to get well, if she could return to writing, if she finally spawned that play about exile, if it worked, if Luis Cesario had been right and she was in fact an artist, if she then went on to be a playwright . . . In short, if all that happened, maybe someday she would write a character like her mother.

As soon as that thought crossed her mind, she shivered. Her very skin shrank from the thought. She tried to find out what that was about. Probably it was not simply "something," but a complicated mix of emotions. Clearly, what she felt was a kind of shame, almost an aversion, before this possibility of emotional nakedness. On the other hand, she also understood that it was inevitable—she could only transfigure what started out as truth. And especially at this moment, confronted by the question of writing about her mother, what she felt was that she could not do it, because her mother would not understand, and would feel hurt or offended at being shown in public, even in disguise, in a way that did not correspond to her own idea of herself. Once again Lena was beating like an insect against the glass pane that separates memory from imagination, fiction from reality. She was back at the point she had argued about so much with Honorio, and verified that avoiding deposition, testimony, or confession did not imply leaving the scene. On the contrary, she was making a stronger statement, being more intensely present, even exacerbating her presence, forced to condense disparate threads in symbolic form. Like dream work, except conscious, which was the whole problem. Or at least partially conscious.

She had also talked a lot about this with old Luis Cesario, though only in terms of artistic creation in general, nothing directly linked to literary creation. It was easier if one did not deal specifically with words. It was a question—in no way simple—of achieving a fully aware immersion in the world, then working it all over internally and extruding it again in the form of beauty. All of it was a lot of work. Whether you then controlled sound, colors, volumes, the strings or keys on an instrument, face or body movements, that depended on your means of expression. But Lena thought that, with words, everything gets more complicated. Because those immediately bring into play concepts that everyone uses every day, that are part of social intercourse, and touch loved ones directly. Right away everybody starts looking for references to reality. Words create a game of hiding and revealing what is real, like any other language, but because everybody uses words, it is within everybody's reach. And then their aesthetic use runs the risk of getting mixed up with their practical uses.

Lena had been thinking along these lines for a while. The more seriously she considered using words in a non-journalistic context, the more the problem troubled her. Language would then no longer serve just for communication, information, broadcasting news in an impersonal way. It would start to express, manifest worlds that exert pressure from the inside out just as one is stating a fact or telling a story. And she became very sensitive to things said and heard in everyday life, finding meanings in everything, as if she were suffering from an incurable disease that made her see hidden meanings where others just saw transparency. As a consequence, she was choosing her words ever more carefully. She noticed she was less and less inclined to speak, keeping ever-greater spaces private. Or else, in emotionally charged situations, she would shoot closer to the target. With irony, or sarcasm, for instance. Or with a joke. Just like a musician humming or whistling, or a painter doodling while he chats, like a potter shaping soft bread at a restaurant table, she, too, before she got sick, had begun to ply her craft absentmindedly, and was surprised to find herself doing it. Sometimes Alonso called her attention to it, after the fact: she had been ironic, sarcastic, borderline aggressive toward someone, fencing with words against an nonexistent or unaware adversary. Something between aggression and cowardice. It was hard to explain that, for her, it was not gratuitous, however much she regretted it. These things happened because of a subtle awareness of hostility or antagonism, something that hurt her and that, immediately, unleashed in her a defensive battery. It could even seem a bit paranoid, but it was just a question of excessive sensitivity, an acute awareness of words.

On the other hand, she realized that she needed to dig deeper into her thoughts about her work. She had discovered a pitiless law: censorship, too, is one of the writer's raw materials. A curse: censor yourself or isolate yourself. Other artists might be able to exercise their talents with greater freedom. But a writer can't. The meanings of words are immediately conceptual and linked to external referents. If a writer is among friends and decides to play with words happily, the result is humor, and success. If a writer handles words in pain or when hurt, the result can be irony—a social disaster. Unless there is self-censorship. And not just in the moment—later, too, when it is time to write things down. If Lena started to tell about her unhappiness as a child, she would hurt her parents. If she started on what had hurt her as a friend, she would hurt other people she loved. But pain was what she most needed to talk about. So she had to censor herself, and to learn to invent new ways of getting around that censorship, just as she had had to do for so many years with the police proscriptions at the newspaper during the dictatorship. Would it be possible to do that? Or would she have to hurt herself and muzzle herself in order not to hurt those she loved? It might even be the case that those worries were part of the illness that now kept words away from her in that painful way. Maybe she was inventing this unconscious way of not being able to write without feeling guilty. Or until she learned to weave a text like a dream, putting one thing in the place of another, one character as a sum of various others, and another unfolding into several. Then the tale might happen despite censorship, and beyond the tyranny of affections. Only, unlike dreams, the work would have to have a natural internal coherence that came from the rules dictated by itself, a harmony, a cohesion, in short, a beauty, that left nothing out. And it would also have to be open to others, an invitation to share an experience, offered in a fraternal communion with a fellow sufferer.

Very complicated. Better cultivate one's garden.

She smiled, remembering that Voltaire had already written that. Or something like it. And she clearly saw the quotable line under the ordinary sentence. There was nothing for it: words were always pregnant, even when unsaid, even if they existed only in someone's thoughts, unformed, unformulated.

And in any case, Lena knew that she could not go cultivate her garden just then. At most she could walk around in her mother's garden. And that was precisely what she would do, now, even if she was still limping a bit.

"Pulling weeds, Mother?"

"Yes. Never mind how many the caretaker pulls, they are always growing back."

"But the garden is lovely, so well cared for."

"It is. The problem is the ants," sighed Amalia. "The jasmine is all in bud, look how pretty! It looks like the rain gave it the last-needed push, and in every little bud here on the stalk a little bit of green is about to pop. Just look. It makes me so sad to think that in almost a flash the ants could destroy it."

"Well, Mother, there is no point worrying about something that has not yet happened and might never happen after all."

Amalia smiled sadly: "I think this year it has already happened about six times, just with this jasmine bush."

"And you can't do anything about it?" asked Lena, her interest awakened.

"I really don't think you can. You treat it with ant killers, you come out at night with a flashlight, looking for their trails, find the anthill, insert a dust bomb guaranteed to spread to all the underground tunnels; it's a lot of work, you think you have taken care of it. Then, a while later, some beautiful morning, you come upon a completely naked tree and find that the ants are back. I get so mad. Ever since I was a child, I have heard people say that either Brazil gets rid of the ants, or the ants get rid of Brazil. And I am pretty close to convinced that the ants are going to win."

More literature comes into my head, thought Lena, and did not quote *Macunaíma*: "too many ants and too little health are the ills of Brazil." She asked: "Could those ant killers be too weak?"

"Not at all, my child. They are so strong that one can't even find them any longer, because the government has banned their sale. At least the good ones, the ones that worked. It seems they harmed domestic animals as well. And there are lots of people around, committing suicide with ant poison. I think they decided to control the substances somewhat."

"Well, yes, it does seem that those insecticides are really very toxic, and have a lot of dangerous side-effects, attacking other animals, plants, even people, and the environment."

Amalia sounded impatient when she answered: "All that talk is very beautiful on paper, in the newspapers, in the city. I always read and think, just let those guys plant something and take care of the land. I'd like to see then if they are willing to cross their arms and let the ants eat everything, let the caterpillars eat the vegetables, and the slugs destroy their plantings. I don't know—every time you turn around, there's a new bug—it's beetles, it's aphids, the lot. No way can one do without insecticides. Great talk, but won't solve a thing."

Lena explained that there might be other resources, less noxious. She said there were teams at the universities and research centers that were developing natural means to control those plagues.

"I think that's wonderful," Amalia agreed. "I don't really like spraying poisons all around me. I just want the plants to grow. When are they going to start selling those natural controls in the stores?"

"Well, that may take a while. You need money for research, education, agriculture . . ."

Lord in Heaven, how tiring . . . There was that need to speechify again. Shit, living in a place where the smallest, everyday problems involve a general situation of underdevelopment, corruption, impunity, bad government, exploitation. A place where any honest thought leads to this sense of impotence and despair, asking yourself what you could possibly accomplish, in the end, when nobody else is doing anything. Or when those who do are so few, and everyone thinks only of himself. It had been like that at the time of the resistance to the dictatorship, as if one were condemned to oscillate forever between heroics and hopelessness, bluster and gloom . . .

Her mother was still talking and Lena tried to pay attention to what she was saying: ". . . there was every type of bird, maybe that's what it was. But they destroyed everything, burning, logging, killing. Of course all that's left is grubs everywhere. There is nothing left that will eat them. Sometimes I think, you know, that there have always been that many ants in Brazil, even in prehistoric times, among the dinosaurs. This must have been their own country. That was why God put anteaters here, to eat ants, or else, how do you explain that this is the only place in the world that has anteaters? You, who are always reading—have you ever heard of this, read it anywhere?"

Lena smiled. "I have never heard of it, Mother. But I swear it is an interesting idea. Makes a lot of sense. That's how it must have been. This is where there had to be an eater of ants because there were too many ants. Luis Cesario used to say that Brazil is the only country in the world named after a tree and the one that cuts down the most trees."

"Named after a tree?"

"Sure. Brazilwood. Or have you forgotten?"

Amalia laughed, really amused. "You mentioned Luis Cesario. But I am not the one who is going to answer him. It's your father who will do that. Because he always says that Brazil has fire, as in a brazier, in its name because it is an incendiary country, always setting fire to things, can't see anything working well without burning it."

"Could be," said Lena. "That's probably how it is. One dreams and imagines that this is a land of beautiful trees, but in the end it is really the land of trees cut down to dye fabric. But this is a funny idea— Brazil a land of fire."

"Not mine, Alberto's. He used to talk about that from time to time. He pointed out that the Indians practiced slash-and-burn before the Portuguese arrived. And that the land was settled by burning. Even now, the Brazilian way of cleaning a field is not with a tractor, as in other places, but by setting it on fire."

As they walked toward the house, Lena thought about those observations. Then, by herself, she continued to consider the Brazilian brazier. It is true that it also provided warmth, and how cozy and good that was! What is it, tender and loving, that connects us to the land this way? So that you feel a tightness around your heart when you are away from it, and miss it as if there were a deep hole in your soul.

She went back to the conversations with Maria and Antonio in Italy, the nostalgia she felt while in exile, the uprootedness she had seen, read, and heard in the accounts she had collected during that trip and that she recognized from her time away. To uproot yourself is not just to cut yourself off from the land and feel stifled. It is also carrying that fire in your chest. It is a sleeping, covered ember that insists on burning on, and you blow on it in secret, in silence when night falls and others are about to sleep, to keep it alive and burning inside because, without it, you die.

Some of her notes from the accounts she had collected could not hide all of this, much as they tried to. All she had to do was open her pad at random and read any passage:

"I spoke to Juan, from Uruguay, about sixty, an old militant now living in Sweden and staying at our hotel. He was invited to participate in a debate here in Rome and grabbed the opportunity with both hands to spend a few days in a Latin country, enjoying any resemblance there might be between Italy and Uruguay. About ten years in exile. He grumbled endlessly about Sweden, resentful and very aggressive. He complained about its excessive materialism/capitalism, which cannot fathom voluntary work for the common good and has to pay for everything: information, help doing translation, overtime, an interview on the radio, any talk by a professor. I argued that it was only fair and respectful; after all, we have all fought hard for that. But obviously his resentment is deep against the society that sheltered him, against the moral pressure for him to feel grateful, against the realization that the utopia he had dreamt of might even exist but that his people were barred from paradise. He told the story of a friend, a woman from Chile, a fellow exile in Stockholm. When she had a baby, she produced too much milk and decided that she would donate the excess to a milk bank. A few days later she received a check in the mail, from the government, for the milk she had donated, and had a crisis, feeling that instead of being a mother who shared life, she was being turned into a cow selling her milk. Juan is very excited when he tells that, inflamed, shaking. There was a group of Swedes at the breakfast table, and they all listened in silence and with great respect, which only made him angrier and more resentful. He claimed that this was nothing but coldness disguised as politeness, that they were icy, with no emotion, that they heard someone criticize their country and did not fight. It was very embarrassing to watch him as if he had a steam engine inside, hissing and whistling like that. It got worse. I reminded him that Uruguay was redemocratizing and that, just as Brazilians and Argentines were able to return, his time would come as well. I said it was time to prepare to return, that it would not take long. And then I blew his emotional fuse for good. As he tried to argue in response, he calmed down and his eyes filled with tears, and he cried: he was unable to plan to return; he could no longer imagine himself living in Uruguay. He has worked for many years in Europe, has all the citizens' rights, social security, retirement, an assured old age. He knows he won't have the courage to return. And he will stay. Grumbling and attacking. But transplanted, unable to be Swedish, unable to be fully Uruguayan again."

There was note about somebody else from Uruguay:

"I have given my Rio phone number to Helena, from Uruguay, who is returning. Or preparing to return. She is worried about how her children will adapt, speaking a language different from that of the other children, used to all the resources of a developed society She is afraid they will be turned off by the strong smells, the dirt, the noise, the lack of punctuality, the disorder, all the hallmarks of our Latin America, and that they will be unhappy. She is just a mother who does not want to subject her children to pain and suffering. But she also trusts in the love and the force of happiness; it is touching: she talks about music on the streets of her country and the games the children will play with cousins and her friends' children. Then she asks about how those who stayed will accept her, if they are likely to be hostile, if the competition in the workplace will be very harsh. You can see she is afraid of being hurt by the possible resentment of those who stayed and suffered through the dictatorship and did not leave. I try to encourage her, and she mentions the case of a Brazilian playwright who worked for years in exile, garnering great respect, success, and international prestige, and who, as soon as he returned home, had his work destroyed in an act of aggressive and gratuitous retaliation, purely personal and nasty. Helena is an artist, extremely sensitive, and afraid she would not be able to stand a similar massacre, and keeps asking herself why she insists on returning, if she thinks it will not be good for her children and fears that her work will not be recognized and her fellows will see her as an intruder and a threat. She tells of another case, a Uruguayan writer who achieved recognition abroad, denouncing the dictatorships, the repression, and the bloody historical exploitation at the root of all the misery on the continent. Well, according to Helena, the more successful he is, the more books of his are translated, the more hostile the other writers are to him, accusing him of having nominated himself an international spokesman for Uruguayan culture, of playing at being a superstar, of hogging the limelight and castrating his fellows as they try to make themselves known. At first I am amazed at all these references to submerged rivalries among intellectuals of the opposition, splitting into factions: *those who stayed versus those who left versus those who were arrested,* and so on. I say that I have no experience of this phenomenon. But then I shut up, remembering that it happened in Brazil as well, though in a more diffuse way, hitting a priest here, a politician there, or a filmmaker, anyone who had been able to be heard abroad. The censorship, the authoritarianism, and the intolerance of the dictatorship had brought on that additional pain: they had often been incorporated by the militants themselves, who had fought against them but modeled in their fight their behavior toward their comrades. Whether or not they had been exiled. Eventually, I realized that I could not comfort Helena very much. And since she wanted my phone number as a contact, for support when she came through Rio on her way to Montevideo, I ended up giving it to her."

But she had not called. Lena did not know whether the woman had decided not to return, and thus had not needed the support, or whether she had not stopped in Rio on her way. She read on:

"Gilda is from Chile. The Chileans belonged to a different wave. They arrived after all the others. They were the last to go into exile and they had fallen from a greater height. They had seen their dream close to coming true or had even managed to live for a little while in their utopia. They did have their problems, sure, but in the end, they had believed that it was possible, in Latin America, for a popular government to be voted into power and that it was possible to build a society that was both just and democratic. It was because of them that we, too, had believed. But it was precisely because they had come closer that they suffered more when they fell. Gilda was a teacher back home. She now owns a bookstore founded by an exiled Spaniard. When he died, he left the business to his children. When the Franco regime ended, they returned to Spain, leaving the store in the hands of another exile, this time a Uruguayan, who had been a merchant in Montevideo, who did not care all that much about books, but had kept the business going as well as she could. Till her turn came to declare an end to her exile and return to Uruguay. She turned the business over to Gilda, who cannot muster indifference to this history of exile that marks her store and her activity. She presides over a roomful of Iberian and Latin American books and themes, on a small side street in the university quarter in

Paris. Very specialized, catering only to natives or scholars of these cultures. And it is not going well, undergoing a financial crisis. It had been an important, very busy center of cultural resistance, at first hosting exiles from Franco and Salazar, then turning into a home for South Americans in general. Peruvians, Bolivians, Argentines, Brazilians, Uruguayans, Colombians, Paraguayans, Chileans, all came to peck at the latest in culture on its newsstands, to leaf through the magazines, to look for books, leave leaflets, or just to find people with whom they could exchange ideas. Little by little they started to go back. Now there are only Chileans left, some Colombians, and Paraguayans. Gilda says that this is very good, a sign that there can be an end to exile and that someday everybody will return. But, at the same time, she is sad to be constantly taking leave of people, to see that everybody else is going and only she is staying. And of course this reduction in the reading public also means that business is bad for her. She is there whenever there is a gathering of exiles, insisting that they buy books, that they support the effort to keep alive the written word in their languages, keeping alive their little island in an ocean of European culture. She appeals to them, asks that they pick up books, journals, magazines, that they show an interest, that they read more—otherwise, she will have to close the bookstore, she won't be able, financially, to keep it going. But she thinks it will be very difficult to survive, not only because Latin Americans don't really have the habit or the taste for reading in general, but because, as she explains, she notices that she is starting to be seen as a kind of vulture, trying to make money from a national catastrophe, exploiting the nostalgia and the thirst for knowledge of her compatriots just so she can sell her books. Of all, this is what hurts her most. As she talked to me, she came close to tears. She spoke a lot about how badly we handle money, that we are the direct heirs of Iberian colonialism, with its paternalistic and slave-supported system, in which culture is connected to official state honors and visions. We always think that teaching is a kind of vocation, publishing is charity, and that to request a text from someone or invite someone to give a talk is to honor them . . . We accept any kind of reasoning that will make paying for intellectual work an insult to the person who did the work. Gilda insists, vehemently, that this way of thinking only serves the colonial powers, those who want to suppress independent thinking. She spoke of domination and imperialism, mixed clichés and emotional outbursts drawn from the depths of her own self. In the end, eyes lowered and tears flowing, she confessed that she had gotten so used to the life of the bookstore that, if she had to close it, she would feel it as a second exile—once more expelled from Chile, this time from the little Chile she had rebuilt bit by bit on the banks of the Seine, where her beloved araucanos* live on the printed page and where all the Spanish American accents come together."

Through a friend who had gone to Paris some months later, Lena learned that the bookstore was gone. In its place there was a store selling ponchos, alpaca and vicuña wool sweaters and hoods, South American crafts and tapestries. From afar, and without news of her, Lena wished for Gilda's success. She hoped Gilda would not have had to go into a new exile, but had found a way to make this deracination bloom into another activity that, if not nourished by the written language or the culture of books, could still connect with the motherland and help her bear her time of waiting.

"Alda is Bolivian, looks quite Indian, but is very thin, almost emaciated from generations of malnutrition. No way of telling how old she is—she looks atemporal or eternal. As she talks to me she is so overcome by emotion that her face gets covered with red blotches and she trembles uncontrollably. I don't understand this shyness, because earlier she had behaved in a startling manner: at the morning roundtable she had almost caused a commotion because all of a sudden she had risen from among the general audience, gone up on the stage, asked to interrupt the proceedings in an unplanned way, and started an exalted speech, saying she could no longer stand to see films, TV documentaries, news reports, speeches, books, whatever, produced by Latin Americans themselves, that showed a Latin America made up of nothing but war, hunger, and misery. She begged the exiles not to forget the joy of life they had known before they left. She insisted that their works should not ask for solidarity, but for admiration and aesthetic

---

* Araucania is a wide area, covering parts of Chile and Argentina, that was originally inhabited by the native Mapuche.

pleasure even if the reader or viewer did not understand it logically; that did not matter, we have a different logic, but if we had learned to understand their European stuff, than they, too, by reading, listening, and being charmed by what is ours, if they tried not to just analyze, they could be enriched with all that. She may not have put it in exactly those terms; her language was much more direct and concrete, but the force of what she was saying was undeniable and the vehemence with which she defended her idea was completely irresistible. Fluent, burning, secure. At the end of the session, I sought her out so we could talk and found her painfully shy; she said it was the only time in her life she had ever spoken in public but she had been unable to contain herself. Now she was ashamed of it. But eventually she told me a few things. She had been an elementary school teacher in her country. In exile, she works as a cleaning woman. But she keeps up a strong connection with the children in this diaspora. And she says a few interesting things. For instance, she had noticed that the little Latin Americans, when they draw a landscape or a house, always put a colorful and smiling sun in the sky; they can't conceive a world without the sun. Even when they are born in exile. A drawing by a European child may or may not have a sun. Drawings of our children always have it. Alda guarantees it."

Somewhere in her notes there was someone else who spoke about children. It was in another notebook, the one with the Brazilians, and Lena searched till she found it. She knew who had said it. She would never forget the deep emotions linked to her meeting with Cecilia, which had happened after recommendations from common friends, exchanges of letters, so many things.

"Finally I managed to meet up with Cecilia, but we are friends already; it's an old and affectionate thing. We talked a lot; I tried to have her give me details of her work at Curumim, how it started, what it is.* After all, she does not have children, and had never thought of working with children. And suddenly, in exile, she bursts out with this beautiful thing. She explains that she started on an impulse. She had just arrived in Paris after the standard trail of disillusions leading

---

* *Curumim* is an Indian word meaning "child." It is often used in Brazil as a term of affection toward a child.

through Santiago and Stockholm. She went to the home of a friend, Brazilian as well, who had small children. Someone asked the children what they wanted to be when they grew up. Quickly, one of the little ones answered: 'I want to be French.' And explained right away: 'The French sleep in beds, sit in chairs, keep their clothes in wardrobes, take their children on vacations, some of them have cars . . . And the parents have parties and know the songs the children sing in school.' The boy's notion set them all thinking. They saw that, in truth, in the homes of the Brazilians he knew, people slept on mattresses on the floor, sat on cushions, used suitcases and trunks every day, and had no way of going on a vacation or buying a car. As for parties, none of them celebrated the *Mi-carême*, or Bastille Day and their Easter was much less cool than those of any of their friends. Cecilia could not stand it and decided to organize a back-country party for the children, even though it was already August.* She ended up involving a large group of parents. They improvised peanut brittle and even coconut candy, boiled corn, and any food they could think of that would resemble what was traditional for the feast of Saint John's Eve. They rehearsed a quadrille with a guitar and a mouth organ. They decorated a room with streamers and pennants. They played fortune-telling games. The only thing they did not have was bonfires and firecrackers. But she decided that the following year there would be those too. 'And then, Lena, I realized that was the first time in exile I was planning for the coming year, far from Brazil. I cried all night because of that. But I saw that I had learned something from the children. Or many things. For instance, the coming year could be cheerful. And I decided to organize the Curumim Club so all the children could meet on Saturdays and play happily at being Brazilian.' They told stories, sang, danced, put on costumes, read books, had parties, collected Brazilian postcards, played ring-around-the-rosy, and from time to time someone prepared our Brazilian food. I will never forget the light in Cecilia's eyes as she told me all these things and said, 'I thought it was good for the kids. And I also think that it was good for the parents. For me it was wonderful.'"

---

*Traditionally these country parties take place in June, from the 14th (Saint Anthony's Day) to the 29th (Saint Peter's and Saint Paul's Day). The most important of these is the feast of Saint John's Eve, on the 23rd.

It was great to see someone who had managed to get out of the hole that way. Now, from afar, Lena followed Cecilia's work, after she had returned and opened a little art school, studying art education, turning toward the future. Many plans for the coming years, and now without pain.

Still with her notebook in her hand, Lena found another account she had written down, from a Brazilian as well. She remembered the calm and solid woman with whom she had talked in a café: elegant, well dressed, with a German surname.

"Well, my real name is not Anna Fischer, but Sebastiana. Sebastiana Conceição de Araújo. Right away I turned into Anna; nobody was going to be able to say a name like mine, long, different, full of tildes, cedillas, *j*s. When I got married I immediately became Frau Fischer, my husband's name, and nowadays even I forget about Conceição and all the rest. But I actually think that she was a different woman, who stayed behind, a shy little girl who arrived here afraid of the police and of everyone, who had to flee across the border without documents, who suffered hunger and cold in Buenos Aires till she found some friends who got her a false passport and a ticket to Europe, who did not quite understand anything that was going on. I was in high school, had a boyfriend who was a law student; we were arrested together, he tried to flee and was killed, and I was caught. I got beat up a lot, was tortured. When my family managed to find out where I was and went to find me, my father searched out the major and told him that he should beat me more so I would learn. He said that right in front of me. That's when it got really bad. I almost died. Then, one day, they let me go. I have no idea why. I never quite understood what was happening—I was very stupid, only got involved because of my boyfriend. I did not even live in the South Zone. My family was from Nilopolis, and I was born and raised in the lowlands. At first, I suffered a lot here. I did a bit of everything, don't even like to think about it. But then I met Klaus, who was lovely, a real father to me, a tender husband, who gave me a new life, I could not ask for anything better. I became a real German; my children speak only German; I want to leave that nightmare behind. But one day, a couple of months ago, the children brought home a book from the library with stories that took place in Venezuela. And it was full of pictures of running children, barefoot or in sandals, among the banana trees. I had never thought that something like that could happen. When I saw those feet without socks, and those hills covered with banana trees, my throat and my heart tightened up, and tears rose in my eyes, and I missed Nilopolis, and wanted so badly to run barefoot all over Brazil; it was such a strong feeling that I found myself sobbing, crying aloud like a weaned calf, as my mother used to say. But that was just then. Because I know quite well that, for me, Brazil is finished forever, just like my childhood. I will never again live like that. Every once in a while I go there, but I know that deep down, I am a tourist. I am a foreigner in the city; I can't tell where it is dangerous, I can't recognize the sounds that should alarm me—do you understand? If I were an animal returning to the forest, I would die before I reached the first clearing. Before, I would go to classes in the lowlands, I would go to parties on Saturdays, I would get back late, and I was never afraid. Now, it's not like that; I am afraid of Brazilians; I am frightened by the aggressiveness of people; I don't recognize my own people; I feel tense in the part of town where I was born and raised and where my parents are still living. I am afraid of being attacked, robbed, killed. I feel I am in danger all the time, but I don't know where that comes from; it is so strange. I think I am Brazilian only by language now, and because I read a lot in Portuguese; I work as an executive secretary for a Brazilian shipping company, and I spend the whole day speaking Portuguese. If I change my job, I will enter a German orbit right away and finish killing Brazil inside of me. That would make us even, because Brazil does not want to have anything to do with me, and has killed me to itself. I have no idea why. I was not even twenty and nobody missed me."

But this kind of reaction was not very frequent. And Lena knew that this kind of story was not very frequent. Most of the time everybody wanted to go back. One or another might form ties abroad, but they were rarely strong enough that they could not break them. In general, what happened was that people lived in a permanent state of inadequacy; they did not belong to the world around them and less and less did they belong to their native country (or else they were deathly afraid that this would be the case). And every individual case varied according to each person's circumstances and personal experiences, their emotional entanglements, and their chances for professional advancement. Love and work—that was so important. Lena thought of two Brazilian journalists she had met: same profession, same nationality, such very different stories.

Raimundo was from the northeast, from a humble family, young, a brilliant reporter, aggressive, and had not even got his degree when he was arrested with everybody else at that clandestine student meeting. He was a leader at his college, was part of the governing board of a student organization, and it was a long time before he was released after the triage. When he was finally set free, he had missed classes and exams, did not have a chance to try again, and lost the year. The police came back to look for him at the boardinghouse where he was living. He was not in then, but took it as a warning. At the paper, a friendly boss decided to send him to work in Peru for the time being. While he was there, two things happened: he was fired, and there was an earthquake where he lost everything except the clothes he was wearing and his camera. Always a reporter, he took amazing photos, and managed to send them off, together with a wonderful writeup. Thanks to that and to contributions from friends, he ended up with a ticket to Paris and the injunction not to return to Brazil any time soon, because he was being sought. He turned up in France, completely lost, speaking not a word of French, no warm clothes, no prospects, no job. For a while he stayed with one or another exile, feeling humiliated, and eventually moved to a charity's homeless shelter. Or a solidarity shelter, which, as far as he was concerned, came to the same. He found work at a circus in Lyon, and spent six months cleaning up elephant shit. Huge. Then he managed to return to Paris, on another job, and spent another number of months washing corpses at the city morgue, where he introduced the term *jambon* to designate the "hams"—Rio police slang for the bodies in the refrigerator drawers—a sign that he was starting to speak some French. But all he thought of, night and day, was going back. Finally, he could not stand it any longer. Nobody knows how he did it, but he got a ticket that took him to South America so he could try to enter Brazil clandestinely. And he managed. Two months later, he was killed by the repression at a farm where he was working in the backlands of the state of Pernambuco, turned in by someone who had taken him for someone else.

Antonio was from the northeast as well, of a poor family, a brilliant, aggressive reporter. Not all that young. And he had not gone back yet. Lena thought he would never return. That is, he would go to Brazil from time to time to see old friends, feed his nostalgia, get back in touch with the culture, stay for a month or six weeks, never more than that. He had left right after the Institutional Act 5, when he understood that he could not bear the weight of the dictatorship, and managed to have his paper name him correspondent for some European capital.* He was a journalist of exceptional quality, made the most of the position, and gave a new meaning to his work in the structure of the paper. He developed valuable contacts and made himself almost irreplaceable. He kept his post. His children went to school, grew up, married, gave him European grandchildren. And, had he decided to return, after the relaxation (known as the "opening") of the dictatorship and the beginning of redemocratization, all the paper would have been able to offer him, that would allow him to live as he had till then, would be a bureaucratic position as a managing editor. For someone like Antonio, who was used to keeping his own hours, going after the stories he chose, this would be equivalent to professional death. He had been a reporter all his life and loved his work. If the price of returning was putting his behind on a chair, hanging from a phone, going to meetings with other managers, and bossing around other reporters, he'd rather not return, and would enjoy his children and grandchildren in a place where his profession was respected. His umbilical cord might be buried in the dry backlands, but he felt that someday his heart would rest in earth that had been worked by Romans and Etruscans. And that was no longer painful to him. On the contrary. Every time Lena traveled and saw her friend again, she felt that she stood before a person who was tranquil and at peace with himself, with a tranquility unexpected, given common ideas about typical exiles, and rarely found among most people anyway, even those who had never been chased out of their own countries and, impelled by some life force, had gone looking for the chance of happiness somewhere else in the world. Except that, for all

---

* Known as the AI-5, the act gave the government enormous powers, took away civil liberties, and initiated a period of extremely severe repression.

that serenity, she also knew, for they had spoken about it a few times with Antonio, the flame had never quite gone out. Someday, out of the blue, a sudden breeze would bring it back to life, and it would leap up. It could singe you, could set you afire any time. And then Brazil would ache in every one of your nerves.

There were other successful professional people who had tried to return. Lena remembered Adalberto, for instance. He had been a highly regarded medical doctor and university professor in Brazil, a productive and pioneering research scientist, but had run into mean-spirited obstacles to his work. His rights were taken away, he was forced into retirement, and persecuted. He moved to France, with his talents and knowledge. There, they gave him a team—which included other exiled scientists—and more stimulating working conditions. After twenty years of dedication, his work brought him prizes, international recognition, everybody's respect. But the fire did not stop burning, consuming Adalberto—he wanted to offer the results of his efforts to his people and to his country; he wanted to share the harvest that had cost him so much effort. As soon as there was an opening and the least sign of interest in his return, the embers turned into a conflagration. He was rational about it, and negotiated the necessary conditions to develop his work, settling for the minimum necessary, abandoning any ambition of more sophisticated research, asking only for the most basic support. With everything guaranteed, he dismantled the life he had built abroad and traveled back. He found that the mean-spirited obstacles were still there, with added bureaucracy and resentment against his fame, general hostility. He packed his suitcases and returned to Paris and, in perfectly good humor, during a quick conversation with Lena at a café, he remarked that he had hardly had the time to satisfy his nostalgia:

"Well, it was worth it. I had a chance to dot the *i*s once and for all. And I found out all the *i*s come in capitals: Inefficiency, Incompetence, Ignorance. But above all, Insensitivity, and Incomprehension."

Lena tried for a joke, for hope: "Maybe your return was premature, Adalberto . . . Who knows, with a little more time they could develop a capital *i* for Information, and things would improve."

"No way, girl. All I still needed to do was add the *i* for Irresponsibility. And it would be absolutely irresponsible for me to keep going from here to there and back, disbanding the teams, interrupting research that involves the sustained work of many people, just for sentimental reasons because over there is my country and I miss it and my people. I can't do this; I don't have the right."

Looking sad now, he went on: "There is something else as well. It is no longer possible to return to doing science as an isolated activity, even if I decided to be stubborn about it and found a sponsor or a source of funding for that particular investigation. Either the whole nation values the search for knowledge and this is reflected in a consistent policy of support for science and technology, or there is no point in trying. Because otherwise, you end up working alone, with one team here and one team there, on disconnected projects. There is no exchange, debate, circulation of information, a kind of daily commerce of common learning and information through discussion. I come from a time when one had a classical education in school. And I can assure you that this evil had already been diagnosed by the ancients and, in the present circumstances, it would be an ironic paradox for me. Because staying in Brazil would subject me to what the ancient Romans called *dementia in exsilio,* madness in exile, which here, in my exile, I could not possibly come to suffer from, because here I can't have this 'madness of isolation.'"

Lena did not know what to say. He went on: "Another very apt Latin expression teaches us that *in delitescentia non est scientia.* There is no hidden science. If you lead a clandestine life, far from knowledge, you never reach it completely. I really have to exile myself for the rest of my life. But in the end, you know, science is universal, and what one discovers ends up benefiting all of humanity."

Lena was about to say that technology is not universal, that he should think again about that decision of his because Brazil needed him, yet she didn't. She couldn't. All she needed was to look at his face and she understood that she had to be quiet. Because she saw anguish, sadness, tension. In one word, pain. A pain without cure in a man who would give his life to help find a cure for everyone's pain. And at this moment, his eyes filling with tears at the echoes of the ocean that separated him from his country, he said:

"I can't return. It would be irresponsible. But when I leave the lab, get back home, and sit down to relax, there are times when I feel something burning inside, consuming me. I think I will die of it."

It was that bed of embers. She knew it well. It was always there, deep down, different for each person, but a permanent presence. She glanced at the notebook, looking for the references to Paulo, dear to her, who carried his fire openly like the urchins who sold roasted peanuts on street corners, carrying their buckets by the handle, filled with burning coals so the paper bags of peanuts would not cool off. While she turned the pages, Lena had to smile, moved by memories brought up by those lines. Paulo, the enthusiastic, confident, faithful friend. Of course, his story was one of pain as well, full of anxious moments. But Lena could only remember him with tender thoughts, seeing before her the picture of her friend, the walking fireball carried by an urchin in the middle of the night:

"Lena, we are talking here under the eaves, in the middle of this grey Paris, but we could also be chatting like this on a bench by the beach there in Rio, and it won't be long . . . I feel it right here, inside, that it is almost time to return. People laugh at me because I keep talking about this all the time, but I can't give in. Sometimes it is hard. One day I met a little old Spanish guy and it was such a downer, depressing, him talking about how he had been exiled for almost forty years and had spent the first thirty saying he would return the next day. But, damn it, Brazil is different. We are not that bloodthirsty; soon this will pass. I've got to believe it. That's why I am always prepared. Ready. I will be the first to return, that I promise. Every year I say this is the last time, I will never again spend Christmas away from home. Every spring I want to pass on the winter coat and the heavy winter clothes that I think I will never need again because I will return before another winter comes around. The only reason I don't do it is that once I did and then I had to scrounge about to find another set. Every New Year's Day I say again that this year will really be new, and I will return. And I have not returned yet. But it is certain that I will. As soon as it opens the least crack, I'll return. I will be the first to land at the Galeão airport; you can write it down and I will sign it. I swear. I can't take it anymore; all I think about is this. I don't buy anything on credit, so I won't have to deal with the remaining installments. I don't accept any jobs that ask for a longer engagement. I renew my lease almost by the month, as if I were here for just a short term—I know this is not good for me, that I end up paying more, but I insist on being able to leave any time. I was careful not to get emotionally involved with anyone here, at most a short little affair, so I would not feel sorry to leave someone behind with whom I'd be in love at the time of returning. Even if I end up alone. This may seem strange, you know, but for me, missing Brazil is stronger than solitude; the desire to return is bigger than everything; Brazil is bigger and I end up thinking about nothing else. It was lucky that I met Roberta in Chile, that we found each other, stayed together, had these two wonderful children that sustain me. Because I would never have been able to have a real relationship with a French woman, I am quite sure of it, for she would try to keep me from home. I put together the money for the passage, bit by bit, my father helped, everything is ready, put away in a savings account and at any time I can take it out, we buy the ticket, pack, take the plane, and get out in Rio. As soon as the lawyer gives the green light and my mother calls. Every time the phone rings late at night, I think that's it, they are calling because it is time to return, because when she calls it is always quite late because of the time difference. And then, when they call, everything is ready to go, all they have to do is tell me to go, that I can go and not be arrested, or that I'll just be questioned and released. Then I'll go, you just watch me . . ."

He had a good lawyer, smart and with a fine sense of the situation. Because Paulo was indeed the first to disembark legally in Rio, an unbelievable sign that times were indeed changing and the "opening" that everybody was talking about was for real.

Lena remembered the day well, remembered the early morning and the arrival, remembered even what had come before.

She had been at the newspaper, in the middle of a working afternoon, when the phone rang: "I don't know if you remember me, Lena . . . It's Celina."

Lena thought: "If it starts this way, it's because one really won't remember. It has to be one of those annoying people one meets once and who think themselves unforgettable. Or else it's somebody asking for something."

"Which Celina?"

"Celina. See if you can remember. We met about four years ago, at a dinner at the house of some common friends. At the Lagoon."

It was not the voice of a young person. But the tone was assertive. She was not omitting things to be annoying or because she enjoyed mysteries, but for discretion. At the Lagoon? Whose house would that have been? Ah, yes, of course, Dr. Augusto. How could she forget? Paulo's mother . . . She answered carefully, like someone who knows the code, the fear of tapped phones.

"I do remember, yes. You are Camilo's grandmother."

"That's it. They arrive Saturday, and asked me to let you know."

"At what time? What airline? What flight? Wait a moment, let me get a pen to write it down." And to gain time, compose herself. What a jolt! Her heart was racing with happiness, worry, fear. All those thoughts coming to her mind. Was it safe yet? She wrote down the information, mechanically, while she said things, anything, to avoid silence on the phone. "Wow, Dona Celina, how wonderful. You must be on pins and needles."

"Not really, child. I am more than happy, of course. But calm. Everything will be all right. We have been preparing for this a long time."

It had been a long time, of course; everybody had been preparing. Nobody had been ready to go. But for the return they had been in permanent, daily training. Clearly the news of the return had been no surprise. The last time they had seen each other, a couple of months earlier, was when she had taken down his account for some future purpose that she herself did not know, in a mixture of diary, reporter's notes, and history, in that little apartment in the Marais section of Paris, and he was definite: "In August I leave. I can't stand it anymore. My place is there."

In the all-purpose kitchen, sitting, and dining room, as she cleared the table and passed him the plates to wash, Roberta tried to season his dream with a pinch of reality: "You mean, if they give you the passport."

"They will. You know, Helena, I filed an injunction. After all, by this time there are laws, precedents, whatever they call it. And after that report in *Veja** we already managed to get passports for the children. It has to work. We are going home with the children."

---

*Important news magazine, whose name translates as "Look."

The children. In his high chair, Camilo was stuffing himself with *carotte rapée*, the grated carrot he had learned to love in nursery school. From the bedroom they could hear the little voice of Ernesto singing "*Sur le pont d'Avignon.*" Some day that would turn into "*Passa, passa, gavião.*" Now they were real Brazilians, with papers and all. All they needed was to get to know Brazil. And the parents' papers.

All that had been just the other day, such a short time ago.

And now Dona Celina was saying they were returning. And Lena thought of Paulo an even longer time ago, when he was still in school, a good student, interested in everything, restless, getting the best grades on exams, great friends with the other students, the most demanding on the teachers. And of the course he had not been able to finish, his career slashed before he could start on it.

And now they were returning. On Saturday. She could hardly wait.

On Friday she had been invited to a party, and did not go—she could not concentrate. She spent the night thinking about her friends, feeling like explaining to the others: "I can't be distracted, go to parties, anything. Tell everybody that I can't. That tomorrow morning is the first return flight. No, not tomorrow! Today! Right now they are leaving their apartment to go to the airport; they are checking their luggage; they are entering the plane. How can I pretend to go to a party here, if all through it I will be far away, with Paulo and with Roberta, with Camilo and with Ernesto, somewhere in the night, thousands of meters above the Atlantic? I can't imagine how Dona Celina is doing . . ."

It was impossible to sleep. At three she was wide awake, afraid of not hearing the alarm. At four she decided to get up and just walk the halls at the airport. She could not stay home doing nothing, and she wanted to be right there, to see, to make sure that they had arrived as they should and that nothing had gone wrong. "Boy, if I am in this state, I wonder how Dona Celina can take it . . ."

Even though she arrived very early at the airport, she saw that Paulo's mother was there already, keeping vigil. She must have spent the whole night there. Ever since they had left Paris.

Lena mentioned she had not slept. "Neither have I, Helena. I couldn't. I thought it best to be here early. But I took a lot of tranquilizers." And after a pause: "To speak the truth, for the last week I have been taking tranquilizers nonstop. Even at lunchtime, instead of water, I have passionfruit juice or chamomile tea."

Maybe that was why she seemed so calm, so enviably controlled amid the general tension of the other friends and relations that were arriving, especially after the plane had landed, when the first passengers started to come out, and they hadn't. Suddenly someone identified them: "There they are, look, there are the children!" "Camilo is huge!" "Roberta had her hair cut, she looks different . . ."

Outside the glass partition, his younger brother, left behind when he was still a small boy, looked just like Paulo had when, a few years before, he had had to disappear and leave. The family resemblance appeared in other faces. From both sides of the glass wall, there was a ceaseless exchange of waves, gestures, blown kisses. Dona Celina asked again: "Don't make too much of a commotion. Don't do anything to call the attention of the men. One has to cover up, look as if one does not care. As if they were just returning from a vacation, after a short time."

At this point, the children had already run out, gone through the scanners and then the doors. They were a little dizzy with all the Portuguese and the unknown faces, but bit by bit they were finding people they knew, telling about the flight, getting hugged by uncles, grandparents. Roberta and Paulo were still inside, taking such a long time . . .

"Everybody has come out, except for them. Do you think something has happened?"

"Don't worry, Aunt Celina. It must be just customs."

"They have a lot of luggage."

"Then it might be best to tell them to leave the suitcases there and come out anyway. We'll find them clothes later."

"Can't tell them through the glass."

"Nonsense, Mother. No need for any of that. It's just the bureaucracy."

"They say there is a computer in there, it shows the names of the people on a screen. Do you think there is a problem with that?"

"But they have nothing on them, Mother. There is no suit, no conviction, nothing. Don't you remember how the lawyer explained it so many times? Let's go ask him again."

"No, don't distract him now. He has to pay attention to what is going on in there."

"It's just customs, you'll see. In a moment they'll come out."

"True. The guy is already putting a chalk mark on the suitcases. Another minute and they'll be out here."

"People, be careful, don't create a commotion, for the love of God. Don't call the attention of the men. Speak quietly, greet them quietly."

They were coming out. They had gone through. Right at the doors, Paulo and Roberta were being smothered in hugs, passed from the warmth of one body to another. Dona Celina, from a bit further on, was waiting her turn, repeating: "No commotion."

Paulo hugged his brother. He stepped back a bit and they looked at each other. "Shit, man, you've changed. If I saw you on the street, I would not recognize you." Instead of tears, they all burst out laughing: "But he looks just like you, Paulo. It's like you were looking in the mirror."

Friends came closer: "How good to see you here! There's a thousand things to talk about later. Drop in at our place when all this uproar is over."

Only Dona Celina, from afar, under firm control, holding up, was waiting her turn. Then, suddenly, Paulo turned away from all the rest, and shouted, as loudly as if his voice had to cross the whole ocean and all the exile days of separation: "Mother! Didn't I say I would come? Look at me here!" And his hug lifted her off the ground, tight in the arms of her son who whirled her round, whirled till she was dizzy, turned and turned in a child's reel, through the electronically controlled, air-conditioned, glassed-in, bullet-proofed airport aisle, singing aloud like a child: "I've come home, I've come home, I've come home . . ."

Laughing and singing, dancing and turning, crying now, bathed in tears, Dona Celina still tried to say: "Look at the commotion, son . . ."

Hard to imagine anything less discreet. Everybody at the airport had to notice that noisy young man who was singing and dancing, and making himself the focus of everyone's attention. A strange bird.

They distributed the luggage and the people among the cars. Time to go home. Paulo was shouting, as he entered the elevator that would take him to the parking lot, indiscreet, uncontrollable, scandalous, celebrating.

"Did you hear me? Attention, everybody! I am going home. HOME, PEOPLE!"

On the way, along the bay, between the Maré slum and the Galeão air base, an elegant heron traced the end of its solitary flight and landed in the mangrove. My soul sings, I see Rio de Janeiro, I miss it so, Rio, its sky, endless beaches, Rio, you were made for me, Rio de Janeiro that is still beautiful, Rio that is still Rio, January, February, and March . . . Before April and the coup. Rio before cement trucks and coups. Motors, power saws and nightmares. And above all the songs of Tom Jobin or Gilberto Gil, there was that of Paulo that followed the flight of the heron, the day of grace, the poise, the repose. And announced the new temptation, of just looking up to the sky, waiting for the rest of the flock, of the wide, generous flight, the tribal feast in which the new song they sobbed out would no longer be a solo with a damper on: "I have come home, I have come home, I have come home."

In the mangrove, on the border of infinite green, the white speck of the heron corrupted and corroded the flock of vultures.

IX

Eu também já fui brasileiro
moreno como vocês.
Ponteei viola, guiei forde
e aprendi na mesa dos bares
que o nacionalismo é uma virtude.
Mas há uma hora em que os bares se fecham
e todas as virtudes se negam.

(CARLOS DRUMMOND DE ANDRADE)

I, too, have been Brazilian,
brown like you.
I strummed a guitar, drove a Ford,
and learned around tables at bars
that nationalism is a virtue.
But there comes a time when the bars close
and all virtues are negated.

It—or perhaps she—had been standing beside the house for so long, she did not remember anything earlier. Must have been born there, in that very place. After all, trees don't travel. But she had heard something; it seems she had arrived as a small sapling, with the others. It must have happened as with those bougainvilleas that had been planted by the fence some years before. Only two or three had lived, brick-colored and purple. Ants had eaten the rest. Or caterpillars. From where she stood, she could not tell. But it must have been ants—they are the greediest. They tear off any little leaf one manages to grow; it's horrible. It does not help to tell oneself that they are not the ones eating the leaves, that they just take them home to feed to the aphids. Whatever they do with them, it is horrible. In her life in the garden, she had seen ants do in a lot of bushes that never managed to grow into trees. Hers was turning out to be a long life; people kept going away, disappeared, did not come back, the animals passed, only she stayed on. The old man, for instance—he had not been there for several summers. And the children to whom he had taught so many things had all grown up and almost all even had their own children. And now it was his daughter who had white hair, wore glasses, and went about the garden pulling weeds, cleaning out beds, and showing flowers and leaves to new boys and girls. Strange how well she remembered the old man, who had not even lived there, after all this time. When this one who is there now, lying with her foot up, was small—small but not so small, there was even a time when she was taller than the tree, she remembered all at once, seeing again the adolescent with the braids measuring herself against her—but in any case, the girl had been younger and the old man had disappeared and the tree was still there and remembered a day when they had talked a lot about herself. The girl had asked: "And this one here, Grandpa? What is it called again? Dona Teodósia says that it is the anut tree, I always call it an almond tree, and the fishermen call it a chestnut."

The tree listened to the answer: "In the south they call it an umbrella tree, because of the compact shade this species gives."

"Shade? This little nothing speck?"

The old man answered in his slow speech, lengthening the first syllables of the longer words or the beginning of sentences, to keep from stuttering. But even so, he'd repeat some sounds uncontrollably. Those who were used to it did not even notice. "It's because it is still young. But when it grows, you'll see. And since it is a tree that grows really well by the beach and can thrive in sand and withstand the wind and the sea swells, it gets to be typical of a large part of our seacoast. That name of umbrella tree calls attention to that use it has."

The girl insisted: "But then it is not a chestnut?"

"It is that too. Almond tree, chestnut tree, castagnole, even this 'anut' of Dona Teodósia's; all these names refer to its fruit."

"It has fruit? Can you eat them?"

"You could. Some people do. But it is not tasty, though bats really like it. And horses. When it grows, you will see it covered with fruit—

chestnuts or almonds, if you will—after the flowering season; the flowers are delicate, light-colored."

"But what is it called, in the end?"

"You can call it any of these names. Or you can call it 'terminalia,' as it is also known, a term derived directly from its scientific name."

The girl wanted to know more: "Ah, is that its family?"

"No, the family is the combretaceae, which has many representatives in Brazil and in other tropical countries, and is quite different from the European almond tree, which is a rosacea and turns the Mediterranean landscape pink in spring. It so beautiful, my child; someday you will see . . ."

But almond or chestnut were the names they called it most frequently around there, with the freedom of intimacy. Old Teodósia, the local healer, came for pieces of its bark for a tea or a plaster to close wounds, or for the fruit or "anuts" against diseases of the chest. The children picked the fruit to use them in their games, as ammunition or make-believe food served with its leaves torn into little pieces. Along the years, the umbrella tree had been a trapeze, Tarzan's jungle, a pirate ship's mast, a cowboy's horse, a plane for parachutists to jump from, and all the rest that the children's imagination or the heroes of the day would suggest. In almost no time it had grown taller than the children, the adolescents, all the adults. Then its highest branches came even with the roof and, soon after that, it was taller than the house. Now it looked upon the entire yard from high up, and on the street beside the house, the path to the fountain that went along the back of the house, the sand on the beach in front of the house, the sea stretching to infinity, and on the other side the forest extending out of sight, sea and forest separated by a tree cover dotted with roofs. So many new roofs appearing in all those years. She had watched as the thatched covers were replaced by ceramic or asbestos tile. And she even saw the appearance of the first boxy apartment building, an awful cement square with no pitched roof, three piled-up unnecessary floors that offended the landscape. And she had withstood it all, solidly planted, shading the garden without depriving the house of sun, helping time to peel the walls, darken the roof tiles, bend some of the people, stretch out others. She had sheltered the children who came to eat at the rough table they had built in the garden, a stage for barbecues, birthdays, crab fests for Sunday lunches, and a permanent shelter for the small fry who preferred not to break up the day spent out in the air, even to eat. And as new small fry replaced those who were growing, she had sheltered young love, stealthy smoking, the gang gathered for endless talk to the sound of radio or guitar, leaving surfboards to dry in the shade as they came back from the beach, and one summer she was even a garage for an upturned boat on two trestles, pulled up from the sand while its engine was being repaired. When there were many people, they would park their cars under it. And always, before, when the owner still lived there, it was from that lowest branch to the fork on the right that he set up his hammock and rested after lunch, the sacred silent time, when all the children's ballgames were suspended in the neighborhood, which did not happen when anyone else in the house used the hammock for reading or rest. And she was always there, steady, growing, shedding her leaves twice a year, breaking out into new twigs, offering herself in buds and tender leaves, shading, watching over the house and the family like a protective spirit, contemplating each of its inhabitants with the sweetness of an old friend who knew every one of them and embraced them in her shade like a guardian angel. Just as she did now, for the oldest girl, now become a woman, who had come out of season, in September, the month of high tides and awakening green, limping, hardly moving, spending all that time with her eyes closed or shuffling papers, looking sad like someone who is really in need of a guardian angel who guards the territory of childhood.

"Carefully folded in my wallet I keep a thin sheet of airmail paper with the outline of your bare foot. On a diagonal, of course, since otherwise it would not fit on the sheet. Do you remember when I drew it, so long ago, in Mother's dining room? I was still using a fountain pen, and that royal-blue Parker ink that you insisted on. You can rest assured that it is kept safe. If at any time you should need a pair of shoes in a place where everyone has small feet, you won't need to worry. If you find a way to send me word, I will have it made to measure, though I cannot guarantee that it will compare to the Italian boots you did not have the money to buy that time we met, in the chill of exile, the boots that fed all your fantasies in the ad promising that it would be (in Italian) *morbida* and *foderata*. Or, maybe, should I someday find, in Cabo Frio, a pair of those sandals made by Malaquias that you liked so much, big ones with a strap around the heel, then I can buy them and keep them till there is someone to take them to you. I have tried it a couple of times. But he never had your size. Sometimes I think he never will. It is all much, much smaller. Ridiculously shrunk.

"On my shelves I keep some of your books, those you like best, so they won't disappear as the world borrows them. Stendhal by the side of the Cananéia sugar mill and its country ball—the volumes are near me, but know that 'cananeus,' Fabrício, and Julien/Julião live in your body's inner pockets, squeezed between Fabiano and Macunaíma. Most of what was on your shelves and did not get lost went to the attic of Grandmother's house in the mountains. But I know that the books that were your home don't have to be mourned: under the pressure of time they turned into skin, and it is not necessary for anyone to worry about keeping them.

"For a long time I kept, all washed and folded, that huge judo outfit with the dark band—you must agree that it was a nuisance. It took up a whole shelf. But someone turned up who needed it, and off it went. And, anyway, you can't keep turning things into relics, and there is no occasion for it. It is being useful to someone who is learning how to fight. And what does it matter, why keep it?

"*I kept the streamer so carefully, that she threw at me, she was a beautiful columbine and I was nothing but a poor pierrot* . . . Remember that trashy musical comedy from the Atlantida movie studio we went to see at the film club and there was a gentleman wearing a 'summer suit' singing that song amid balloons and confetti? Well, my dear, I have no streamers left, even though I can't help seeing some resemblance between you and a pierrot by Prevert-Carné-Barrault. I imagine your mocking face reading this and classifying me as a columbine, eternally undecided, unable to fuse thesis and antithesis into a synthesis. But if I don't keep the streamers (and I won't lie if I tell you that I always keep all the confetti so I can throw it at whatever you come up with to do next), I did take good care of all your vinyls by the guys from Bahia. And even now, when I miss you most, Caetano and Gil bring me the clearest memories of you, shouting, '*Let's go walk on the avenue (so long as Mr.*

Wolf does not come)'; advising us, *'Mother, Mother, have courage'*; antici-pating *'The day I went away'*; announcing, predicting, denouncing. The tropicalists are put away, beside Luis Gonzaga and Caymmi, Paulinho da Viola and Cartola, Chico and Ismael. And whatever comes out that is new and good, we will copy to a tape when you return. And to get a start on the new stack of things to keep, I sent your boy a new album by Chico, for children,; you'll like it.

"Speaking of which, of course I keep in an album all the photos I can get of your son. There are not many, but one can follow his grow-ing up. If I knew where, I would send it to you. If you return before he does, you can get an idea of how the boy is growing, with your long body, your large eyes, his mother's mouth, and the determined expression of both of you. He is losing his milk teeth and he already knows how to read. Small, strolling along, he is curing in Africa the Chilean asthma that got worse in the European winter. I am keeping for him our memories of what boys are like and the stories and the history of his father. One day I will tell him about the beach-apricot tree in Grandfather's yard, where every grandchild had one branch and nobody really owned anything. And about the almond tree at home. And I will tell him about the dragnet that all the fishermen pulled at, passing it from hand to hand, and singing at their work that ended only when they had shared out all the fish they had caught. And I will sing and tell of you as a teenager, how you belonged to the student association at the high school and were the editor of the newspaper, and played soccer, and made trouble (do you remember when you hid the bell from the little church under the sacristan's house?), or danced during Carnival, argued about politics, and blew up so easily, so people called you Mate Leão, the brand that's scorched in the box.

"In every detail—and someday I will tell the truth to everybody—I remember that Friday the 13th. The radio was on, the man was talking, we were listening in silence. Your fury. Your gesture punching the air. Your suddenly snapping out of the relaxed relief you felt, like an animal just released from its cage. Your stronger connection to the rest of the flock, still kept by force in the pen, despite orders to the contrary. Your outcry: 'Fuckers! But these sons of bitches will see. I will get them out of there. I don't yet know how, but I will.'

"You did. God knows how. And at what price. We all know, but since the story has been told so badly, I am also keeping for history what really happened. Some day we will tell.

"After that I didn't keep anything else of yours. Nothing that they could take away from me. Only the memory. And this faith that nobody can destroy, this hope that nobody can extinguish, this love that nobody can tame. Faith, hope and love, just as in Sister Zoe's catechism before first communion, in the "Sacred History" comics that you used to read and reread, in the anthem that the simple people on the beach sang, out of tune, in the little white church on top of the hill after the ceremony of pulling up the mast for Saint Sebastian or Saint Anne. Faith, hope, and love that no guards can unguard, my guardian angel, my brother."

In the end, she had never given Marcelo that letter to read. There was no messenger to take it, she did not know where he was, whether exiled in the world or clandestine in his own country. And then, with amnesty and her brother's reappearance, they had so many new things to talk about, so many projects for the future, so much to catch up on, that she forgot all about the letter. Only recently, as she poked around in her things looking for material for her play, did she find the paper. She reread it and found it confusing, personal, too personal, she could not use it or try to publish it, for nobody would ever understand: it rested too much on personal memories, on a code shared by siblings that could not be shared with anyone else. But it did awaken memories in her, particularly of Friday, the 13th of December, 1968. Marcelo had been freed the day before. The writ of *habeas corpus* and the order for release had been granted in the morning by the Supreme Court. Together with that of other four students, in alphabetical order. The other four were to be dealt with in the afternoon. Her father had taken a plane immediately with the documents already issued, going from the capital to the military fortress where they were being kept. Another lawyer remained on call to take the papers that would free the others in the afternoon.

A whole day of negotiations and pressure had to be spent with the head of the jailkeepers, who did not want to accept the orders from the judiciary and, although—or perhaps because—he had a high post in the military, refused to follow the order of the Supreme Court and free the students. In the end, he had to give in and allow the five to leave. But later on, when the other lawyer arrived with the *habeas corpus* writs for the others, he delayed and temporized and did not free anyone. He said that working hours were over for that day; they should return on the next one. On the next day, he said that December 13 was Navy Day, a military holiday; nobody was at work, he could not free anyone. What nobody could imagine at that point was that the prisoners had been transferred to another fort in the night, in another city, in another state, and while the lawyer argued with the commandant, there was no longer anybody there to be freed. The military knew what was brewing; the civilians had no idea.

Marcelo and the others who had benefited from the alphabetical order of their names were lucky that they had already left. And there was a plan to take them out of São Paulo and get them to Rio, separately, which was safer. By car, and by taking turns as passengers, which was essential so they would not be arrested again. Fernando, for instance, had left the fort with Marcelo in his car. He stopped at a gas station on the road and, according to plan, exchanged his brother for another passenger. When Marcelo left the toilet, he entered another car, of a friend who had been waiting, and they drove off without being noticed. A few kilometers ahead, Fernando was held up by the police, under pretext that they wanted to have a look at his papers, and he had to spend the night at headquarters while the men communicated to their superiors that his fellow traveler had disappeared. And in this way, stealthily, Marcelo rang the bell to his sister's apartment in the morning. When she opened the door, there he was, all smiles: "Hi, Lena. I'm coming to spend a few days with you. May I?"

The emotion was strong. In the middle of the tight hug, tears in her eyes, a knot in her throat, she could hardly speak: "Of course, how wonderful! As long as you like, come in . . ."

A bath, coffee, a coded call to her mother, indicating that he had arrived safely. Then a long talk, tenderness, the affection necessary to help along what one might imagine would be a return to normalcy and freedom. And all day long, instead of the full celebration of being at large, the tension about the political climate in the country, the anxious wait for news of the others who had not been able to leave the day before. The phone calls did not bring any relief; on the contrary. In addition to news of the detention of Fernando on the road, the voices coming through the line told only about the lawyers' efforts to be heard by the authorities in command of the fort, their inability to have the judicial order obeyed, an exasperating ploy to wear them down. And slowly they also became aware that, as the morning papers had hinted, the whole day was exceptionally tense everywhere. Radio and TV were on all the time. The whole country discussed the result of the vote in Congress the day before. Despite all the threats, and against the opinion of the Judiciary Committee in the House, the representatives had decided to confront the military authoritarianism. In an all-night session, into the small hours, with what the press called an "unusual *quorum*," the representatives kept their vigil and finally, on the 10th, Thursday, by a large majority of 216 to 141, they denied the request to indict their fellow whose head the military had demanded. The spectator galleries were jammed; citizens stood, singing the national anthem. According to the dailies, that night, all over Brasilia, there were celebrations of the independence of the National Congress, despite the threats to his life that the congressman had been receiving. The entire climate was one of civic resistance. The national anthem was playing as a background in everyone's head; all one had to do was close one's eyes and see the green and yellow flag flying against the blue sky of the land. One felt the time had come to say "enough" to government caprice; congressmen and the judiciary had just given the example, and nobody was going to bow to it. The sword was not going to be stronger than the law or the ballot—or at least so one thought.

But the dream did not last long. The reaction of the authorities was announced in the news as well. At night, on the radio program called *The Voice of Brazil,* the official voice of the government, the Ministry of Justice, broadcast an official announcement to the nation, and the entire country waited to hear who had declared himself its voice, without any legitimacy or popular mandate.

With the radio on, Lena made a light dinner, not much more than a snack—it was hot and nobody was hungry. Only Marcelo ate: "After the prison glop, Lena, one cannot refuse home cooking."

"This isn't home cooking, Marcelo. It's more like coffee and bread-and-butter at the corner pub."

"And could you want anything better than a fresh bun with butter melting on it? Just smell . . ."

Lena had always admired her brother's vitality, that love of life that manifested itself in every little part of his day. He took clear and open pleasure in the senses—smells, tastes, even in comfortable temperatures. She remembered that Amalia used to state that Marcelo lived like a Saint Francis in permanent prayer. Except that instead of being a little brother of everything in nature, he was forever celebrating the pleasure of every little thing—a new bar of soap, clothes freshly washed, writing in a virgin notebook, a soft pillow, the smell of wet earth, the sausage in the beans . . . Her father laughed:

"He is no saint, Amalia. You are spoiling the boy with these things. What he is, is a certified hedonist, a sensualist lost in the revolution. Pretty soon you'll explain that he goes out at night spray-painting slogans because he likes to shake the spray can for the sound of the little ball dancing inside it. Or for the fresh air before dawn."

And Marcelo joked back: "That's it, Father. And the sound of the paint squirting onto the wall, the color showing, the smell. I love the smell of the ink on the pamphlets as they come from the printer . . . But truly, what I really like are the strong emotions." And he aped the text of a TV commercial: "I like to live dangerously . . ."

With a sinking heart, Lena remembered those family games while she put lunch on the table and thought that the dangers were getting too great, the emotions going beyond what was bearable. Little did she know that things had not even started yet and that the greatest threat was about to hit them in a few minutes.

It came through the radio. In the voice of a professional announcer that Lena was never again able to hear without wanting to throw up. The military was fighting back, decreeing the end of what was left of the constitution. And they promulgated a new "institutional act," the fifth, that later became known and execrated simply as the infamous IA-5. And they shut down Congress, censored the press, revoked the mandates of elected officials, punished members of Congress, judges, secretaries of state, journalists, intellectuals, students, workers, anyone who, at any time, had had the nerve to imagine that the country could ever live in any way other than under the boots of the military.

Between her husband and her brother, Lena heard in silence the reading of the entire document on the radio. It was the end of all hope, she thought. What would become of Brazil now? From time to time she heard an exclamation from Marcelo or Arnaldo:

"Fuckers!"

"What cynicism!"

Suddenly, when the announcer stopped speaking, she noticed that Marcelo was pacing from one side of the room to the other, like a caged lion, punching the air and cursing: "Bastards! They already knew, and that's why they kept fucking around. Sons of bitches."

He was speaking of the jailers, she realized. Those who had not followed the judicial orders and released his companions, the friends with whom, till the day before, he had shared the narrow cell, cut off from the world by brick walls and iron grates and who now, while he was outside, were still shut in, just because they came later in the alphabet.

Marcelo went on, furious: "But this is not how it will be, not at all! These sons of bitches will see . . . We will drag the guys out of there. I will take them out, one by one, you can count on it. I don't know how, but I will . . ."

Marcelo paused. And facing his sister and his brother-in-law, who sat silent and cowed by the violence of the IA-5 they had just heard, dizzy from the blow, not quite aware yet of all it implied and could lead to, he continued, still punching the air: "And, in case you doubt me, I will get Guilherme out too, as an extra."

That was a private obsession of Marcelo's. Under any other circumstances, Lena would even have smiled. Guilherme was an old-time communist leader from the northeast, a man of the people, aged now, and of an admirable peasant dignity. In 1964, just after the coup, he had been arrested and dragged through the streets tied to a jeep or a truck, in an attempt by the military to demoralize and humiliate him publicly. Marcelo was fifteen at the time and was deeply disgusted when he learned of it. He talked about it for days and never forgot it. More than five years had gone by and old Guilherme was still moldering at the bottom of some cell. Marcelo did not forget, though he did not know him, though he lived in another city, was a member of another generation. For him, Guilherme was a symbol. A saint on his private altar, Amalia would have said. And at that moment, when the years of terror were officially beginning, announced by the voice on the radio, on a hot summer night in Rio, Marcelo reminded them all that, in truth, for so many people, the terror had started almost five years ago, at various points in the country. And he was promising to himself that he would fight it with the meager means at his disposal. Or, as the poet said, he would make a big elephant with the few resources at hand.

Right away, however, there were several concrete things to be done. Marcelo was the first to realize the extension of the evil that lay ahead and the gravity of those new times. He got up and started to pack the little suitcase he had emptied in the morning. He called his brother-in-law: "Could you please go to this address and say that I am here and have to leave?"

Lena wondered: "Leave? Didn't we settle that you would stay a few days, that it was safer? Do you think it is prudent to leave now?

"My dear, this is safer than Father's house. But it is the second place where the men will come to look for me, here and at Teresa's house; you are my sisters. And the hunting season has started, I can't lower my guard."

Her husband left, and Lena helped her brother, worrying about what could happen to Arnaldo on the street, apprehensive about what he might find at that address where he had gone, scared at the idea that her house was not a safe place for Marcelo. And, by extension, for her.

"It would be good if you cleaned out the house, Lena."

"Clean out?"

"That's it. Wake up, girl, stop running around in a daze like an idiot, repeating what I say. You have to think quickly and do things in a hurry."

"Do things?"

She could not stop herself from repeating. She found everything strange, could not understand what was happening.

"Yes, Lena . . . The men will come knocking here, it's just a matter of time. And I have to be far away when they come. But they are going to search everything. You can't have anything in the house."

"Anything what?"

Marcelo stopped what he was doing, looked at her, sat on the edge of the bed, and called her, patiently: "Come, sit here." She sat. She was indeed in a daze, feeling that she would do anything anyone told her to, and nothing if nobody ordered her around or decided things for her. Marcelo explained, stroking her hand:

"Excuse me if I am a bit brusque; maybe I am giving you the shock treatment. But I think I will have to destroy your innocence, Lena. Times have changed, the pot is boiling, the hardliners have just staged a coup in the country."

"But hadn't they already?"

"Now it's the coup inside the coup; it will get much worse. No more speeches, no more demonstrations, no more gatherings, no more articles in the press, no more little courses by professors who criticize things, nothing more . . . I left that narrow prison for a bigger one, and you, too, are jailed. Of course, we are better off than those who stayed inside, because we can do some things. And we are under an obligation to do them, because if we don't, we will never get out of this."

She still did not quite get it, and asked, "What do you want me to do?"

The answer was quick: "The first thing you have to do is control yourself, stop this childishness. You can't stand around like a dummy now. Or ever again. Because if you go on like this, like a dizzy cockroach, you won't be able to do the most important thing, which is to survive."

That got her attention: "Survive?"

"Survive to organize. Or organize yourself to survive, whatever, I can't know everything all at once. I only know that one has to be alive, free, and organized. That means that we can't allow anything to happen to us. The men will come here, that's for sure. First of all, they can't find me here. Second, they can't find anything that incriminates anyone. That is why you have to clean out the house, Lena. Do away with that poster of Guevara, which is only going to irritate the men and make things worse for you. Get rid of some of those records, hide the books. And be very careful with anything written down—addresses, pamphlets, rough drafts of articles; I have no idea what you have lying around. Not just your things, but any paper belonging to anyone else that could be a problem. Get it?"

"Got it. Tomorrow morning I'll take care of it."

"You did not get it. You can't wait. You have to start right now."

She started. And it seemed to her she would never stop. Arnaldo came back with a message from a girl who was waiting downstairs to take Marcelo somewhere else and none of them could know where. Her brother took leave with the warning: "Tell Mother that I am going to a safe place. If needed, somebody will get in touch with you. And there is one thing I want you never to forget: if there is no news of me, that's because I am well. For everybody's good, you should not know anything about me. If anything happens, you will know right away. So it's the old saying: no news is good news."

At the door he hugged Lena hard, and added: "Don't be scared. We have been preparing for these kinds of eventualities; there is a whole organization behind me. You, however, don't have one. So take care, girl. Start by cleaning out the house. And don't forget that toilets get clogged, garbage is searched, and fire creates smoke."

Lena closed the door after him and threw herself, crying, into Arnaldo's arms. Lately she had been like that, tense, sensitive, feeling that she wanted to wake from a nightmare. She suffered for Marcelo, for the others, for herself. She had always been so close to him, the older sister, the protector. And then suddenly, that night, she saw the roles reversed. He had called her "girl," had given her orders, advice, as if he were the guardian. And he was. Suddenly, the boy had left, and the man had appeared in his place.

Arnaldo stroked her hair and left her arms.

"Lena, what he was talking about is serious. We can't waste any time."

All night long they shredded papers. The smaller pieces they threw, little by little, into the toilet, afraid that it would clog, that the neighbors would wonder about the noise of all that flushing. They burnt some of the larger pieces at the bottom of the bathtub, but had to stop, coughing with the smoke, afraid that suddenly someone would call the fire department in the middle of the night. They finally decided to trust luck and leave part of the job for the next day, dumping things out at a time when the apartment building's incinerator was going. If the men arrived before then . . .

They didn't. It took them another few days to arrive, which was lucky. When they came, they turned everything upside down, broke things, threatened a lot, but that was all. The surely knew already that Marcelo would not be there. And that first day they had had a lot more work checking out other places. It was a full war operation; they arrested tons of people. The 14th was a Saturday. The newspapers, heavily censored, resisted as they could. They published news items as if they were telegrams, squeezed in, in tiny type, literally between the lines of obituaries: "So and so has been arrested; whosit has been arrested." They used tricks of pagination to indicate to readers that things were going badly. They used ambiguous headlines, captions with double meanings, odd photos that had nothing to do with the topic. The *Jornal do Brasil*, for instance, in a brave show of resistance, published classifieds randomly throughout the paper, instead of censored news items. It informed readers that Congress had been ordered into recess and printed the full text of Institutional Act 5. As an illustration, it printed a huge photo captioned, "Dramatic Moment," showing an old soccer game in which Garrincha, who was known as "the Joy of the People," was being expelled from the field. Other sports photos peppered the issue. Instead of an editorial, under the title "Herculean Task" there was the picture of a small child trying to knock down a large world judo champion. And everywhere, among classifieds and letters to the editor dislodged from their usual places, there were photos of gorillas* and other allusions to the situation in the country. Like the old photo of the Brazilian World Cup team at their training camp, with the caption, "Warriors at rest—Brazilian players happy with the facilities, taking it easy," a subtle way of telling readers that there were many people in prison. Lena had kept the paper. Actually, Amalia was the one who'd

---

*The military were commonly referred to as "gorillas" at the time.

kept it and given it to her later. But even without the printed pages before her, she had never forgotten that first page where every upper corner had a message, right beside the traditional fonts. On one side was the information that "Yesterday we celebrated the Day of the Blind," overtly referring to the celebration of the feast of Saint Lucy, patroness of vision. On the other side, a threatening weather forecast, warning of black clouds on the horizon and other dangers, clearly given the lie by the sunny beaches that drew everybody to the seaside, the only place where it was still possible to gather, discuss the casualties, try to find out who had been arrested and who was in hiding. A shameless summer sun, torrid, the image of a tropical paradise, indifferent to the terror that had installed itself in the land, ironic traitor to the national anthem and its assurance that "And at that moment, the sun of freedom shone its brilliant rays from the homeland's skies."

Now that same sun, in the garden at the beach house, was milder. September sun, just like on the day of the proclamation of Brazilian independence that the anthem referred to. But it was still an early spring sun, sweet and freshened by the breeze. Lena put the undelivered letter to Marcelo back into the folder, and leaned on the post of the verandah to go down the steps to the garden and the sunny lawn. Even limping, she felt it was nice to take a short walk around the house. She was walking better, more securely, and that was a good sign that the foot was healing. Getting over it. Surviving. She had to be thankful for life. She had survived a few times. Survive in order to get organized. Or the other way round, as Marcelo had told her, in time. At the moment, Lena was just surviving. Completely disorganized. If she really wanted to live, she had to put herself in order. She had to fight back, straighten out her head, straighten out her papers, prepare for the day when she would be able to straighten out her words, sentences, ideas, and write the text. Even if, to do that, she had to risk stopping the medication and go back to falling. She knew she would get there. When she had gathered her courage. But there was still a ways to go. At the moment, it was time for another glass of milk and a pill. She really could not walk for too long. Then she was going to pick up the letters and reread them for a while. There could be material there for the play; all she would have to do was a triage and some changes.

Dearest Mother,

Paris, March 7, '70

Everything is going well, despite the initial trouble of getting settled and this cold weather that won't go away, though it is almost spring. But everything indicates that we will stay around, rather than go on, as we had planned. Alfredo's two friends have been wonderful and we are sure that something concrete will come through with their help, probably a fellowship for Arnaldo and a job for me, or the other way round. Meanwhile, we are living very sensibly on the bit of savings we brought along. Go on writing to the same address. We'll leave the hotel in Holy Week and spend fifteen or twenty days at the house of some friends who are going to Italy. That way we save some money; it's not easy, living is very expensive, our money is worthless; and since we don't know when anything is coming in, we have to live like misers. But I have already sent two pieces to the magazine and the branch office said they will publish them. It's a beginning . . . As they are going to pay over there, Dad will have to watch out and see if the money comes in at the end of the month.

The search for a place to live has been depressing. Everything very expensive, tiny, falling apart. But with patience we'll end up finding something. Teixeira, from the paper, told us yesterday about a couple—he is an actor and she a journalist—who want to return and pass on the lease on their apartment. They would need someone to give them three months' rent that they have paid as a deposit and that the owner returns only at the end of the lease, to the new renters. This would pretty much clean us out, but we'll see. Depending on the condition of the apartment and our prospects of finding work, it could be a possibility.

We really miss you but are also greatly relieved. The other day Arnaldo celebrated the first week of being able to sleep, without nightmares or insomnia for either of us. Just that alone makes up for all the difficulties and any longing.

Kisses,
Lena.

Dear parents

Paris, May 5, '70

Now one can really tell that spring is coming and that this city is beautiful, like an MGM musical, despite the grumpiness and aggressiveness of its inhabitants. We are finally settled, in a charming "mansarde," a fifth-floor walkup amid the surrounding roofs, and on the table a little bouquet of "muguet" looks at me from a glass of water. It turns out that on May Day everybody gives out muguet in the streets, for good luck. I will have luck, we will all be lucky, this is what the little white bells seem to say (what do you call them there, lilies-of-the-valley? I don't know). Arnaldo managed to get an internship in a hospital; for the time being it is not paid because, as I told you in my last letter, his degree is not completely valid here. But it is like a residency (another one!) and he gets his meals plus the chance to meet colleagues and get to know the environment. Silvia guarantees that he will get the fellowship, which should come out in September, at the beginning of the school year. Then he can continue to work there, and be paid as a fellow. I am making do as I can. Apart from work at the magazine (the first piece came out last week and I am sending you the clipping. Of course, it did not have a byline, but it was very exciting to see something I wrote published in French), and this month I will start to do some translation and research about Latin America for the library of a Catholic organization. They pay little, of course, and it is a lot of work. But I can set my own hours, and often work from home. Speaking of magazines, in April I sent four more pieces over there. I am keeping up an average of one per issue and, from what I can see, all of them are being published . . . What's happening with the pay? Could Dad put on a bit more pressure? We really need it. Especially since Patricia and Eduardo (the couple who was living in this apartment before) left behind various unpaid bills, from telephone to dentist, and asked us to cover them and they would reimburse us later from a payment she should receive here through Teixeira, for some work she had sent to Brazil. Since they are super-friendly with Alfredo and Teixeira secured it as well (after all, the paper is going to send the payment directly to him, here in Paris, and Patricia left a written authorization for him to draw the money and give it to me), we are sure that there won't be any problem. Only it's taking a while, and it's getting tight over here. After all, it's been 250 dollars and we have nothing more in reserve.

Write often and a lot, ask everybody to write as well. We miss you all intensely, and we get worried when we don't have news from you, given that what one knows about the country is so discouraging.

Kisses,
Lena.

Lena, my dear
Rio, May 20, '70
This is just a short note, because I am in a huge hurry. But I want to avail myself of the opportunity of having a bearer who is also bringing you fifty dollars in addition to the beans and beef jerky. This is a present from us to you. It's not much, but it's what we could get. I hope it will ease things for you. At least a bit. We are hatching plots to pry out that money of yours. Dad thinks that payment for the articles in the magazine is now a question of days; there are only some administrative and bureaucratic complications. And since that bitch Patricia arrived and stopped the transfer of funds from the paper, everybody is putting moral pressure on them. Alfredo has already had a very serious conversation with them and has come up with a great idea: he will give Eduardo a big role in the movie that he is about to start producing right now. And as soon as the production gets some financing, he will pay him ahead of time so that the money can go off soon. See? If you have friends, you are never alone. Now it's just a short while.

As for news of the country, you must be reading it in the papers over there. We heard that they even had the news on TV. Did you see it? The bearer will tell you more and give you details in person. Kisses, longing, from your sister,

Teresa.

My dear parents,
Paris, June 18, '70
Wonderful that for once there is great news about Brazil in the papers here! But first the homeland had to put on cleats . . . We had a party to celebrate. We watched the finals on TV, at Teixeira's, and then went out on the streets to celebrate with a bunch of Brazilians who turned up from all sides, with flags and drums and wearing the national soccer team shirts. Can you see me dancing the samba in June, under the Arc de Triomphe, in the middle of a monumental traffic jam? Well, close your eyes and imagine the scene. After that we went to dine at an Italian restaurant where we had made a bet with the owner. These Italians are great . . . We got off the subway at Mabillon, walked to a narrow back alley, sort of a dead end; the restaurant was closed for a party, packed. You won't believe it, but they were celebrating second place in the championship . . . And had left a special table free for us, as the representatives of the world champions. I felt that all of us, here, there, on the island, in all the other countries—who knows where there are Brazilians?— but all of us were together, cheering at the same time and following the game together. It does not matter that they are trying to get political mileage out of it over there. What matters is that we need something to be happy about together. That's why my heart was on its knees beside Jairzinho as he laughed, arms raised high, wearing the team's yellow shirt on that green Mexican field.

Maybe we will get out of this apartment at the end of the month. We will meet with the landlord tomorrow and talk. It's the official end of the contract, and given how black things look, the best will be to get the money from the deposit and try to find something cheaper, even if it is further away and not furnished.

When the money from Patricia and Eduardo arrives, we will
buy some furniture. Or maybe we will pay off some of our debts,
because until it comes and the magazine pays (what is happening
there, by the way?) we are having to borrow and I have asked for
an advance at the library. But today I don't want to talk about
these things; I am still celebrating the championship. Kisses to all,

Lena.

Lena, dear sister,
I was hoping to write to you today, on July 14, a day when
a small-cap bastille might have fallen here. But it was not
possible. We finally managed to find out what happened. Alfredo
advanced Eduardo half of everything he would be paid for his
work on the film, so he would be able to send you the money
right away. He did not send it. That was when I ran into him
treating a huge table to whiskey on the porch at Antonio's and
there was that scene that mother wrote to you about. I know it
was not a high-class performance, but I could not help myself. I
let him have it, loud, so everybody would know, but it's no good,
the guy is truly shameless. However, everybody at the restaurant
was talking about it and Alfredo found out that he had not sent
the money. So the next day, he went with him to the bank, gave
him a check in the amount of the money he owed you, again,
an advance, on the half he still had to receive at the end of the
filming, so he could send it off right away. And Alfredo did
more: he stood beside him while Eduardo filled out the forms
to send the money. That was why he called right after that, to
say the money was on its way. But what happened was that he
took his eyes off the proceedings when the documents were to
be delivered to the teller, and that son-of-a-bitch Eduardo, right
by his side, put the check in his pocket and did not send it off!
I have never seen such baseness. It is hard to believe that a guy
who socializes with all of us, is friends with everybody, can be so
dishonest, show so little solidarity, be such a crook. I don't know.
I think it will be really difficult to get this back; those two are

truly worthless. And now, knowing that you are pregnant, I am really at a loss, because you will really need that money badly, there will be a lot of expenses and things are really ugly here.

Adriano thinks that the best would be to beat up Eduardo. I think that nothing will work; the guy is really worthless. But Alfredo thinks you could try one more thing. Patricia is expecting their second child and they could be mollified by that. So Alfredo suggests that you write a long letter, setting down everything that happened and insisting that you really need the money, and send the letter to him, Alfredo, and he will deliver it personally and put the pressure on Eduardo one more time. He thinks it will work, that Eduardo is not as bad as he seems, that he is just a little irresponsible, inconsistent, but has a good heart and political solidarity. It does not cost anything to try, and you really need it . . .

Many kisses to you two, and take good care of that little belly that has probably not yet stared to show.

Teresa.

It was too much. Lena would not be able to read on; she knew that. The exile was over, the hard times had ended, the marriage had ended. But the pain was still there, solid. She had not kept a copy of the letter to Eduardo and Patricia. She remembered it well, but would rather forget it all now, not think about how she had explained to them that she was pregnant, that she really needed the money that she had lent on trust and that they were then able to pay back. Now she wanted to forget everything. She felt fragile all over again, and would never be pregnant again. That child that had never lived, created when there were no resources for it, lost after months during which, every day, she tried to extend its life a little longer inside herself, that child she had dreamt up and that had disappeared, that emptiness, none of that would ever be filled again by a child from her womb, cuddling warm and soft in her lap, nursing from her breast, warming her heart.

"Tell that woman to stop bugging me! I am not going to fucking pay a penny . . . Who told her to be such a dupe? As for pregnant, so is Patricia."

And he did not pay. He stayed in Brazil, drank his whisky, turned into a good film director and a TV soap-opera star, made his leftist films, took up positions in the government with his wife by his side when there was the redemocratization, and left in Lena, more than the memory of a swindle, the shock of being confronted with absolute dishonesty and the certainty that a new society has to be ethical. He helped her lose her innocence. And great part of her hope for humanity.

All of that was painful, even physically. It weighed on her chest, and suffocated her. Her nostrils burned with the tears that she did not want to shed. She swallowed with difficulty, and felt as if what she swallowed would not go down her throat. And her chest felt tight, closing up, as if she were being crushed. And maybe that was indeed best, to give in and let the pain crush her and put an end once and for all to all that. The tears flowed, the sobs rose, she did not want to shake or make any sounds; she was struggling not to moan, to keep from making any movement, to control the vibration of her vocal cords. She heard the phone ring. And right after that, her mother appeared: "It's Alonso . . ."

She could not, she could not stand it, she could not talk now. Amalia noticed immediately; all she had to do was see her daughter's expression: "I'll tell him you are in the bathtub, let him call later."

And then she came back, all instinct, and did not say another word.

X

Lá em Londres, vez em quando, me sentia longe daqui
Vez em quando, quando me sentia longe, dava por mim
Puxando o cabelo,
Nervoso, querendo ouvir Celi Campelo pra não cair
Naquela fossa
Em que eu vi um camarada meu de Portobello cair
Naquela falta de juízo
que eu não tinha nem uma razão
pra curtir
Naquela ausência
de calor, de cor, de sal
e de coração para sentir.

(GILBERTO GIL)

Over there in London, from time to time, I felt far from here.
From time to time, when I felt that way, I'd find myself
Pulling out my hair.
Fidgety, I felt like listening to Celi Campelo, so I wouldn't fall
into that trough
that swallowed my comrade from Portobello.
Like that, unreasoning,
for I had no reason
to enjoy;
in that absence
of warmth, color, salt
and of a heart to feel with.

* * * *

I came around to say yes, and I say
But my eyes
go looking for flying saucers
in the sky.

(CAETANO VELOSO)

A tiny ember broke the line that separated the dark blue from the darker blue. Inflamed. Showing itself more clearly, in its fiery roundness, untouched by the seawater from which it rose like a baby's head growing out from between his mother's legs at the time of birth. In a moment all of it would be visible, born, complete, full, plain. Rising slowly in the sky, it would exchange fire for gold and then turn into the celebrated silver disk of so many songs and poems. Into everybody's moon. But this one, now, scarlet, bursting out of the vastness of the ocean, demanding that everything stop to contemplate it in silence, in the swift tropical dusk, this one was the privilege of a few.

Every time she saw the full moon rise, Amalia felt she was praying. She prepared herself, in a ritual. Once a month, the moment could be total, if the sky was not clouded over. She arranged the chaise on the darkened porch or on the beach, depending on the wind, but turned toward the east. Then she put another chair behind the house, turned toward the woods that covered the hill on the sunset side, sat down and waited. She watched the sun lying down, stretching, trying to stay a little longer and extending its vigil in gold, orange, pink, and lilac, in all nameless warm colors. The moment it finally disappeared, Amalia rose and went to the other chair, on the opposite side. To see the moon rise. She had known that from a child, and remembered her grandmother telling her what she was now teaching her grandchildren: "When the moon is full, it is born the moment the sun dies."

The day before it had been a little earlier. On the next day it would be a moment later. Only on the very day of the full moon there was that double bill in God's movie theater, as the grandchildren's joke went. That was why she never did without this monthly ritual, this

unique moment when she admired the beauty of creation and meditat-
ed on her own life. The moment was unique but cyclical, and that was
one of the things Amalia prized the most. There was a certain security
in the thought that it would always return. As her grandmother had
seen it, at the time when there were still slaves in Brazil, and as her
grandchildren would see it in a time when, perhaps, there would not
be so much misery.

On this particular day Amalia really needed a beautiful moonrise.
Helena Maria's crisis had been difficult, crying that way without telling
her why, unable to say anything, not even wanting to talk to Alonso afterward. But now she had given her daughter a tranquilizer and
she would certainly sleep till the next day. And when she woke, all
would be gone. She had never seen Lena like that; she wondered what
could have put her into that state. She even thought of calling a doctor,
of asking Alonso, when he called for the second time, whether her
daughter had been having many such crises lately. But Lena implored
her not to talk to anyone, and especially not to say anything to her
friend, and assured her that it would all pass once she took the pill.
And it did. Now Lena had been asleep in the house for several hours,
and all was quiet. It was as if a wave had passed, as if the tide had come
in and emptied out again.

The ocean had cycles too, thought Amalia. That might be why she
felt so at home near it. There she was, all year, by the sea, almost alone
in that large house, and felt that it kept her company. They understood
each other. It was salty like tears, like whey, like the sweat from the
work she had done all her life, like the liquid that, inside her, had cra-
dled each of the children she had birthed. Like a woman, the ocean,
too, regulated its ups and downs by the moon. It was a living being,
a huge animal, with a rhythmic breath and different moods. But the
changes were cyclical. The calm after the storm, as her grandmother
used to say. After the flood, the ebb. After the high equinoctial tides,
in March and September, the small tides of the long nights around the
Feast of Saint John, or the long days near Christmas. All returned to
how it had been before. And the sea was there, always the same and
always different. Always so vast and wanting to grow still, to spread

over the earth, sending in lazy waves to finger the sand, invading the air with ethereal spray, sound waves to wrap sleep in its surge, waves of smell to fill the lungs with the tang of ocean. Alive, mutable, companionable. By the sea, she was never alone.

Now she was looking at the moon that stood high and clear in the sky, covering the sea with silvery scales. The night breeze refreshed her skin. She decided to go in for a shawl and protect herself somewhat. On the way, she peered into Lena's room to see if her daughter was well. She was asleep, breathing slowly. What could have shaken her so? Those papers she was messing with. She opened the folder and looked. Old letters, newspaper clippings, notebooks, loose papers. She picked up some typed sheets stapled together, the easiest to take along, just one item. She closed the folder and, while waiting for sleep, read on the verandah:

(Setting: Ricardo and Vera's apartment in Paris. Sitting on the floor, with a portable typewriter on the trunk, Vera types. The phone rings; she answers.)

VERA: Hi, Tiago, how is it going? Is Tania well? And that baby? Is it behaving? *(pause)* Yes, I did call but you had left. I worried a lot whether Madame Audard was going to mind my asking her to give you a message, but decided to risk it because it is urgent. *(pause)* No, no, nothing happened; everything is fine; it's just the following: an apartment is going to be free in our building here, because the girl was transferred to Marseille and has to leave right away. The landlady does not want to have it empty even for a day, and in order not to charge the girl with a penalty, she wants to rent it out right away, even if it is at the same price. It's pretty cheap, so I thought you might be interested . . . It's really small, just one room, a studio. But it would be all right for you and the baby, at least for one year. *(pause)* God willing, she'll return . . . *(pause)* And there is one advantage—it was all redone, has a great bathroom, and a nicely equipped modern kitchen; it's in really good shape. *(pause)* She said she could leave the key with the concierge, you can ask for it downstairs.

(Ricardo comes in from the street carrying the mail and waving one of the envelopes. He takes off his overcoat, hangs it up, kisses Vera, puts the letters on the trunk, while she goes on speaking—all but the special envelope that he holds onto.)

VERA: Well, I don't know about that, but I don't think there was any. I think all the apartments in this building are unfurnished, which is why they are so much cheaper. But the girl who is living there has her own furniture and might be willing to negotiate if she can get a good deal; after all, she gets out of a hefty penalty if you come in. *(pause)* Fine, and afterward you can come here for a cup of coffee and can tell us how it went. Bye, a kiss to Tania.

RICARDO: Was he interested?

VERA: Of course. After all these months of searching for a place, and living in that dump at the end of the world . . . He said he's coming right away because he is in the area. What was that envelope?

(She looks for it among the others and does not find it. Ricardo brings it out from behind his back, where he has been hiding it, and jokes, waving it around.)

RICARDO: An envelope with a little window . . . All transparent . . . All that's missing is the vase with flowers. Look, look what a beautiful decorative font. A lovely envelope. *(He hands it to her and she examines and then opens it.)*

VERA: Paris National Bank . . . I can't believe it . . . *(suddenly worried, in a different tone)* Or could it be a bill?

RICARDO: No way a bill, we have no bills like this. Open it!

VERA: I have! It's money, finally. Six months' worth, all at once. And I think Dad rounded it up some, because it's more than we were expecting . . . *(She kisses the envelope and dances around the room.)*

RICARDO: This deserves a celebration. How about a real dinner? A steak?

VERA: Forget it. We can celebrate sensibly. Fish or hamburger, you choose.

RICARDO: Meat. And a bottle of wine.

VERA: And some flowers to cheer up the house.

RICARDO: And that's all, so there will be some left for your coat.

VERA: And your boots.

RICARDO *(hugging Vera and dancing her around the room):* And our table, Vera! Our table.

VERA: Right! I never thought a table would be so hard to do without. You can get used to not having a bed, a chair, even a wardrobe, but it's so hard to do without a table.

RICARDO: A wardrobe too; Vera, I can't get used to it. I think if we look carefully and get lucky, it might be enough for a table and a wardrobe.

VERA: It might. All we need is a very simple table, cheap, a kitchen table. Just a place to put the typewriter at a good height and be able to put one's legs under it. Typing on my legs or crouched is killing me. I'm no Hindu.

RICARDO: And no yokel either. Jeca-tatu sitting on his heels at the door of the general store . . .

VERA *(looking over the other letters):* There are letters from my mother and from your father. Take yours, then we'll exchange. Ah, what a great day! Letters from home and money in the bank . . . *(They open the letters, read, comment on them.)*

RICARDO: Neide's daughter is getting married.

VERA: Adriana has a loose tooth, I can't believe it, it goes so fast. You turn around and the small fry are all grown up . . .

RICARDO: Lucy and John moved to a new apartment; they say it's huge, on a side street of Rua Augusta.

VERA: Aunt Cora is very ill, what a shame! And she is quite old . . . Will I still get to see her some day?

(She lowers the letter and looks around, with a melancholy expression. Ricardo finishes his letter and puts it back into its envelope and then into his pocket.)

VERA: Here, do you want to read it? Let me see yours . . .

RICARDO *(taking hers):* Nothing worthwhile, I've already told you the news.

VERA: What's this now? Are you keeping little secrets? Or did something bad happen? Was somebody arrested? Did somebody die? What was it, Ricardo, tell me . . .

RICARDO: Nothing, nothing happened, I've told you.

VERA: You can't fool me, I know you, I know there is something you don't want to tell me.

RICARDO: All right, there is. But don't I have the right to keep something to myself? To read something in a letter from my father and not tell? Do you have to know everything?

VERA: All right, but you don't need to attack me just because of that. And I will be thinking the worst; I am sure it was bad news and I think it is silly of you to try to protect me in this stupid way. I will end up finding out anyway, whatever it is. If it is that bad, it's better to learn it through you than suddenly through some stranger.

RICARDO *(impatient):* OK, read it and see for yourself. It's not bad news; it's the same as always, just more insistent this time. I can do without his advice. And I thought it best not to bother you with it.

VERA: Is it that old story that I am paranoid and am spoiling your career, keeping you far from your father's house and from the pleasures of family intercourse?

RICARDO: Yes. But you don't need to exaggerate. He does not put it into those terms. He just thinks that everything is going very well; there is no reason why we should be here pinching pennies when the country is developing so fast, living a real economic miracle . . . He believes it.

VERA: Sure. Everything is going really well. The men arrest everybody, torture them, disappear them, kill them, but that's progress, right? We are the bad patriots, and don't love our country, right? They are the heroes. It's the greater Brazil.

RICARDO: He believes it, Vera. He is making a lot of money, everything he had never been able to earn before just through honest work. In a few months of investments, he is now, for the first time in his life, raking it in. It's not his fault. John, too, is swimming in money. Dad is sorry for us, that we are not there to take advantage of it, Vera. His nagging is annoying, but it comes from love, because he is fond of us and worries about our situation.

VERA: And is it possible that he does not see what is happening with the others? The wretched salary crunch that guarantees all that crazy speculation by one part of the middle class? The brutal repression, the prisons, the torture so that nobody will complain, nobody will organize, nobody will yell? The deaths, the violence, the military apparatus?

RICARDO: No, Vera, he does not see it. It is not written about in the papers; everything is censored, have you forgotten?

VERA: But you can always find out; someone sees something, someone tells. Whoever does not know does not want to know, prefers to be an accomplice.

RICARDO: It's not quite like that. They may even know, but they don't see any connection between the economic miracle, censorship, and torture.

VERA: But the miracle only exists because of the repression; without it there would not be a Greater Brazil, Ricardo . . .

RICARDO: We know that, but people who are not informed don't see it. That's why censorship is so indispensable to the dictatorship. Everybody thinks that those few times when someone is arrested, it was an evil bandit, a cruel terrorist, and they thank God that the military is putting the country in order.

VERA (after a pause): Does your father think we are terrorists? People who kill little children, that kind of thing? Or does he think that we are bad Brazilians? That story Tania told us, that now there are all those cars driving around in Brazilian cities with bumper stickers speaking ill of us: Brazil: love it or leave it . . . Brazil deserves our love . . . As if we did not love Brazil till our hearts hurt.

RICARDO: I don't believe he thinks any of this, if you really want to know. It's just that he does not understand anything that is going on. And he would like us to come back and be near him. It's because he does not think we did anything wrong that he keeps calling us back and says that there is no reason for us to be here.

VERA: But I was arrested; you were arrested.

RICARDO: Sure, but we were released. He thinks that this wiped the slate clean; it was just a mistake.

VERA: So he is not afraid that we will be tortured so we'll tell things? Or so as to blackmail my brother and make him give himself up?

RICARDO: No, Vera. I've explained this over and over. He does not think so. He does not believe that there is torture. He thinks that if you don't owe, you need not fear.

VERA: Well, in that case Brazil has a lot to fear, because it owes more every day. The way these guys are picking up money here to finance all of that, they will win the World Cup in debt too.

RICARDO: You are right, of course. But Father does not know any of this; he does not see it; there is no place where he could find out. And he is really happy because, after a life of hard work and sacrifice, he may get himself enough money to finally be able to afford his own apartment. And he does not want us to miss the party, that's all.

VERA: This party is a bit macabre for my taste.

RECARDO: But for those who see nothing but the party, it's great fun. The rest of the letter speaks of nothing but the stock exchange, the shares he bought, how much they have risen. The numbers are really impressive.

VERA: They must be. Even Mom's letter mentions economics, as you will read.

RICARDO: See?

VERA: Indeed . . . She says we sound like Martians. That all we ever speak about is when our ship will come in . . .

RICARDO *(astonished):* We do?

VERA: Yes indeed. Every letter says we are waiting for the fellowship, depending on the fellowship coming in soon, and we must be the only Brazilians who, when they talk of the economic situation, are thinking of "bourse" in the sense of fellowship instead of "bourse" in the sense of stock exchange.

(Both laugh. The bell rings. Ricardo opens the door, and Tiago steps in.)

RICARDO: Hi, Tiago, welcome! Come in! So, have you come to see the apartment?

TIAGO: I've had a look. It's great . . . Small but really neat. Tania will love it.

VERA: And also, with us so close, it will be so convenient. When the baby arrives, I can give you a hand, and you won't be so isolated.

RICARDO: So when do you move in? If it's at the end of the week, I can help.

TIAGO: Well, that's the problem . . . I don't know if we will be able to take it because of the money.

VERA: But the girl said that you could keep it at the old price; it's pretty cheap. I don't think you'll find anything else at that price.

TIAGO: Sure. I know that. The problem is not the rent itself. It's that the landlady will only rent if the present tenant recommends the next one. And the girl will only recommend someone who can pay her the money of the deposit, three months' rent. Then, at the end of the lease, the landlady returns the deposit to the new tenant.

RICARDO: That's fair . . . It's still a good deal, and the simplest way of doing it for everybody concerned.

TIAGO: The only thing is, we don't have that kind of money.

VERA: Can't you ask for it from Brazil? Couldn't your parents or Tania's parents send it to you?

TIAGO: Sure, they could. And we are about to get some from some land that Tania owns and is trying to sell—the person who has the power of attorney has already signed the security, and they are going to sign the deed next week and send the money. But the woman wants it now; she is in a hurry and has given us a deadline two days from now.

(Vera and Ricardo look at each other; she discreetly touches the envelope from the bank, with a gesture that consults him. He nods; she raises her thumb in agreement.)

VERA: Tiago, maybe we can solve that one, if it is really just a question of days and you will be able to pay us back soon.

RICARDO: Sure, there is no point in your missing an opportunity like this by a couple of days. We can lend you the money.

VERA: When you get the remittance, you'll pay us back.

TIAGO: You? You have that kind of money? Aren't you always saying that you are broke?

VERA: Well, we always are. But today we are not. We got some this very morning; look, the note from the bank is right here.

RICARDO: It's something Vera was supposed to have received all along, for months of work at the magazine; it accumulated and has just come in.

TIAGO *(would like to accept, but still hesitates):* And you can really do without it? Are you sure?

VERA: Absolutely. Don't worry. We were going to buy a table and a few other things, but we have waited so long, a couple more days is no big deal.

TIAGO: Gosh! This is so great. Thank you, guys. You are real friends, I am sort of shaken . . .

VERA: I have to go to the bank to draw the money. But I can go now and give it to you this afternoon. You can come back then.

TIAGO: Boy, this is so wonderful. I can't believe it. Tania will be *so* happy. We are so uncomfortable in that place, it's an awful hole. You can't imagine . . . OK, so I'll call, and tell the woman that we'll take it.

VERA: And I am going to the bank. You just come back this afternoon.

TIAGO *(hugs both of them):* Thank you so very much. I will never forget this. And you can rest assured, as soon as the money comes in, the first thing I'll do is pay you.

(Vera takes leave of them with a kiss for Ricardo, and exits. Tiago goes to the phone and while he speaks the lights dim and the stage darkens as his voice fades.)

TIAGO: Hello. *(pause)* Madame Dupont, s'il vous plait . . . Oui . . . Ici c'est Monsieur Silva, à propos de l'appartement . . . Oui . . . Eh, bien, j'ai l'argent, nous pourrons . . .

It amused Amalia to read this. She knew the story well. In a way she had been part of it, since she had been the one to send the money abroad to her daughter. Or part of the money. They had to have more than one person send money to more than one person because the law did not allow remittances above a certain amount. And after all the time her husband had spent fighting to receive the pay for the reports to the magazine, the amount that finally was paid out exceeded the limit the bank would allow them to send. And she remembered the story very well, except that the guy had not been named Tiago but something else that she did not remember right now. But she knew that they had really paid, as promised, a couple of weeks later and had even cooked a thank-you dinner for Lena and Arnaldo; they had become tight friends. It was only later that everything changed, and Amalia knew how deeply that had upset her daughter. She knew that after a while Lena and Arnaldo had begun to be shunned; everybody avoided them, and seemed to run away from them. Nobody invited them to anything. When they approached, people fell silent or changed the subject. After a while, Lena lost her job at the library and Arnaldo found out that the famous fellowship they had waited for so anxiously and which they had been assured he had pretty much gotten (she thought that the first month had even been paid out to them) had been cut, no explanations. And both the job and the fellowship had been arranged with the help of other Brazilian exiles who had been there longer, had lots of contacts, belonged to well-established organizations.

That had been the beginning of her daughter's worst time in exile; Amalia knew that well. It was when she had just got pregnant and without money, without resources and without friends; they had eventually lost the baby. Helena Maria's life would have been so different with a child. She had wanted it so much. All would have been different. Surely she would not be as she was now, neurotic, in tears about nothing and everything. Maybe she would even still be married to Arnaldo. It's just that one cannot change these things. God has his own plans. But Amalia was certain that few things had hurt Lena so much as this business with these friends; their names were not really Tiago and Tania, but she could not remember, she had blocked it. But the fact was that after a while Lena had found out that they had been spreading around to everybody that she and Arnaldo were really strange, and must be plants from the police or be working for the Secret Service. That they passed themselves off as hard up and then could come up with lots of money on short notice. And they had managed to find an apartment for Tiago and Tania—OK, let's call them that—in the very same building where they were living, and surely they must have had an extra key, just so they could spy on them better, and the apartment was so cheap that they must have been paying part of the rent directly to the landlady, so they could attract others to the same building. And furthermore, they did not belong to any party, any organization, had nobody to vouch for them, which was really suspicious in that community of exiles where everybody was in some way connected to some kind of movement. Only Lena and Arnaldo and that other nice couple that had a small boy (what was their name again? Amalia had met so many people when she visited her daughter in Paris that she couldn't remember everything; she had kept the faces, but forgotten the names; she only recalled that the woman had been institutionalized for some mental disorder), only they did not belong to any organization. And it was through them that Lena had learned of the nasty slander. Somebody had mentioned it to her, and she had objected, assured the person it was a lie, and even traced the gossip back to its origin and then told Arnaldo. It was a really sad thing. At least that one couple had stuck with them. The only true friends that had not let them down in all that time in Paris, as she remembered Lena saying when she returned.

But what was the idea, now, for Helena Maria to be reading and writing these things? That must be why she was crying about nothing. Amalia felt like hiding these papers, making the folders disappear, for the good of her daughter. But with Lena she never knew what the reaction might be; she was afraid of unleashing a storm. And also, at this time in her life she knew that sometimes one has to stir up all these painful things and make them burst; it does not work to spend all your time pretending that it does not hurt or that there is nothing there. You have to let it rise to the surface, like an inflamed abscess, full of pus, that bothers, hurts, throbs till it ripens and one can lance it, burst all that putrid garbage inside, purge it, drain it all till only blood comes out and one knows one has gotten to the bottom of it. All you have to do then is clean it out completely so it won't reappear somewhere else. And that's it, a great relief. Maybe that's what it was. Maybe her Helena Maria needed to drain this infection, slowly, lest she have to undergo more drastic surgery. Perhaps that's why she was like that these days, talking about the past all the time, of things she had not

mentioned for ages. And she, too, Amalia, realized now that she wanted to remember more, to let memory dive into memories and let them
rise slowly like the water at the spring behind the house, which one
reached by walking through the trees and which pooled endlessly, surrounded by coarse white sand, and reflected the sky in its small mirror
where dragonflies and hummingbirds came to bathe, carrying petals
from the flowering trees down to the brook, along the lazy bends with
which it flowed through the village till it rode into the sea among the
rocks where lobsters lived, by the mangrove where the grandchildren
set traps to catch prawns.

That's what it was. Like water rising from a spring. If it is to follow
its path and dissolve into the green vastness of the sea, the earth has
to drain its water. Memory was a bit like that. And at times it was
imperative to remember, just as they had been doing these last days, at
all times, talking about times past. Or even without speaking—at least
on her part, the memories were rising very vividly. The months after
AI-5, for instance, had stayed very clear in her mind, when, as soon as
she was able to sigh with relief at her son's release, she had had to learn
to live in a new reality that she had never imagined possible—that of
his needing to live in hiding. She had learned so many things in that
time . . . The value of silence had been one of them. She had had to get
used to the idea that the lack of news from Marcelo was a good sign.
And that she must not speak of him outside of the closest family circle.
And to think of her son all the time and do all the housework while
praying for him, delivering into the care of God the safety and the life
of that boy of hers, all grown up and far away.

At least she was able to learn gradually. In the first months he would
sometimes send news. He might call, or send a friend over with a message. On one or two occasions it had even been possible to meet, with
a thousand precautions, but at least face to face. On her birthday, she
had received flowers, with a note from him. And on the day before he
turned twenty, they even had lunch together in a little hole-in-the-wall
eatery on the edge of town.

But then everything stopped. And what she had learned in the previous months proved useful. She couldn't have said anything anyhow,
even if they tortured her to death, because she really did not know any-

thing. She did not know where Marcelo was living, what he was doing, what he called himself, even; who were his friends, what he looked like, whether he was wearing glasses, whether he had turned blond, whether he had a moustache. She knew what he smelled like, the temperature of his skin, his voice, but none of that could be part of a description and help the police to arrest him.

The new phase in her life had started abruptly, like a nightmare, and was going to last for ten years, up to that sham lying amnesty that applied to almost nobody and whose only function was to assure any torturer or terrorist he would never be punished. Good thing the law had been so badly written that big holes started turning up in it and, battle by battle in the judiciary, it ended up being extended to almost everybody. And she had dreamt so long about a holiday, a collective national party to celebrate the end of the terror, with all the prisons being opened to release all the political prisoners, with flights of planes and fleets of ships bringing back all the exiles to general rejoicing, as she had seen happen when the soldiers returned who had fought in World War II and paraded through the center of the city in open cars under a rain of tickertape. Amalia thought that the end of the dictatorship would be something like Bastille Day in France, or April 25 in Portugal: the creation of a new holiday to herald a new epoch.. Even if it was not so clear an event as the fall of the Bastille or the uprising that marked the Carnation Revolution in Portugal. But no. It was so slow, gradual, and plodding that it never ended, and if, on her private calendar, she could mark in red the day when her son returned, finally amnestied, she could not forget that there were still some who had not received a complete pardon. Or that the government was still packed with people in high posts, who had served the previous regime with the same enthusiasm. Or that one still did not know when the next presidential elections would happen, something that she had not seen in thirty years at least. And especially, she could not forget that all those who had repressed, beaten, arrested, bombed, and killed during the years of terror were still on the loose and scattered among the population, never having been punished in any way, and often never having been exposed to public opinion. Add those to all the thieves and all the corrupt officials who had engaged in every kind of malfeasance and shenanigans till the country had come to the economic calamity in which it found itself then, and it added up to a crowd of people enjoying perfect impunity. That was why at times Amalia felt deeply depressed when she thought about Brazil. She told herself that now things were better because the press was free to cover these financial scandals, the elected officials were free to denounce them (though mostly they did not denounce anything, and instead just got involved in new ones), the parties were free to constitute themselves, and everyone was free to have opinions without being persecuted for them. In short, it was a much more democratic situation, no doubt. But until she saw justice done, she really could not believe that times had changed. Unless, of course, she just let herself be selfish; after all, she had good reason: her children were well, alive, free, at home. Thank God! Everything was going very well . . .

XI

Quando vieres de torna-viagem
Trarás a cabeça exangue
E a lembrança inútil
Dos que freqüentaram o inferno
Trarás a cabeça
Como os caules amorfos
E o teu coração beijará os perfumes da tarde

(OSWALD DE ANDRADE)

When you return from your travels
You will bring back a head bled white
And useless memories
Of the regulars in hell
You will bring a head
Like shapeless boles
And your heart will kiss the fragrant afternoon

When Lena awoke, the sun was high in the sky. She was off schedule for the first batch of medications, she thought, alarmed. She had to make up for it, take them all, right away. Her whole body ached from the previous night's tension, the muscles in her back, her shoulders, her arms and legs. Her head felt heavy. It felt as if she were coming down with the flu. Or as if she had taken a beating.

It had, in fact, been a beating, she thought. Mugged by memories. But she refused to start her day thinking of it. She rose and opened the window. Right in front of her, the almond tree greeted her by existing, all in new, tender leaves, green and shining, with bunches of tiny white flowers opening and fluttering off in the wind. The tree was still giving her daily lessons in regeneration, she thought. She remembered her grandfather's explanation:

"The almond tree is a true vegetable phoenix . . . It is reborn from its own ashes as often as necessary. When it notices that the weather is turning cold, it sheds all its leaves to conserve sap and save energy. That rapid loss is a kind of defense."

And the girl Lena asked: "How does it know it is going to get cold?"

Her grandfather was always ready to teach, and answered slowly, to control his stutter: "All living beings have a kind of biological clock. The ants know if it is going to rain a lot and they move away from the rivers to where the flood does not reach. Mammals, like squirrels, know when winter is going to be especially cold, and grow an extra-thick pelt, or they know when the winter is going to be very long, and store up a lot of food. Every species regulates itself in its own way."

Lena insisted, interested in her favorite tree and the beautiful spectacle it offered: "And the almond tree? How does it know and decide whether to turn yellow or red?"

"It's as I told you, it knows biologically . . ."

The girl did not quite understand, so he went on:

"This is a very sensitive species. At times it needs only a very small climatic variation to start shedding its leaves. It begins to save its chlorophyll, and the green shades into yellow, and you get this golden symphony. Then the chlorophyll is all gone and what is left is totally red, fiery, brilliant, glowing. Then it looks as if all the leaves had really burned, because they dry out and drop. The almond tree undresses completely to brave the winter, when the nights are longer and sun and water are less generous to feed it. When it has no leaves, and looks dead, that's because it is getting ready to grow, burst into life, covered with new buds." The old man would pause and say: "A vegetable phoenix."

The girl Lena did not know what a phoenix was. She only learned later, when she grew up. And the woman Lena thought that it was what she needed to be, a phoenix. At some point, she would have to do that, be reborn, whole. Like the snake that sheds its old skin, leaves the empty shell behind it, and buds out from within itself, new, while remaining itself. Not like the butterfly that leaves its chrysalis, keeping nothing of the caterpillar it had been. To be reborn without a metamorphosis, faithful to herself. A permanent challenge, to achieve living, surviving and organizing herself, as Marcelo insisted.

Physical effort helped. And because her foot ached less every day, she could walk some, take advantage of the ebb tide to stroll on the hard sand by the sea. She did need her mother for support getting there, so she could walk on the softer, dryer sand further from the water where vegetation gave out. Just a short stroll. If all went well, maybe the next day she would venture further, and walk to the other side of the village, toward the little shipyard where they repaired and built boats. Not this day. She had to push the limits slowly.

At the breakfast table she talked with her mother about her walking plans. Amalia was relieved to see the grey depression from the previous day lifting. As soon as Lena declared the meal over, they left.

"Now you go back, Mother. Let me go by myself for a stretch . . . ." she said when they came to the hard sand.

"Are you sure you can do it?"

"I can and I want to. I need to, Mother. Please."

Amalia knew she needed it. And she was sure that her daughter was able to walk for a while there. She was worried about her head, or her heart, not her foot. But she could do nothing at the moment. She agreed to be left behind and suggested, almost as a sign of respect for Lena's independence:

"Then I will go in for a moment and bring out a chair for when you return, OK? That way you can sit, rest a while, sun yourself by the sea. When it gets too hot, you'll come in."

"Good idea, Mother. What I'd really like is a swim in the ocean . . ."

Amalia smiled at her daughter's spirit. "Easy does it. If you want to swim, you have to start by making it through the breaking waves. Not a good idea with this foot. You could lose your balance."

Lena agreed. She really longed to feel the sea against her skin, but she was still very fearful. Not because of the foot—that was the least of it; if she made a false move, she'd recover. But she was afraid of the dizziness, of falling down suddenly in the water and losing the sense of what was up and what was down. She would drown, maybe, because in those cases she lost all her points of reference. True, she had not fallen in days, but she was still not free of the panic she felt with the falls, that sense of complete helplessness. No, it was better to stay on dry land. "If you fall, the ground will stop you," her grandfather used to say to encourage her when she was small and tried, fearfully, to climb the lowest branches of the guava or apricot trees.

Amalia went in and sat on the verandah, watching her daughter without being seen. Lena limped along on the sand, happy to be walking by herself and by the sea, remembering her grandfather's saying; he was always pushing her to overcome obstacles and grow up.

If I fall, the ground will stop me. When she grew up, she learned that you could, in fact go past the ground, be buried below it. In exile as well as in those months before she left the country, one of the greatest sources of anxiety usually started that way: *So-and-so fell . . .* It was a way of saying that So-and-so had been jailed. And from there on, more pain.

She pushed away the thought. She had to busy her mind with other things. Think about the grandfather, the cousins, childhood. But you can't order thoughts about; she couldn't. Maybe think about Alonso as well. That, too, was painful. If he did not call today, during the day, she would in the evening; after all, he had tried to talk to her the day before and she had not taken the call. Beat as she was, it was best not to say anything and pretend she had been sleeping. She was missing him to death. Resolved: she would call in the evening. And if he was not alone? If the other girlfriend answered? It was a risk she had to run; there was no other way. And in any case, it was not worth worrying about it before it happened.

She tried to think of nothing, just feel the wet sand under her feet, follow the flight of a seagull diving after fish, rest her eyes on the horizon, and fill her lungs with sea air. She was sure this little outing would do her good. It was, already. Also, she thought, there has to be some compensation, some balancing out. The first world could not have everything. The country is in miserable shape, democracy long in coming, economic dependency absolute, but we have this great climate, magnificent landscapes, this tropical paradise so delicious and unbelievable that one is almost ashamed to relish fully and intensely the pleasure it gives.

The same in her personal life. Her health was a shambles, the work she loved best was forbidden, the man she loved preferred another, the child she dreamt of was hidden in the folds of eternity, the words she needed escaped her and dissipated like smoke. But there was still the house by the beach, that reliable refuge, and her mother's clandestine tenderness and this childhood soil, the home range forever, mother country to which one could return from any exile, with no sudden jolts. And that was a privilege, a blessing. It recharged the batteries and forced her to get back on her feet. She was increasingly sure of that. She would have to get up, by herself, no chemical crutches, facing the dangers, paying to see. The moment she felt strong enough, with the least possible support, just a point she could lean on as a lever of herself. But not yet. She couldn't yet. She could hardly walk as far as the point, in front of the house, where her mother had set up the chair. She sat, tired but content. The next day she would walk some more.

Not now. Now she was going to sit and look at the sea and the sky, relaxing and feeling her strength return. The intensity of the greens and blues was striking, and she thought of her friend Luis Cesario, forever attentive to colors. Attentive to everything, that warlock, who could see through mysteries, foresee future needs, and send messages across long distances without material support.

It could be amusing. Lena had gone to their house one afternoon, but he was out, spending the day at a friend's farm, about two hours' drive away. He was supposed to return the next day. She could not even be disappointed, because it was also a special pleasure to have Carlota to herself. There were times when Lena thought she had never loved any person as she loved Carlota. It was as if she had two mothers, Amalia and Carlota. But with the acquired mother there was a rare affinity, difficult to explain; they understood each other without having to speak, despite the forty or more years that separated them. They could spend hours almost silent on the porch together, stroked by the sweet smells of the afternoon. Or they could talk for hours about everything. It was Carlota who gave her the diaries of Anaïs Nin to read, it was Carlota who told her about Lou Andréas Salomé, it was Carlota who introduced her to the works of Hermann Hesse, and it was with her that she argued animatedly about the trajectories of Narcissus and Goldmund, as if both were re-creating them. With Carlota she had learned how to make jabuticaba jam, whole-wheat bread, and home cheese. Carlota showed her the Brazilian beauty in the music of Alberto Nepomuceno and the universal fury of Stravinsky. And with Carlota, who had lost an infant daughter, she could share her deepest hurt, her most recondite dreams, her most childish pleasures.

That was why she did not mind not finding Luis Cesario. Carlota was a fulfillment all by herself. And that afternoon they rested on the porch and wandered through the garden, setting some fern cuttings, transplanting tender little shoots of African violets, planting begonias. And while they did that, they talked, discussed the political situation— Carlota was vehement like an adolescent in all her pronouncements. Lena had to moderate her from time to time. At the top of the stairs leading to the porch, right in front of the front door, Fifina the dog was sleeping, indifferent to the activities and the arguments of the two women.

Suddenly, Fifina raised her head, and pricked up her ears. She whined once and started to bark. She ran toward the gate and once there started to chase her tail as if she intended to bite it. Then she stopped, barked a lot, and lay down again, in the yard, by the gate.

Carlota interrupted what she was doing, looked at the dog, and said: "When we are done with this begonia, we'll go in." Lena was surprised: "Didn't you want to finish with this bed?"

Lena could not believe the matter-of-fact answer: "It's that Cesario decided to return today. We should go in and into the kitchen. I think I will make the vegetable soup he likes, for a more substantial dinner." Lena looked surprised, but she went on: "When he comes back from a trip like this, he always likes a good soup. He says it helps him relax . . . Especially if he leaves at this hour, he'll have to do some night driving."

Lena looked at her watch. Twenty-five to six. She asked: "Carlota, I don't understand. Where did you suddenly get the idea that Luis Cesario is driving back this evening?"

The old woman laughed as she collected the gardening tools. Lena opened the garden spigot and, while they washed the soil off their hands, Carlota explained: "Sorry, you don't know about his . . . I am so used to it that at times I forget that other people may not know . . . But it's Fifina. She and Luis Cesario have all those secret communications, they talk to each other in corners, I have no idea what happened in their last incarnations . . . Every time he leaves it's the same thing: as soon as he starts on his way home, she lets me know. She does all these things you saw her doing—she runs around, barks, chases her tail, and then waits at the gate. Even when he only goes downtown, I know when he is getting on the tram down there, and ten minutes later he is home, I can put the food on the stove to warm it up. When it is farther away, I can't predict it quite as accurately; there can be traffic, or there can be something unexpected, it may rain on the road, things like that. The only thing one can know for sure is that he left wherever he was at that time."

Though she was well acquainted with Luis Cesario's magical powers, Lena could not quite believe it.

"You mean you are going to make dinner for him just because of that feeling?"

Carlota did not miss a beat. "It's not a feeling, child. I know he is coming, and when he gets here he will be hungry."

And he was. Shortly before eight, Lena heard a horn. The headlights in front of the gate to the garage showed that old Luis Cesario had arrived. Carlota returned to the kitchen and Lena went to open the gate, avoiding Fifina, who ran around her legs, looking out for the first breach that would let her throw herself out into the road; she couldn't wait to greet her master. As Lena pushed open the heavy iron gate, she thought how surprised her friend would be to find her there. He entered, turned off the ignition, and ran to hug her.

"I knew you were here! I came back early just so I would find you."

She made a weak attempt at a joke: "How did you know? Did you hear Fifina bark?"

He laughed. "It's Carlota who needs Fifina to learn things like this. Not me. I know, and that's it."

She thought she'd test it: "At what time did you leave?"

"About five-thirty. Around four we went to see the new plants in the nursery; beautiful, someday I'll take you there and you'll see. Then, suddenly, it happened."

He looked positively roguish, full of mischief, making affectionate fun of her. He winked and said: "There was a beautiful orchid, just lovely, the kind you like . . . And right beside it, a ratty begonia, without a single bloom, its leaves looking burnt. The orchid reminded me of you. But it was the begonia that told me you were here. So I decided to hurry up, finish what I still had to do, pick up the honey, and then I packed and at about half past five . . ." And while they were still climbing the steps to the verandah, he asked: "Did Carlota make the soup?"

Naturally, Lena answered: "She did. It's in there, being kept warm."

"Then let me wash my hands so we can eat, because I am dying of hunger. But first I have to talk to Fifina . . ."

And while he bent to pet Fifina, who was lying on her back, paws in the air, delighted, Lena asked herself whether the two old people were putting her on or whether what she had just witnessed was really true and she had just watched another one of her warlock friend's magic tricks.

But she should not have doubted it. As time went on she witnessed more of Luis Cesario's friendly witcheries. A few months after AI-5, for instance, on a cold and rainy winter's day, when it got dark early and at half past five was night, one of those days when all one wants to do is stay home, reading under the covers, or at least having a cup of hot chocolate, Arnaldo was surprised to find that one patient who had made an appointment with him under an unfamiliar name was in fact old Luis Cesario.

"What a surprise to see you here! My assistant announced an entirely different name . . . Luis Neves."

"I thought it more prudent."

Arnaldo did not argue, greeted the old man, and, still curious about the mystery, indicated a chair, inviting him to sit down. "So, how are things? Is Dona Carlota well?"

"Thank God, we are all in good health."

The doctor thought that was strange. "Well, what brings you here?"

Old Luis Cesario looked serious and gave him a grey envelope, all folded up till it had turned into a small package, with something inside. "I wanted to give you this, but thought it would be better to do it like this, in this neutral way."

Arnaldo unfolded the envelope till it opened completely. He looked inside. It was an old key. Or an antique key. One of those that make you think of old mansions or trunks in church vestries, a long key with a looped bow, a cylindrical shank, perpendicular to which there was a bit with its wards. It certainly predated the modern cut keys everybody used.

Before Arnaldo could ask, Luis Cesario explained: "This is the key to my house. It opens the side door to the study, from the porch. But it also opens the gate to the outside."

Arnaldo said nothing, used as he was to listen professionally, waiting for further explanations. Luis Cesario clarified: "It is so that you people can come in any time of day or night, should it be necessary. Even if there is nobody home. And I changed the position of the easel, which was always in the way, so nobody will bump into it. I hope it won't be necessary, but it is best to be prepared."

Arnaldo was still a bit perplexed; he did not quite understand, and did not know what to say.

"Thank you. This is an enormous proof of trust . . . But if we need to go there, we will call, and only go if you are home."

Patiently, as if he were speaking to a child, old Luis Cesario tried to be even clearer: "Son, I have lived through two world wars, one occupation, and one other dictatorship. I have lived through one resistance and I know what is needed for that. I will be seventy shortly, I am not in good health, and I can't get involved in some clandestine fight, as I should; I would end up being in the way. But there are things that I can do. One of them is this: I can offer my house."

"But we aren't . . ."

The interruption was blunt: "I don't want to know. All I know is that we are together, and I want to help. Carlota and I talked for a long time and decided to do this. It is a well-thought-out decision. Tell Lena that I sent her the key. She can do with it what she wants, give it to whomever she wants; I trust your wife completely, my son."

Arnaldo could not argue any more. Moved, he thanked him, and promised to get the key into Lena's hands. The old man went on: "Tell her she is free to use it as she wants. There is one condition, however, a somewhat sad one . . ."

"Which is . . . ?"

"Maybe it is best if we don't see each other for a while. So as not to threaten the security of the hiding place. This way nobody will suspect, in an emergency, that we are such close friends. But we will have to put up with missing each other. Carlota and I will be thinking of you every day, praying that all will be well for you. And from time to time we will run into each other at some opening, or at a concert."

Arnaldo was beginning to wonder whether the old man was really in such good shape, or whether he was a slightly delirious, making up this spy-movie plot. And he was still more surprised by the last request from Luis Cesario: "And now, my son, to do things exactly *comme il faut*, you will write me a prescription in the name of Luis Neves, which is a family name of mine that only appears on my identity card. It was the name I used to make this appointment, and with today's date on it, it could someday be your evidence that I really came here in need of your professional services . . . To get something for my gout . . ."

In the evening, as he told Lena about it, Arnaldo suggested that maybe the old man was having fun with his game of make-believe mysteries and adventures. Lena put the key away carefully in her handbag, in the zippered compartment, and almost forgot all about it.

About a month later, Amalia called and asked: "Lena, my child, could you come with me on Thursday to Del Castilho?"

"Del Castilho, Mother?"

"Yes . . . I found a fabric store there selling some really cheap stuff. I want to have some shirts made for your father, and as you know he only likes those very fine *fil-à-fil* fabrics that one can't find anywhere. And when one does, it costs an arm and a leg. I also want to get some fabric for Fernando so I can have some pajamas made."

Her mother went on talking, and Lena sighed. Amalia was like that. She was always finding extraordinary bargains in faraway places, and one of her daughters always had to go with her, for company. At least this time she had given her some warning.

"Fine, Mother. I will arrange things at the newspaper, and tell them I will be a bit late."

"We will go in the morning. By one you will be back, having lunch."

Indeed, at one they were back. But they had had lunch at eleven, in a working-class eatery on the outskirts—which, by the way, was not Del Castilho—with Marcelo, whose birthday was the next day, and who had sent a message setting up that meeting with his mother. Amalia brought him a gift, a warm coat for her son. But Lena was caught unawares. She was not prepared for the encounter. Deeply affected, she wanted to give her brother something, and remembered the key. She handed it to him, and explained where it was from, and where the house was. She recommended:

"For the love of God, don't pass this on. It is only for you, your emergency exit, your bridge, if you need to retreat. I feel better knowing that you have this false bottom where you can hide. But I am very worried about the two old people, so be very careful."

She saw that Marcelo was touched. Much more than she had imagined. And he answered: "Don't worry. I will not open up to anyone. And will only use it as a last resort, if all else has failed and I am desperate. But it won't be necessary. We are well organized, with a good support structure; the organization takes care of security. I accept only because one never knows, right? And this gift from you, so thoughtful, means a lot to me; it means that you are really on my side—it is a lucky charm. It will be my talisman. But now we should go. I will take you in my car to where you parked yours."

Marcelo's car was a fifth-hand little VW beetle, falling to pieces. It choked, coughed, sputtered; whatever could go wrong probably would. That day it stalled, suddenly, at a red light, right beside a police car parked at the corner. No way would it start. Lena and Amalia were flooded with anxiety; their legs went weak; their hands trembled. Marcelo ordered:

"Stay calm!"

He waved to one of the policemen and asked: "Do you think you could give me a hand here and give the car a push? There is a little problem with the starter."

The policemen got out of their car, gave the VW a push, the engine started, and off they went, putt-putting along the pot-holed street of the working-class quarter, almost floating on their sighs of relief.

"You are crazy, son, doing something like that," Amalia scolded. "You should not tempt fate that way . . ."

"That's not how it is, Mother. The way things were, they would be coming over anyway, and they might have approached showing their power, asking for papers; we would not have been able to do anything and the situation could have gotten out of hand pretty quickly. They stay on street corners so they can start a raid, ask anyone at any time to get out of their car, hands up, to be searched while they hold a machine gun over them. They want to show results. But the thing is, by taking the initiative and calling the men over, I disarmed them for a moment. I put the police in the position—short term—of a guardian and protector of the citizen, these things they say they are. I caught them unprepared. They were paying more attention to the car than to me."

The two women were still worried.

"Well, yes, but it is still very risky. You should get another car."

"I should, but how?"

"I don't know. But at least you could take this one to the shop, for a good overhaul. We could get the money for that; we'd lend it to you."

"We'll see. If I need it, I will ask."

A few weeks later, Marcelo looked up Lena and asked her to lend him her car. He had finally decided to take his to the shop; it was really impossible to go on like that; it would end up causing a bigger problem. As he was leaving, he asked: "Do you have a second key for this car?"

"I do."

"So let's do the following: I think the best way of returning the car is to have it parked at some prearranged place. For instance, that square in front of the newspaper offices. If I can't go, I'll have someone park it there. Every day, you'll look. When the car turns up, you use your key, get in, and drive away."

She thought this was strange. "You'll have somebody do it? If you can't? What is this all about?"

"Lena, dear, I can't explain, and I don't want to lie to you. All I'll say is: don't worry. I am not irresponsible, and I like you very much. I won't do anything to harm you. But I will also not tell you anything. If it turns out to be necessary, you'll stick to the truth, and tell everything you know. It's the best way."

He gave her a big hug, long and tight, as if he were taking leave forever. She felt her heart shrinking, suspecting something she could not imagine, and felt like crying.

"Now leave without turning back."

They were at a busy corner. She had known that the meeting would be short. She left, a growing emptiness inside her.

A few days later, Jorge came to lunch at her house. It was an early lunch, in the middle of the week, because Lena had a free day in exchange for having been on call at another time. And she wanted to chat with him on that Thursday, without distractions, catch up with her dear friend, who had just arrived from France a few days before, after two years of graduate studies over there. He was on vacation, spending two months in Brazil before returning to finish his thesis. And though she did not have a lot of time that day, she did want to chat with him, enjoy his being in town. Then, on another day, they would have a longer talk.

The lunch was light, and the conversation animated. Jorge spoke about the course he was taking, the thesis he was working on, the very French life he was leading at a provincial university where he had no contact with other Brazilians and spoke French all the time. So much so, that he was speaking a heavily accented Portuguese, rolling his *r*s, swallowing word endings, sounding almost like Luis Cesario. But the old man had lived in France for twenty years, and there were good reasons for his accent. Not Jorge. Two years were not enough for that effect. Lena thought it really amusing, sure that the accent was a conscious effort on her friend's part to impress. He even pronounced his own name as if it were French and as if it were spelled *Georges*. And he told a long story about what had happened to him in line at some government department where he had gone to renew his passport, and he kept saying *passeport*, and Lena was laughing to herself.

Shortly before dessert, she observed: "You are really doing very well over there, aren't you, Jorge? It looks like you are really turning into Georges. I am glad to see you so assimilated. When I remember how you left here, how desperate you were . . . Boy, you are in so much better shape!"

Jorge laughed happily. And then he said: "You know, I am still not entirely over it. I know that she married, had a child, went ahead without me. But I thought that my secret dream, my *rêve d'amour*—yes, I know it sounds like that chocolate sweet—was to run into her suddenly, on the street, and she would put her arms around me and say that she wanted to stay with me."

"I don't want to be a spoilsport, but would like to remind you that there is not the least chance that this would happen."

Jorge agreed: "I know that. But I really feel like traveling to Ouro Preto, wandering around there and hunting for her ghost. Even if only to exorcize it."

Lena took the dishes to the kitchen, put them into the sink, opened the refrigerator to take out the dessert. As she went back and forth from dining room to kitchen, the story of Jorge and Teca played quickly through her head. They had met a short time before he went to France. It was a sudden, overwhelming passion that carried all before it. She was engaged to someone else, one of those long engagements that drag along and never resolve themselves. She left her fiancé, her job, her studies; she left her parents' home and ran away with Jorge to Ouro Preto. They spent a few weeks there, lost themselves in that colonial paradise in the mountains, in a love affair beyond time and any conventions, loving each other, drinking each other, devouring each other, submerged in one another. As the day for his trip was approaching, they had to return. Teca decided to break off the engagement and go to France with Jorge. But after talking to her fiancé, she did just the opposite: she set the wedding date for a few days hence, and informed Jorge that she would not see him again. Their friends never found out the reasons behind this completely unexpected decision. The explanation she gave to Jorge, or the one he passed on to his friends, did not explain anything. It said something about the need for security, a fear of the unknown, the certainty that she would be able to keep up a good standard of living if she married the fiancé. She swore that Jorge was the only true love of her life, the only person who really mattered, and that she did not want to spoil that great passion with the wear and tear of married life. And all of this was communicated two days before the trip, when Jorge was sure they were going together. At that point, Teca went into hiding; she simply disappeared. And he was crushed, maddened, searching for the girl everywhere, drinking all day long, attacking people, and he ended up being taken to the plane almost by force by Teresa and Adriano, who knew that their friend had to show up in France for the beginning of classes, and that his ticket was discounted and he would lose it if it were not used for that day's flight. It was a generalized suffering among his friends, who had to witness Jorge's pain unable to do anything, and all of them trying and unable to find Teca, and arguing about whether it would not be better to let Jorge miss his flight and lose his ticket and go after her, but all knew that he could not afford another ticket, and classes were about to start, and he could not lose his fellowship that he had fought so hard to get and that would be so important for his career. Poor Jorge.

Those were very disordered days, as Lena remembered with fondness for Jorge. It was good to see him doing so well, calm, self-possessed, teaching at the French university, publishing articles in specialized journals with an international reach, finishing his first thesis and starting to work on an idea for the second. As for Teca, she had really married that fiancé, she had a one-year-old, and was not all that happy. Jorge knew this. What he probably did not know was that she had recently separated from her husband. But Lena would not tell him that at this time. She did not want to see him that desperate ever again.

As she served dessert, she changed the subject and asked: "Have you seen Teresa and Adriano?"

"Of course. As soon as I got here. They picked me up at the airport. And it was your sister who gave me your phone and new address— have you forgotten that?"

Lena had forgotten. In fact, Jorge's best friend was indeed Adriano, her brother-in-law. They had been at college together. And because Jorge's family was from the country, it was at Adriano's parents' house that he would stay when he came to Rio; that was where he always stayed. But Jorge was going on: "Yet they, too, are full of secrets. So far, you are the only one who is not being mysterious."

"What do you mean mysterious?"

"There are times when it seems as if I had the plague. Everybody is avoiding me. Or they are full of secrets."

Lena was puzzled. "What a crazy notion, Jorge. Where did you get that? It's absurd for you to think that."

"It is. Adriano and your sister are cool, and they are my very good friends, and I know that they like me a lot and all. But sometimes, I say something, and they look at each other when they think I can't see; then they fall silent or change the subject. I was at their house, the phone rang, I was sitting right beside it so I answered, she jumped up and tore the phone from my hand. All she said was for the person to call later, and she hung up, excused herself, and did not explain a thing."

He paused and then went on: "I am glad I can talk to you about this because I think it is really weird. Even at Adriano's parents' house, where I am staying, there are some mysteries I have never found before. Like yesterday, somebody rang the bell, I went to open the door, but Dr. Nelson looked at me very seriously and said I'd better go to my room and stay there till they called me. It was obvious he did not want whoever it was to see me, or for me to see anyone. By the voices, it was three people, at least. They stayed there for an hour, talking in the living room. And me, locked in my room, like a child who is not supposed to show itself when there are visitors. I was very hurt."

Lena understood right away what it was all about. She tried to explain: "It's a question of security, Jorge. As things are now, the less anyone knows the better."

At that he got really mad: "And they think that they can't trust me? I am mature, responsible, and on their side. Is everybody like that now? The other day I was at a bar, ran into Alfredo and Paulo at a table with other people. First, they acted as if they had not seen me, or did not recognize me. Damn it, I have been away two years, I could not have changed that much. I did not think anything of it; I was so happy to see them. Then, when I approached, they said something in a low voice to the others at the table, and everybody got up and went away. Only the three of us remained. We talked a lot, it was cool, but they had already spoiled my evening."

Lena insisted: "Jorge, times are very different. For the good and safety of each one of us, it is better not to listen to conversations, not to see people, not to know who was where. That way the risk is less for everybody. In one way or another, everybody is trying to resist, to help, to do something. But the repression is very hard, and nobody knows what to do or where to start. There are people who live in hiding, under a false name, never turn up at the places they used to go. It is good not to risk knowing about those clandestine people, which only exposes them to danger, uselessly. And there are people like us, living a pleasant life, with a steady job, a well-known address, but we are always sailing around in waters full of these icebergs of clandestineness. One has to be careful not to bump into them so as not to sink everybody. Especially us, who have bumped into them. Because the icebergs are at times so big that they just sway a bit and go right on. But not us. All we need is a good crash and down we go. We don't belong to any organization that can hold us up. We have to be really careful."

Jorge helped himself to more coffee. Lena saw that he was not really persuaded and was in fact hurt. Again, he complained: "But you don't need to treat a friend this way, *n'est-ce pas?*"

"It's just little things. You should not take it so seriously."

"Little things? You call that little things? It's because they are not doing it to you. Little things! *Ça alors . . .* That was all I needed."

Visibly furious, he seemed to hesitate and then said: "I wasn't even going to tell you about it, because I find it offensive for people to humiliate me like this and I did not want anyone to know. But I will tell, and you'll see if these are little things." And he told her than on Sunday evening he had gone to Henrique's place for a chat, and had been careful to call in advance and make a date (he insisted on saying *rendezvous,* which she found amusing). He thought his host was distracted the whole time and tense. Suddenly someone knocked on the door. Henrique told him to be prepared to jump out the window and run, if it was necessary. He looked through the peephole and asked Jorge to go into the back room. He did not want to go. Henrique pushed him in, closed, and *locked* the door to the hall and went to receive his visitors.

"Can you believe it, Lena? He locked me in so I would not turn up in the living room. My friend, doing this to me . . . Well, then I did look through the keyhole. He was not doing anything much. All he did was give some dark glasses and one of those masks they give you on airplanes so you can sleep to that journalist friend of yours, Honorio. The guy left and he let me out. Of course I was offended and wanted to go off immediately. And then Henrique did not let me. He said I had to wait ten minutes or so, could not leave so soon after the other guy. And closed the door to the street. He locked me up twice in a row! *Mais c'est fou, ça . . .*"

Suddenly Lena was furious as well: "Jorge, I'm sorry. If you do not want to understand, or are unable to understand, that's too bad. But you don't have the right to go around telling people these things. I did not need to know that Honorio knows Henrique, or that he was there last night."

"Is it a secret?"

"It must be, if Henrique did not want you to know. Honorio quit his job at the newspaper a few months back, and disappeared, went into hiding; nobody knows where he is. I really would prefer not to have learned about this, not to know what they gave or received one from the other, not to know anything about it."

"But why doesn't anybody tell me these things? Henrique could have told me that Honorio went underground; I know how to keep a secret. You know me; you know I won't go around telling, I am not a gossip. I, too, have a political position, I am against all those gorillas, I do have courage. In May of '68, when the students occupied the Odeon, I dropped everything and went there. We confronted the police, picked the *pavés* up from the street . . ."

And Jorge calmed down. Or maybe just changed the rails on his anger. He started to talk about the things he had gone through the past year. He always said *"mai soixante-huit,"* and it was *"événements de mai"* here and *"policie"* there, all so very exciting, so thrilling, a wonderful epic film enjoyed in the past tense; he was animated, posing as the charming hero of the *Quartier*. Maybe that was what he needed, thought Lena, to tell some of the thrilling moments he had lived. She was going to listen attentively while she had the time. She could do that for her friend: be an attentive audience for the romantic narrative of the Parisian student rebellion from the previous year. She could listen quietly, especially since her only attempt at saying something had not been all that successful. It was when she said: "But it is very different here, now, Jorge. We are being governed by a military junta. The general who was playing at being president got sick and they did not allow the vice-president they themselves had chosen to step up. It was like a coup within a coup; there is no end to it. And when someone is arrested, he is tortured. In the end he will tell what he knows and also what he does not know."

Her comment did not even register with Jorge. He just went on recounting the story of all the adventures he had lived on the banks of the Seine. He did not want to listen. He wanted someone to listen to him. And Lena was there as a silent audience.

Suddenly the bell rang. She stood up and went to open the door, in the middle of one of Jorge's sentences, and the "*événements de mai*" were left hanging. Through the peephole she saw Roberta, the sister of Gabriel, one of Marcelo's guardian angels. She looked at her with frightened eyes and in a whisper asked: "Are you alone? Can I come in quickly? It's urgent . . ."

"Wait a minute."

She turned to Jorge and could not help finding the situation a bit funny. Now it was her turn to be mysterious; what could she do?

"Jorge, there is an emergency. Could you go into the kitchen for a little while? I promise I won't lock the door, but come out only when I call you."

Jorge looked as if he was choking on the tail end of *mai '68*, but he went. Roberta came in and said quickly, in a low voice: "I need your help. We have to hide a person, a journalist, and an object, most urgently. I don't know where. All the places I had are taken."

"Can't you use your grandmother's cellar? Where your cousin's band rehearses making all that noise with the drums?"

"No way. The other day I was there and wanted to talk to my cousin for a minute. I went to the basement and found out that all that noise—drums, saxophone, cornet, all of that was a tape. What they do there is put out a clandestine newsletter, pamphlets, things like that. They even have a small press. It's just not safe."

Lena thought for a moment. She could try to hide the person in the house of a colleague, Ivan, a university teacher who lived by himself and might well be home at the time, because he only taught in the morning and at night. She said: "I might have a place for the person. But I don't have a car right now. What is the object?"

"I have a car, no problem about that. We can hide the journalist right away. The other thing I have to get rid of is a typewriter."

"Drop it anywhere. Throw it into the sea from up the rocks."

Roberta was very nervous. She almost yelled: "It's no go! Somebody could see!"

"Maybe at night . . ."

The girl interrupted her: "Lena, there is no time to wait for darkness. We have to do all this very fast and then be very quiet and wait to see what happens. Can't you see? Or haven't you heard?"

Only then did Lena notice that the urgency in her voice was unusual, even for the tense days they had been living through. So she just repeated: "See what happens? Why?"

It was Roberta's turn to be surprised: "Don't you know? Haven't you been listening to the radio? Hasn't anybody told you?"

"No, I was having lunch here quietly with a friend. I didn't have the radio on. What happened?"

Roberta looked deeply into her eyes and said just one sentence that filled the silence and took up all the space of that moment and kept reverberating in Lena's life for all the years to come:

"The American ambassador was kidnapped this morning."

XII

Atenção
Tudo é perigoso
Tudo é divino-maravilhoso
Atenção para o refrão:
É preciso estar atento e forte
Não temos tempo de temer a morte
Atenção

(CAETANO VELOSO AND GILBERTO GIL)

Attention
All is dangerous
All is divine-marvelous
Attention to the chorus:
One must be alert and tough
There's no time to fear death
Attention

Films have cuts. Sharp ones. When a scene has a strong impact, the director or the editor can interrupt it all of a sudden, splice it to another scene that happened at a different time and in a different place, and there you are. In time the viewers understand what is happening as they follow the rest of the narrative. The theater has a thousand resources—all you have to do is turn off one light, turn on another, everything changes. A life has nothing like that. No comparable suspension of the narrative. Lena had thought of that many times when she felt like cutting a scene. Interrupting. Waking up from the nightmare. Taking her eyes off the page. Changing the station. Turning off the TV. And taking it all up much later, at some other time, after a breather in which she could recover in order to go on.

Not possible. One had to live every hour with all its minutes and seconds, all the small daily chores jumbled into them, and was not allowed to choose only the facts one wanted to stand out. When they came to arrest her, for instance, she was frying a steak. She had to think about the meat that would be scorched in the kitchen if she did not turn off the burner. And before they took her, she had to turn off the record player. Just as, before opening the door, she had thought of quickly shoving under the rug a note from Alfredo that she did not want anyone to see.

There is no way to control memory. Theoretically, you can cut, interrupt, swerve. In practice, however, you can't boss it around; it is the boss. Or else it disappears and hides, no matter how hard you try to pull it out.

Lena had gone out for a walk on the beach, for exercise, to contemplate the infinite horizon, clear her thoughts, sweep away the sad thoughts from the previous day, clear away the pain of exile, of illness, of barrenness. She was having a few good moments, feeling happier than she had in the last few days. Suddenly memory played a prank on her and offered on a tray a full recall of that moment.

Strangely, it was not a memory of pain. Just of a great fright, as if time had been suddenly arrested and every fact around her had become very distinct, each detail etched onto a hard medium. So many years later, so many lives and so many deaths later, as she missed Luis Cesario, Carlota, and Alfredo, with whom it was no longer possible to chat in this world, Lena remembered clearly every detail of those days. All as clear as if it were happening right there, before her at that very moment under the bright sun of that September morning.

It was a different September. Independence week. The junta that had just taken power from the general-president, who had not been elected either, was preparing huge festivities to commemorate Independence Day. They had appropriated all the national symbols as if they alone owned them. Even the phrase "our country" sounded ridiculous, delivered into the wrong hands, alienated from its rightful owners, who would only recover it many years later. Same for the anthems, the flag, the green-and-yellow colors. None of that spoke of citizenship at the time. And it was in this climate that Independence Day would be celebrated, September 7, three days after Roberta had come to Lena's house and given her the news. It had been a complete surprise. Evidently, as the country was entirely dependent on the United States, the military would have to put away their independence festivities for another time.

"Kidnapped? By whom?"

"The radio did not say. Kidnapped was all it did say."

Lena's first reaction was to feel threatened: "This is some bright idea from the far right, so they'll be able to accuse us and go around arresting everybody."

Roberta, who had had a chance to consider the matter, agreed, but only in part. "I don't know. I thought that at first. But then I went over it again, and I don't think so. Our right wing is tied in so tightly to the States that they would not risk displeasing the boss; not even as a ploy."

"You are right. That seems clear . . ."

Roberta interrupted: "But Lena, you are right too. Whoever did this, there is going to be the hell of a repression and we can't waste any time."

"You've said it. Go down and wait for me in the car. I will go in and change my shoes and then meet you downstairs."

She closed the door and called Jorge. While she got ready, she told him the news. She called Arnaldo, who hadn't heard either. Then she gave her friend some advice: "Jorge, we are going down now, but not together. You'll leave by the kitchen door about five minutes after me. Just close it, and it'll lock."

"Can't I go with you to the newspaper office? That way I'll be able to get the news as it develops. And you should not be walking around by yourself."

"Thank you, but there is no need. And I am not going directly to the paper. It's best to do as I say. Bye."

From the door, she added: "If the phone rings, no need to answer. And I am sorry, Jorge. Tomorrow or the day after we'll talk."

She could not have imagined then that they would not talk again till five months later, in a café in Paris, when she was just arriving, starting her exile, and he came in from the provinces to meet his friend.

At this moment she had some urgent tasks. She went down, got into Roberta's car. In the back seat, a young man was covering his face with his hands.

"It seems I did something I should not have done," said Roberta. "When you were coming out of the building, he saw you and recognized you, and got a fright. I had not told him anything and he did not know that you were the friend I was looking up . . ."

"Sorry, but so what?"

"So he does not want you to hide him or to know where he is. He does not want you to turn back to look at him. He won't say anything so you won't be able to recognize his voice. He said that your neck is stuck way out in this, and you are in greater danger than he is."

That startled her. She could not ask anything, so she just repeated: "Me?"

Roberta confirmed: "Yes."

"Then it must be because of my brother."

"Of course. And in that case, I, too, am at risk, because my brother lives with yours."

From the back seat they heard a muffled voice: "Are you two going to settle down for a good chat now?"

"He is right, Lena," said Roberta. "We can't delay. I leave you where you suggested, and you get rid of the typewriter. And I will see what I can do to hide him."

"No need," said the voice from the back seat. "I'll take care of myself. You just open the car door, I'll get out, Lena closes her eyes so she won't see me, and I leave. Good Lord, how did I get myself into a tight spot like this? Of all people, I had to fall into Lena's hands . . . If what I suspect is true, I am fucked."

They did as he had told them. Lena's uneasiness was growing. They had to get rid of that typewriter right away. She did not like that at all. She wanted to help people, of course, but she was feeling very insecure, being dragged along like this, little by little, toward things, and she did not know where they would end. She felt alarmed, like an animal in the woods that has scented smoke in the distance. She felt like putting up her ears, flaring her nostrils, trying to decipher the danger signs so she could protect herself. And she was unable to do so. She was not ready for this. And she had nobody to turn to, except people as unprepared as she was.

They arrived at the building where that professor lived. Lena took the elevator to the eighth floor, carrying the case with the portable. She went to the end of the hallway, turned on the light, rang the bell. Inside, silence. But she thought she heard a muffled sound. She rang again. She had the clear sense that there was movement behind the peephole. Somebody was looking at her. Ivan must be home. But he did not open the door. She rang again and whispered: "It's me, Lena. Please, open, it's urgent."

The door opened, but it was not the owner. It was a strange face, bearded, with sunken eyes.

"Come in quickly. Officially, this apartment is empty. I was not going to open, but I recognized you. Aren't you that journalist, Marcelo's sister? I saw you once at a demonstration, and someone told me who you were."

She hesitated. It was a relief to have the door open, but at that point she could not go in with a stranger, not knowing what was going on: "So where is Ivan?"

"He has not come back from the university yet, but he'll be here in a minute."

Just then she recognized the stranger, behind his beard and glasses. He was an important student leader, one of the most intensely searched for, who had not been seen in public for months. She took two steps into the apartment, half-closed the door, quickly explained that they had to hide the typewriter, and took her leave. As she was stepping out, she asked: "Do you have a radio?"

"No. There is a TV, but I try not to turn it on, because I am afraid someone will hear. It has to seem as if there is nobody home."

"In that case, turn it on. There might be a special newsflash. They have kidnapped the American ambassador."

The boy let out a high-pitched whistle, using all the air in his lungs. "No shit! It's going to get even hotter."

He wanted details, information, things that Lena could not give him. He turned on the TV, took her to the door again, and suggested: "I think it would be wise for you to hide. Sorry to speak without being asked, I know nothing about any of it, but when the men get angry and can't get their hands on those they want, they take anyone they can find, just for revenge. It could get really ugly."

Though it was her day off, Lena decided to go to the offices of the paper. She knew there would be work to do, and every extra hand would be welcome. In truth, journalism is a full-time job that requires total dedication. Her place was in the newsroom. She had no car, so she took a cab to get there more quickly. On the way, she thought about the situation and what she had just heard from the student. It was really good advice. And considering the panic of the other guy, the one who preferred to run away from the car and try to hide by himself so he would not be in their company, it was clear that the danger was real. But what could she do? She had no intention of going underground, living another life, with another identity, another history, another profession, new friends. She could not quit the paper or stop working. Arnaldo, too, had his job at the hospital, worked for a few hours in a colleague's private practice, was trying to get a fellowship for specialty training in Europe, and there was no sense in throwing all of that away just so they could protect themselves. Or was there? How great was the actual danger? To what extent were people at risk who did not really do anything, except offer a little help here and there?

At the paper they had more information. The ambassador had been kidnapped in his car, on his way to work, on a route that he took every day at the same time—except on that day there was an open market on the street he used and the stands were in the way of traffic; the car had to slow down, and the kidnappers took advantage of that. Lena could visualize the scene; she knew the market well, on a little street right in front of Uncle Gustavo's house. All had been very quick and efficient; not a shot had been fired. And the kidnappers had already gotten in touch with the press; it seems there was a manifesto the police were looking at and it made some demands for freeing the diplomat.

Regardless of how interested she was in the case, Lena had work to do. She was not covering that story. They told her to prepare a big piece for something else to come out in the Sunday edition. She had no time to waste. But she could not concentrate. Every so often she would get up, leave her desk, and, like everyone at the paper that day, peek into the political section, or general reporting, trying to find out whether the other workers had any fresh news. The kidnappers did not want a ransom, properly speaking. They asked that censorship be breached for the publication of their manifesto to the nation. The government acquiesced. And they announced that they would free the ambassador in exchange for the freedom of fifteen political prisoners, whose names they would give out as soon as the military agreed to their conditions. The prisoners should be placed on a special plane and taken to Mexico. As soon as they arrived there, and the international news agencies confirmed their arrival with photos, the diplomat would be freed, safe and healthy. At least, those were the terms they proposed.

At the paper nobody doubted that the government would accept the terms. It had no choice. It had been caught entirely by surprise and could not run the risk of displeasing the United States, which, after all, provided the support necessary for the government to exist. The guerrilla action had been totally unexpected. Never in the world had anyone dared to get hold of an American ambassador in order to denounce a dictatorship supported by the United States and, at the same time, used him as exchange currency in a prisoner swap. It was not just the spectacular action, creative and daring. It was also a play with marked cards; there was no way the junta would fail to give in— for that they would have had to be less dependent on the U.S. But if they had been less dependent, they would not be imposing their will on the country. All the analyses by the journalists, at their tables, in the hallways, in the corners of the newsroom, agreed on that point. Nobody even considered that the government might not accept the conditions. But everybody also knew that, as soon as the ambassador was safe, they would unleash the most violent repression the country had ever experienced, and it would be every man for himself. As for the long-term political consequences, opinions were divided. Some thought it would be the beginning of an increased popular resistance. Others argued that the repression would be so complete that nobody would dare stick out his neck.

Lena tried to get some work done; her attention, however, turned toward the news. Bit by bit information was coming in, mixed in with rumors about military maneuvers, American pressure, offers of mediation by religious leaders. There was news that the government was giving in to the demands, and news that it would never agree to them.

It was late at night, after midnight, when Lena was back in her house, that the manifesto was read out on a national TV and radio chain, the first time that viewers and listeners learned that the authorities were beating up, torturing, and killing political prisoners. The next day all the newspapers printed the manifesto. It was a sign that the first condition for the release of the ambassador had been met. Now they needed to publish the list of the prisoners who would be exchanged for him.

All day long, at the paper, Lena worked on a culture story she was preparing for section B, trying to keep ahead of her tasks, but always with an ear out for the latest news. In the morning, an anonymous phone call had told them where to find a note by the ambassador himself, together with a second message from the guerrillas. And finally, by mid-afternoon, in another phone call, there came the list with the names of the prisoners. Lena was at her table, the typewriter before her, working, when a very young reporter, still a student, came by and whispered: "Did you see the list? Everybody is on it . . ."

"What do you mean, everybody? Aren't there only fifteen?"

"The leadership, Lena. Valdir and the others."

Cheerfully, he reeled off the names of the four student leaders who had been kept in prison despite the *habeas corpus,* the time when Marcelo had been sprung. Lena had a fright on top of her initial fright. She jumped up:

"Where is that list?"

"Barros has it. But there is a copy floating around the office—look, on that table with all the people around it . . ."

Like a sleepwalker, Lena went to the table. And she saw. On the table, held by various hands, behind various heads, a list of about fifteen names. The second was Valdir's, followed by the other three. But it was the first name of all that worked for her like a signature. It was that of old Guilherme. "I'll get them out of there, one by one. And if you doubt me, I will get out old Guilherme to top it off." Marcelo's words echoed in her memory. God in Heaven, he was taking them out. And then? What would happen next?

She had to tell her parents what she had found out. They had to study the situation, evaluate the consequences. Meanwhile, everything indicated that the police still did not know who the kidnappers were. But it was just a question of time. And when the man was freed, it would be the law of the jungle.

Lena was unable to organize her ideas, examine clearly what was happening. She returned to her typewriter, finished her report anyhow, and turned it in to the editor with a confused story about how she had to leave so she could check on some facts for her next story. As she was leaving the building, she almost ran into Alfredo, who was coming in.

"What are you doing here?"

"I've come for the news; I could not stand it. Is it true that old Guilherme is on the list?"

"He is."

"How wonderful! This kidnapping was the best gift the country could have wished for."

Unsure, still stunned, she asked: "You really think so?"

"Of course. For the first time someone turns up to defend the people in the middle of all this violence, someone with the guts to confront the gorillas, Lena. I don't know, it's been as if every time a little defenseless child leaves home, it is beaten up by the bully on the corner. This is the first time the child did not have to leave home alone. The big brother went along, and for a change beat up the bully."

"Yeah, sure."

Alfredo noticed she was on her way out. "Are you leaving already?"

"I am. I'm leaving early, because I have no car and don't want to get home late. I still have to drop in at my mother's."

"I'll give you a ride, wait a minute. I'll go up quickly, all I want is to see the full list and learn the latest news. In five minutes I'll be back. Then we stop somewhere to celebrate, and I'll take you . . ."

"Celebrate, Alfredo?"

"Sure. The city is partying; it's as if Garrincha had shot a goal, a victory for Brazil at the world championship, something like that. You spend your time shut up here at the office and have no idea of what is happening on the streets."

Lena hesitated: "But I am in a hurry. I'd better get going."

Alfredo would not let go: "Why? Is something wrong? I've told you I'll take you afterward, to any place you like. If you take a bus, at this time, it'll take you much longer. Wait, I'll be right back. And while you are waiting, you could call Arnaldo, and we can meet at the Dirty Foot."

And he caught the elevator before the door closed. Lena decided to wait. She liked the idea of being with a friend and also of meeting up with Arnaldo at that time. She called her husband, and set it up. She was so dazed by the sudden realization that Marcelo was one of the kidnappers that she could not think straight. It would be good to return home with the two of them, though she was not sure she wanted to celebrate anything.

At the café, however, she caught the general festive mood. It was an unpretentious neighborhood dive, cheap, Portuguese, a long counter on one side, two rows of little tables with marble tops in front. And it served wonderful fruit-and-cachaça drinks, in addition to straight cachaça from a clay still, very special, from private suppliers. Every once in a while they'd meet up with Alfredo there, for a late-afternoon chat downtown, when traffic ebbed and it was possible to talk quietly. But on that day, the mood was agitated, nervous. The bar was full, all the tables taken, a lot of people standing in the hall holding glasses, laughing and toasting each other.

"No toasts! No toasts!" the Portuguese owner kept saying, frightened, though of course he appreciated the business and the profits.

"Just one more toast, to finish up, people!" Alfredo ordered loudly above the noise at the bar.

"One more, and that's all, please," the owner pleaded. "And, please, watch what you say . . ."

Alfredo raised his arm, with his glass in his hand, and shouted: "To all of us, who just found out that we have an older brother! And the health of the older brother!"

"The health of the older brother," some echoed him over the generalized euphoria.

Arnaldo, too, was very excited: "Well, Lena, what a relief. I never thought that someday I would be able to watch the military having to swallow all their arrogance and release a few prisoners. And everybody will find out that they are not the good guys they keep saying they are."

"Sure. We'll talk about this later."

"But Alfredo is right. Now we have someone to go to. If someone pulls something like this kidnapping, it's because they are strong, and able to do more. Now at least the game comes to a draw."

One could not really talk in those surroundings. She would tell Arnaldo later. And right now, she could not tell anybody. The later people found out, the better. But her parents had to be warned. Carefully, but soon. She called out: "Can we leave now?"

It was going to be hard to get Alfredo away from the party. But Arnaldo noticed that she was not well and decided that the two of them would take off. As he left, Alfredo called out once more: "To the older brother!"

Lena repeated the toast like a prayer. From that day on, Marcelo had become, for all time, everyone's older brother and protector, as she had noticed him earlier, becoming that for her; the boy had become a man and the little brother had turned into her own Robin Hood, fully adult at twenty.

On the way home, she shared her discovery with Arnaldo. He could hardly believe it, but she knew he was just trying to gain time as he got used to the idea. Now she would have to tell her parents. When she arrived at their house, her mother came to the door, looked carefully at Lena, and realized that her daughter knew. On the way in, she managed to whisper: "Don't say anything to your father yet."

Lena went in, talked to Claudia and Cristina, who were watching TV in the living room, and went in to kiss her father. As she did, she wondered how Amalia had found out. Lena only suspected it when she saw the list of the prisoners to be exchanged and remembered what Marcelo had said when the AI-5 had been read out on the radio. Amalia had not been there then. She had seen her son only a few times since then. The last time had been at that birthday lunch, and they had not talked at all about that. How could she have guessed? Or maybe she did not really know and had been talking about something else?

She entered his room and gave him a hug. He looked over her shoulder, saw that she had come in alone, and said: "I can see by your face, that you know, right?"

"Know what?"

"Don't play innocent. I, too, know that it was him. But let us spare your mother for the time being. Tomorrow we tell. Today everyone is so happy, why spoil the party?"

Lena was amused. "Father, she knows too. I think the best is for us to face it, sit down and talk. At least then nobody will be caught by surprise." She called out: "Mother, come here!"

When Amalia came in, Lena closed the door and said: "Sorry, this is how the party works, all mixed up with danger and fear."

"My child, what are you talking about?" Amalia was still trying to avoid it, delay the inevitable words spoken aloud that would articulate what the heart already knew.

"The three of us know, and I would really like you to tell me how you found out. And I hope nobody else has found it out too."

"About Marcelo?" asked Amalia.

"Right . . . ," said Alberto. "How did you figure it out?"

Amalia explained: "I had a huge scare, because I never imagined. I had heard the news, I had talked about it, and had no idea. But when I heard the manifesto, I knew."

"How?"

"Who knows? It sounded just like him. I know my son, the way he talks, the way he writes. There are things in there that don't sound like him at all. There could have been more people writing it. But there are a couple of sentences where it's as if they were in his handwriting, in his voice, with a signature below. I know he was the one who wrote them. And he even mentions the Bible, that part in the Old Testament that he spoke about the other day, at lunch."

Lena tried to remember: "What part?"

"Don't you remember that he thanked me for the Bible, and said that, after reading just the New Testament for so long, he was now discovering the Old one? He even referred to one verse. Well, I got home and looked it up. It's the same one that crops up in the manifesto: an eye for an eye and a tooth for a tooth."

Lena smiled. So that's how it was. "You could teach stylistics at the university, Mother. I just hope the police are not as efficient. And you, Father, how did you figure it out?"

"I, too, could not have imagined it," said Alberto. "I heard the news, thought it was a brave and very bold act, fantastic timing, and I just admired it and tried to analyze the implications and the consequences of the act, didn't even think that soon I would learn that my son was in the group, and start feeling as I do now, very proud and deadly anxious . . ."

Now Amalia pressed him: "But how did you find out? Was it also because of the manifesto?"

"No, it was because of the watch. But I think the first thing that caught my attention was the name of the street."

"The name of the street?"

"Well, yes. When they started to broadcast the news in more detail, describing what had taken place, one of the stations kept talking about Marx Street and I registered it with some surprise, partly unconscious, since I did not know that there was a Marx Street in Rio."

Lena laughed. "That was confusion on your part. It's not Marx, with an *x*, it's Marques, a very nice Portuguese name. And what does all of this have to do with Marcelo?"

"Well, that's when I remembered it all. Many months ago, as soon as he left your house, Lena, after the AI-5 . . ."

"When he was released from jail?" Amalia asked.

"That's it. Back then he spent a long time hiding in Gustavo's house."

"Uncle Gustavo? Your brother? I would never have guessed."

"Well, yes," said Alberto. "It was best that nobody should know. One morning I went there for a chat, as was my habit. While we were talking, I saw that Marcelo kept looking at his watch. Suddenly he got up, went to the window and watched the street from behind the shades. Then he half-smiled, looked at the watch, and smiled broadly. I looked out and all I saw was the heavy traffic in front of your uncle's house, and a street market in full swing on that tiny street that starts in front of his building."

"Well, and so what?" asked Amalia, impatient.

"Well, then Marcelo said something about people who lead such a methodical life that you can set your watch precisely by what they are doing at any one time. Something like that; that was the general idea. I looked again and saw a huge black car with a little banner in front, the kind that embassies use, turning the corner and entering the street with the market. There are a lot of embassies there, one sees those diplomatic corps cars all the time, and I registered having seen that one but did not pay a lot of attention; what I wanted was to chat with Marcelo, and there was not a lot of time."

"And Marcelo?"

"He was amused by some idea, finding something funny that I did not understand. He even mentioned that Marx once said that very organized people who insist on planning everything never come to a good end. I thought the citation was strange, so very un-Marxist. He laughed and said that Karl Marx had in fact never said that, it was somebody else. An unknown Portuguese called Marques . . ."

"And it was only now that you got the joke, right, Father?" said Lena. "That's what is called a slow wit."

"But it was really not easy to get sooner. And today, I confess that when I finally got it, I did not think it was so funny. But I recognize Marcelo's style, as your mother would say. It's the aesthetic touch in that action, the exquisite casual touch, maybe, that irony in perfectionism that only half a dozen people are going to get, but that he appreciates in silence."

Worried, Amalia asked the question that summarized everybody's concerns: "Well, and now what do we really know? And what do we do?"

There was a short silence, and then Alberto decided: "Now we act as if we did not know, and we swear, cross our hearts, that we know nothing. And we get prepared. If the men find out that he is mixed up in this story, we will hope that they come after us. Because if they come after us, it's a good sign, because it means they don't know where he is . . . And since we don't know either, we won't be able to tell."

Lena felt a shiver going down her spine. Alberto concluded: "There isn't really anything much we can do, except wait and try not to think about it all the time."

"And pray," added Amalia.

"And pray a lot," Alberto agreed.

A little later, Amalia brought in a Bible. "I know that each one of us is going to pray for him always, all along, all the time. For him and for

all of us. But I think that now, at this moment, it might be good for us
to pray together. At least read a psalm or two. And she began:

The Lord is my light and my salvation—whom shall I fear?
The Lord is the strength of my life—of whom shall I be afraid?
When the wicked, even my enemies and my foes, came
upon to eat up my flesh, they stumbled and fell.
Though an host should encamp against me, my heart shall not fear;
Though war should rise against me,
even then will I be confident.

Silently, she passed to book to her husband, who read the following
stanza. Then it was Arnaldo's turn, till they came to the verses meant
for Lena, from another psalm, that she remembered well, from having
read it again and again all those years, even through her entire religious
crisis, through the feeling of being abandoned by God that she had
in exile, when she watched on TV the arrival in Algeria of one more
group of prisoners exchanged for one more kidnapped diplomat and
saw the state they were in, from being tortured. She remembered in
particular a young woman in a wheelchair, crippled by all she had gone
through. And she could not forget how angry she had felt and how
betrayed by God, a simple-minded reaction, since she had made prom-
ises of special worship if they all escaped, taking communion weekly
thinking of the prisoners and the fugitives. The TV showed, briefly,
in a few seconds, the physical state of those who had been freed. And
Lena, sitting in her living room, in her Paris apartment, saw what Brazil was not seeing and was refusing to see. She saw the young woman
carried down from the airplane by a companion because she could no
longer walk. She saw the scars on Honorio's body, in closeup. She saw
the legs and forearms of Rodrigo, atrophied, suddenly thinned, from
hanging on the "perch." She saw Gabriel's gums raw and bleeding, one
big wound, from electric shocks. Tears tried to keep her from seeing
more. But she had to see everything, it was the least she could do. See,
so she could later tell. See for herself and for Roberta who, at that time,
somewhere in Brazil, clandestine already, must have been celebrating
the freeing of her brother. And for Teca. And for Julinho, Rodrigo's

brother, so young and a prisoner already, no more than thirteen or fourteen years old, in solitary confinement, and living through all the horrors that caused the results she now saw, through tears, on French TV. And for their mothers. And the others. And for all the mothers and sisters, fathers and brothers, children, friends, acquaintances, and strangers, for all who had had the misfortune of being born in Brazil in that generation so completely abandoned by God and crushed by a handful of men in the service of the strategic interests of another country. But even at that moment, when she decided that she would no longer believe, not in anything, not in any god that charged such a ridiculous, stupid price for the wish to be free, she could not stop herself from repeating the psalm for Marcelo, as if his whole salvation depended, superstitiously, on those who loved him weaving a safety net with words, thought, and emotion, over distances and obstacles. And in despair, when the newscast ended, Lena resolved she would never again go to communion or even to mass. But she went looking for Psalm 90 in the Bible and reread it, sobbing, remembering the first time she had read it, with her parents and her husband, in the old apartment where she had grown up:

> *You who live in the shelter of the Most High,*
> *who abide in the shadow of the Almighty,*
> *will say to the Lord, "My refuge and my fortress;*
> *my God, in whom I trust."*
> *For he will deliver you from the snare of the fowler*
> *and from the deadly pestilence;*
> *he will cover you with his pinions,*
> *and under his wings you will find refuge; his*
> *faithfulness is a shield and buckler.*
> *You will not fear the terror of the night,*
> *or the arrow that flies by day,*
> *or the pestilence that stalks in darkness,*
> *or the destruction that wastes at noonday.*
> *A thousand may fall at your side, ten thousand at your right hand,*
> *but it will not come near you.*
> *You will only look with your eyes*

and see the punishment of the wicked.
Because you have made the Lord your refuge,
the Most High your dwelling place,
no evil shall befall you, no scourge come near your tent.
For he will command his angels
to guard you in all your ways.
On their hands they will bear you up,
so that you will not dash your foot against a stone.
You will tread on the lion and the adder,
the young lion and the serpent you will trample underfoot.

And now, once again repeating those words in her mind, back home, assured that the dictatorship had ended and that Marcelo had never been caught, Lena admired Amalia's wisdom in having found this well of strength to hold up herself and her family in those very dark times. And she also noticed that now, under the sun, where the Bible itself says there is nothing new, the words of the psalm did indeed have a new meaning for her, as if they were there to instill the confidence she needed so badly to take care of what was coming apart in herself. And that was good.

But it was not time yet. The morning had been tiring, and there was a lunch table waiting for her with little bottles filled with capsules and pills of different sizes, all lined up beside her plate. She was going to take them all, obediently, like a well-behaved young girl who was following every recommendation of her doctors and getting much better. She had even managed to go for a walk along the beach. And if she went on like that, pretty soon she would be able to refresh herself by plunging her body into that lovely ocean before her, with no fear of being unable to get up and out when it was time. And the falling would be behind her. Forever. As would the child she had dreamt of and the words she longed to reach and order.

XIII

Alguns, achando bárbaro o espetáculo,
Prefeririam (os delicados) morrer.
Chegou um tempo em que não adianta morrer.
Chegou um tempo em que a vida é uma ordem.
A vida apenas, sem mistificação.

(CARLOS DRUMMOND DE ANDRADE)

Some, finding the spectacle barbaric,
Preferred (they were sensitive) to die.
The time has come when there is no point in dying.
The time has come when living is an order.
Just life, no mystification.

The basket weave was regular and tight, the strands crossing perpendicularly and forming a zig-zag design. Indian wisdom, transmitted by example to all the country craftspeople who had gone on making baskets for daily use along the years. The bottom showed that it all started with a flat square that kept growing outward and that suddenly, when it reached the proper size, was rounded up at one corner and started to rise in flexible straw walls till it grew to the height of a hand span, and received a bamboo finish that gathered the strands in a closed arc sewn up with fine bast fibers, like the rim of a sieve. The basket cover was in fact a sieve, and if Amalia wanted to, she could use it as such in the kitchen. Lena had already told her that, to be able to teach her how to make the jabuticaba jam she had learned from Carlota, she would need a sieve, and those made with bamboo were better than metal or plastic. More flexible, to let through the juicy pulp and hold back the stones. But Amalia was not going to break up her knitting basket and dirty the lid with sweets; she'd rather buy a new sieve at the old market by the quay in the neighboring town. She had to remember to add it to the shopping list later on. When she went to buy the jabuticabas. Their season was starting, and she was going to see if she could find some, not just for the jam, but also for Lena to eat. They were one of her daughter's favorite fruits, from when she was a child. She remembered her, a little kid, gorging on the small, round, black fruit, as bright as her eyes, and playing at repeating a funny sentence that she liked to call "my magic words": "Buddy, this'll bust my tummy" . . . Sometimes Amalia feared it really would. Lena threw herself on the fruits with such abandon, ate so many, swallowed so many pits, that she expected a monumental tummy-ache to follow. But fortunately, it never happened. Not even on the great-grandfather's one hundredth birthday.

"Do you remember, Lena, great-grandfather's hundredth?"

"Not me, what happened?"

"You were about five, and my grandfather had already died, but he would have been a hundred if he had lived. So my father, your grandfather, decided to have a party for him, in São Marcos, where he had been born. He rented two buses and the whole family went along, children, daughters-in-law, sons-in-law, grandchildren . . ."

"I remember very vaguely. There was a moving bridge, right?"

Amalia laughed: "It was a ferry, to cross the river. Really precarious, but that's what was available. And we did not care. Just think, a trip that takes less than two hours by car today, took us a day and a half, on that same road."

"A day and a half, Mother? From town to São Marcos?"

"The road was not paved and was one long mud track. The buses had to put chains on their wheels so as not to skid. We had to sleep on the road. And there were no bridges over any of the big rivers; all the crossings were done by ferry, often after a long wait."

Lena tried to remember more: "I think I forgot everything. I remember that funny bridge, with the buses on top and all of us on foot, outside. Now you say it is a ferry, and I understand. But the only ferry I do remember, when I knew what it was, was the one we took to the cacao plantation, when I was older."

Amalia insisted: "You really don't remember anything at all?"

"There is one thing I remember well, and we were on a bus, but I don't know if it was that trip. I remember jabuticabas."

Amalia confirmed it with a small nostalgic smile. "That's what I was wondering if you remembered. I was sure you would never forget."

"And I didn't. I think it was the first time I'd seen a jabuticaba. Before, I had only heard of the fruit, but never seen one, and I know I was always curious about what it was like, such a funny word, and everybody always saying that I had jabuticaba eyes. Then the bus stopped, with all those people on it, and Grandfather said everybody had to get out and eat jabuticabas."

It was an amusing memory. Lena almost felt, all over again, the little girl's curiosity and excitement, remembered jumping down the high step from the bus onto the muddy ground, looking around and not seeing any fruit at all, not a stand, not a basket, not a table; she could not figure out where they would be eating those jabuticabas in the shade, by the roadside, under a bunch of tall trees all in a row, on both sides, many with ladders leaning against them. Then she saw the uncles and the older cousins running to the ladders and climbing. And she noticed that up there they sat on branches. But even on the trunks she could see, attached by their short stalks, hundreds, thousands, infinite numbers of shiny little black fruits, round like marbles, stuck, it seemed, directly on the wood, almost stemless. She just stood there, gaping, and her father came and patiently taught her how to bite into the fruit, suck out the juice, and spit out the pit and the skin.

Aloud, coming back from the warm, fragrant memory, she said: "Never again in my life have I seen so many jabuticabas. It looked like something magical, a vegetable Aladdin's cave, a wonderful treasure. And someone said: 'This is endless jabuticaba . . .' And someone said: 'It will be the end of me, all right . . .' And all of that was fantastic, like a story, a fairy tale, with those words running through it, and that wonderful taste, that abundance, that view from atop the tree, beside Dad, afraid of falling, the surprise of seeing everybody sitting in the trees, even Grandfather, and a lot of laughter, a big party. Funny, up to now I never knew what that memory was about. Sometimes it comes to me and I think I dreamt it, or imagined it. I was not sure it was something that had really happened."

This time Amalia laughed out loud: "Not at all. Your grandfather had rented the trees for an hour. Over there, in São Marcos, he had run into the farmer who owned that orchard. He suggested renting the trees and the man accepted, left everything ready, prepared, waiting for us, the ladders collected from the neighborhood and all gathered there for the use of the entire family. It was a wonderful idea, an unforgettable feast."

They were silent for a while. Then Lena noted: "Strange. It's the second time I've thought of grandfather today, each a very strong memory. I think he gave me a lot, taught me a lot that I'll never forget."

Amalia was happy about this memory of her father, but not disposed to get sentimental. She decided to change the subject: "Want me to teach you something? Look."

She lifted the lid of the round Indian basket that sat on the little table beside the rattan chair. In it there was a huge variety of skeins of wool, in all colors, in all sizes, brilliant colors and pastels. "I am making an afghan. Do you want to learn?"

"Is it an easy stitch?"

"The easiest of all, Lena. The basic crochet stitch. I can teach you how to attach it so you can make these little squares."

There was no way out. Lena hated it when her mother decided to teach her handiwork. Amalia was the least patient person for this kind of thing. At least in Lena's case, she was sure of it. Amalia got exasperated about nothing, complained that Lena was not handy at anything; they always ended up annoyed with each other. Whenever she could, Lena tried to avoid that kind of situation. But now there was no way out; she would have to try. Amalia was so happy, remembering her father and the excursion, that it would be a shame to break the mood. Lena was going to make an effort.

"Let me see."

Amalia showed how the hook in the crochet needle guided the wool, made a loop, formed a pattern, generated another like it. Lena sighed with relief. It was really a very basic stitch, one that she already knew; it would not be necessary to learn anything very complicated; all she needed to figure out was how to hold the pattern so she could turn the corner. She had not done any crocheting in a long while, but she knew these things were like swimming or riding a bike—you learn it once and never forget it; it turns into an automatic movement, and all you need is a minute to get used to it again.

"See, it's easy. Try it . . . ," Amalia insisted. And gave her the wool and the needle.

Lena held it so awkwardly that she almost undid the last stitch. It was always like that, thought Amalia. How could it be that a daughter of hers was so fidgety, so clumsy? Herself, even if she tried, she would not be able to hold anything so wrong. No wonder Lena was always stumbling into things, if she could not even do something as elementary as hold a needle properly without letting the wool slip away. At times Amalia thought it was really impossible to be so awkward, and that Lena did it on purpose so nobody would ask her to do anything, just out of laziness. Deep down, that made her really unhappy, to see her daughter so incompetent, so sloppy with everything domestic, so useless. And then, to top it off, she could not stand criticism, went into an immediate sulk, got moody, answered back. Or else, she teared up, her lips trembled, and if you said the least little thing, she could well burst into tears.

"See? I did it right. I still remember the stitch. Funny; all I need to do is start, and my hand does it all by itself," said Lena, very proud of herself.

It does it pretty crookedly, thought Amalia. But she did not dare say it aloud. She controlled herself and just said: "Try to hold the needle from a different angle. And guide the wool with another finger. Let me show you. Like this, look. See? It looks different right away, all finished, not that sloppy stitch you were getting."

Lena sighed. Amalia noticed and was unsure whether at that point a sigh wasn't one of the more insolent and ill-bred ways her daughter had always found to react to any suggestion. But she decided it had been involuntary. She looked again at Lena's hands, holding the wool and the needle in such a crooked way that it made her uneasy to watch.

"No, no, not like this, child! Now you are making it too tight, it will pull . . . I don't get it! You are smart, speak various languages, went to college, know so many things, and can't learn to do a little crochet so simple that any illiterate woman can do it without even looking."

Lena blew up: "No, Mother, I really can't. I never could, I'll die without learning it! There are lots of things that illiterate people do better than I and there is no shame in it at all . . . Everybody does some things better than others. And now I know why I don't, because all my life I have been clumsy and worthless. And now I have a certificate for it, Mother. A medical certificate so I am allowed to miss handiwork class if I want to. I have a dysrhythmic node in my brain that affects my motor coordination, you hear? I am sick, I am not well."

Amalia was startled. She had not wanted this to happen. Lena was always so unpredictable. Now she was crying again, on her feet, tossing away the crochet.

"Let me do it my way, Mother. For pleasure, do you understand? I don't want to do anything as a punishment, as an obligation, as a way to be perfect . . ."

"But that's not it, child, you don't need to . . ."

"And one more thing: I don't ever again want to feel guilty because I can't do everything just so. I can't, and that's it, OK? Nobody can. Why do I have to do it right and be perfect in things that I don't know how to do? You said it yourself, I studied, I know other things. With those things, I earn my money. And I can buy as many afghans as I want, do you hear?"

Amalia thought it best to shut up and not speak about the pleasure one has in doing things with one's own hands, about the value of an object that is unique. Lena was really intractable, and it was best not to insist. But even though she had been so careful, the milk was spilt. She was hobbling toward the door of her room and closing the conversation:

"Enough, Mother, please. I am tired of all this. It has nothing to do with you, I hope you understand that, but I can't take it anymore. Leave me alone for a while, please."

And she closed the door, in tears, all upset. On the outside, Amalia was stymied. If Lena were a child, she would get a spanking or at least a time out. So she'd learn. But obviously, she had grown up and had not learned. She got furious, beside herself, when Lena made scenes like that. She felt like jumping on her, and shaking her by the shoulders till the anger went away. It was like a curse on her that she would have to put up with this kind of behavior from a child of hers, even in her old age; she'd never be shut of it.

In her room, sobbing into her pillow, Lena's thoughts were running on parallel tracks to her mother's. Would she never be rid of that pressure to be what she was not? Would she always have to go into battle to defend herself against the accusation of not being a perfect, gifted housewife, like her sisters and her sister-in-law? Would she have to be tested, all her life, till she died, on domestic virtues and good behavior in order to become worthy of Amalia's love and approval? Was it that hard to accept her as she was?

And then, as always at that point in her life, her sobs eased and gave way to more rational reflections. Amalia, too, had to be accepted as she was. She would never change those ways, and, in fact, she had changed a lot along the years. Asking her to be patient about these little things was indeed a bit much. She had spent all her patience on the big things, if you can call a Spartan stoicism a kind of patience. But Lena knew that it was she, the daughter, who would have to give in. She was the one who had gone into analysis, and she was the one who was more aware of those complicated emotional paths. She was going to get up, leave her room, and apologize.

Apologize? Even thinking of the word lit a spark of her old resistance. But she was not guilty of anything! The old familiar mechanism always made her feel guilty in the same way, whenever the machine cranked up, however well she knew that she was not. Not guilty. One of the most welcome and tenderest parts of her relation with Alonso was the certainty that it was not necessary for her to feel guilty, and the implacable clarity with which he detected any sign of that rage for self-incrimination she carried from her childhood. This was helping her greatly in getting over, little by little, the feeling of incrimination that characterized her relations with her mother.

She turned over in bed, lying on her back, counting the slats in the ceiling, as she had done so often as a child. Her breath came more regularly, and she decided to get up. All she needed was to be clear to herself; she did not need to prove anything to anyone; she did not need to persuade her mother of anything, to play anyone else's game. She knew she was not guilty of not being a traditional housewife. And she was not going to feel guilty for defending her territory like a cornered animal. Or take her illness to the point of feeling guilty for feeling guilty. Apologizing did not necessarily mean she accepted any guilt. In a dialogue between mother and daughter it was just a kind of ritual, a formal expression that meant the desire to turn the page, to indicate that it was worth it to her that they should live well together. To make peace. Be friends, as they had done as children.

She left the room, hugged Amalia, and said: "I'm sorry, Mother, I got excited about nothing."

Amalia accepted the hug, rigidly, but did not turn away, a sign of assent. She had always had the greatest difficulty expressing any kind of physical tenderness, especially toward her daughters. One day, when Lena was a preadolescent, she came running home, headlong, happy, and kissed her mother all over her face, and Amalia had complained loudly about that child popping her ears and licking her cheeks. Hurt, the girl had retreated and, for a long time, never kissed her mother, hoping that she would miss it and ask her for it. But that never happened, and six or seven years later, Lena decided to get over the incident. But she was always careful about loud or wet kisses. And so she knew that her mother was not going to return her affectionate gesture. But now Amalia did not avoid the hug, which showed that she, too, was inclined to bury that latest scene under a stone.

Indeed, she did more than signal it mutely; she said: "I did not mean to hurt you. I was just thinking of your own good. It is good to make something with one's own hands, it keeps your mind busy with something, does not allow it to think nonsense."

Lena agreed: "You are right."

A slightly awkward silence fell between the two. Lena decided to suggest another kind of handiwork: "I think I will do some drawings."

Amalia was almost enthusiastic: "That's it, child. Great idea! You have done such good drawings here. You could do some boats again, like those you gave to Luis Cesario, remember?"

"I do remember. But I feel like drawing something else, at random, just like that. Some bottles, a pitcher, something with geometric forms, a study of light and shadow, something simple."

"Oh, like the drawing he gave you, then?"

"Which one? A drawing by Luis Cesario? You must have it mixed up with something else. He never did any drawings, Mother, only as studies for paintings; he only did paintings."

Amalia insisted: "But he did give you one, one day, a huge sheet of paper, how could you have forgotten?"

Then she thought a bit longer: "Maybe you did forget, because you never took it with you. The drawing stayed here, with me, somewhere; I don't know where I put it when I moved from the city apartment. I must have brought it here, but don't know where it is."

"Are you sure? I have no idea about any of that. Why did I not take it to my own home? When was that?"

The answer explained it all, in one sentence: "It was the drawing he gave you the day before you were arrested."

"Of course. You are right. I had indeed forgotten."

But now she remembered. While she went to look for paper and pencil, rooting around in the drawers of the desk that had belonged to her grandfather, Lena wondered about the coincidence that had made her think once again, on the same day, of the events from that week. As if she were under an obligation to live through all of it again, all at once.

Three days after the kidnapping of the American ambassador, the manifestoes of the kidnappers had been broadcast, the prisoners whose names were on the list had been released and banished to Mexico, and the photos of their arrival sent to Brazil. And then, on a late winter afternoon, when it was getting dark early, the ambassador was released in a square in the North Zone, where he took a taxi and arrived, safe and sound, at the embassy. The news was on radio and TV, and right after that, censorship was reestablished.

Shortly afterward, Lena's phone rang. It was the dear voice of Luis Cesario, who announced, somewhat laconically: "I am calling to tell you that the drawing I promised you is ready. It came out great, just as you wanted it, if I may say so myself."

She had not asked for any drawing; he had not promised anything; she had no idea what this drawing could be all about. But she thanked him, cautiously, and waited. Her friend went on: "You need to come and pick it up soon, because the sheet is huge, and can get crumpled. We are home, why don't you come over?"

"Sure. I'm on my way."

The old man added: "But don't worry about the size. It is not framed. You can roll it up and carry it easily. I know you don't have a car right now, but you can take it anyway. I am dying to show it to you, so don't delay."

Lena hung up and told Arnaldo. "It was Luis Cesario. He wants me to go there right away, to pick up a drawing that he promised me. It's urgent."

"Now? Can't you do it some other day?"

"He was very impatient."

"But this makes no sense, Lena. On a day like this, with the police running around like mad searching everybody and everything, you'll go out now, without a car, to go to the other side of town and pick up a drawing, that's just crazy."

Lena paused, looked at him, and said:

"Arnaldo, he never promised me any drawing. And he knew perfectly well that I have no car."

"So? Another good reason not to go."

She insisted: "But I do think that I have to go. Precisely because of everything you said. I think the drawing was a pretext, in case the telephone was bugged. For real, it's something else, and urgent."

That caught Arnaldo's attention: "Like what?"

"Do you remember that key to his house? I gave it to Marcelo, and he said he would only use it if things got desperate, and if everything went wrong. And he still has my car."

Arnaldo jumped up: "Holy shit! Then let us go there right away, before they find the car some place over there."

"Not us. I am going by myself."

"No way! What if something happens?"

"If something happens and we are together, it will happen to both of us. It will take forever till anyone learns of it. It is better for me to go on my own and for you to wait so you can alert the world."

It was obvious that Arnaldo did not like that one bit: "I don't know. Why don't we do it the other way around? I'll go, and you stay here and sound the alarm if I don't return."

"We could do it that way. But I still think it's better if I go. I am his sister, the car is in my name, I was the one Luis Cesario telephoned. In short, I think it would be much easier for me to explain my role in this as normal."

Much against his will, Arnaldo finally accepted the plan. But he imposed conditions: "OK. But this is how we will do it. I'll take you there and wait for you somewhere nearby, in a place we agree on. If you don't return in time, I'll know something happened."

With everything arranged, they took off. Two or three blocks from Luis Cesario's, as they cased the area, they saw Lena's car parked in a side street. Apart from that, everything looked perfectly quiet. They separated, according to plan. At her friend's house, she found her brother, as she had surmised. And all was very quick; they hadn't a second to waste. Right away, she told him that she knew he was involved, and so did their parents.

"Well, yes. It would be best if you also did not have to know where I am. But we had a hole in the security system, we can't trust it, and I thought it best to use your emergency exit. And we have to get that car out if here right away, or it gets really dangerous."

"Did you use my car?"

"In the action? No, don't worry. But one of the companions who was out of the loop used it, drove right in front of the house where we were staying and that the police were watching. They could have written down the license and that's where there could be a problem."

He looked at her and said, fondly: "I am asking your guardian angel to look after you, as Father would say. If anything happens, don't panic, Lena. Tell the truth up to the point where it might incriminate someone. All I ask is that I be notified right away. Let us have forty-eight hours to set up another system. Then you can open up, because I will be gone."

She swallowed. It was like a nightmare. She asked: "And the owners of the house?"

"In that case, I'll set up an exit that makes it seem as if they had been forced to shelter me, you can be sure of that. Nothing will happen to them. Or to us, for that matter. Nobody knows I am here, and there is not the slightest chance they will suspect it. I arrived a little more than an hour ago, and you are off with the car, and there is no sign of anything left. Just keep calm; that's the most important part."

She hugged him, and felt like crying. "God keep you. And know that I am very proud of you."

"One more thing. How did people react on the street? Were they really happy, as I was told?"

"From what I saw, it was a party, in secret."

"I am glad. Bye. When I can, I'll get in touch. Tell the old people that I am well and, if there is no news of me, that's good news."

As she left, she embraced Luis Cesario and Carlota with tears in her eyes. The old man said: "I am happy and proud to be able to help, Lena. I thank you very much, my dear, for having given us the opportunity to do something for freedom in this country at this point in our lives, at our age . . ."

"Forget that, my dear friend. I am the one who does not know how to thank you."

"He has character in addition to courage. When he arrived, he introduced himself and told us the truth. He did not hide the risk, he did not lie, and he let us choose freely whether we wanted him to stay. He can stay as long as he needs to. And he'll only leave if he wants to. So long as we are alive, we will not let anyone take him away—you can rest assured of that."

She was indeed sure. And this certainty worried her the most. But she could not linger; she had to leave right away, take the car somewhere far from that part of town, meet up with Arnaldo at the time they had set. She kissed Carlota and left. Luis Cesario called her back: "The drawing!"

"What drawing?"

"This sheet here. Didn't you come to pick up a drawing? You can't return without it."

The roll was placed on the back seat of the car. She almost forgot to take it in when she got to her parents' house, sometime later, to give them the news, after getting through a number of roadblocks with her car, fearing, each time, that she would not make it. And she had completely forgotten her intention to retrieve, someday, the sketches by old Luis Cesario that her mother had carefully kept on top of the wardrobe. She even forgot their existence. But that was not surprising. Other things had occupied her mind in the hours and days that followed.

That night she slept badly, a light and fitful sleep, haunted by fear and nightmares. The day after, as she was frying a steak for lunch, she was arrested.

She was lucky not to have been tortured, despite the constant threats meant to intimidate her. To help herself concentrate and not allow her imagination to call up possible scenes of horror, she mentally repeated texts she knew by heart, as if they were magic words. One of them, in particular, gave her unexpected strength. The moment she was being taken to the police van, in front of her house, she saw a man walking down the street. Her most beloved poet, whose words had so often rescued her and fed her. She saw the scene from the outside, as if she were a spectator: she under arrest and he walking by the car, oblivious. She remembered some of his verses:

Prisoner of my class and clothes,
I walk in white on the grey streets.
Melancholies, merchandise stalk me.
Shall I carry on unto nausea?
Can I rebel without the weapons?

She realized that, in the few seconds it had taken him to walk past, she had been able to think of something other than her fear, and that, for a moment, had done her good. She saw the poet walking away. He was gone. More lines came to her:

The first love is gone.
The second love is gone.
The third love is gone.
But the heart remains.

She kept repeating: "But the heart remains, but the heart remains, but the heart remains." Heart, courage. The same thing. *Cor, cordis,* Latin for heart, third declension. Cordial. Cordiality. Learning by heart. To accord, to record, to hearten. Heart, courage. The heart remains, life remains. Prison could seem like the end of the world, but it was not. The heart remains. In it there were Marcelo, Luis Cesario, Carlota, who needed her wits and her courage. She would think of that, of the poem. And try to remember the rest, and other poems. By other poets. They all had much to tell her at this time and she needed to listen.

And so she was taken away. While she waited in a room for her turn to be questioned, they saw them throwing in a young guy she knew by sight, from the beach. He had been roughed up and was pushed away by two men, through the door. He fell to the floor, was kicked, and a third man handcuffed him to the leg of the bench where she was sitting. She and another young man who was waiting in the same room bent down to him. He managed to mumble his name and where he worked, a weekly review. The other guy said:

"They are picking up any journalist they can get their hands on. The say that one of the kidnappers is a journalist, that the manifesto was written using a way of abbreviating words that we are the only ones to use. And it seems they already know it was written on a portable typewriter belonging to someone who works there in a newspaper and had already written a lot of articles on it at his home. They are searching for the guy and the typewriter also . . ."

"Shut up over there! Do you think this is some kind of a parlor?" interrupted a guard, opening the door. "You feel like talking? You'll be talking a lot right away . . . You there, girlie, it's your turn."

And she went. Five men took turns interrogating her, some harsher and more threatening, others less so. But they did not touch her. They wanted to know about her car. She confirmed that she had lent it to her brother. She did not know what he wanted it for. She imagined it was for a date; he had not said anything, and she had not asked. That's how she was brought up, a sister had no business asking her brother where he was going or what he was going to do. The men understood that perfectly. Then they wanted to know whether she knew where the car was. She said she did. That took them aback. They all stopped what they had been doing and gathered around her to hear the great revelation. Their suspense was so visible that she was afraid of the anticlimax that her answer would bring about: "It was parked in front of my house. Didn't you see it when you came to pick me up?" When one of them explained that it had been another group, she realized the roles had been reversed for a moment. She was being interrogated.

But she had just asked a question and the interrogators had answered. Confusion reigned. They gave orders that someone should go and see if it was true. She prepared to wait for a few hours till someone went and returned with the information. She thought that was good, since she had to give Marcelo those forty-eight hours he needed. But they were quick. In a few minutes the answer came back, that the car was there all right, right in front, on the right side of the street. The speed told Lena that her house was under surveillance. And she prepared for the worst: now she would have to explain how the VW bug had gotten there. But nobody asked. They interrupted the interrogation and took her back to the other room, which was now completely empty. She waited for a few more hours. They came back for her. They read her the transcript of her testimony, asked her to sign it. And, late at night, ordered her to get back home. She went back, called her mother, took a pill, and went to sleep, exhausted, expecting that the following day they would discover the flaw in the interrogation and pick her up again.

As soon as she woke up, and before she really felt like it, she came into the middle of a conversation between Arnaldo and the lawyer in their living room. They were evaluating the situation. The day before, her parents' house had been invaded as well. Everything had been searched and her father had been arrested, but they had not done anything to Amalia or the younger children. Fernando had been detained as well, and interrogated in the town where he lived, but had already been freed. They had looked for Teresa at her home, but she had not been there—she had been warned and gone to sleep elsewhere. Alberto had been released late at night. But they had arrested him again early in the morning. Another group. The building where Lena lived was under ostentatious surveillance. Everything indicated that she was about to be arrested again. Unless . . .

"Unless what?" she asked.

"Unless they released you on purpose, to serve as bait."

"How is that?"

The lawyer explained: "Lena, they know that Marcelo had the car all those days. And, suddenly, here it is, back with you. It follows that you had some contact with him, or that you know how to get in touch with him. So they keep Alberto locked up, so as to cut any communication between Marcelo and his father. And they let you loose, closely watched. You make a wrong move, give them a clue, and they find Marcelo."

"Don't you think this is a rather fanciful hypothesis?"

"I don't think so at all. I am convinced that this is what is probably happening. Their action had a lot of security flaws. At this point they know who participated, where they kept the ambassador, what cars were used, on what typewriter they wrote the manifesto, all of that. They have gone into the house and collected a ton of fingerprints. All they need is to find the people, and that's just a question of time. They will be able to trace some of them. Others seem to have evaporated. And they must be pretty sure that you can take them to Marcelo. Now, it's just a question of being patient."

"Are you sure?"

"Nobody can guarantee something like this, Lena. If they come back to arrest you again, right away, it's because they chose to go for the stupid solution, and use force, beat you up and make you talk. But now, almost twenty-four hours since they arrested you, there has been enough time for Marcelo to be warned and to have created a way of leaving where he is, if that's necessary. From the point of view of the repression, it is smarter to let you go, thinking that it is all over. They are going to encourage you till you let your guard down and lead them to your brother."

"And what should I do?"

"Act as if you had not noticed. Lead an absolutely normal life. Go to work at the usual time, go to the market on the usual day, go to the movies with your husband, visit your family, all as you always do it. But keep alert, especially to see who is watching you at any one of those places."

Lena tried to make a joke out of it, never realizing how close it was to truth, to what her movements would look like in the coming weeks: "You mean I'll have to turn myself into a professional paranoid. Should I start finding people following me wherever I go?"

"We'll help you, Lena. You are not alone," Arnaldo reassured her.

"And for you this hypothesis is much better than the brutal and stupid solution, remember this. Though it might be more dangerous."

"It's not that bad, don't exaggerate . . ."

The lawyer was firm: "I am not exaggerating; I am warning. All through my professional career I have seen incredibly determined people, who could bravely withstand the worst tortures without giving up a secret. But few people can withstand strict surveillance without betraying themselves, without relaxing for that one fatal minute. And you'll have to watch out for twenty-four hours a day, we don't know for how long. Watch out on the telephone, or when greeting acquaintances on the street with a warmer smile. You, too, Arnaldo, of course. It's as if you were carrying a fatal virus that does not harm you but that is highly contagious and could be spread by any person you come across."

Lena shivered. "This is awful. I feel as if I were carrying the plague."

"A ticking bomb," said Arnaldo.

"That's it, precisely. A ticking bomb, ready to explode at any moment, but nobody knows when."

Thoughtful, Lena asked: "I need some time to get used to this idea."

The lawyer touched her hand kindly and said: "OK, so long as it is a short time. Go off by yourself for a few minutes, take a bath, get ready, and get going. You missed work yesterday, and should not be late today. And you have to catch up on what you did not get done. Carefully. Remember that everybody at the paper knows that you are the sister of one of the kidnappers, and everybody will want to talk about it. You have to cut it short, for the sake of everyone's safety. But few people know that you were arrested yesterday; maybe nobody knows."

Nevertheless, as soon as Lena arrived at the office, one of her fellow workers came up to her and said: "Good to see you here. I did not think they would release you so quickly."

Surprised, she answered: "What are you talking about?"

He pulled out a pass and said: "Look, I edit the police newsletter in my free time. I am very well informed. I know that they arrested you yesterday because of your brother's car."

She was firm: "Sorry, but I don't want to talk about it. I need to get to work."

She went to her desk, opened the drawer, started to move some papers around. Another co-worker came up to her, looking mysterious. She knew him only from greeting him; they had never really talked. But he sounded very solicitous: "Careful about that guy who was talking to you. We think that he is a police informant. What did he want?"

Suddenly she had a funny feeling. She noticed the new climate in which she was now condemned to move. She just answered: "Please, I need to get to work."

The guy insisted: "What was that card he was showing you? Be careful about him, Lena. If you need anything you can count on me; I am here to help you."

"I thank you."

"I know you are going through a difficult time, but I want you to know that I am your friend and am on your side. Do you need anything? Would you like me to call anyone? Give anyone any messages?"

Something caught her attention in this, and she felt a suspicion arising about what the others in the office would confirm months later, when she was already in exile. Those two were working as a team: the one, fairly openly an informer, and the other ostensibly a friend and helper. All she said was: "Thank you very much. If I should need anything I will be sure to ask. It is comforting to be able to count on people in times like this one. But now I have to get to work."

And she did plunge into her work. And into the infected life she started living till the day when she could no longer take it and left the country. It was a life in which she had to flee everyone she loved, outside of her family, to protect everything she knew. First of all, Marcelo and those who had hidden him. But much more. Whoever owned the typewriter that had been used for the first manifesto, for instance. Or who had provided the blindfold and the dark glasses used to keep the ambassador from seeing where they took him when he was kidnapped. And she also had to protect other people. Adriano's parents, who had helped get Teca out of the country. Ivan, the college professor who had sheltered a fugitive student leader in his home. Even the fugitive, who had trusted her and opened the door on the afternoon when she was hiding the typewriter. Roberta's grandmother, in whose basement there was a clandestine press, and not even she knew about it. And so many people who did not even know her or imagine she knew so much. And for that it was necessary to keep her eye on the rearview mirror and watch for cars following her when she left for work in the morning. And observe the sign the man at the newspaper stand made to the doorman at a neighbor's building. And the solicitude of the waiter at the bar. And the readiness of the taxi driver who had rejected a fare at the corner and come to pick her up. And the clerk at the store . . . but no, it was not possible, she was imagining things, it was impossible that she should be watched like that, she was going crazy, paranoid, she had to relax. And at that point she remembered the lawyer saying that everybody ends up relaxing some day and giving a watcher a clue. So she tensed up again, refused invitations from friends, gave people one-sentence answers, afraid they would tell her something and she would then know even more, afraid they, too, would be followed and run into trouble, afraid, afraid, afraid. But the heart goes on. But the heart goes on. Goes on. She thought she would really have gone mad if Arnaldo had not found a cargo ship whose charterer wanted to collaborate, just think, and was offering a cabin for nothing, to get her out of the country. And so they left behind the land of the palm trees where the thrush sings. Just like Marcelo had left, by land, three weeks before. But they had not known that then. All they knew was that he had left Luis Cesario's recently. And for her and her friends' safety, she was not to go there, not even to take leave of him.

XIV

Debaixo do sol observei ainda o seguinte:
a injustiça ocupa o lugar do direito,
e a iniquidade ocupa o lugar da justiça.
Então eu disse comigo mesmo:
"Deus julgará o justo e o ímpio,
porque há tempo para todas as coisas
e tempo para toda obra."

(ECCLESIASTES 3:16–17)

And I saw under the sun
that in the place of law, there was injustice,
and in the place of justice there was iniquity.
And I said to myself:
"God will judge the just and the impious,
for there is a time for everything,
and a time for every deed."

Pus-me então a considerar todas as opressões
que se exercem sob o sol.
Aqui as lágrimas dos oprimidos,
e ninguém para os consolar.

(ECCLESIASTES 4:1)

Then I saw all the kinds of oppression
that are done under the sun.
Behold the tears of the oppressed,
and no one to comfort them.

That had to be the most beautiful little newsstand in the country. Not because it was huge, or well ordered, with an abundance of imported magazines, or serials just in from the bindery, or books, picture stamps, old issues from series, newspapers from other capitals, or all the wonders that the big stands have room to keep, protected from bad weather, those well-lit, inexhaustible metal treasure troves of printed matter. Not at all. It was smallish and modest, with a few newspapers and rare weeklies amid farming manuals, crossword puzzle collections, comics, and countless sealed plastic bags that did not quite hide pornographic magazines. And everything old, weathered by sun and sea breezes. But Lena doubted there existed another stand in so wonderful a location, under the sun hats, right on the sand, amid the beached boats.

When she was a child there had been none of that. The newsstand was a recent novelty. But even weathered, faded, it was more than a novelty. It was an invitation. It said: "See? Now you can come live here and you won't be isolated; come, come write your play, put your characters on paper, and I'll guarantee you two daily doses of contact with the rest of the world, whenever you want them; a portable connection you can use anywhere, on the sand or under the trees, free from the slavery of the set times of the news hours on radio or TV, bullies that they are, imposing their reading and keeping from you the pleasure of discoveries between the lines."

This morning, for instance, Lena had decided to sit on the little seat at the stern of one of the boats to read the paper. Every day she increased somewhat the distance she covered on her morning walk. Today she had reached the village, walked all the way to the stand to buy her paper. She was happy to have made it, though she had had to rest her foot a while before starting on her way back. But she was conquering new territory every day. Soon she would even be able to reach the small shipyard at the end of the beach. And, if she went on that way, she might even, any moment, and with company, dare go into the water. Those were the advantages of taking all her medicines, like a good girl. She was no longer falling. The days were slowly left behind, those days when she suddenly found herself on the ground, with no sense of balance or idea of a horizon, without the least notion of how she had gotten there.

She glanced at the first page, read the summary of the main news of the day. It was too windy to open the paper completely; that made it harder. She folded it and chose her favorite bylines, reading quarter page by quarter page. The world went on; the country went on; life went on. The heart goes on, as she knew and had recently remembered. But it was good to follow history every day as it dripped from the pages of the newspaper. Lena was a voracious reader, and faithful. She read everything that fell into her hands, but could not do without *her* paper, going through it from end to end, politics, the economy, local, international, sports, culture, leisure, letters to the editor, editorials, fashion, recipes, every single section. And she compared news, established relations among apparently disconnected items, demanded clarity, explanations, honesty. It made her furious when the police blotter condemned someone without benefit of a trial, especially when two days later a different commissioner came up with a different hypothesis and nobody thought of clearing the name of the first suspect. A well-written article made her happy; she savored every sentence, read it aloud to anyone who happened to be near her, quoted it all day in conversation. A well-researched article made her proud, when the reporter focused on what was pertinent and not on what some clever source wanted him to see. At times she wished she could be just an ordinary reader, so she could write to the editor praising and complaining as she pleased. She felt great tenderness for those in her profession. And for that very reason, she was pitiless about the faults that betrayed what she considered to be the essence of journalism: to inform honestly. She knew that, during the dictatorship, the environment in the office, like everything else, had reflected the times. At the newspapers there were worthy people and bastards. And, as was the case everywhere, the military regime provided the ideal soil for the blossoming of the latter. As well as for the lesser bastards, the enablers. At that time, she had lived and seen, with her own eyes, episodes that she was ashamed to even recall. A news editor receiving bribes from gambling bosses. A reporter denouncing colleagues to the police. An editor forbidding, as if on orders, the publication of news items that the censors had forgotten to suppress. But she had also witnessed the solidarity, the courage, and the professionalism that investigated the right-wing coup, denounced scandals, questioned the official version. And she had also witnessed beautiful individual acts of professional creativity and quiet bravery in resistance. She knew that, if the dictatorship had finally ended, it was to a great extent thanks to the dedicated work of her colleagues. It was gratifying to observe now that often the old bosses, who had co-operated with the dictatorship directly or indirectly, were slowly being replaced by more capable journalists and worthier people. For Lena, these were some of the clearest symptoms that they were all living in new times. And few things in the press had the same symbolic value for her as being able to open *her* newspaper every day and happily find a column signed by the same intellectual whose name had been barred from mention in those very pages by a veto from Barros.

In fact, Barros was a master of those things. Once he had come to the point of calling a meeting with all the subeditors to inform them that a certain big shot, scandalously corrupt and incompetent but well ensconced in power, had bought a large number of shares in the pa-per. But that was confidential information, he'd said, which under no circumstances could be mentioned, because it was all done through a front man, and it would not look good, you know how it is . . . Still, they needed to know, so they could avoid any criticism of the individ-ual in question. And this situation went on for a long time. Only years later did Lena find out that it had all been a lie. That Barros, who at the time had been having an affair with one of the big shot's daughters, had decided to protect his extramarital father-in-law.

Nevertheless, this same Barros had made some beautiful gestures. He had taken advantage of his position and his prestige to get news about some imprisoned journalists so he could inform their families. And on at least one occasion he had been able to find a colleague in a particularly difficult situation, wounded and in prison, tortured while hospitalized—Barros's intervention had been crucial to protect him. And later, when Honorio was exchanged for another kidnapped dip-lomat and banished from the country, at the time when kidnappings were no longer surprising and had begun to be routine, involving ever less important diplomatic personnel and more violent action in ex-change for ever fewer prisoners, in negotiations where the government drove an ever harder bargain, spending more than a month temporizing before rejecting the list so the kidnappers had to accept the freeing of other names that had been on the second list—well, at that time, when everything was very hard and difficult, when most journalists preferred to act as if they had never heard of Honorio, Barros surprised everyone. As soon as banished Honorio had set foot in the land of his exile, Barros had started to send him a copy of the paper every day so he would stay connected to his country. That same paper that Lena could not now do without and spent so much effort to secure every day, at the little stand by the sea. She smiled at the thought. She would have to tell this to Honorio, someday. For the sake of fairness. Because he may never have known the risk Barros had run for his sake, or the kind solidarity of the gesture.

Just like Barros, other coins had their two faces as well. A bit of a cliché, thought Lena. You could say that about anyone. But she was thinking of another term: two faces. Maybe that was too strong; she did not want to seem judgmental. She had lived with other professional groups in her life, and had observed environments that were more envious, more destructive, more scheming than journalism. But she had never seen such distinctive and at the same time such contradictory traits as in her profession, especially in those times. Contradictory and incoherent. Maybe even now. As in strenuously defending free speech and being unable to bear the least criticism, arguing, as soon as anyone raises any objection to a report that they are restricting the freedom of the press. But back then it had been more complicated. And the conditions allowed for someone like Barros, shallow and friends with torturers, to insist on keeping a former guerrilla, exiled abroad, abreast of events at home. And the same conditions allowed Teixeira and Maria Alice, leftist militants, with a family history of courageous and commendable activity in the resistance, to intercept this information and not allow it to reach its destination.

For Lena that discovery had been a shock. And it had cost her one of the two closest friendships she had made in exile, a very high price. Like all exiles, she and Arnaldo were hungry for news from Brazil. And Teixeira, as a correspondent for a Rio paper, received the publication every day. Every once in a while, after reading it, he would lend it to Lena and Arnaldo. As their friendship became closer, based on affinity and real affection, those borrowings became more regular. Eventually, they had developed a ritual: on the weekend one of them would go over to return a week's worth of papers and collect the latest issues. One of those times Teixeira remarked: "Look, you can keep the papers, lend them to others. No need to return them."

Immediately, Lena thought of the professional angle: "But don't you want even the first section? Or cuttings? For your files? It could be useful; you don't have the collection available otherwise for consultation, should you need it . . ."

Teixeira explained: "No, you can keep it. We have doubles."

"Doubles? How come? The paper only sends one; there is no room in the bag for more."

"Well, yes, theoretically. But in reality, Barros found a way, no idea how, and we get two every day."

Arnaldo got excited: "But this is wonderful. Lots of people want it, and we could circulate this."

"No," said Teixeira. "Nobody is to know. And these papers belong to someone."

And then he showed it to them, behind the curtain. It was a pile of newspapers, open on the floor for stability, almost as tall as Lena. It was obvious they had not been touched, or crumpled from being read. She thought that was really strange. "What is this?"

"Well, Barros sends an extra issue for us to send to Honorio in Argel."

"Don't you have his address? I do. Look, you can write it down."

There was an embarrassed silence. Little by little, with some words from Teixeira, completed by Maria Alice, they explained. They were afraid that the Brazilian government would somehow get wise to the correspondence reaching those who had been banished. And if they saw papers arriving regularly from Paris, then they themselves would come under suspicion. But they did not dare tell that to Barros or to communicate with Honorio to see whether there were any alternatives. Lena had a suggestion. "Look, I have an idea. I can talk to someone at that library where I work. It is run by the church, and they are just so eager to help. I am sure they would be able to organize a weekly shipment, in an official library mailer, and even pay postage. I am sure there would be no problem."

The unease became palpable. "No need to bother, Lena," said Maria Alice. "You are so busy anyway."

"It is no bother at all, and it would be so important for the guys there in Argel. I can take these tomorrow . . ."

Now there was a wall between them. You could not cut it even with a knife. Lena decided to act as if she had not noticed, just so the papers could reach their destination.

"You'll have all this bother for nothing, Lena," Maria Alice insisted.

"It's not worth it," said Teixeira.

Arnaldo burst in: "Do you think Honorio knows that Barros is sending him these papers?"

"I don't know," said Teixeira. "But Barros said it was Honorio who asked him."

Lena said, even more firmly: "I am sorry, but I don't think we have the right to let this pile grow without doing anything. Either you tell Barros that they won't send it on . . ."

"But how, Lena? He is the boss. We can't refuse."

"Yes, you can. You have the right to say no, if you are afraid. He is not giving you a professional order."

"It's not fear; it's caution."

"Whatever. Either you refuse, or you send on the papers. I can't see a middle way."

"Nobody needs to know," Teixeira said, feebly.

Lena came to a decision. "You are right; nobody needs to know."

Teixeira looked at her and guessed what she meant. "What? Are you going to send it anyway?"

She assented, serious. "I am. But you need not know. I will send ours, those you just said we could keep, and need not return. And this way it is all solved. No risk for you."

"You have no right to do this! Everybody will think it was us."

"I'll put down my name as the sender. It is not a crime to send an old newspaper to an exile, not even in Brazil."

"Everybody will know that we are the ones who get it here."

"OK, then."

Lena decided to give in. She did not need to say what she was going to do. She'd just do it, and that would be that.

But Teixeira was not fooled. Never again did he lend them or give them a paper. If they wanted to read one, they would have to do it there, in his room, by the growing pile. And later, not even that. Every time Lena and Arnaldo came to visit, the others were just leaving. If they called ahead, the couple had an appointment and would not be there. And they themselves never called. On one rainy night, when there was a strike at the metro and Lena was on the street, near their apartment, pregnant, with no money and no way to get home, she went up and asked whether she could sleep in their living room or borrow ten francs for a taxi. They could not help. The money that she could see on a shelf was for some payments they had to make early the next morning, and a friend of theirs was about to arrive any minute and might need the couch in the living room, since the metro was on strike. At least, that was what they said. Just as they had told Barros that they would send on the papers that Honorio had never received. Oh, well. But the friendship that had thus melted down left a painful scar.

Now all were back. Each living his or her own life, chatting cordially when they ran into each other, as if nothing had happened. Neither the warmth of the friendship nor the disappointment of the break. Weird people, journalists. But she was leaving it behind, to an extent, having decided to cut down on day-to-day business at the newsroom in order to work on her play. And then there was her illness, which now extended her leave beyond anything she had envisioned. Don't think about that. Look ahead. Look at the ocean, the horizon, the waves forming all of a sudden, from nothing, and breaking hard on the beach, as the tide rises, eating the sand greedily, hungry to swallow it all, to cover, possess, impregnate every pore in the sand, holding, enlacing, embracing. Alonso . . .

Do not think of that either, do not think of him, push away that other cup that insists on being carried slowly, carefully so it won't spill, a ritual offering to a hidden godhead, silent and indifferent. An elixir she did not want to drink willingly. Blood. Push it away. Do not think.

She decided to get up and start on her way back home. She stepped on the good foot, pushed against the rim of the boat, stood up, stepped out of the frame, and onto the sand. She remembered that her mother had asked her to buy something at the greengrocer's stand. Some greens for a salad, fruit, herbs, she did not quite remember what. Good thing she had made herself a little list like someone who knew she could not trust her banged-up memory for anything. At least not for recent events, because the earlier ones occupied her whole memory, stubborn and obsessive. Maybe that was why there was no room for anything demanding attention in the present.

She dug into her pockets looking for the list. After a while she found the piece of paper, carefully folded with the money. She stopped at the stand, contemplated the shiny skin of the oranges, the glowing bulk of the tomatoes, the purple moonlight of the eggplants. She appreciated the fake dew on the small watercress leaves, recently sprayed with water. She unfolded the paper and glanced at it to see what she had written down on the list her mother had dictated to her.

No way of knowing. There was nothing to read.

She looked again, her eyes misting over. The same. Those were not the scratches of the illiterate, because the letters were there, clearly drawn. But they did not form words. At best, one or another random meaningless syllable. Their only meaning was the disease.

She turned her back to the vegetable stand, took a few halting steps toward the beach, and let herself fall on the sand anyhow; she opened the paper once again, and looked. The letters did not spell out anything. She looked at the newspaper, folded in her hand. She could read it all. She was reduced to semi-illiteracy. She could read, but she could not write. Even when she tried it like this, absentmindedly, just a succession of nouns, a list of fruits and vegetables. Something was happening on the way between her brain and her hand; some orders were not being followed, traps set. She thought she was writing, was certain that this time everything would come out right, and immediately realized that all she had traced was an illegible scrawl. She was being tripped up by herself, tricked by the feeling that the words were flowing, the reasoning was a logical chain, ideas came when called. She had in fact noticed that she was not able to really formulate them all that well; the sounds got tangled up, tripped over each other, replaced one another without being told, searched for others like them. She noted: in daily conversations with her mother, Amalia concentrated to decode her utterances, as if she were a foreigner with a heavy accent, and garbled sentences. At times she did catch her own stutterings, the substitution of phonemes, the difficulty in finding a word she knew should be there but wasn't. But she was sure it was a motor problem. Her thoughts were lively and sharp. She imagined she was lucid and in control of her ideas. She thought that the physical difficulties were small and temporary and were certainly getting better, like the broken toe slowly healing. Time and rest. But no. Now she saw that it was just the opposite. Before she had come to her mother's house, in her attempt to write the release for Paulo, she had replaced words with others that sounded like them. But now it was much worse—nothing resembled anything on her list, apart from the arrangement of the scribbles in rows of useless letters. Words continued to flee from her, but the speed and efficiency of the flight had increased. Now they were able to get so far away that it was impossible to retrieve them.

The tide was rising, the waves breaking hard, the water coming close to Lena's feet. Close to both, the good one and the broken one. Careless, like a road coming to retrieve her, open, offering itself wide to relieve her. For a world without words and without pain. Right there, silence. On the other side of the wall of noisy, wild, foaming waves, eddies pulling, calling, exploding into vertigo—vroom! Drawing her into peace. Into where words were unnecessary, or balance.

Loose on the sand, the newspaper was being unfolded and carried away on the wind. Lena threw the list of vegetables after it, or that thing that should have been a list. It was light and taken farther away. The instant it touched the sand, a wave picked it up and it disappeared, leaving no trace. So quick, so simple. Just as it ought to be.

She lay down on the sand and closed her eyes. She felt tired through and through. As in the poem by Fernando Pessoa: "supremest tiredness, -emest, -emest tiredness." Never to open her eyes again, letting herself be taken away, once and for all. Lay down the arms she had wielded all her life, feinting against that force, day after day, that was so much stronger, more insistent, more patient than she was. And it was not worth going on against it. What for? She was not going to write that play; now she knew it for sure. She was not going to have the child she had wanted so much, that new life in her shared womb, her own and Alonso's cells fused to change the course of future time. She would not even be able to go on with her small life as before, writing for the newspaper in words she had chosen, walking, dancing, traveling, going to the beach like any well-balanced thinking biped. Or chatting, easily, like any normal person who opens her mouth and says what comes to her mind in the most natural way in the world. Without effort, victory, struggle. As if it were a hereditary right. She was very tired. Exhausted. With no will at all to fight that hopeless fight, running after what should be naturally hers. With no inclination even to rise now, walk to the ocean, speed up the response to the call of the full tide. No strength to open her eyes and chase away the dog that was sniffing at her, his cold muzzle against her skin.

But eventually she could not stand it—it was too uncomfortable. She sat up, stretching out her arm, away from herself, as if to tell the animal to leave. He paid no attention at all, licked her hand, and curled up on the ground beside her. Just like Fifina used to do by Luis Cesario's side. Missing her friend, Lena stroked the dog's head, passed her hand down his back and along his neck. She felt an artery pulsing strong and slow. But the heart goes on, goes on. She recollected herself. In order to get up without help, she had to crouch, like the animal she was. Conscious of that, she was amused, like the person she could not but be.

Like a person. Erect, on two feet, one in front of the other, returning home. Even though she was limping, making slow progress along the little dirt road that bordered the beach, since the tide was high, and the strip of sand had narrowed and softened, offering little support. Slowly, looking at the sea, listening to the sea, feeling on her skin the moisture and in her mouth the briny taste of the sea air. Ever-present animal, panting. God enchanted in liquid form. Absolute energy.

Slowly, trying not to think of the remaining distance, knowing only that every minute brought her closer, slowly—or further from what she was leaving behind. As on a sea voyage, on her way to an unknown exile of uncertain duration. Anything would be better than the hell she was leaving. Big Brazil, little Brazil. It had the size of the dictatorship.

Bigger than any dictatorship. Survivor of any dictatorship, except of the one subsisting inside of it.

It was a long journey, a difficult trek. Like hers, about which Honorio did not want to know anything. Different from the zip-zip of a jet flight, overnight, go to sleep here, wake up there, in a different time zone, a different climate, a different language. Like Jorge, thrown anyhow into a plane, semi-doped with drink so he would not complain, convinced that he would find some ghost waiting for him in Paris, and all it was, was the ghost of freedom. And he only understood what had happened months later, when Lena arrived and they met to collate the different angles of the story.

On the day of the kidnapping, after leaving Lena's house, he had gone to a library, where he wanted to check some data he needed for his thesis. He had spent the whole day there. When he left the library, he noticed the subdued glee in the city, celebrating something, nobody knew quite what, a fleeting and diffuse difference. He went into a bar and joined the party. And since he had not the faintest idea of how close to the eye of the tornado he had been, he just gave himself over to the secret euphoria that warmed those clandestine hearts. He was happy he had returned to watch his people resist, close enough to see the first steps on the way to their liberation. It was just an embryo, but one could see that it would grow, and make the "*événements de mai*" take on the proportions of a children's game. He spent the next few days reasonably buzzed, floating on the divine-marvelous clouds of the festivities. And then it happened. His most secret dream came true.

It was on the night when the ambassador was freed. Jorge was returning to the house of Adriano's parents, light and cheerful, when he saw before him, from the back, walking quickly along the pavement, Teca's beloved form. He hurried up and caught up with her. He put his hand on her shoulder, and she turned quickly and gave him a push that almost knocked him down. Then she cried out: "Jorge! How wonderful!"

And before he could recover from the shock, she was hugging him, burying her face in his chest, and saying: "Take me away from here! Quickly! I want to be with you now! This instant!"

"Right away . . ."

She did not have to ask twice. He had been waiting for this for over two years. He put his hand on her shoulder, and enlaced, so one could hardly see Teca's face hidden by her long hair and the collar of Jorge's jacket, on the shoulder where she was nestling, they walked another half block and arrived at where he was staying. The owners of the place had gone out. Jorge took his beloved, so painfully lost and then found again, into his room. Without questions or explanations, he enjoyed with passion the gift that destiny had put into his hands, Teca, suddenly returned, trembling in his arms like a frightened rabbit, and repeating over and over: "Take me with you. Don't let anyone take me . . ."

"Of course, my love. Relax, nothing will happen to you, I won't let it . . ."

They did not leave the room, not even to have dinner, not even to talk to anyone in the house, having found each other, desperately and passionately, unreal. After Jorge fell asleep, Teca got up, found Adriano's parents, and asked them for help. She was dating a journalist and had participated in the kidnapping, though indirectly. When they left the house in different directions, she had been followed, like all the others. She did not know whether she had managed to lose the tails. She had left the car a few blocks away from there and fled on foot, mixed in with the crowd, not knowing where to go. That was when Jorge had turned up, pushed her into an elevator, and saved her, and she'd found herself in the home of friends of her parents.

They did what they could overnight. Her father was notified; they found another, more secure place to hide her, and after some time she was able to leave the country clandestinely, leaving behind her young child, and taking along a lot of pain. But for the sake of everybody's safety, Jorge could not be told. He would have wanted to follow, have made a huge fuss. So it was necessary to make believe that nothing had happened, try to convince him that it had all been a drunken hallucination. And stand up to his fury, the scenes, the aggression, the certainty of someone who would not allow himself to be fooled and still carried the marks of the night of love too clearly on his body and in his memory to accept any other version. And once again he was carefully saved by his friends, once again placed by force on a plane to

France against his will, again because of the same woman. This time with much more secrecy, forbidden from even mentioning her name in public, thanks to a minimum that they had had to tell him, to make sure of some level of security. A few days after landing there, he learned some more. But it was only when Lena arrived, several months later, that he learned the details that could complete the romantic story of his turbulent love.

It really does take a long time to complete a love story, Lena thought. Was hers with Alonso coming to an end? Could it be that the other woman was really settling into his life, occupying a space that Lena had left empty because she had not noticed or because she could not fill it? And was that woman burrowing in? It was a very present risk. And a permanent risk when one thinks one can walk that tightrope of leaving space for the other one to soar, of not holding him back. Ah. Alonso, Alonso . . . The idea of losing him was a black hole, a silent void, a pain without measure. She did not think she could bear it. Too many fronts to fight on at the same time. But what about the love she felt? In herself and in him? What were they going to do about that? How could one imagine that something as alive, as throbbing, could be shutting down? Feelings change slowly; they don't die all of a sudden, of an accident or a heart attack. Can they die at all?

She got home a wreck, almost dragging herself along. With difficulty, she climbed the steps to the porch and lay down in the hammock.

"What about the shopping?" asked Amalia.

"I forgot."

Her mother looked at her, unbelieving. "And the newspaper? Did you not go out to get it?"

"That's right . . ."

She did not feel like explaining. She was in no condition to try. Amalia noticed and did not insist.

"Alonso called twice while you were gone. He asked you to call back as soon as you arrived."

"Thank you, I will."

But she didn't. She needed a few more moments lying down, to recover, to allow for the tide to flow out in her, and then she would try to get up and go on to the next flood tide. Vague waves, adrift.

The phone rang again. It was Alonso, explaining: "I did not answer a while ago, because I was in the shower. But I knew it was you."

Why tell him it had not been her? In a way it had. Calling all the time, wireless, from afar.

"How are you?"

Trying to sound jaunty: "The foot is getting better all the time. Today I managed to walk all the way to the newspaper stand. It almost does not hurt anymore and I am not getting as tired."

"I did not ask about the foot, Lena. I asked about you."

Silence. Why tell? She was not going to pretend. She did not want him to know the truth. She tried to think of something neutral, but all she managed was some sounds not even she understood. Then she articulated: "And you?"

His pause was almost imperceptible. Then he said: "I'm OK. Well. A lot of work." Another pause, and then: "I'm missing you a lot, my little fish."

"Me too. A lot."

"When are you coming?"

"I don't know yet. Why?"

She wanted so much for him to tell her to come soon, to hear "little fish" again, or something like it. But none of that came: "For nothing, just to know. If you are doing well over there, getting better, close to your mother, resting up, I think you need to enjoy it and stay as long as you can."

"Yes. I'll stay . . ."

"That's it. Eat well, rest, so you'll heal quickly."

"Don't worry. I am resting all right."

"Sometime soon I'll call again. And you keep in touch. When you decide to return, let me know."

"Don't worry. I'll let you know."

"Oh, I almost forgot. That friend of yours, Paulo, called yesterday and asked for your phone over there. It seems he has a job for you; I don't know if you are interested, if you could do it now . . . Anyway, I gave it to him."

"A job for me?"

Paulo had some weird ideas! He knew better than anyone about her blockages, the barriers between her and words, the shame, the powerlessness, the pain. Alonso was still talking: "That's right, little fish. It seems there is a gallery somewhere around that wants to set up a retrospective of your friend Luis Cesario. And Paulo thought you could help. You know his work so well, you know where the most important pieces are, what they are, all those things . . ."

"Maybe. I'll wait for him to call."

"All right. I'll call again tomorrow or the day after, OK? Take care, my little fish. A huge kiss."

"Bye. A kiss to you."

She wanted to ask: "Don't hang up, don't hang up, stay a little longer, I want to hear your warm voice a little longer, come closer, come here, take me away, that's enough playing around, that's it, it's time to go back, to go home . . ." And to feel the comforting embrace, the end of the nightmare, just hear: "It's all over, little fish, what was it? Wake up, it was just a bad dream. I am here, with you, it was nothing, nothing will happen to you, I won't let it . . ."

But there was none of that for her to hear. Only the sea and the wind out there, one bird or another in the trees. And memories, and the spirits, that make no noise. Luis Cesario, Carlota, Alfredo. Hearts that could not take it and broke.

Carlota, bathed in the perfumes of true jasmine and Madagascar jasmine, on the lace-railed verandah, saying: "The beautiful thing about life is the force with which it carries us."

Luis Cesario at night, chatting on the terrace, and suddenly ordering: "Shhh . . . Quiet for a moment. Have you noticed? This very minute the land wind is beginning to blow. I think this is wonderful. To know that every night there is moment when the wind changes and the sea breeze turns into a land breeze."

Alfredo, who always knew of anyone in any kind of difficulty: "We have to do something for him."

Even though she heard nothing out there, Lena now felt the presence of her friends caressing her. The three of them were coming to her rescue. It was the phone call from Paulo, whom she had met through

Alfredo. To organize the exhibit Carlota had wanted so much and had already explained so often to Lena, exactly how it should be. They should show Luis Cesario's paintings, indisputable landmarks of Brazilian art, and still so far on the margins of any commercial circuit, unknown to the great public, given the seclusion in which he had always lived, working at home, selling his works only to those who already knew of him and went looking for him where he was, hiding from all hype or publicity.

Lena remembered the many times they had talked about it, when she and Carlota had tried to convince him to have a show.

"What for? I don't need any of that."

"But the country needs it."

"People need to get to know your work, Luis; we have talked about it so many times . . ."

"There's no hurry; the time will come."

Lena insisted: "When? What are you waiting for?"

"For when I have the time."

"What do you mean, Luis Cesario? The paintings are all done. It's more than half a century of work without ever having had a show. You have to show it."

And he, immovable: "When I die, you can show it. Now I don't have a lot of time. I have to paint; I can't worry about catalogs, selecting paintings, giving interviews, photos, openings, conversations with dealers, cocktail parties—just thinking about it makes me nervous . . ."

"But we'll help, Luis Cesario," Lena assured him. "I promise I won't let them bother you."

"Do you really promise?"

She got all excited: "Sure I promise."

"Then let me paint. This business of showing, notices in the papers, parties, that's for the young, who have a lot of time ahead. I don't. I need every minute that is left me. To paint and to see, before painting. To think about painting, understand beauty, live. Otherwise, how am I going to paint?" And he concluded with a word that was just like him: "A show does not give a painter a painting. When the time comes, you can do it."

And he would change the subject, talk of other things. Of trees, of birds, of the dog Fifina, of a spiderweb he had seen in the morning on his way to get water at the spring in the woods—because all his life, though they had water piped into the house, he had liked to drink, when at home, that pure and fresh spring water. Or else he would talk about the political situation, discuss literature or music, distill his view of what was human. Always very firmly planted in everyday life and with clear and strong opinions.

"It's absurd how the papers fell for those gorillas' line and insist on calling the resistance terrorism. Not even the Nazis, not even the fascists, not even the occupation forces were that cynical. I am a pacifist; I understand that at times someone might feel like condemning armed action; nobody could reasonably desire it . . . But sometimes there is no choice. Even the law recognizes a right of self-defense, after all."

Carlota added some oil to the fire: "Come on, the law, Luis Cesario . . . It's a long time they have been trampling on the law; they could not care less for people's rights."

"That's just it. And then they call the opposition subversive. They were the ones who subverted everything, knocked down the constitutional order, deposed a freely elected president, flouted the constitution, put some sort of quilt in its place, and then they say they won't tolerate subversion . . ."

"But there is also pressure from the outside, Luis Cesario. This kind of position is in the interest of the Americans; they are exporting this kind of ideology everywhere in Latin America, and we are in their sphere of influence. It's all part of the military education over there in their academies, where our officers go to study and come back having learned that stuff. They call it the doctrine of national security."

Luis Cesario went on, more and more excited: "That's all nonsense, child. We aren't the ones who are threatening national security, and if they think about it just a little they, too, can see it. And this business of security and development isn't just from the Americans. Our military has had this urge to ape foreigners for a long time, even before the United States grew up, when it was still in diapers. Earlier, it was France, and positivism was the big thing. Security and development are just the presently fashionable names for 'order and progress,' which they wrote on the flag when they created the republic. Wouldn't it have been much better to choose 'peace and justice' for the national motto? When a nation wants to live unperturbed, what it wants is not order, but peace. And can there possibly be progress or development without justice? Only in the heads of those who like a dictatorship."

"True, but even in the rest of Latin America, which did not suffer a positivist influence the way we did, this ideology is now being sold by the United States . . ."

Luis Cesario interrupted: "The rest of Latin America is the rest of Latin America; it's not Brazil. We can have a lot in common, we are brothers, we suffered through a lot together, we were bled in the same way by the colonizers, but we have different histories. Their Indians built stone cities, had calendars, were goldsmiths, wove wool, had writing and math. Ours were nomads, made baskets and feather art, knew no metals. Different. The Spanish had a university in Lima in the sixteenth century, printed books, and right away their Indians were writing epics and being published on this side of the Atlantic. Different, different . . ."

Lena agreed: "True again. We had to wait till the nineteenth century for the first university."

"And for the first Brazilian press, with Lobato," added Carlota.

Luis Cesario went on: "Those native civilizations built roads, and had good communication among their cities. Here, the Portuguese forbade opening roads, to keep people from deflecting gold from their control." And he repeated: "Different, different. Very different."

Lena would argue: "But now, as the various countries slowly move toward redemocratization, one can also note that there are similarities, aren't there, Luis Cesario? That is, Chile is still under violent repression, and so are Paraguay and various others. But Argentina, Uruguay, Peru—and we as well . . . Don't you think this corresponds to a different moment in the American position toward the continent? Don't you think that Somoza fell in Nicaragua and Baby Doc in Haiti only because the U.S. allowed it? That now their overall strategy has changed, but they still treat us as a bloc, as if we were all the same?"

"That may be, child. But it does not invalidate the observation that we are very different. If we say we have nothing in common, we are playing the enemy's game, sure. But if we say we are completely

alike, we are doing the same. For instance, to get back to the beginning of this conversation, this business of calling resistance terrorism.
That came from the right, to confuse people. Here it was resistance.
In Argentina and Uruguay it was not resistance. Their forms of armed
struggle, the actions of the montoneros, of the ERP—or popular revolutionary army—of the tupamaros, and of other groups started before
the dictatorships and in the end helped the dictators settle into their
positions of power. At the time there were all sorts of ways to protest
over there. There were elections, Congress was in session, and so were
the courts, the constitution was in operation, there was no surveillance
of correspondence, unions could be organized, parties could meet and
speak out: in short, peaceful forms of making demands and trying to
change society had not been exhausted. Not here, Lena. When your
brother and his friends kidnapped the ambassador there was none of
that. All had been tried and thwarted. There was no other way, except
for walking to the slaughterhouse, head bowed."

Carlota completed the picture with a very feminine analysis, involving the heart: "And another thing I find important, Lena, is to
remember that those boys did not need to do it, if they were just thinking of themselves. It was a very selfless and generous impulse, of the
sort that only young spirits are capable of. Personally, what was any of
them losing with the dictatorship, apart from the freedom to throw a
tantrum? In general, they came from the middle class; they were university students about to enter the professions. They could do what so
many did, think of themselves only, egoistically, graduate, and get on
the security-and-development bandwagon, shout, 'Brazil is the greatest,' and go make a bundle on the stock exchange. But they chose to
stay on the side of those who were being left out when the pie was cut,
those who did not even get the crumbs. I think that was very generous.
To abandon comfort and risk their lives for the sake of others? That
wasn't for just anyone."

Lena was happy that they thought so. After all, during the entire
time of her exile, having left without taking leave and always imagining that her friends, who were old, could die before they'd meet again,
she had chatted with them in her thoughts, somewhat worried that
they had been suddenly thrown into the fire when Marcelo had needed

to hide in their house. When she returned, along numerous and repeated conversations, she had felt the total solidarity of the old couple and that helped her in her constant need to take stock, to analyze, to understand, to find the truth.

That same need had taken her to inquire of Marcelo, the first time they had met, in exile, two years after the kidnapping: "Listen . . . Excuse me for asking, but there is something I have always wanted to know. If the government had not given in and agreed to free the guys, were you really going to kill the ambassador?"

Marcelo turned very serious, then looked straight at her and answered thoughtfully: "I think that was the question we all asked ourselves most often. Aloud and in silence, alone, within each one of us. Before, during, and after the kidnapping."

She insisted: "Well, and what is the answer?"

"There isn't just one answer, Lena. There is more than one. The first one is theoretical. It was not just a game, playing around; it was an action, for real. In that case, we had to be determined. If the government did not give in, we had no choice. But there was also the practical concrete answer, deeper within us. I think we were all sure that there was no danger."

Lena was astonished: "What do you mean there was no danger? Few people risked what you did, and you are telling me there was no danger? Have you forgotten?"

"No. One does not forget something like that. What I mean is that we were sure there was not the least danger that we would be pushed against the wall and forced to liquidate the man. There was not the most remote possibility that the military junta would decide not to agree and not to do everything we asked so he would be released. Because of that, there was no danger."

"How could you be so sure?"

"If we had been wrong, then the entire analysis of the situation in the country would have been wrong. And we knew it wasn't. We knew, without a doubt, that it was the American interests that were in charge, that the generals were fully supported by them, that the regime depended absolutely on the United States, and that the government was going to do everything necessary to please its boss."

"But what if the United States decided that it was not appropriate to give in?"

"Well, that's where the power of the surprise factor comes in. It was the first time anything like that had happened in the world. Nobody had imagined it; they were not prepared. They did not know who we were and could not risk paying to see. And they did not have the time to analyze all the possible consequences. They had to act fast, act first and think later. Just like the military likes it; if I am not mistaken, it's Shakespeare himself who says, in *Othello*, that the commander who killed poor Desdemona did so more because he was trained as a military man to act without thinking than because he was jealous. Anyway, you are the one who knows about the theater . . ."

She returned to the matter at hand: "OK, but they could always find that the price was too high."

"The price was high? What? Fifteen dirty-ass *cucarachas* for an American diplomat? Your innocence is amusing, Lena. At that point, 15,000 would have been cheap. You are forgetting that they think themselves the center of the universe. Or they did, back then. We find it hard to evaluate things like that, because nobody respects us anywhere, we are really shit anywhere in the world, and our own government would never move a straw to defend a Brazilian citizen. Human life is not worth a whole lot in Brazil—heaps of children die of hunger, poor people waste away with disease, pedestrians are run over, husbands kill their wives for nothing, any argument brings out guns, or knives, or broken bottles. In a land where any landowner has his henchmen to teach the people their lessons, where ambushes are normal, where one has always hired available guns to eliminate adversaries, one ends up thinking that being a citizen isn't worth much. And Brazilian citizens aren't really worth much. But an American citizen? All you need is for one of them to be arrested anywhere in the world, and they bring in the marines . . . As for an ambassador, no questions asked. Of course they would give in quickly. What would they lose with it? The demoralization of some South American generals? There are so many of them. All you have to do is put another one in his place. That is why we could be sure that there was no chance we would have to eliminate the man who, by the way, behaved with all possible dignity. No risk. At least that time, which was the first and where the surprise was complete. After that, it could get complicated. But that is another story."

Another story, other stories, the same history that flows without interruption, connecting all that happens under the sun. It was in the Bible, and Lena remembered having read it, though she did not recall the precise words. The sun rises, the sun sets, one generation comes, another generation goes, men pass, earth abides. Hemingway had written a beautiful book in that key. But she looked around and saw things differently. This generation seemed to want to do away with earth. And for the first time in history might even be able to do it. The nuclear threat. The spread of ecological devastation. Economic inversion, concentrating more and more resources in the hands of the military for the benefit of an arms race and to the detriment of the productive forces in the nation, which would necessarily harm the general welfare of the society. It was all just the opposite of what nature requires, instinct asks for, morality demands. It was all moving too fast. In just one generation they had killed off the trout in the rivers where Hemingway used to fish, animals that had lived free for millennia in the forests, trees, plants, even the centuries-old forests where she had walked with her grandfather when she was a girl. Maybe it was better not to be stubborn about surviving the destruction, and just fold oneself into the general disappearance of the earth. And so long as it held out, to live like an animal, a lazy lizard, eating, drinking, and lying in the warm sun.

XV

Fiz um verso tão bonito
que carrego na lembrança
nunca mais eu vi o mundo
com meus olhos de criança.

(CACASO)

I wrote such a pretty poem
that I carry in my mind
I've never seen the world again
as to my child's eye outlined.

Another sunny day. Lena woke up early, and slowly anchored her consciousness to the habitual morning sounds. In general she woke in good spirits. But that morning she was still suffering from the previous day's despondency. And probably also from more recent experiences. Why wake? Why does the heart go on? Possibly one could tell why, but what for? To take medicine, to extend the illusion of normalcy, to be able to stand up? To insist on walking, maybe all the way to the shipyard that she liked so much? Smell the good smell of freshly cut wood, walk on the sawdust, play with the curls of the shavings that fell from the planes . . . Look at the insides of the boats being built, those vessels full of infinity, cathedrals pointing toward the sea, pregnant with all the possible routes. Listen to the work, hammers and nails, saws and machines, and the human voices laced into them. Sniff like an animal, trying to tell the acrid odor of tar, the pungent aroma of vegetable rosins, the penetrating smell of paints and solvents, the sea perfume of ship's shellac, that promised all the horizons and every one of them an absolute subject to the salty ocean smell, carrying in seaweed and seashells with every breath.

Why visit the travel-pregnant shipyard when pregnancy and all high flights were so impossible? Better give up. Give up the morning walk and the play she had dreamt of, the word that would never be incarnate on a stage to bring back old conflicts. What was the point of reading sketches and letters, statements and notes, if she was now certain she would never write again? Better abandon the project once and for all, get rid of all those folders, notebooks, and envelopes, shred all that paper and throw it into the ocean, with the courage to finally accept the impossibility and stop fooling herself.

Unless she had the courage to risk the vertigo. Exchange balance for the word, barter the plumb line for the abyss.

She picked up another passage she had written and reread it. Was it worth falling again so as to save that? To dive more deeply into pain? To throw footlights on those who had been disinherited through exile, those nobody remembered, of whom no one wanted to know?

She glanced quickly over the written pages, on a slant, just to see what they were about. Some scenes showed the progressive isolation of the Vera-Ricardo couple, as they tried to maintain their independence, avoid joining a party. Other exiles set traps for them, taking advantage of the fact that they were helping create records denouncing torture. They tried to expose their names, burn them somehow, so that they would have to abandon their dream of returning soon to Brazil. As if they needed the greatest possible number of exiles on their side, the better to bear it. The idea that some members of the community had not been indicted and that there were cracks in the doors that would allow them to sneak into the country before them seemed unbearable. As if they were drowning and needed to pull someone down by the neck so he, too, would drown.

Another scene picked up the Sergio-Diana couple a few years later. Vera and Ricardo had already returned to Brazil; she was passing through Paris as a tourist, staying with some friends. Now they had a better apartment, with furniture, a steady job, a good situation, another small child, a normal and stable life. Diana was serene. Vera was happy. She was about to meet with Roberta and Paula (she would have to change their names when she made them into characters), who had completed a complicated circumnavigation, an odyssey starting in Chile, and were now living in France, still outside Paris. She was telling Sergio and Diana that she would be meeting her friends soon; they would call from the station when they arrived. Diana's reaction was violent. Something like "You gave someone our telephone? Our address? You had no right to do that! Who authorized that? What about our security?" A sad, hurt speech, by someone who felt betrayed and could no longer trust anyone. Sergio's position was that, objectively speaking, Vera was right, she had not done anything wrong, but Diana had to feel that at least that nest of hers was inviolable, a closed territory, which nobody would know about if she did not want him to. Both were very sorry, but they had to ask Vera to pack her bags and move. She had been unworthy of their trust and friendship. It did not help to argue. Never again had they answered a letter; they moved without telling where and were lost forever, despite all their affection and friendship.

Was it worth harping on it? Picking it up again, telling, preparing it so that someone else could live through it in the theater?

A wren chirped, hopping on a branch of the almond tree. Lena went out, walked a bit, and watched, leaning against a chaise in the shade of the tree, almost lying down, contemplating the high lace of the leaves, the play of light, green brushstrokes against the blue sky, a rustling painting in the breeze. They were going to have a show of Luis Cesario's work. It was as if he were calling. She had to help. She had promised. And not only by providing information on where the paintings could be found, but supervising the production of the catalog, so it would be well done, placing the artist and his work in their context. She would have to write. For the sake of her friend. But she could not . . .

The wren sounded again. No, it was another one, answering the first one's call, with its little agitated air, its chest a rosy brown, hopping without letup. Its companion was on the ground, scratching for something in the sand, interrupting itself to sing back with its round little black eyes turned upward.

When she was a child, her grandfather used to call her a little wren. Because she was small, with lively eyes, brown, and would not sit still, always running from one side to the other. He would not recognize her now, under the same tree where they had talked so often, a big woman, dimmed, trying to erase herself, so far from that granddaughter who was eager to live, insistent on taking part in everything, even those things that the grownups wanted to veto at all costs.

Like the walk in the woods.

Lena had already lost hope when her grandfather pulled his watch by its golden chain out of his waistband pocket, which he called a pouch. Imperturbably, as if he had not heard the argument when the girl insisted on her point, almost crying before her cousins and her uncle. He checked the time. He placed the back of the watch in the palm of his left hand and wound it with his right, turning a little pin back and forth on the crown of the gold circle. He did not say a word, did not look at his son or at his grandsons, only at the white dial with its Roman numbers, even the four, which was a IIII and not a IV as one learned it in school. But despite the silence, Lena sensed that something was imminent, just as one feels that a summer storm is about to break, moments before the first drops free up the smell of earth. And she waited. The period was about to be added to the sentence. After the grandfather had spoken, nobody was going to go on arguing. And she was going to have to say good night and keep her tears for the pillow and the darkness. She was not going to give all those men the pleasure of laughing at her and saying that she was a crybaby. Then for sure they would not let her go to the woods with them.

"It is time to go to sleep," the old man said, putting back his watch. "Tomorrow we will have to leave very early. You, too, Helena Maria, if you want so much to go with us, you should be in bed already. I am not going to call anybody twice."

"Good night, Uncle. A blessing, Grandfather," was all she could say, her heart pounding with emotion.

"God bless you, Helena Maria."

Her grandfather said that with such a solemn air that it seemed he was really giving her a message from God, more so than any priest preaching a sermon at mass. After such a leave, Lena did not even have to pray before going to bed, which she did with her clothes on so she would not be late the next day. All she needed was to put on the high boots she wore to protect her feet from thorns, nettles, and any snake that might be lying on the path. Not really a path, since the forest had no paths, just trails, and sometimes not even that. Her grandfather had already taught her that much. How wonderful that he was letting her go with them! And the uncle and cousins must have sat there with long faces, after that big quarrel about not wanting her to go.

"I don't know what you are going to do there. There is nothing that might interest you in that forest. You'll just be in the way."

From the start, her uncle's reaction to her request had been very clear. She could not go, and that was that. He had no idea why she kept insisting.

"I want to see the forest."

"We'll bring you a twig to see," Luis Carlos mocked her. "Do you want a twig with thorns or one with a wasp's nest?"

"There is nothing to see. There is a dense forest, mosquitoes, heat, thorns, snakes. Nothing that could interest a girl."

Her uncle was always surly and contrary. Good thing he was only her uncle, not her father. But when her father was away, Lena had to argue with him instead, and he did not think that children should argue or, as he put it, talk back to their elders.

"I want to see the same things you are going to see. If you can go walk in the forest, why can't I? I promise I won't be in the way."

"Walk? Do you think this is like going for a walk? Do you think this is a matinee movie about Africa? That you will run into Tarzan, and Cheetah will come play with you?"

Everybody laughed, while Ze Roberto hopped around the room scratching himself, imitating a monkey behind Luis Carlos, who let out high-pitched hysterical screams in the role of a woman in distress. Then Carlos Eduardo started to sing and the other two fell into the song as Uncle Vicente smiled:

Let's go walk in the forest
so long as Sir Wolf doesn't come.
Let's go walk in the forest
so long as Sir Wolf doesn't come.
Sir Wolf, are you home? What's he doing?
Sleeping? We've got time, lots.

Let's go walk in the forest
so long as Sir Wolf doesn't come.

Lena felt like falling on her cousins and punching them, kicking them, pulling their hair, even though there were three of them. But right there, in front of Uncle and Grandfather, she did not dare. And she knew that, if she did, that's when for sure she wasn't going to the forest with them the next day. That's why she also had to endure the definitive explanations and the categorical tone of her Uncle Vicente, which she hated even more than the teasing by the cousins. Because she could not even hope that at least some day, later on, she would be able to get back at him and attack him and punch him and kick him.

"Helena Maria, it's no good. This is not a stroll. Father and I have to go see about the cacao, deep in the woods. We will go by way of the river and the forest because it's a shortcut and we can use the early morning hours. Then we return by road in Salustio's truck. We have a lot of work, and the forest is dangerous; it's not a stroll and it's not child's play."

"Then how come they are going? Luis Carlos is my age, and Ze Roberto is only one year older."

"They are men, it's different. They have to learn early."

"Women have to learn too. I'll learn. Grandfather always says that I learn everything quickly."

Lena knew she was bending the rules of the game. She had mentioned the grandfather to see if he would be touched and raise his eyes from the papers where he was writing, sitting at the mahogany desk that he adored, with all those drawers and pigeonholes that were full of surprises and that appeared suddenly when someone raised the rollup lid that curved and slid into the top. Not at all. It was as if the old man were not even in the room. It seemed that he did not actually enjoy going out with her when he went to survey some land, chain in one hand, theodolite, light silk sunshade, red-and-white striped posts, and a whole lot of other tools. Lena knew she was not in the way. She sat quietly wherever he told her to. Or she looked for new rocks for her collection. Or she gathered different leaves so she could learn from her grandfather later.

"This is serrated; see how the edges look like a saw. And notice how they grow differently on the stalk. When one leaf is like this, in front of the other, they are opposing. Now these here, see, are alternate. Pay attention, Helena Maria, so you won't forget."

She paid all the attention she had. And she did not forget. She loved it when her grandfather asked: "Do you know the family of this plant? Look carefully."

She examined the flower, compared it mentally with others, remembered the guava tree in the yard, and said: "It's in the family of the myrtaceae."

He laughed and praised her: "Very good, child. A true member of the myrtaceae. Now, as a reward, you can eat the fruit. It is called araçá; it's a little sour guava."

Lena was very proud of herself. The sourness of the araçá tasted like honey coming from her grandfather's hands. And she did not forget the day she got the highest praise. In the vegetable garden, she had just identified the cucumber as belonging to the same family as the watermelon: "It's a cucurbitacea."

The old man burst into laughter, stuttering a bit.

"Cu-cu-cucurbitacea, great! Yes, ma'am! This granddaughter of mine learns everything really fast, and learns even more than I teach. Cu-cu-cucurbitacea, that's a good one."

That day the grandfather, who always took her everywhere but rarely touched her, did something unforgettable: he put her in his lap after dinner and spent a long time playing at asking her the family of plants:

"What about beans?"

"Legumes."

"Pineapple?"

"Bromeliaceae."

And every once in a while, he would return to it, as if he had forgotten: "And what is the melon, again?"

Lena answered, "A cucurbitacea."

And he laughed and laughed as she had seldom seen him laugh, just shouting with laughter. Then he hugged her and stroked her curly hair, and it was good. And while she smiled with all the gaps left by her milk teeth that were in the process of being replaced, he repeated, delighted, one of the few words he had never been able to say without stuttering: "Cu-cu-cucurbitacea . . . This little miss granddaughter of mine learns everything. It's a pleasure to see!"

So how come now Uncle Vicente dared say that only the male cousins could go to the forest because men have to learn? That was why she had sent her grandfather a disguised cry for help. At the time, the old man had not said anything. He went on sitting before his desk, leaning over the papers, marking something down in his regular, right-slanting handwriting. He seemed not to hear the grandsons teasing Lena: "Just give it up. You're not going, fold the deck, it's not in the cards."

"That's it. Girls are weak, gutless, slow, keep stopping, you'll just make us late."

"You'll complain about mosquitoes, cry because you are afraid of frogs . . . Or have you stopped being afraid of frogs?" asked Carlos Eduardo to provoke her.

Lena knew she'd better not answer. Anything she said was risky; they might put a frog in her bed again, as they had done the summer before.

Luis Carlos fulminated: "Worse. She'll get tired, whine, ask to be carried. She'll hang back and make everybody late."

And all three started singing in a chorus: "I want you to carry me! I want you to carry me!"

And that was when, as Lena was about to give up and start crying, the grandfather decided to look at his watch and send everyone to bed.

And lying down in all her clothes and not even saying her prayers, just barely thanking God for the happiness of having such a grandfather, Lena closed her eyes, for just a little while and right away woke again with someone knocking at the door:

"It's time!"

She heard the knock repeated at other doors and her grandfather's dry voice calling again. She was the first at the breakfast table, all ready, to drink the coffee her grandmother had just made and was serving in the green glazed coffeepot with the flowers that went with the sugar bowl and the mugs. While she dunked a buttered roll into her coffee, the grandfather arrived. The grandmother asked, with the air of continuing a conversation that had started earlier: "Are you sure she can go?"

"Let's not talk about it anymore," he answered, looking at the door as if signaling. Uncle Vicente and the cousins were coming in. The grandmother saw it, understood, and was silent.

And it was in silence that they started on their journey. It was still dark when they left and went to the bank of the Rio Grande, the Big River, where two locals were waiting for them with a canoe at the ready. Lena made herself comfortable at the bottom of the canoe, near her grandfather's legs where he sat on the bench, and kept very quiet. Even though she lived in the city, she saw no great mysteries in these canoe trips. Every vacation she came to the hamlet by the river, which at that time was really small and did not even have a bridge. They would stay in the house by the beach, but there was always a trip of a few days to the plantation further inland, where the grownups inspected the cacao. And to get to the plantation, it was necessary to spend the night in the hamlet, after the crossing on a ferry. Or by canoe, when the line of trucks was too long and her uncle asked for a driver to wait for them and ordered a canoe to transport the people. The canoe had the uncles' monogram painted on its hull, like that on the cattle in the barn or on the embroidered towels in the bathroom. The canoe was deep and narrow, cut out of one single tree trunk, and it crossed the Rio Grande real fast with its outboard motor, with so many others that went by loaded with people, as day broke with streaks of light behind the forest. And that, even when the sun was high, would go on all day, from one bank to the other, from one rustic quay to the red clay cliff, up and down the river, taking people from here to there. Women with parasols, protecting from the sun the babies they carried curled up on their laps. The German priest, fanning himself, red-faced, his cassock rolled up and showing his spindly legs rising from his black boots. Groups of workers, each with his neat bundle made up of a very clean dishtowel, embroidered in chainstitch or cross-stitch, borders in crochet, wrapping up two soup dishes rim to rim, that protected the lunch the wives had prepared early in the morning. The agronomist and the employees of the Department of Agriculture, who worked on the other bank, in the Section for the Promotion of Agriculture, busy about cacao and indifferent to the set fires and the logging that daily bled the forest in the form of huge logs of hardwood, against the law, a hemorrhage transported openly on rafts and carts. The elementary school teacher, tiny, thin, always impeccable in her print dress and cologne, up to the daily miracle of teaching the alphabet, reading, and sciences to a band of urchins of all ages, crowded together into one room that did not even have desks and where Lena had helped once, playing at being a teacher on a day when the real one had laryngitis and could not speak, and discovering a Brazil that was not in the books taught at her own elementary school. It was a Brazil where schools had no books, no blackboards, no recess, and no school lunch, where grown boys could call her, respectfully, Dona Helena, and that she, eight years old, at the dawn of her own life, beside Dona Aurora, was not able to understand.

All of them crossed the muddy waters of the bridgeless Rio Grande in their canoes, balancing the load, careful not to rock it. All greeted the monogrammed canoe with respect, and her uncle and her grandfather returned the greetings with a wide wave or took their hats off and put them back on, in silence. All you heard was the noise of the outboard motor, the water flowing and the voices of the sailors, at times, saying things that one could only rarely hear.

The canoe moved upriver, as if there were a highway in the water, one-way lanes going in opposite directions, and no vessel ever bumped another.

In a moment the best part of the excursion would start. At least as far as Lena knew. The Rio Pequeno, the Little River. She had never entered the forest on foot, so she did not know what that would be like. But the Rio Pequeno was one of her passions. She had gone upriver often, when there was enough time or when there was no available car and they had traveled the whole way, more than two hours, till they came to the plantation, on the bank of the New Lake, where the river had its source. And every time, Lena liked it better, and wanted the trip to last, for that beauty to be eternal. Being happy forever must be something like forever riding up the Little River in that canoe. And it was about to start.

The boat coasted along the bank of the Rio Grande and suddenly entered the Little River. Everything changed all at once. They turned off the motor and that was the end of the constant tut-tut-tut that had accompanied them from the time they had entered the canoe. The force and speed of the water diminished so much and so quickly that at the first moment it seemed that they had stopped. And in a way they had. But only for a moment, until they got used to the new rhythm and started to row against the new waters that ran more slowly in their lazy, shallow, and narrow bed, full of sneaky curves that demanded the rowers' full attention. At some deeper parts it was even possible to turn on the motor, at a slow and careful pace. But there were other stretches where the sandbanks and the sinuous course of the shore forced the rowers to stand, pushing the oars against the bottom as if they were the thin legs of a strange animal that traveled with its back to the ground and its belly to the sun, supporting itself against the earth to lurch ahead along the water. Like a man crawling on his belly and his elbows, silent till he took someone by surprise.

The Little River was full of mysteries and surprises. The clear waters showed the light sand at the bottom, where at times one could see the ripples formed by the current. But its mysteries and charm were not in secrets hidden by muddy waters, as happens in the large dun-colored sludgy rivers. They resided in its very transparency and apparent silence, teeming with life. In the intimacy between earth and water. In the multiplicity of nooks and hiding places, in the play of light and shadow. In the roots of the large trees that held up a cliff, which would otherwise tumble into the current. In the petals of the purple glory trees that fell slowly onto the current, floating toward the swirling waters of the Rio Grande. In the heavy trunks that had settled at the bottom, resembling alligators and providing hiding places for fish. In the light tree trunks that dragged by and had to be pushed aside by the rowers with their oars. In the water plants that gathered into colonies so compact they were frightening, despite their blooming beauty, as if they were deceptive islands that would close in around the canoe and paralyze it. In the places where pacas and capibaras came to drink and where once somebody had seen the tracks of a jaguar. In the small monkeys that squealed in the treetops and sometimes threw fruit from way up high onto the travelers who glided along down on the water. In one or another heavily antlered deer that swam, then ran away, startled, as the canoe approached. In the bands of parakeets and parrots that filled the air with their squawks. In the birds of all colors and kinds that bathed by grazing the water or that sang in the woods. In the nests hanging precariously over the current. In all the lianas that overhung the water from the trees, like snakes, among the Spanish moss. In the tropical mistletoe that covered tree crowns and shrubs. In the red bromelias, golden cow-horn orchids, and orchids of all hues, in the moonflowers and ginger lilies and all the seasonal flowers in their calendar of colors and fragrances. In the huge trees that formed tunnels over the river, and the small shrubs that bent over the water and made everyone lie low in the canoe to avoid them. In the chirping cicadas, buzzing mosquitoes, horseflies, and beetles with their heavy flight, light dragonflies barely touching the water. In the fish, who owned the river, tiny, dancing in their rapidly swimming schools, or bigger ones, alone, seeking the cooler waters, and protection in the shade. Fish that could hold almost still in the current, stemmed against the force of the water with the undulating movement of their fins and that, suddenly, in one quick move slid away into the distance. The charms of the Little River were endless; Lena was never able to remember them all. All together, they were a feast for the senses, unique and incomparable. Playing in the cool water, with her fingers hanging over the rim, sprinkling her face with drops from the river, looking, listening, smelling, and feeling on her skin all that she could perceive, the girl had disconnected from her uncle and her cousins, from the world of people who bossed others around and thwarted their desires. She did not yet know that the traces the Little River had left in her mind would one day help form the cosmopolitan woman she was going to invent for herself; little Helena Maria de Andrade was entirely busy, that moment, at the art of being happy forever.

With a jolt, the canoe stopped. One of the rowers jumped onto a trunk on the bank of the river and with both hands pulled up the big dugout in which they were all traveling. Everybody started talking at the same time:

"Careful! Hold on over there!"

"Push the oar hard into the ground, there! Don't let the current carry the boat."

"Sit down, kid!"

"Wow! That was close!"

"Did you hear me? Sit down! Easy."

"Hand me that bag there . . ."

"Give me a hand; let's go!"

Soon the boat was unloaded and the occupants on dry land. After brief farewells, the rowers pushed the canoe into the middle of the river, and took off downriver, on their return journey. Father and son stood on the edge of the woods with the four children and one local man. Now they would take a shortcut through the forest and enter the cacao plantation from the back. For the girl, that was the beginning of the adventure.

Lena had entered the forest several times before, with her grandfather or with her father, uncle, and cousins. Little by little she was learning the basic rules for orienting herself, to follow the position of the sun, observe reference points, decipher the simple markers that other travelers had left—a machete cut on a trunk, a broken branch pointing in the right direction, two palm fronds laid down as an *x* closing the way at a crossroads. She knew some things about how to walk in the woods, though she had never gone by herself. But she had never entered the forest.

Right away, she found it all different. The trees were very tall. There was a huge number of lianas, vines, and creepers, aerial roots hanging from on high, Spanish moss, a variety of parasites and leaves twining themselves around the tree trunks. A profusion of branches, trunks, roots, and vines closing the trails but, in a way, the sensation of there being less underbrush than in the woods to which she was used, the masculine woods with nettles and clumps of thorny bushes. In the woods— *Were woods more like girls and forests more like boys?* she had asked herself when she was younger and still stupid—the paths had been closed too, but the impression had been different. It was not as if a lot of thorns had grown there to bar the way, like in the story of Sleeping Beauty that her grandmother used to tell. It was as if under the great trees there now, there existed an ever-renewed cemetery of more ancient trees, of their fallen branches and felled trunks, of their dead leaves, rotten fruits, and tumbled twigs. And at the same time, that cemetery was a nursery, a hatchery, a seed plot. The soft vegetation dissolved into the earth and turned into humus, the seed pods opened and scattered their grains, the worm-eaten fruit let go their seeds and all germinated, budded, stretched upward searching for the light that did not come down to them, and demanded a great effort and will to be reached.

Lena walked on, looking at the ground, careful not to step on a snake, not to stumble over a root, not to scrape against a stump, not to step into an anthill. On the first stretch she hardly dared to look up, and only had a general idea of what was around her. Her eyes were glued to the ground, and she struggled to keep pace and not be left behind or do anything wrong, so the cousins would not laugh at her. She hardly noticed, from time to time, all the different mushrooms and tree fungi or the profusion of spiderwebs with insects caught in them. Then she began to get used to the environment and feel more at ease. And she did not have to worry about walking fast: everybody was going slowly because they were tromping through a portion where the trail was less traveled and beginning to close up again. From time to time it was necessary to cut through it with the machete, and everybody waited and watched the accurate and efficient blows of the farmworker who headed the line. Then came the grandfather, holding back one or another of the branches so it would not hurt the girl, who was following close behind him. And from time to time, a warning: "Watch out for the hole!" Or "Careful, there's a stump." She watched out, avoided the obstacle, and then looked back to pass on the warning to Carlos Eduardo, who was walking behind her and would pass it on to his brothers and to Uncle Vicente, who brought up the rear.

Nobody talked much, just said what was strictly necessary, as they began to breathe harder. The forest imposed its own silence made up of ceaseless sounds, bird cries, cicada chirps, insect hums, the cracking of twigs, the noise of the wind in the leaves, something falling from the top of a tree. The heat became more intense as well, despite the deep shade. One's shirt was glued to one's body, sweat ran from one's forehead and burned in one's eyes. It was a humid, heavy heat, inhabited by mosquito stings, no-see-ums, gnats, midges, all must have been represented; one could not imagine any one of them missing. Suddenly the grandfather said, quickly, in a low voice so she hardly heard him: "Over there is a cattleya."

Lena looked where he was pointing and saw a beautiful white orchid on a very high tree branch. She almost asked to be allowed to take it home. But she saw how high it was and figured that she should not interrupt the walk, noticed all at once that her grandfather had spoken almost as if he were telling her a secret, and was afraid that the uncle and the cousins would say she wanted to delay them for the sake of picking some silly little flower. And she was proud of herself and understood that she had grown up that very moment, that she had not followed her impulse but had been able to see the white orchid, admire its beauty, and keep it all to herself, all she had thought and felt, silent in the general silence.

Further on, the trail went around an immense tree trunk, the hugest Lena had ever seen, or would ever see in her life. Her grandfather stopped, raised his left arm, and said: "Halt!"

He was telling them to stop, but the girl thought she was supposed to look up. She bent her neck far back and looked. She almost got dizzy. The huge trunk rose till it was almost out of sight in the vast canopy. Around it, all the large trees in the forest, enormous as they were, seemed half-grown, like ordinary city trees, planted in a sidewalk. One could not even see all of it, as the branches of the smaller trees covered it up. All of them stopped, speechless, looking up. Then the grandfather introduced it: "This is a jequitibá. The king of the forest."*

Lena thought it was more than a king. A god. If anyone ever managed to climb it, he would reach the sky. And from up there, he would be able to see everything—the entire forest, the Little River, the Rio Grande, the sea, far away, all the cities, the little airplanes flying way down there, the curve of the earth.

"Imposing. Looks like a cathedral," said Uncle Vicente.

Palace, castle, cathedral, church, like that and more than that. And the rays of the sun that managed to penetrate that canopy of leaves and reach the ground were so few, so well defined—straight lines of brilliant light—they looked exactly like the illustrations on the first communion missal, showing God in the eucharist. Maybe that tree really did reach heaven and came to one of its gates. Surely, up there, one would see the little angels singing.

* *Cariniana ianeirensis,* a hardwood that grows only in Brazil.

"Three men can't embrace its trunk," said the grandfather.

He took a few steps toward it and leaned against the tree with his arms open. Uncle Vicente and the employee did the same and held his hands, one on each side, as if they were about to play ring-around-the-rosy, three large men who suddenly seemed very small in a children's game with the king of the forest. And they could not embrace the tree. "You come too," the uncle called, reaching toward Lena. The children came up, with difficulty, climbing over roots. Uncle Vicente held Lena's hand firmly and she thought it was good, as if he had never groused at her and were a friend who would take care of her. On the other side, Luis Carlos grabbed his cousin's wrist and she did the same to his, feeling she would never want to break away and always stay together, in the shade of the jequitibá. Only then, as Ze Roberto and Carlos Eduardo completed the circle with the employee, did they manage to circle the tree. And for a moment they held still, holding hands in the heat of the forest, leaning against the trunk and standing on the roots, their feet sinking into dead leaves, silent as if they were praying.

"Some animal!" exclaimed Uncle Vicente, breaking the spell.

All let go the hands they had been holding and went back into Indian file as before to go on with their trek. Before they started again, the grandfather gave a last glance in the direction of the tree and said a mysterious thing that Lena did not understand: "This tree should be called Machado de Assis."*

That was the name of her school, and she did not understand why that should be the name of the tree. For such an important tree to be called "axe" did not make any sense. She did not get it, and neither did she ever ask. On the other hand, she never forgot. And many years later, when all of a sudden she recalled it and realized the meaning of the comment, she had to smile at the tricks of memory that unexpectedly brought back an opinion of her grandfather's, dead by then. But there, in the middle of the forest, when she heard it, it was just one more mystery in a morning so full of emotions.

They went on, with little talk. Lena was beginning to feel tired and to mix up sensations and discoveries, all somewhat submerged in the en-

---

*Considered the greatest Brazilian writer, 1839–1908. In Portuguese, *machado* means "axe."

chantment of being in the forest. She saw a biggish bird, yellow-breasted, brilliantly colored, with a tall tuft of feathers on its head, vertical on the trunk of a tree. She pointed it out: "Look, Grandfather, a woodpecker."

"No, that's an oropendola, which they call japu, or japira, or also japim. This one is still young."

Lena waited for her grandfather to say something more, completing the lecture, as usual. For instance, saying that the bird sang well (sometimes he even imitated the song or chirp), if it ate fruit, if it made some special kind of nest. Nothing. It seemed that on that day the old man did not feel very much like talking. Maybe because in the forest one should not get distracted. Maybe because of the cousins or the uncle, so they would not think he was wasting his time chatting about little flowers and little birds with a girl. Lena found it odd.

Suddenly, again, the grandfather lifted his left arm and cried: "Halt!"

This time Lena did not even think of looking up, she was so busy looking at what was in front of them. A little river, even smaller than the Little River, running among boulders and branches, down in a ravine, with its crystalline waters. From one bank to the other, a large fallen tree was the only way to get across. The worker stepped on the end of the improvised bridge, cautiously at first and then pushing down as if testing its strength. It passed muster:

"You can go, Doctor, the log is firm."

Go? Lena was scared. The trunk seemed so narrow, so round, so slick . . . Only a monkey could walk there without falling. Down there, the brook rushed along. It seemed higher than the guava tree she used to climb in her grandfather's orchard. And all those rocks, in the icy water, in the middle of the forest, maybe there were alligators . . . She felt like giving up, like crying, like waking, anything that would get her out of crossing that abyss over that log.

"I think it would be best to cross further up, at the ford. For the children it is safer. Especially with this one there. It's better to lose some time and cross somewhere else. I told you I did not want to bring the girl, but since she is here . . . That's the only way."

For once Lena was relieved to hear her uncle. He was being as negative as ever, which she hated, but it gave her some hope that she would not have to go this way.

The grandfather, however, seemed not to have heard. He was silent, as he had been all morning. He sat on the log where it rested on the bank, right at the edge of the cliff, as if he were about to get some rest. Then he started to unlace his boots. Could his shoes be bothering him, and was he going to relieve his feet? Lena looked on, with no idea of what would happen next, divided between fear and curiosity.

"Take off your boots and socks."

The order was dry, in a tone that allowed no questions. Lena sat down beside him and in a moment was barefoot. In the same voice he gave another order, to the worker: "Take this to the other side for us."

And then, changing his voice, with that air of telling her a secret in which he had shown her the orchid back there, he turned to his granddaughter: "Turn your feet out a bit, like the clock at ten to two. Don't worry about the river down there, and don't look down. Make believe that the whole log is resting on the ground. It is very easy: all you have to do is not think about the danger, look where you step and look ahead, where you want to arrive."

She opened her eyes wide, felt her heart pounding, *ka-tuck, ka-tuck, ka-tuck,* as if it were about to jump out of her mouth or her ears. But she had hardly any time to think of anything. The old man had already started to cross on the log, in the direction of the worker who was waiting for him on the other side, with their shoes in his hands. If she were not quick about it, she ran the risk of being left behind, far from her grandfather, in the middle of those teasers. She watched the movements of the old man carefully, stepped on the log, and did the same thing. And there she went, her feet slightly splayed, arms out to the sides, one step after another, every four beats of the drum in her chest, *ka-tuck, ka-tuck, ka-tuck,* farther and farther away from the cousins, closer to the grandfather who, at each one of her steps, smiled a bit more broadly under his thin grey mustache. The girl looked at him, at her destination, his blue eyes sweet behind their lenses, opening his arms to receive his grandchild when she managed, *ka-tuck, ka-tuck, ka-tuck,* another step in the direction of the old man, tense and almost smiling on the other bank, one could almost hear him clearing his throat despite the yelling of Uncle Vicente on the bank behind her.

"Father, this time you overdid it! I am sorry, but this is irresponsible!"

She's not going to manage! Helena Maria, come back right away. No, no, don't come back. Stay there till someone comes to get you. Bend down! Sit down on the log, come on, one leg to each side, it's easier. Come on, Helena Maria, don't be stubborn!"

She's past midway, *ka-tuck, ka-tuck, ka-tuck,* one more, *ka-tuck, ka-tuck, ka-tuck,* and knowing where you want to arrive.

"Good job, Helena Maria, well done, you are almost there."

At the end, almost at the other bank, *ka-tuck, ka-tuck, ka-tuck,* one more step and a little hop, almost a run to her grandfather's lap, who hugged her and just said: "I liked to see that. Now, put on your boots."

"This girl is something else, isn't she, Doctor?"

His comment went unanswered. The old man was already bent over, putting his shoes back on, beside his granddaughter. He did not even look up to see the cause of a lot of crying and confused yelling on the other bank. Lena tried not to look either, but could not hold off. Trying not to give herself away, she checked and saw that Carlos Eduardo insisted on crossing right away and his brothers did not want to. The uncle was giving contradictory orders. Finally, he yelled: "Enough! I've made up my mind. We cross here. I'll go first and you'll look on and see how it's done."

But even then it took a while. Lena and her grandfather were ready, standing beside the worker, waiting while the arguments and the indecision went on at the other bank.

"Look, Helena Maria, there is another orchid. This one is a laelia," her grandfather showed her. "Do you want to take it along? We could pick it."

She did not really have to answer. The glitter in her eyes spoke for her. Her grandfather reached up, carefully detached the plant that was growing in a fork in the tree a little above his head. He went on, all animated, showing in his hands that heap of roots, the fleshy leaves, the three lilac-colored flowers, with a bit of pink in them and intensely purple at the center: "Look carefully, this orchid is an epiphyte. This means it grows on a tree branch. But it is not a parasite; it does not feed on the sap of another plant. The roots are aerial; they take the food they need from the air."

"The petals are beautiful," said the girl, charmed.

"Not all of them are petals, look," the old man explained, "An orchid has only three petals, these two and this other one in the middle, which is modified and curls around the sex organs and is called the labellum. These other three, that look like petals are in reality sepals, because in orchids the calyx opens, and they take on the same color as the petals."

"Labellum," said Lena, savoring the word. It was pretty, and easy to remember.

"Look here," her grandfather went on, "look carefully. Inside the labellum, there is this column, which is the organ for reproduction. Look how long and narrow it is. Because of its shape, the ideal pollinating agent for an orchid is the hummingbird. That's why orchids and hummingbirds live so well together in this forest."

On the other bank, the crossing was starting. All in a row, like a little train, there came the four of them, riding the log, holding onto the trunk for dear life and pushing themselves along with their hands. They helped themselves along with their legs and their behinds advanced slowly. First Carlos Eduardo. Then his brothers. At the tail end, Uncle Vicente huffed along. But Lena hardly had the time to take in the scene. The grandfather had already turned his back on the brook, saying: "Let's go."

They went along for a little distance on the trail, one after the other. This time it was the old man, the girl, and the worker. The others were left behind. Shortly, the forest made way for the cacao plantation, shaded by the great trees left over from the forest. But at eye level, the view no longer had that tangled diversity as before: the golden fruit glued to the trunks, the new pink leaves, the pleasant shade, the sweet smell, the softest carpet in the world of dry leaves in layers and more humid layers, decomposing. As the trail opened into more space, the grandfather slowed down and let the girl catch up with him. He held the orchid out to her.

"Take it. When we get home, ask your grandmother for help, and we will tie the laelia to some tree in the garden. It does not even have to be a big tree. Maybe that lady-of-the-night by the front gate. That way you will always have a reminder of this day."

Lena embraced the orchid with her right arm, as if she were holding a puppy or a doll, firmly and carefully. She felt her left hand in her grandfather's knotty one, with its blue veins and thin skin. Hand in hand, sixty years between them, they went on, stepping on the soft cacao leaves. Against the girl's cheek, the colorful laelia. A remembrance from that day. As if it were necessary. As if the remembrance ran any risk. As if the memory were not to outlast the grandfather, the orchid, the lady-of-the-night, the garden where they had been planted. It would live longer than the cacao plantation, the forest, and the log bridge. Even longer than—how painful that was!—the jequitibá with all its royalty and divinity, which were unable to impose respect on the burns that destroyed life and created grazing fields where orchids and hummingbirds had disappeared, pacas and capibaras no longer came to drink, deer no longer bathed, and the little rivers shifted their courses into the memories of those who had known them, their sources in their hearts, *ka-tuck, ka-tuck, ka-tuck,* watering their words while they still existed, fragile, balancing on the log, so simple, so easy, all you have to do is look where you put your feet, *ka-tuck, ka-tuck, ka-tuck,* and know where you want to arrive.

Way up on the tree, the wren, the cambaxirra, was still singing. Lena shivered. It was getting cold in the shade, and her skin reacted to the stronger wind that shook the branches of the almond tree. Like a Romantic poet braving the lightning of a stormy night, she felt like testing the imponderable. She wanted to consult oracles, to decipher the auguries in the flight of birds. Or of the wind in her almond tree. She offered herself as a sacrifice. She asked for a sign. A dead leaf floating down, a branch rustling, a limb falling on her. But the breeze might be too weak yet, though it was fresher. And the tree just dropped a few petals, small and white, on her lap. Was that an answer? A sign? No way to know for sure. Amalia interrupted her, calling out: "Come, child, come have your coffee. It is getting cold."

On the table, the row of little bottles with her medication was waiting as well. And suddenly, she decided. She cut the dose of all of them, in silence, without saying anything to her mother. And she decided to go all the way to the end. To go back home. To *her* home. To fall down in her own corner, the next time she lost her balance. Close to the doctor who had promised to take her on. And close to Alonso, if he was willing. Or without him, whatever the case might be.

All she said was: "When is the next plane for me to return?"

"At ten," Amalia responded, somewhat surprised.

"Could you call and see if they have a seat, while I pack my bags?"

They did. She put all her papers in the bottom of her bag, and her few clothes on top. In a moment she was ready. As they were locking up the house, Amalia looked at her closely, and said: "But are you going, like this, as you are? This seems very strange."

"Why?"

"Your hair has some dirt in it, specks of something. Let me put on my glasses . . ."

And then: "Go brush your hair, Lena. Your head is covered with flowers from the almond tree."

She answered, with a half-smile: "Leave it be. It's the same inside."

She turned her back to the house that stood there, solid and sunbathed. She lifted her bag to her shoulder and, with a slight limp, walked to the car that would take her to the airport. So simple, so easy, the heart goes on, *ka-tuck, ka-tuck, ka-tuck,* all you have to do is look where you step, *ka-tuck, ka-tuck, ka-tuck,* and know where you want to arrive.

Después de este desorden impuesto, de esta prisa
de esta urgente gramática necesaria en que vivo,
vuelva a mí toda virgen la palabra precisa,
virgen el verbo exacto con el justo adjetivo.

Que cuando califique de verde al monte, al prado,
repitiéndole al cielo su azul como a la mar,
mi corazón se sienta recién inaugurado
y my lengua el inédito asombro de crear.

(RAFAEL ALBERTI)

After this disarray imposed on me, this rush,
this urgent, necessary grammar in which I live,
may the right word return to me, all virgin,
and the virgin exact verb, with the precise adjective.

So that when I call the hill green, or the meadow,
and echo the blue of the sky or that of the sea,
my heart will feel as if just now opened
and my tongue the ineffable wonder of creation.